a dose of PRETTY POISON

USA TODAY BESTSELLING AUTHOR

KELSEY CLAYTON

Editing by Kiezha Ferrell at Librum Artis
Proofreading by Tiffany Hernandez

To Renee McCleary
Thank you for everything.
This book wouldn't be what it is without you.
I love you & I'm so grateful for our friendship.

CONTENT WARNING

This book deals with sensitive topics that may not be suitable for all readers. As some readers have said they find descriptive trigger warnings to be spoilers, I have provided a link to where you can find all of the trigger warnings for each of my books. Please read safely.

For trigger warnings: Please go to www.kelseyclayton.com/triggerwarnings

Laiken

CHAPTER ONE

THE FIRE BURNS HOT IN FRONT OF ME—THE LEVEL of heat where it turns a light shade of blue—and all I can think of is throwing her into it.

Right, I should probably explain who *she* is.

Her parents would call her a nice girl.

My brother calls her his ex.

But me? I call her Satan. It's fitting, especially when she's the reason my brother was almost sent to prison.

He was only defending her honor. After a night full of drinking and having a good time, some creep wouldn't stop coming on to her. Cam told him to back off a few times, but his efforts were futile. When the guy wrapped his arms around her and tried to pull her away, my brother had enough.

One perfectly executed punch was all it took to knock the guy flat on his ass, but no one planned for the way he slammed his head against the curb on the way down—or the intracranial hemorrhage that took the charges from simple battery to aggravated assault. All the provided witness statements were in his favor. Everyone saw how belligerent the guy was being, as well as his lack of common decency for women that want nothing to do with him. However, none of them saw exactly what happened after they left the party.

None except his ex.

We all thought it would be simple. That she would provide her statement and the police would drop the charges. After all, he was just protecting his girlfriend. But when Cam went to her house to find out why she hadn't done it yet, she dropped a bombshell on him that none of us saw coming.

Perfect little princess didn't want to get involved.

And if that wasn't bad enough, she broke up with him because she "can't be involved with a violent criminal."

Cam was devastated.

My parents hired a lawyer.

And I started thinking of all the ways her death could look like an accident.

"Laiken!" Cam shouts, his face only inches from mine, pulling my attention back into the now.

I jump and nearly fall off the bench. "What the fuck is wrong with you?"

He breaks out into a fit of hysterics, laughing so hard he's struggling to breathe. I cross my arms over my chest and shake my head at him.

"You know, now that I think about it, I wish you *were* given jail time."

That's a lie. I love my brother. He's that one person who has always been there for me. We've stuck by each other through some shit, and I'm just as protective of him as he is of me. Call it joint sibling rebellion in a religious household—there's no way to make it through alone. You need to have each other's backs.

But that doesn't mean I won't fuck with him when given the chance.

He flips me off and laughs when I pretend to grab it. "As if you didn't cry the hardest when you found out I was only getting two years of probation."

"I told you," I insist. "I was still drunk from the night

before. I was crying because I remembered that Taco Bell exists."

Cam smirks and looks back at his friend Aiden. "You believe a word of this shit?"

He shrugs. "I don't know, man. Taco Bell to a drunk chick is like free porn to us."

The two of us stare at him in disbelief as we try to figure out what the hell goes on in his brain. Cam and I glance at each other, and I raise my hands in surrender.

I'm not touching this one.

Cam must have the same thought because he just shakes his head and mutters something under his breath before dropping the topic entirely—just in time for more of his idiotic friends to show up to our celebratory bonfire.

Because not having to wear an orange jumpsuit for the foreseeable future is something to celebrate, dammit.

"Whoop, whoop!" Owen calls as he walks toward the back of the yard.

He's carrying a six-pack on each shoulder while Lucas and Isaac follow behind him. Having been on the same hockey team with Cam since they were younger, I've grown up around these guys. But that doesn't mean I like them. To be honest, there's only one of his friends I don't find completely revolting.

"Congrats, man!" Owen tells Cam as he hands him one of the six packs. "My present to you."

At six foot four, Owen looks intimidating. The tattoos on his arms along with the muscle he's built from going to the gym every day, it's easy to think he's some rebellious badass. In reality, he's a total teddy bear—a ladies' man, but the kind that cuddles after a one-night-stand.

"Because *that's* what he needs—to get drunk and assault someone else," I drawl.

All of their attention turns to me and Lucas coos. "Don't

worry, Baby Blanchard. If he gets locked up, I'll be your new big brother."

I stare back at him pointedly, waiting for the catch—because nothing that comes out of his mouth is *ever* from the goodness of his heart. "Oh yeah?"

"Yeah." He smiles. "And on a completely unrelated note, how do you feel about incest?"

And there it is.

Lucas has been hitting on me for years. He's shorter than the rest of the team, so in his man-brain, he needs to overcompensate for that by being completely obnoxious. He's cute, in that *looks like a preppy rich kid* kind of way, but I watched him chase Cam around the yard while he tried to piss on him. They were eight, but that kind of thing sticks with you.

Rolling my eyes, I don't even need to say anything, as Cam predictably comes to my defense. He takes one of the bottles from the six-pack and holds it upside down by the neck, swinging it as if he's practicing.

"Are these beers for drinking, or for breaking over Lucas's head?"

Owen looks between Cam and Lucas, and his grin widens. "Look at that. You don't even need to be drunk to want to assault someone."

"Fuck off," he snaps back, but the way he chuckles shows he isn't actually mad.

Feeling extra lonely and co-dependent, I slip my phone from my pocket and text my best friend.

Where are you? I'm dying over here.

It only takes a minute for her to respond, much to the relief of my codependency issues. Can anyone really blame me, though? Sitting by myself while my brother's friends fail at trying to flirt with me isn't my idea of fun, surprisingly.

In your driveway, drama queen.

Thank fuck.

While the guys get lost in a conversation about hockey plays and opposing teams, I slip away and head for the driveway. It's not that I'm not comfortable being alone around my brother and his friends. They've all been coming around for as long as I can remember. It's just that once I hit puberty and grew an ass with a pair of tits to match, they started treating me differently.

I'm not just Cam's little sister anymore. I'm the hot former head cheerleader they can't manage to get into bed, no matter how hard they may try. Although, I don't know how you could want to sleep with someone and still call them *Baby Blanchard.*

Vomit.

The second Mali gets out of her car, I throw myself into her arms.

"My hero," I swoon with a fake southern accent.

Mali and I have been best friends since we were in preschool, when she told me my bow was pretty so I took it off and gave it to her. She's the epitome of a ride or die. My call-in-the-middle-of-the-night-to-get-rid-of-the-body kind of person.

She grunts from trying to hold us both upright. "Yeah, yeah. I'm your favorite person. Your whole world. But didn't we learn that *this* is a bad idea from the time we fell and you skinned both your knees?"

I find my footing again and pull away. "We were nine. This is hardly the same thing."

"I'm just as weak now as I was then."

"Now that's the first true thing you've said since you got here."

The back of her hand hits my arm, but it lacks malicious intent. "I should just go home and leave you to fend for yourself."

"Don't you dare," I growl. "That's just mean."

"You could come with me."

My lips press into a line. She and I both know exactly why I won't be doing that—something she just loves to fuck with me about.

Bitch.

"I hate you."

She chuckles and tucks a strand of hair behind my ear. "Aw, babe. That's so sweet."

We make our way back toward the fire, finding Aiden trying to balance a full beer on his head. When he seems to be doing a little too well, Mali sneaks up behind him and screams. He startles, and the beer that was still halfway full tips forward and pours beer all over his lap.

"Oh, what happened?" she says with a fake pout. "Did you have an accident?"

He glances down at his pants and sure enough, it looks like he pissed himself. He throws his head back and groans while Mali goes over to Cam and gives him a hug.

"Congratulations."

"Thank you," he answers sincerely.

"You must be so relieved. Hell, even *I'm* relieved."

My brows furrow. "Why are *you* relieved?"

She looks at me as if it's obvious. "Because if they locked him up, I'd be the only one left to deal with you. Duh."

Cam strokes his chin, thinking. "Now that you mention it, maybe I should have let them send me to prison."

"Har har," I clap back. "You're such a comedian."

My phone vibrates on my lap and being as the only other

person to ever text me is sitting to my right, I know who it is before I even look at it.

My ex, Craig.

Just seeing his name on my screen is enough to make me nauseous. You'd think he would have understood that I have no intentions of answering him by the first ten messages I ignored, but nope. There must be some kind of brain eating amoeba in the water around here.

One that only affects men.

"Not going to answer that?" Mali questions.

I drop my phone back into my lap and shake my head. "It's not worth my time. He's only texting me because he's back for the summer and wants to look like he's still hot shit in front of his friends."

She nods approvingly. "That's the queen I've always known you are."

My breakup with Craig was anything but pretty—it never is when the guy will fuck anything that walks. Everyone thinks they want the hot quarterback in high school, but I've been there and done that. Trust me when I say it's not all it's cracked up to be. The whole high school fairy tale where the quarterback and the cheerleader are meant to be together is just not for me. Give me the option and I'll choose the hot hockey player any day of the week.

As if fate is solely controlled by the inter musings of my mind, a familiar truck roars as it pulls onto the grass beside the driveway. The rumble of the engine grabs all of our attention, except for Mali. Hers stays laser focused on me.

"Is that a chick in his passenger seat?" Isaac asks.

Owen squints. "Looks like it. I didn't even know he was fucking someone on the regular."

Remember when I said that there was only one of Cam's friends I don't find completely repulsive? Yeah, it was Hayes sex-on-legs Wilder. And by *I don't find him completely repulsive,* I mean I'm disgustingly and embarrassingly in love with him. What can I say? There is no happy medium with me. But even the possibility that he brought a girl with him makes my stomach sink. To be forced to watch him hold her and kiss her and whisper things in her ear? I'd rather throw *myself* into the fire.

"Must be serious if he brought her with him," Aiden muses.

Mali nudges me, probably to see if I'm okay, but I shake my head. I've gone the last three years without anyone finding out I low-key wish he would be more than just my brother's best friend, and I don't plan on that changing—girlfriend flaunting or not.

"All three of you are fucking morons," Cam says as the girl hops out of the truck. "That's his sister."

Relief floods through me like a tsunami while Mali whines. "What the hell did he bring Devin with him for?"

"Damn, Mal. We don't have to worry about you rolling out the welcome mat," I say with a snicker.

She narrows her eyes at me. "She's annoying, and she clings to you like a goddamn koala. The position of your best friend is taken, thank you very much."

Her possessiveness makes me laugh. "Come on. She's not that bad."

"She is, you just don't see it because you—"

I swing the heel of my foot into her shin, effectively shutting her up before she blurts out the only secret I've ever successfully kept from my brother.

"Ow!" she yelps. "That hurt!"

But I can see the smirk hiding behind her facade. Messing with me about anything involving Hayes is her all-time favorite hobby. When it first started, she even wrote a secret admirer letter and slipped it into his locker. She learned that was going too far when I stopped talking to her for a week straight.

I'm thinking she might need a refresher course in the boundaries.

"Aw, you really *are* just as weak as you were when we were nine," I tell her.

Before she can respond, Devin comes over and sits on the other side of me.

"Hey Laiken," she mumbles.

Devin always has been shy. She was a gymnast growing up and never really had time for friends outside of those who trained with her. But her hopes to go to the Olympics died with a broken femur in the middle of a national competition, leaving her with a ton of free time she's never had and doesn't know how to fill.

"Hey, Dev," I greet her sweetly. "How've you been?"

"Good," she answers. "School sucks, though."

"That's right. I keep forgetting you didn't graduate with us."

Mali scoffs quietly beside me, but I don't acknowledge it. Devin exhales. "One more month. I can't wait."

"I bet. The only good thing about that school was getting to check out Mr. Taylor." I glance over at Mali. "*Someone* used to masturbate to the thought of him."

A bark of laughter shoots out my best friend's mouth. "Funny you should mention masturbation. Hey, Wilder!"

My breath gets stuck in my lungs, and I look over to see Hayes walking toward us. As if his mere presence wasn't enough torture, his biceps flex as he carries two bundles of firewood.

Fuck me.

"What's up?" he asks Mali.

If I didn't know her for as long as I have, I'd be worried about what she'll say next, but Mali is anything but stupid. She may test the boundaries at times, but she knows that telling Hayes anything about my feelings for him would end our friendship.

At least until I got over the humiliation and sting of rejection.

"When's the last time you man-handled the ham candle?"

Okay, that *may be even worse.*

He freezes and looks at her like she's gone insane—honestly, she may have. "What?"

"You know, polished the banister. Shucked the corn. Had a threesome with a couple of no shows."

The more that comes out of her mouth, the deeper I want to crawl into myself.

"Jesus Christ, Mali," Cam groans. "Just say jerked off!"

She scrunches up her nose. "That's so dirty."

"Right, and calling it a ham candle is *so* much better," he counters.

Pursing her lips, she half shrugs, and I'm hopeful the conversation will end there, but she's not about to let me off that easy.

"So?" she presses, looking at Hayes.

Don't answer it.

Don't answer it.

Don't fucking answer it.

"This morning," he tells her, as if it's the most normal question in the world. "Why?"

Mali smirks. "Just wondering. What about you, Cam?"

"Okay," I interject. "I do not need to know that information about my brother, fuck you very much."

"How do you think *I* feel?" Devin asks.

She has the same look on her face that people have when someone mentions their parents having sex—simultaneous horror and disgust. Meanwhile, I can't get the image of him jerking off out of my mind. I'm guessing that was Mali's plan.

Evil bitch.

"Oops. Sorry, Dev," Hayes says, and then brushes off the topic as if it never happened.

Something I wish I could do right now.

I wonder who he was thinking about when he came.

Fucking hell.

After congratulating Cam, Hayes goes around to each of the guys and does their little bro-handshake. When he's done, he sits down and looks at me. Between the heat of his gaze and the images that are playing on a loop inside my head right now, I have to press my thighs together to bring myself back to reality.

"Potter," he greets me.

I roll my eyes, momentarily over him. "For the last time, Harry Potter didn't live in the attic. He lived under the stairs."

"Who lived in the attic then?"

I'm about to say *no one* and put an end to his incessant need to make fun of my bedroom, when Mali answers for me.

"Mrs. Rochester."

He raises a single brow. "Am I supposed to know who that is?"

She sighs, as if not knowing classic literature is a disservice to humanity.

"She's a character in the Charlotte Brontë book *Jane Eyre*," she explains. "Basically she's a mad woman who lives in an attic. Some even call her a demon."

Hayes smirks and turns his attention from her to me. "Well, that's fitting."

"She's insane!" I argue, but that was the wrong thing to say.

He lights up like a fucking Christmas tree. "Even better!"

I shake my head slowly. "You're dead to me."

He puts a hand on his chest. "But I'm your favorite."

"Who the hell said that?"

Looking around, he glances at all the other guys and then comes back to me. "The competition isn't very fierce."

Okay, fair point, but I can't let him win that easily.

I consider my options and decide to go with the one guy he likes the least but tolerates for the sake of the team. "Isaac. You're my new favorite."

Hayes's jaw drops as Isaac holds up his beer bottle. "Cheers, dude."

As desperate as it makes me sound, I secretly yearn for these fake little arguments we get into. It's the only time we ever really talk, and pathetically, the part of me that doodles my first name with his last will take everything she can get. Needless to say, she and the me that hated his guts from age thirteen to fifteen don't get along.

"Wait a damn minute," Lucas argues. "Why the hell is he allowed to mess with Laiken but we aren't?"

Hayes chuckles, and it takes everything I have not to get lost in the sound of it. Meanwhile, Cam tosses another log into the fire and sits back down.

"Because Hayes knows his boundaries. There's a difference between messing with her and hitting on her." There's a momentary pause before he adds, "And I like him more than I like you."

Lucas finishes chugging the rest of his beer and tosses the empty can at Cam, only for Isaac to intervene.

"Careful. Haven't you heard?" He looks Cam up and down, as if he's a rabid dog. "He's a violent criminal."

Everyone chuckles and Cam flips him off. Anyone who knows my brother, knows that he would never intentionally hurt anyone. Not without a really good reason, at least. He may joke around with his friends about it, especially now that court is over and the fear of going to jail is gone, but I know it bothers him. People in this town literally watched him grow up, and yet now at least half of them think he's a sociopath.

Fucking Satan.

My phone vibrates, and being too wrapped up in my thoughts, I open it before I can stop myself. A text from Craig stares back at me.

> Stop pretending you aren't seeing my texts. Isaac just told me you have your phone in your hand.

For the love of fuck. "Isaac!" His head snaps toward me at the tone of my voice. "Did you really tell your fucking brother that I have my phone on me?"

Hayes bites his lip to conceal his smile. "That was short lived."

Isaac looks like a kid who got caught with his hand in the cookie jar. "Is that bad?"

I pinch the bridge of my nose and take a deep breath. "If you were going to give him a play by play on me while you're here, you should've just brought him."

"Do you want him here?" he asks excitedly. "I can call him. Guarantee you he'll come."

"No!" Mali and I yell in unison.

Isaac frowns. "Oh, come on. He missed you while he was at school, and he's really sorry."

"For which time? When he ditched me at a party to go fuck someone else, or when he meant to send me a video of us and accidentally sent me an amateur porn of him and his lab partner?"

He stares back at me, dumbfounded.

"Oh, I know," I continue. "It must be for the time he screwed another girl on my bed and left me the condom as a present. Besides, it's not even like we recently broke up. If he was sorry, he should have apologized *seven months ago*."

Everyone stays quiet as his mouth opens and closes a few times, not saying a word. After a moment, Cam breaks the silence while inspecting his empty bottle.

"Maybe you *should* get him here," he says like it's a decent idea.

"Easy, badass," Hayes warns. "You just got put on probation like five minutes ago. Let's wait a bit before we violate it, okay?"

Cam looks between Isaac and Hayes. "No promises."

"Didn't ask for one," Hayes answers, because he knows better than that. "Now, who's up for some beer pong?"

Everyone nods in agreement while he gets up to grab the table from the back of his truck. Meanwhile, Devin looks at my beer as I take a sip, and she grimaces. I can't help but chuckle.

"What's wrong, babe?"

She drops her head. "I don't really like beer."

Mali snorts, muttering *of course you don't* under her breath. For the second time in twenty minutes, I drive my heel into her shin. She does a good job at concealing the grunt she lets out from the pain.

Devin may not be anywhere near as close to me as Mali is, but I don't want her to feel uncomfortable around us simply because Mal is a possessive little shit who never learned how to share.

"Come on," I tell her, standing up and putting out my hand. "We can make you a mixed drink. You can sip on that."

That seems to cheer her up, and she smiles as she puts her hand in my own. As we start to head toward the house, I notice Mali walking on the other side of me. I raise my brows at her.

"What?" she asks innocently. "If you're making them, I want one too."

Just like that, any bit of tension between us dissipates. It always does.

"As if I wasn't going to make you one anyway."

She wraps her arms around my shoulders. "This is why you're my favorite."

We're almost to the house when I look up and lock eyes with Hayes. He's carrying the folded-up table in one hand and beer pong kit in the other, but all I can focus on is the way he smirks as he passes by.

Isn't it unfair for one person to be *that* good looking? I mean, isn't everyone supposed to be created equally? Because I don't think God got the memo when he made Hayes. Either that or the vial labeled *LOOKS HOT ENOUGH TO MELT ICE* spilled and emptied everything it had into the pot.

I swear, that man was put in my life for the sole reason of torturing me.

"You're drooling," Mali coos.

My hand flies to my mouth, but I should've known she was full of shit. "I changed my mind. No drink for you."

"Aw, come on," she whines. "It's all in good fun."

"What is?" Devin questions.

I throw a hand over Mali's mouth as she goes to answer. "Nothing. Mali is just in rare form tonight."

Opening the fridge, I grab the few things I need—cranberry juice, pineapple juice, orange juice, and most importantly, a bottle of Malibu. It's essentially a bay breeze, but the orange juice adds an extra bit of flavor. Plus, then you can get away with adding more rum to it.

"Mal, do you remember the night we drank entirely way too many of these things?"

She cringes. "How can I forget? We couldn't even drink juice for three months afterwards without wanting to upchuck."

I chuckle as I start to pour in the Malibu.

One ounce.

Two ounces.

Three ounces.

When I still add another splash, Mali hums. "I guess you're planning on repeating that tonight then."

"Eh." I shrug. She's not exactly wrong. "At least then I can blame the shit that comes out of your mouth tonight on you being drunk."

"That's no fun. What if you end up with your soulmate tonight?"

"Mali Elizabeth," I growl.

Devin glances between the two of us curiously. "Wait, what am I missing?"

Fuck.

"Nothing. Like I said, Mali is just extra sassy tonight," I repeat while staring at the perpetrator and hoping she can hear the death threats in my head.

Mali hums as she takes a sip straight from the Malibu bottle. "I'd rather be sassy than horny."

I throw my head back and groan. "Mal!"

Seriously, I'm going to start taking best friend applications if she keeps it up.

Every part of me hopes, prays, and begs that Devin does not catch on to what she meant by that. And I don't pray often. When your parents force you to go to church throughout your whole childhood, your rebellious stage ends up including that in the pile of rejected expectations. But as if I'm getting punished for not going, I literally watch as it clicks into place for her.

"Oh my God," she gasps. "Do you have a crush on my brother?"

"No," I answer, at the exact same time Mali answers with, "Yes."

My head whips toward my almost former best friend, and

I glare at her. "Dude, did I do something to piss you off or did you just wake up and choose violence this morning?"

She rolls her eyes. "Oh please. She figured it out."

"Right, I'm sure she would have put the pieces together even without your lovely context clues."

"You're never going to get what you want if you don't ever tell anyone you want it," she tells me in a softer tone, and now I get what she's been doing.

I finish putting away all of the ingredients and take a deep breath before turning around.

"Okay. Yes, I have *some* feelings for Hayes. But I'm not stupid enough to think that anything will ever happen between the two of us, no matter how much *someone* tries to meddle." I throw a look toward Mali. "It's a pipe dream—fun to imagine but never going to come true."

They both go quiet, not sure of what to say, and I'm okay with sitting in silence for a minute...

Until I hear the sound of Hayes's tailgate closing right outside the open kitchen window.

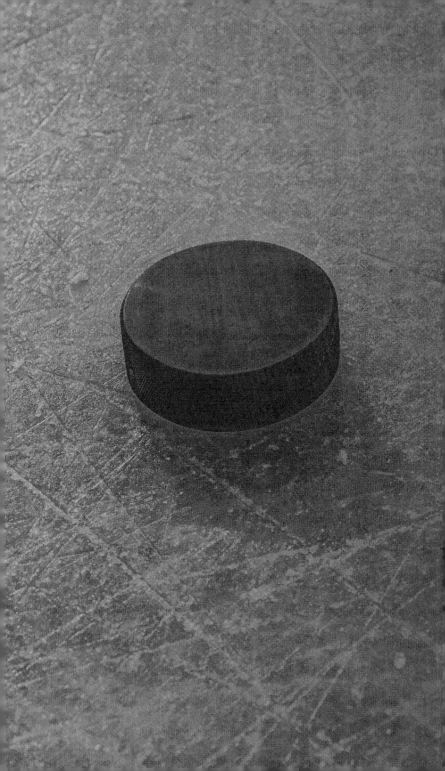

Hayes

CHAPTER TWO

I'VE ALWAYS HAD A TENDENCY TO GET MYSELF IN shit situations. From fights at school to nearly getting kicked out of hockey camp, it's basically my specialty. My resume should read *King of Chaos and Zero Fucks.* Well, that is, if I *had* a résumé. I've never really needed one—the benefit of working at the same surf shop since I was sixteen. The owner has grown to treat me like a son over the years. Now, I run the place since he's never around, and he pays me a substantial amount more than he should. So, at least that has worked out for me.

I don't think I'll be all that lucky with this, however.

It's not like I meant to listen in. I was only coming to my truck to grab the cooler when I heard Laiken snap at Mali. That's not out of the ordinary; being as close as sisters, they're bound to get into it from time to time. But I never expected the answer to the question that comes out of my sister's mouth.

"Oh my God, do you have a crush on my brother?"

I stop, frozen in place, as Laiken says no, but Mali says yes.

Mali has a thing for me?

"Dude, did I do something to piss you off or did you just wake up and choose violence this morning?"

"Oh please," Mali answers. "She figured it out."

"Right, I'm sure she would have put the pieces together even without your lovely context clues," Laiken snaps back.

It's quiet for a second, and then Mali speaks again, this time in a softer tone I can barely make out.

"You're never going to get what you want if you don't ever tell anyone you want it."

And oh—

Oh!

In all the years I've known Cam, I don't think I ever imagined Laiken looking at me as anything more than one of her older brother's annoying friends. Sure, we joke around about me being her favorite, but I never believed it was true. I thought she hated us all equally.

"Okay. Yes, I have *some* feelings for Hayes. But I'm not stupid enough to think that anything will ever happen between the two of us, no matter how much *someone* tries to meddle," she admits, the last part being directed at Mali, I'm sure. "It's a pipe dream—fun to imagine but never going to come true."

Hearing her confession is an experience I can't really process. On one hand, I'm flattered. Even my friends do nothing to hide the fact that they want her. Hell, I'm pretty sure Lucas has blatantly asked her out at least three times, only to get turned down. He keeps trying, though.

But on the other hand, I want to rewind time. Go back and unlearn all this new information. Because nothing good will ever become of it. Cam would slaughter me in front of his probation officer and put the cuffs on himself afterward. Some things are just worth it to him, and his sister is definitely at the top of that list. He's the textbook definition of protective big brother, and I would only hurt her.

Like I said, I always manage to get myself in shit

situations—and relationships are a part of that. They never end well for me.

I'm so out of it and lost in my own thoughts that I don't even think twice as I shut my tailgate, until I hear the sound it makes, followed by a gasp from inside the kitchen.

"Do you think..." Laiken starts but can't finish her question.

"There's only one way to find out I guess," Dev answers.

"What are you doing?" Laiken hisses in a panic. "I can't go out there!"

Shit.

In a quick-thinking move that impresses even me, I grab my earbuds from my pocket and slip them in, just in time for the three of them to come out the back door. They turn to me, and I let my eyes linger on Laiken just long enough to see the look on her face. She looks like she wants to puke.

"Need help?" Dev asks me, trying to act as if nothing happened, and I'm grateful for it.

I pretend as if I can't hear her and take an earbud out. "What?"

Laiken sighs in relief but only I notice the way Devin narrows her eyes for a second.

"I asked if you need help," she repeats.

"Oh. Nah, I'm good," I tell her. "Table is already set up. I just needed to come grab the cooler. We need more beer."

Satisfied, Laiken and Mali turn around and head for the fire, but Devin hangs back. As soon as they're out of earshot, she gives me a no-bullshit look.

"You heard her, didn't you?"

My brows raise. "Heard who?"

It's a decent effort, but she's not buying it. "You literally complained in the car about how your earbuds were dead."

I could keep it going—could try to tell her I was wrong or something just as stupid—but she took the time when we were younger to commit my lying face to memory. There's no point.

I exhale. "Don't tell her."

"Seriously? You're just going to pretend you have no idea?"

"Yeah, pretty much. I don't want her to feel all weird around me."

She glances back at Laiken and then smiles. "Okay, I won't say anything."

Leaving me to return to the fire, I pick up the cooler and adjust it in my arms as my gaze lands on Laiken. She looks a lot more carefree than she did a few minutes ago. As she throws her head back, laughing at something Mali said, the corner of my lips twitch.

No.

Absolutely not.

I don't fucking like this.

The only thing I can do is force it from my mind. I adjust the grasp on the cooler and start walking toward Cam and the guys. Fucking up the closest friendship I've ever had is not going to happen.

TURNS OUT, FORGETTING ABOUT it is a lot harder than I thought. It's not my fault, though. Have you ever watched a chick play beer pong and be good at it? But not only is she good, she's fucking dominating—sinking shots into cups like it's her job and downing the beer like a goddamn champion. I never really paid attention to it before, but tonight, it's the hottest thing I've ever seen.

It comes down to one final game. Cam and me versus Laiken and Mali. If it wasn't for Mali not being nearly as good as Laiken, I'd start accepting the loss of my man card now and preparing for the shit we'd get for losing to them. Cam and I have been the champs at this since our second year of hockey camp. I'm not looking for that to be put to an end by a couple of girls who are two years younger than us.

If I thought for a second that her feelings for me would be a distraction, I would be seriously mistaken. Not a single thing about her changes. She's laser focused and shit-talks us exactly like she did the rest of them. Even her own brother isn't exempt from her verbal assault. Mali sinks a few shots, but most of them hit the rim. Not Laiken, though. She isn't missing a single one—to the point where Cam and I share a look every now and then. We both know what's at stake here and the likelihood of us losing if we're not on our A game.

So much for a fun, careless game of beer pong.

Everyone else stands off to either side of the table, watching with bated breath to see who wins. I wish I could say the guys were rooting for us, but they're assholes. One cup left on both sides, and my eyes meet Laiken's.

"Don't fuck this up," I taunt her. "Haven't missed a shot all game. Would really be a shame if the one you missed was now."

She smirks, not looking away for a second as she sinks it. "You were saying?"

"Marry me," Lucas begs. "Seriously. Marry me."

Cam flips Lucas off as he chugs the beer in the cup. Laiken ignores him completely and focuses all her attention on me, waiting for me to take my shot.

Deep breath.

Aim.

Ignore the way she subtly bites her lower fucking lip.

Shoot.

My eyes close as it flies through the air, until I hear the unmistakable sound of the dunk the ball makes. Mali sighs, and Laiken gives her an incredulous look.

"Yes, Mal. Huff away," she sasses. "Because clearly, you're the one under all the pressure here. It's totally understandable."

Smiling guiltily, Mali wraps her arms around Laiken's shoulders. "I love you a whole lot."

"Mm-hm."

We each set up the three cups for overtime—the third round of overtime, for that matter. With the competitive nature both Cam and Laiken have, I feel like this game could go on all night and neither one of them would cave.

"Who goes first?" Mali asks.

"You do," Cam tells her.

Laiken smiles fondly and rolls her eyes, knowing the same question has been asked each time we've made it to a round of overtime.

They each shoot their shots, with Mali actually managing to find the cup this time. She cheers excitedly as we give them the balls back. But the next shot she takes, she isn't so lucky. The ball bounces on the table, and Cam swats it away.

"The fuck, dude!" she yells at him. "That was going to go in!"

"It bounced. Once it hits the table, it's fair game."

Pissed off, she puts a hand on her hip and glares at him. Meanwhile, Laiken aims the ball and shoots it directly into the cup. The only way Cam and I can win is if we both make every shot, including both making it into the last cup. Cam, however, has another idea.

"Watch this," he says, low enough for only me to hear him.

He tosses the ball, purposely making it bounce before it goes straight for the cup. It's the perfect opportunity for Mali to get her revenge on him, and she lunges for it. Laiken's eyes widen as she tries to stop her, but it's no use. Mali swings to hit the ball away, but instead, manages to send all three cups sailing.

We win.

"Mal," Laiken whines, throwing her head back and staring at the heavens.

She looks confused. "What? It's just spilled beer. We have plenty."

"You lost the game," Owen explains. "It was a smart move on Cam's part, honestly."

"Oh," she replies sullenly.

Laiken scrunches her nose at her best friend. "You're lucky you're pretty."

"Yeah," Mali smiles. "Shame about you though."

"So, you lost us the game and now you're insulting me?" Amusement dances in her eyes.

Mali winks. "Well, I mean, they basically cheated. He did that on purpose."

"Don't be a sore loser," Cam tells her. "It's not my fault you're predictable."

Her eyes narrow as she takes her phone out from her pocket and throws it at him—hitting him directly in the balls. "Did you predict *that*?"

As Cam falls to the ground, Laiken throws her hands in the air. "Now where was that aim while we were playing beer pong?"

I look down at Cam and chuckle as he groans in pain.

And to think he has a thing for that girl.

Chapter 2

THE NIGHT STARTS TO wind down, all of us having sobered up enough to drive home. Laiken stands up and stretches as she yawns. Her shirt lifts just enough to show a small tattoo peeking out from under the waistband of her jeans.

Fuck, why is that so hot?

I force myself to look away. Practically anything would be better than Cam catching me checking out his little sister. I'm not looking to die tonight.

"All right, I'm going to bed," she tells us. "Cam, don't forget you have to follow me to the mechanic tomorrow and then drop me off at work."

"What? No."

She looks confused. "Uh, yeah. Dad didn't tell you? My check engine light is on, and he made me an appointment to drop it off in the morning."

"I can't," he argues. "I have a brunch date."

Everyone goes silent, except for Owen who snorts. "Are you going to sip on mimosas, too?"

I put my hand out in front of him. "Man card. Hand it over."

He rolls his eyes. "Fuck all of you. If you saw this chick, you'd agree to brunch, too."

A part of me wonders if he would even be talking about it if Mali were still here, but she left a half hour ago—she has work early in the morning and said she needs her beauty sleep. I think Cam would disagree, but it's not like he'll ever grow a pair and tell her that.

"I don't know what to tell you," Laiken says.

He sighs. "Can't you just take my car?"

Her brows furrow. "Sure, let me just go clone myself so I can drive two cars at once. I know you think with your dick, but I don't think Mali did *that* much damage."

Cam groans and flips her off. "Son of a bitch."

It all happens in an instant. The idea runs through my mind, and before I can tell myself it's a horrible one, it shoots out of my mouth like it's desperate to escape.

"I can do it."

All heads turn to me, and just like that, it's too late to take it back.

"Seriously?" Cam asks.

I shrug as if it's no big deal. "Yeah. I don't have work until two. Wouldn't want anything standing in the way of your pancakes and mimosas."

He smirks. "What I want to be eating does start with a p, but it sure as hell isn't pancakes."

Laiken gags and covers her mouth. "Cam!"

Chuckling, he nods toward Devin. "Now you two are equal in knowing things you didn't want to know about your brothers. Bond over it."

She looks utterly disgusted. "I wish Mali was here to throw her phone at your crotch again."

"Now that's just mean." He turns back to me. "For real though, man. Thanks."

"No problem." I stand up and pull my keys from my pocket. "What time should I meet you there, Rochester?"

A light blush covers her cheeks, but I'm the only one who notices. "I have to drop my car off at nine."

I nod. "I'll be there. Let's go, Dev."

After saying bye to everyone except Isaac—because fuck that guy—we hop into my truck. As I put the keys into the ignition, I can already feel my sister's eyes on me—judging, suspicious eyes. I put the truck into drive and focus on the road to avoid looking in her direction.

"I really hope you know what you're doing," she tells me.

You and me both.

MY PHONE BLARES INTO my ear, screaming the sounds of VOILÀ at a volume that should be illegal when I'm *this* tired. With my eyes still closed, I grab it and throw it across the room. The thud from it hitting the wall barely registers before I'm on my way back to the comfortable slumber from which I was so rudely pulled.

"And you wonder why you go through so many phones," Devin drawls.

I crack one eye open to find her standing there, arms crossed as she leans in the doorway. Just the little bit of sunlight is too bright for my liking. I flip onto my other side and throw the blanket over my head.

"Go away," I grumble.

She chuckles. "Okay, but you should know, you need to meet Laiken at the mechanic in ten minutes. It's fine, though. I'm sure she won't mind you standing her up."

Fuck.

Jumping out of bed like the thing is on fucking fire, I wince at the pain that shoots through my head, but there is no time for whining. My drawers get thrown open as I grab a pair of jeans and a T-shirt.

"Smooth move, stud," Devin teases, watching me grab my keys and cellphone before heading for the door. "Wait! Aren't you going to brush your hair?"

I turn to glance in the mirror and notice the not-so-attractive mop on the top of my head. Handing her the stuff in my hands for a minute, I run my fingers through it and mess it up a little more, making it fall into place like it always does.

"I hate you," she tells me.

I grab my things back and smile. "Love you too."

It only takes two quick pit stops—one at the bathroom to grab my toothbrush and throw some toothpaste on it, and one at the kitchen for a bottle of water—before I'm gone. I can brush my teeth on the way.

Running out the door this fast reminds me of my senior year of high school, when I used to walk into the classroom as the bell was ringing. My homeroom teacher would give me a dirty look for it, but there was nothing she could do. I was on time. And the sound of my tires screeching as I pull out of the driveway goes right along with the nostalgia.

IF IT WASN'T FOR the construction traffic on Main Street, I'd be right on time. Instead, I'm a little over ten minutes late. I pull up in front of the mechanic shop to find Laiken sitting on the curb, looking bored and unamused. At the sound of my truck, she grabs her purse and stands up.

"God, it's bad enough you have to cheat at beer pong, you have to forget to pick me up too?"

"I'm so sorry," I say ignoring the beer pong comment, because we won that game fair and square. "It's the fucking traffic, I swear."

She gives me a knowing look, and it only takes me a second before I cave.

"Okay, and I woke up just a little late."

Chuckling, Laiken shakes her head and puts on her seatbelt.

"Seriously though, were you waiting long?" I ask.

She shrugs. "About fifteen minutes, but it's fine. I actually found a new career path."

My brows furrow. "By waiting on the curb?"

"Yeah, with the number of men who propositioned me, I realized the bank I could make prostituting," she says with such enthusiasm.

In an instant, my grip on the steering wheel tightens. It takes everything I have to loosen it before she notices.

"You tell your brother about that and let me know how it goes."

Her head hits the back of the headrest as she laughs. "Not a chance. He'd have me locked in a tall tower by sunset."

Not the worst idea, honestly.

We fall into a comfortable silence as I drive through town. Her fingers subtly tap against the door with the beat of the music. I'm actually enjoying this, and it makes me uncomfortable. I force myself to focus on literally anything else, when my stomach grumbles.

"What time do you have work?"

She startles slightly as I break the silence. "A little before eleven, but it's fine. You can just drop me off at the rink. I don't mind."

Instead of doing that, I turn into the parking lot of a popular breakfast spot in town.

"I'm hungry, and you probably didn't eat breakfast either." The guilty look on her face tells me I'm right. "Yeah, let's go. You can't teach a bunch of little kids how to ice skate if you're hangry. You'll traumatize them for life."

An amused smirk forces its way through. "This from the man who told a little kid to get the fuck off the ice last year? And you think *I'm* going to traumatize the children?"

Ouch. "Okay, that was different. We were doing slap shots, and he was trying to grab the pucks so he could collect them. I don't even know how the little shit got into the rink."

"A mix of bad parenting and the TikTok black hole, I'm sure."

Honestly, she's probably spot on. The place always has mothers who bring their kids and don't pay attention to them while they wait for open skate to start. Someone was bound to get seriously hurt during practice, so Coach started locking the gate to keep wandering children out of harm's way.

The restaurant is fairly crowded, but that's nothing new. Luckily, the hostess is good friends with my mom, so she gives us a booth by the window. All of the people that have been waiting aren't pleased, but that's not really my problem. They can take it up with the manager—another woman who is close with my mother.

Good luck.

"French toast?" I question.

She looks at me with surprised intrigue. "Yeah. How did you know that?"

Shit. Was I not supposed to?

As I rack my brain for an excuse as to why I would know something like that about her, I'm saved by the waitress as she comes over to take our order. I get a bagel with cream cheese and a coffee. I never have been that big on breakfast. She writes it down, and I raise my brows at Laiken to order.

"I'll take an orange juice and two slices of French toast," she says, and I drop my head as I chuckle.

"Coming right up, guys."

Taking the menus, she walks away and leaves us to our somewhat-awkward silence. I pull out my phone in an effort to distract myself. A text from Cam waits for me. It's a picture of a girl who looks an undeniable amount like Mali sitting across a table at some fancy restaurant he probably has no business being at.

Thanks again for taking one for the team. 😉

I glance across the table for a second and see Laiken gazing out the window as she daydreams.

As if it's such a hardship.

Wow, you managed to find Mali's doppelgänger. Would've been easier just to ask out the real thing, but maybe that's just me.

🖕 Your sister may not care but mine has a code. No dating your siblings' friends.

I'm mid sip as I read that one and immediately start to sputter on my coffee. Laiken's attention turns from her straw to me, and I smile sheepishly.

"Hot," I explain simply.

The corner of her mouth raises. "The steam coming off it didn't tell you that?"

"Wow." My brows raise in both surprise and amusement. "Someone woke up this morning and chose violence."

She freezes and eyes me with suspicion, and I realize I've repeated her words from last night when I "had my earbuds in." I put on my most angelic face, and she appears to relax. "Is there any other way to wake up?"

"I guess not when you're five-foot-three and need an attitude to make up for your size."

Her jaw drops, and she sticks her tongue in her cheek. "Excuse me, not everyone can be a fucking giant. And you know what they say—good things come in small packages."

I couldn't fight off the smile that forces its way through if I tried. "I bet they do."

The way her breath hitches metaphorically slaps me across the face. I can basically see the gears turning in her head as she tries to dissect the direction this conversation has gone in. What the hell am I doing?

Flirting with your best friend's little sister. That's what.

If I could see my conscience, I'm sure it would be glaring at me, shaking its head, all full of judgment. And it has every right. Cam has been there for me through some of the hardest shit I've ever dealt with. He's the only one I'd call if there was a dead body I needed to get rid of. If I were to betray him like this, the only body that would need to be disposed of would be my own.

"Lai—" I start to apologize, not even sure exactly where I'm going with it, but I'm cut off as the waitress places our food down in front of us.

I wonder if she has *awkward moment* radar. Some sort of intuition that I need saving or something. Regardless, she's definitely getting a good tip.

"Enjoy," she tells us.

Laiken thanks her as she leaves and then turns to me. "What were you saying?"

I shake my head. "It's nothing. That looks good."

She looks down at her plate and bites her lip—a move that goes straight to my dick in a way I'm not proud of. "It does."

Silence settles over us once again, but this one I'm thankful for. Lord knows I can't be fucking trusted to even talk around this girl anymore without risking shit. Stuffing my face with this bagel might be the one thing that manages to keep me alive.

Should've just dropped her off at the rink.

WE'RE HALFWAY THROUGH OUR food when we're interrupted. Craig, Isaac's younger brother and Laiken's ex, comes to stand beside our table. He's wearing his varsity football jacket, like that still means you're someone after you graduate from high school. Laiken hasn't even noticed him yet as he nods at me.

"Hey, beautiful," he says.

Her whole body visibly tenses at the sound of his voice. She swallows and grabs her glass, putting the straw in her mouth as she looks up at him.

"Craig."

He exhales. "I've missed hearing you say my name."

Gag me.

I've never understood what Laiken saw in him. The guy is a damn tool, and after what she revealed last night, I think even less of him now. Shouldn't surprise me. He is related to Isaac, after all. Cam wasn't happy when they started dating last year. He was even less happy when he had to see them sitting together at all of our games.

A part of me wonders what would happen if I let him know about our little guest right now. Something tells me no amount of Mali-lookalike pussy would keep him from storming over here and ripping him to shreds. But before I can even fully consider it, Laiken hums and rests her arms on the table.

"Along with the rest of Calder Bay, right? Or did you only hear them moaning it?"

Ouch.

Craig winces but recovers, like he's used to dealing with her attitude—a fact that irritates me more than it should. "Come on. Don't be like that. I just want to talk."

She looks over at me for a second and rolls her eyes before getting up. "I'm sorry. I'll be right back."

He lets her lead the way and taps on the table before following her. "Tell Cam I said hey."

Oh, I will.

I wonder if there is a record for shortest amount of time taken to violate probation. Honestly, that's probably the only thing keeping me from calling him right now, because as I look outside to where they're standing, it's obvious Laiken would rather be anywhere else.

"All done?" the waitress asks.

Pulling my eyes away from Laiken and Craig for a moment, I notice she's still got half her breakfast on her plate. "Can I just get that wrapped up?"

She nods and goes behind the counter to get a box. I,

however, can't seem to look away from the situation that is clearly escalating by the minute. Craig's jaw is tense, and Laiken looks like she might give Cam's criminal record a run for its money.

I pull my wallet out of my back pocket and throw money down on the table, just as she's finished bagging up Laiken's French toast.

"Thanks," I say, taking it and hustling out the door.

Craig's eyes meet mine, and he quickly shoves his phone back into his pocket. He takes a step backward as I come next to Laiken.

"Everything okay?" I ask her.

She snorts as she glares at her ex. "Fucking peachy. Can we go?"

"Sure."

My gaze doesn't leave Craig as Laiken spins around and starts to walk away, and he makes no attempt to follow her. Maybe the numerous concussions he got while playing football didn't kill all of his brain cells after all.

"You going to tell me what that was about?" I question when I catch up to her.

She hums. "Of course not. I'm trying to keep my brother *out* of prison, not give him a reason to go."

I'd offer to keep it to myself, but she'd never believe that. So instead, I hand her the bag that has her breakfast in it.

"Here. I figure you could eat the rest before work."

She takes it from me with a warm smile. "Thanks, but I don't have much of an appetite anymore. Maybe later."

That's the last she says of it as she opens the door to my truck and climbs inside.

Chapter 2

THE RIDE FROM THE restaurant to the rink is tense. Music plays through the speakers but instead of her tapping along with the beat, she's typing a mile a minute on her phone. I don't even need to ask to know that she's venting to Mali about what just happened. And it's not doing a damn thing to calm her down.

"Maybe you should skip work today," I suggest. "Your hostility isn't good for the children."

Now *that* is the first thing to make her laugh since Craig barged his way into our breakfast. "Or maybe I should just bring you with me. If you're yelling at them, then I don't have to."

I purse my lips as I pull into the rink parking lot, actually considering it for a minute. "I mean, I don't need to be at work until later. I could use a few puck-gophers while I practice my slap shots."

She hums sarcastically. "That's tempting. Really. But I'm not looking to piss off a bunch of parents and get myself fired. At least not today."

"Fair enough."

As soon as I put the truck in park, Laiken leans into the backseat to grab her bag and hops out. I should just let her walk away. Honestly, it's none of my business. But I can't. I have to give it one last shot.

"You're really not going to tell me what that argument was about?" I press.

The smile that appears on her face has no business doing what it does to me. "Bye, Hayes."

She swings the door shut and heads inside, and all I can do is watch her leave. A part of me has half a mind to go back to the restaurant and slam Craig up against the wall. Tell him that if he comes anywhere near her again, it's not Cam he has to be worried about. But that would cause a massive fallout I'm not prepared to even think about.

I only get a few miles down the street before I hear something vibrating. At first, I think it might be mine. In all the years that I've owned a cell phone, I've never put it on vibrate, but maybe throwing it against the wall this morning flipped the switch. However, when I pull it out, there's nothing but a text from my mom from over fifteen minutes ago.

What the fuck?

Pulling over, I turn the volume down and look for the source. It isn't until I get out and walk around to the passenger side that I find Laiken's phone on the floor in between the center console and the seat. It must've fallen out of her pocket when she was reaching for her bag.

"Hello?" I answer it.

Mali's voice comes through, sounding confused. "You're not Laiken."

"And people say you're not smart."

She doesn't miss a beat. "Yeah, well, people say you have a small dick."

"Hey!" I snap in mock outrage. "Four inches is average!"

"Oh my God," she laughs. "There are some things I just never needed to know."

Keeping the phone to my ear, I walk around the truck and get back into the driver's side. "You're welcome."

"Mm-hm. So, where's Laiken? Do you have her tied up somewhere?"

Now *that* is a thought that should never go through my mind, and yet there it is. And something tells me that was Mali's intention. With how she was acting last night and the conversation I heard between her, Laiken, and Dev, it wouldn't surprise me.

I decide to play it safe and not touch that one. "She forgot her phone in my truck. I'm bringing it to her now. I'll tell her to call you back."

"Okay, thanks."

The call goes dead, and I drop the phone onto my lap as I spin around to head back to the rink.

I'D BE LYING IF I said I didn't at least consider reading her text to Mali. After all, with the amount she was texting, I'm sure it has the answers to all my questions.

What the fuck did he want?

What were they fighting over?

Why was she so angry?

But if there's one thing more dangerous than Cam when it comes to his sister, it's Laiken when it comes to her privacy. She'd castrate me with the blade of her ice skate and then make me clean the blood off—which is why I know whatever Craig is holding over her, it has to be something she doesn't want to get out. She takes no mercy on anyone otherwise.

As I walk inside, "Your Body is a Wonderland" by John Mayer fills the entire arena. It's not a massive place by any means, and only has one rink with a couple of locker rooms and a concession stand, but it's our home. I honestly think I've spent more time here over the years than my own house. If I ever needed to let off some stress or just get away, nothing could beat the feeling of my skates gliding across the ice.

My steps slow as my gaze lands on Laiken. She's completely lost in the music, skating around the ice like the professional I know she has always had the potential of being. But she has no interest in going pro. The owner has tried to get her on board more than once, and each time she turns him down, he bitches about it to everyone who will listen.

She's wasting her potential.

When's the last time you saw someone come in here with as much grace as she has?

Could win the fucking Olympics on any random Tuesday, but no. She would rather teach a bunch of tater tots.

It's like that man's biggest failure in life is not getting Laiken to agree to be the next Michelle Kwan. But as I stand here and watch her, *really* watch her, I can see why.

She's fucking incredible…among so many other things.

It's not like I've never noticed that Laiken is gorgeous. My eyes work just fine. But after hearing her confession last night, it's like there is this extra light shining solely on her, making her brighter than everything else and demanding my attention. And I can't find the damn switch to turn it off.

See, there was a time where I couldn't take my eyes off her. When Cam and I first started hanging out, she would walk into the room, and I could think of nothing else. But my friendship with Cam grew stronger, I convinced myself that it was just a puberty thing. That it wasn't *her* per se, but the fact that she was a pretty girl, and I was full of raging teenage hormones.

And now she's making a liar out of me.

Knowing I'm encroaching on dangerous ground, I put my fingers in my mouth and whistle loud enough for her to hear me over the music. Her brows furrow for a second and she skates over to the gate.

"Everything okay?" she asks.

I hold her phone up. "You forgot this in my car."

"Oh." She takes it from me. "Thanks. I didn't even notice."

"I wouldn't have either if Mali hadn't called and made it vibrate."

A look of fear crosses her face before she quickly masks it. "Did you answer it?"

I could fuck with her. Could pretend like Mali exposed her secret. And if she wasn't so fucking off limits, I might have. But I meant what I said to Devin last night. Me playing as if I have no idea she has a thing for me is what's best for everyone—myself included.

"Yeah, but just to tell her that you'll call her back." I pause. "Oh, I also traumatized her a little."

"Oh, God. What did you do?"

Shrugging, I smirk. "I'm sure she'll tell you later."

Joking around about my dick being four inches is definitely not something I'm going to repeat to the girl who seems to be the object of its affection lately. Besides, the whole topic can't possibly lead to anything good, so avoiding it entirely is the better option.

"Mr. Zimmerman has a point, you know," I tell her.

She throws her head back and groans. "Not you, too."

"I'm not going to get on your case about it." I raise my

hands in surrender. "I'm just saying. You're really good, Laiken."

Her features soften, and there is something in her eyes I can't really decipher, nor do I think I should try. "Thanks."

A comfortable silence settles over us as we stand here, until the sound of excited children echoes throughout the arena. Kids come running toward the ice, screaming Laiken's name like they haven't seen her in ages.

"That's my cue," she says, and bends down just in time to hug the first little boy who gets to her. "Hey, buddy!"

"I practiced four times last week!"

"That's great!" She messes with his hair. "I'm so proud of you."

Kids really aren't my thing. They're too naive and full of energy. But seeing the way she treats each one of them like she's their big sister—it's cute. If Lucas saw this, he would probably make some comment about knocking her up and creating a hockey team of their own.

And I would revel in watching as Cam decked him across the face for it.

Without a goodbye she never owed me in the first place, she steps off the ice and walks over to make sure the parents are lacing their kids' skates properly. I let my gaze linger on her for a few more seconds and then force myself to do what I should've done last night—leave her alone.

Laiken
CHAPTER THREE

After eight hours of teaching ice skating lessons, you'd think I would be exhausted. Most of these kids really shouldn't be trusted to walk on their own, let alone balance on ice with metal blades attached to their feet. Don't get me wrong, there are a few who are promising. A few kids I've even moved up to higher age levels to challenge them more. But for the most part, it's hours straight of kids gripping the wall for dear life and falling on their asses when I finally get them to let go.

And yet I'm still dressed up and ready to go out.

I run my fingers through my damp hair as Mali pulls up in front of the rink. The bass from her sound system vibrates the windows as she belts the words to *Since You've Been Gone*. With the way she's singing it, you'd think she's fresh in the angry healing stage of the world's worst break up.

I open the door and stand there, staring at her and wincing at the way she fails to hit the high notes. After a minute, she rolls her eyes and turns the volume down—knowing I won't get in until she does. I'm all for blasting some music, but Mali does it in a way that will have me shouting all night like a stubborn old man who refuses to admit he needs a hearing aid.

"How you manage to not get pulled over is beyond me."

She gives me her best *fuck you* smile. "I do get pulled over, but a little cleavage goes a long way, Laiken dear."

"Right." I nod. "That's how you ended up on a date with that cop who wouldn't stop comparing the size of his gun and his dick. I remember now."

"Ugh!" Her nose scrunches as she pulls out onto the road. "That whole experience still depresses me. He was so hot, but the second he opened his mouth, I wanted to claw my way out of the restaurant with my bare hands."

"And yet you still sat through the whole date."

She scoffs. "Well, duh. I'm not a bitch."

My brows raise. "Really? You're not?"

"Okay, I'm not a *total* bitch. And besides, he was already going to be disappointed about not getting laid. I didn't want to ditch him, too. Talk about a rough night."

Oh, Mali, Mali, Mali. "Could've just had me fake an emergency."

The car comes to a stop at a red light, and she turns to give me a *no-bullshit* look. "Please. You would have laughed at me and then shown up at the restaurant to watch my misery."

I chuckle because she has a point—that sounds like exactly something I would do. Friends are there to get you out of situations you don't want to be in. *Best friends,* however, laugh at you when you get yourself into said situations and only step in when absolutely necessary.

"You've got to live and learn, baby girl."

She rolls her eyes. "Whatever. Tell me about how shit went this morning with Hayes. How did he end up with your phone?"

I shrug, knowing she's hoping for a much juicer story than the one she's going to get. "It fell out of my pocket."

"While you two were getting hot and heavy in the back seat?" She bounces her brows suggestively.

"No, coo-coo-bananas. While I was reaching into the back seat for my bag."

Her smile quickly morphs into a frown. "Well that's no fun."

A laugh bubbles out of me at her disappointment. "I'm sorry. Would you rather I tell you we fucked on the table of the restaurant in the middle of breakfast?"

"Wait. You went out to breakfast?"

Shit. "You would pick up on that."

"Of course, I would!" she shouts. "You went on a date with Hayes, and you didn't lead with that?"

"No, because it wasn't a date. We simply grabbed breakfast before he dropped me off at work."

"Who chose the restaurant?"

I roll my eyes. "He did."

"And who paid?"

"He did."

"Laiken, baby." Her sickeningly sweet tone tells me to prepare myself. "I know you can be a little naive sometimes, but that's a date, sugarplum."

I shake my head and look out the window, wondering if this is even an argument worth having. As long as Hayes and I know it wasn't a date, that's all that matters, isn't it?

Then again, I wouldn't put it past Mali to refer to this morning as a date to Hayes himself, in which case I would die and make sure to take her with me as I go.

"It wasn't a date, and even if it was, Craig interrupting us in the middle of it would make it the worst date I've ever had."

Her eyes widen. "Ouch! I thought he saw you at the mechanic or while you were waiting for Hayes to pick you up."

"Nope," I reply. "Came up right in the middle of us eating and all but begged me to talk to him outside."

Everything goes quiet for a minute, and I look over to see

Mali pouting. Her bottom lip is puffed out, and she looks like someone kicked her puppy.

"Uh, you good?" I ask her.

She shakes her head. "You finally get your date with Hayes, and Craig goes and ruins it. Now I have to hurt him, and I don't want to break a nail. I just got them done."

I pinch the bridge of my nose. "It wasn't a date."

Before she can argue further—an argument I have no chance of winning, mind you—my phone vibrates on my lap.

Dad.

Well, fuck. There aren't many times he calls me as soon as I get out of work. He's always been the type to have my mom call and ask questions, like if I'm coming home for dinner or what my most recent Facebook post is about.

Psst. The answer is always song lyrics, even when it's not.

Honestly, the only time my dad calls me himself is when I'm in trouble. And because I know that little piece of information, I'm able to be prepared.

I press answer and put it on speaker. "Hey, Dad."

"Laiken Rose," he barks.

Yep. Definitely in trouble.

"Ooh," Mali sings beside me. "He middle named you."

I flip her off. "Dad, listen. Before you say anything, you should know my phone only has one percent and is going to die any minute."

"Great," he grumbles. "Just another thing you can't manage to take care of. Whatever your plans were for tonight, cancel them. I want your ass home right—"

I quickly swipe down and put it on Airplane Mode, making it so it says *Call Failed* and not that I hung up on him.

"Oops. Phone died."

Mali laughs as I toss my phone into my purse. "What did you do to get in trouble this time?"

"Who knows," I answer honestly. "I'm sure it has

something to do with my car. I can't think of anything else I did to piss him off lately."

"Well, judging by the way he sounded, we better enjoy tonight," she says. "I have a feeling it'll be your last night out for a couple weeks."

Leaning my head against the headrest, I exhale. It's ridiculous, really. I'm eighteen years old. The fact that my parents still have the ability to ground me is insane. And it's such a double standard. Cam almost went to prison, and all my parents cared about was that their precious baby was okay. But if I blink at the wrong time, the whole world is coming to an end, and I'm responsible for all of it.

"Okay. What did you have in mind?"

Her grin widens as I give in to whatever chaos she has running through her mind. "Well, for starters, we're getting dinner, because I'm starving. And then we're going to Jacob's party."

"Isn't Brittany going to be mad we're ditching her?"

She waves it off like it's no big deal. "She'll get over it."

I can't help but laugh. "It's her birthday!"

"And she has one every year," she says, as if it's obvious. "Jeez, you'd think after nineteen of them she would realize they're not that big of a deal."

Raising one brow at her, the corner of my mouth raises. "So, if I told you I didn't want to throw our annual joint birthday bonfire this year..."

"I'd tell you to fuck yourself," she answers without any hesitation. "I said *her* birthday isn't that big of a deal. I said nothing about ours."

"You know, every day you remind me of why I like to stay on your good side."

"Please. I don't have a bad side." She flips her hair over her shoulder. "I'm flawless."

Shaking my head, I look out the window. "And so modest."

"Whatever. Where do you want to eat?"

"Anywhere cheap," I say, only half joking. "I don't get paid until Monday."

You'd think I'd know better than to say anything like that to her by now, but I never get over the way it pisses her off. As if refusing to assume that she will pick up the bill is calling her a shit friend or something.

"Shut up," she groans. "I'll get dinner, and you can just get me something pretty for our birthday."

Our birthday—makes it sound like we're twins. Then again, if I remember correctly, in the third grade, Mali actually had a few people convinced that we were, and that I insisted on staying in for an extra three days. And when they questioned us on having different last names, she told them our mom got knocked up by two different guys around the same time.

She had it all figured out…sort of.

"You know," I point out, "using your breakfast-with-Hayes logic, that would make this a date."

Glancing away from the road and over at me, she looks me up and down before scrunching her nose. "You're a little underdressed."

Bitch.

Chapter 3

PARTIES ARE OVERRATED. I know, I know—cue the outrage. I said what I said. Don't get me wrong, I'm all for the weekly bonfire or a small get-together with people I can stand to be in a room with for longer than twenty minutes, but parties aren't that. They're a group of morons, most of which you don't even know, who all come to the same house to get drunk and make a fool out of themselves.

They've just never been for me.

But Mali lives for them.

She's always been the type to walk into the room and demand all the attention, while I'd prefer to blend in with the background. It's not like I think I'm ugly or anything. I've had enough guys hit on me to know that's not the case. But being the object of everyone's affection feels a lot like being in a fishbowl. I just want to have a good time and live my life, not put on a show for everyone else.

Mali stands on top of the table, holding up her drink and dancing to the music like she's the only one around. If it wasn't for her being as happy as she is, I'd regret letting her choose tonight's festivities. But as I watch her throw her head back and smile, completely in her element, I can't even be a little mad.

"So, Laiken," Tanner almost yells over the music. "What's going on with you and Craig?"

Just hearing his name makes my skin crawl. After dealing with him at breakfast this morning, I would pay good money to never see or hear from him again. If Cam wasn't on probation, I'd let him deal with it. Getting his ass kicked might do Craig some good, and I have better things to do than deal with him. But instead, I'm left to handle it on my own.

"Other than throwing up in my mouth every time someone asks me about him?" I sass back.

He smiles, showing that's exactly what he wanted to hear. "So, you're single then?"

Ugh. Fuck. "Nope. Haven't you heard? I'm dating Mali."

That gets her attention, and she turns to me with mock interest. "Ooh, do we scissor?"

Every guy within fifteen feet freezes and focuses solely on our conversation. You would think they've never watched porn, and that two girls are a foreign concept.

"Please say yes," Tanner begs. "And then say you'll let me watch."

"If you sold tickets to that, you could make bank," Ben adds.

Mali's brows raise. "I would love a shopping spree."

"Oh my God," I mutter, shaking my head. "You're all incorrigible."

"You started it, babe," Mali says with a wink.

Meanwhile, the guys look disappointed. Like they honestly believed I was serious, and in one move I just crushed all their hopes and dreams. Picture telling a kid that Santa Claus isn't real on Christmas Eve, and then add a little more sulking.

I glance between Tanner and Ben. "As if I'd ever get naked in front of either of you."

"Why not? It's nothing we haven't seen before," Ben says, and Tanner immediately punches his arm as my blood runs cold.

What the fuck?

Closing my eyes for a second, I take a deep breath, and when I reopen them, the tension in the room is tenfold.

"What do you mean, nothing you haven't seen before?" I ask carefully.

Mali hops off the table and comes to stand beside me, putting a hand on my back. Tanner gives Ben a look that silently tells him he fucked up, but no one is saying a word.

"One of you better start explaining, or I swear to God, I'll make everything with a vagina from here to California think you have more STDs than a brothel during a condom shortage."

"Okay, okay," Tanner whines. He knows I'm not bluffing. "We may have seen a couple pictures on Craig's phone, but it's not a big deal."

A dry laugh leaves my mouth. Leave it to a *man* to tell me that having intimate photos of you shown around—photos that were meant to be private—isn't a big deal. That's like telling us childbirth and menstrual cycles aren't that bad.

"He's right," Ben chimes in. "They were very tasteful."

"Mansplain that shit to someone else, but don't you dare fucking come at me with that," I growl. "Were either of you going to tell me he was having his own personal show and tell?"

Their silence tells me everything I need to know. In a question of where their loyalty lies, it's definitely not with me. Then again, being as Tanner was just trying to get with me no more than five minutes ago, I don't think it lies with Craig either.

Or maybe the threesome he had while I was trying to help my parents bail my brother out of jail showed him that sharing is caring.

Regardless, I need to get the hell out of here before it's *me* who is in prison for aggravated assault. I have a feeling I'd be a lot less lucky than Cam was.

All it takes is one look at Mali, and she's grabbing my hand and pulling me out of the house. Calls of my name followed by halfhearted apologies go unacknowledged as we walk out the door and over to her car.

"Are you good to drive?"

She nods. "The beer was warm and nasty. The cup was more of a prop in my hand than a drink."

As she unlocks the car, we both get in and I curl into a ball. Craig mentioned still having the pictures this morning as we were arguing. Said it's the only thing he's able to get off to anymore—like I'm supposed to find that flattering. When the conversation didn't go the way he wanted, he insinuated spreading them around, but I don't think I ever believed he was serious.

I was wrong.

Watching me leave with Hayes after refusing to hear him out must have pushed him over the edge. I just hope it was only Ben and Tanner he showed and not the entire former football team. They *did* say they saw them on his phone, not that he sent them.

"Are you okay?" Mali questions when I'm lost in my thoughts for a little too long.

I look over at her and shrug. "Would you be?"

"Do you want to go back to my house for a bit to cool off, or should I drop you off at home?"

Motherfucker. I completely forgot that my probably-red-faced father is still waiting to read me the riot act. I have half a mind to just sleep at Mali's, but I don't think it would do me any good. If anything, it could make things worse.

"I should get home. Take my punishment like a good little seven-year-old." I pause as Mali chuckles, and a familiar street sign gives me a brilliant idea. "But first, let's make a pit stop."

And judging by the way she smirks, she knows exactly what I'm thinking.

Chapter 3

IT'S NEARLY THREE IN the morning by the time Mali drops me off at home, which is approximately two hours past my regular curfew and eight hours after my dad told me to get my ass home. The naive part of me hopes he's asleep. That he had some time to cool down and realized that he has no business grounding his grown-ass daughter.

But I'm not that lucky.

In a way that could put a ninja to shame, I quietly open the door and tiptoe into the house. I even manage to get it closed without making a sound. But the second I turn to head toward the stairs, the lights flick on and I find my dad standing there with his arms crossed.

"You better be real careful what the first words out of your mouth are, because I am not in the mood for your sass right now."

Between the way he's glaring at me and the tone of his voice, I know better than to push buttons and choose to drop my head.

"I'm sorry."

He grunts. "Do you even know what you're sorry for?"

No, but I can't tell him that. "Everything?"

His eyes roll as he grabs a paper off the counter and smacks it down in front of me. "That's the mechanic bill for your car. It needs a whole new engine. And that," he points to the $7,000 total at the bottom, "is how much I had to pay for it."

"Holy fuck!"

Okay, maybe that was the wrong thing to say.

"Language, young lady."

I smile sweetly at him. "Holy fudge?"

He watches me for a moment then shakes his head. "No. Not this time. The cute and innocent act may have worked when you were five, but you're a long way from that."

Well, it was worth a shot. "Do you want me to give you my next paycheck?"

"You're definitely going to be giving me part of it," he replies as he leans against the counter. "But first, I want to know why you haven't been getting your oil changed. I make the appointments for you *and* give you the money for it. All you had to do was take it there and wait twenty minutes for them to do it!"

He's right, and maybe if the mechanics in that place were hot and not missing half their teeth because they spent too many years on meth, I'd actually go. But I'd literally rather be anywhere else after the one time a guy they call Skid told me he wanted to teach me how to work a stick—and he wasn't talking about a manual transmission.

"You know I hate going there," I try to reason, but it's no use.

"Well, now the only place you're going is your room." He gives me a stern look. "No leaving the house for one week."

"Seriously?" I balk. "I'm eighteen. You can't hold me hostage."

"I don't care. You live under my roof, you abide by my rules."

Neither of us move as we standoff, until I realize there is no winning this one. With a huff, I leave him in the kitchen and storm up the stairs. Fuck being quiet now. There's no point.

As soon as I get into my room, I pull my phone from my back pocket and type out a text to Mali.

Grounded. One week. Seriously, kill me now.

The answer that immediately comes tells me she's already home.

No, thank you. I'd get blood on my clothes.
But hey, at least you got all your anger out
before you got home. 😘

I can't stop the corners of my lips from rising.

She's right.

There is that.

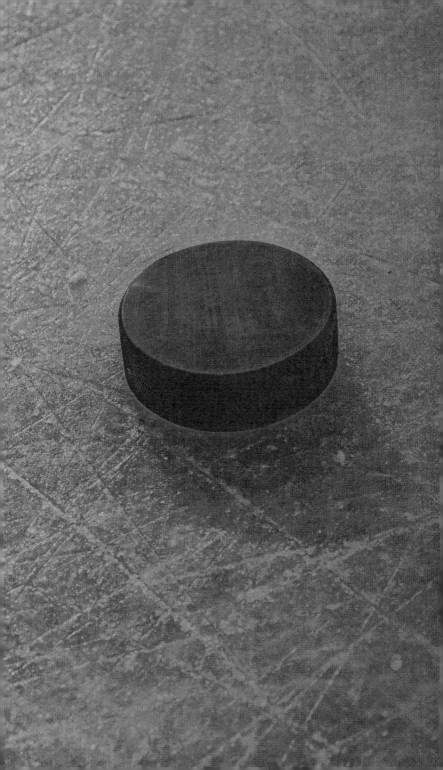

Hayes
CHAPTER FOUR

WHY IS IT THAT WHEN YOU'RE ABOUT TO START closing everything up someone always decides to come through the damn door? I swear, it's like they sit in the parking lot and wait for it to hit five minutes until closing before they come in. And I have to sit around as they finish browsing, like I'm not waiting impatiently for them to leave.

By the time I finally get out of work, it's almost an entire hour past when I was supposed to lock up, and all they bought was a fucking sticker to put on their car.

Because you don't have to actually be *a surfer girl to look like one.*

Sure, catfish. Whatever you say.

As I pull away from the surf shop, I send Cam a text letting him know I'm on my way. If he has a problem with how late I am, he can take it up with the chicks who tried to suffocate me with their perfume cloud.

My truck roars down Main Street as I drive through town. People stop to stare at me as I pass—some giving me dirty looks, while others smile because they recognize me. That's the problem with living in a place where the population is low enough to fit everyone inside a basketball court. Everyone knows everyone, and they constantly think that your business is their own.

No fucking thank you.

I turn into the driveway my truck has spent more time in than my own and throw it in park, grabbing the box off the passenger seat and heading inside. Cam is standing in the kitchen with his phone in his hand when he looks up and sees me.

"Look who decided to show up."

I roll my eyes and shove the box against his stomach. "Fuck off. I tried texting you."

His brows furrow as he looks down at his phone again. "Oh yeah. Guess you did."

"Too busy texting your mimosa chick from yesterday?"

He grunts. "Nah. Don't get me wrong, we had fun, but I'm not interested in seeing her again."

Now *that* doesn't surprise me. "Not Mali enough for you?"

His eyes widen and he looks for Laiken, but when he notices she isn't around, he relaxes. "No, asshole. She's just too high maintenance for me."

"So, you're looking for the Toyota of women?" I quip.

He closes his eyes for a second and shakes his head. "I don't know what's worse—that you're an asshole or that what you just said makes sense."

I grab an apple from the bowl in the middle of the island and take a bite out of it. "Neither. I'm fantastic."

Before he can spit back some smartass response, Laiken comes storming down the stairs. You can tell by the look on her face that she's not in the best of moods. And when Cam is blocking her way to the fridge, I'm almost concerned for his wellbeing.

"Can you move?" she sneers.

He glances at her and then back at me, with an expression that says even he knows not to fuck with her right now. He steps out of her way, and she grabs a bottle of water before stomping her little ass back to her room.

Only when she's finally out of earshot do either of us find it safe to breathe again.

"What the hell is wrong with her?" I ask.

He shrugs. "She got grounded, so now it's Hurricane Laiken around here for the next week."

"Ouch."

"Yeah, tell me about it. No one is safe from her wrath."

Cam puts the box on the island and opens it up, pulling out one of the bars of surf wax. One of the perks of being sponsored by the owner of the surf shop is he gets all the wax he wants for free. And one of the perks of being friends with me is that it gets delivered to his house. The rest of those fuckers can come pick it up at the shop.

"Perfect," he says. "Thanks, man. Would you mind putting this in my room though? I've got to head out."

For the first time since I got here, I notice he's all dressed up—or at least as dressed up as Cam gets. "I thought you said you weren't seeing that girl again."

"I'm not. I have a dinner date," he explains.

Out of all the years I've known Cam, he has gone on a total of maybe five dates. And that includes the year he was in a somewhat-serious relationship with Sienna.

"Okay, what the fuck is going on?" I chuckle.

"What do you mean?"

"I *mean* you've been going on a lot of dates lately, and yet none of them get a second one."

He slips his phone into his pocket and grabs his keys off the hook. "I don't know. I can't risk being at parties, so for the next two years I have to spend my time elsewhere."

The corner of my mouth raises. "And the fact that they all seem to look like Mali is a total coincidence?"

Instead of answering, he heads for the door and flips me off. "Later, douchebag!"

Cracking on him about her is my favorite hobby. And honestly, I've never really understood why he won't just ask her out. I've seen the way they glance at each other. If she were to say no, I'd be shocked. But I guess we'll never know, since he won't ever grow a pair when it comes to her.

I grab the box off the island and head up the stairs to put it in his room. Clothes are strewn all over his bed, suggesting he put a little more effort into this date than he wants to admit. Who knows, maybe he actually likes this one.

Or maybe he's just avoiding the obvious.

Just when I'm about to leave, I hear singing coming from the second set of stairs. Laiken's voice carries throughout the house as she belts out the lyrics to Taylor Swift's *All Too Well*. It's never been a secret that she can sing. She's performed the National Anthem at our hockey games more times than I can count. But there's something different about the way she hits all the right notes when she's alone versus when she has an audience. It's like she's willing to push herself a little further when she's in her own little world.

I take the stairs two at a time until I'm standing in the doorway to Laiken's bedroom. It's funny because I've always teased her about having a room in the attic, but as I stand here, watching her dance around with her eyes closed and earbuds firmly in place—I can't help but be a little jealous. The moon shines through the skylight, making me wonder what it would be like to fall asleep while staring up at the stars.

Leaning against the doorway, a smirk appears on my face as I watch Laiken and listen to her sing. Her hair is curled, her makeup done, and the loose shit with a plunging neckline is definitely not the T-shirt and sweatpants she had on a few minutes ago. But before I can figure out what she's up to for myself, she opens her eyes and sees my reflection in the mirror.

"Jesus Christ!" she shouts. "What the fuck are you doing?"

"Enjoying the show," I answer simply.

Cocking a brow at me, she takes out the earbuds and puts them back into their case. "How long have you been there?"

"Long enough to hear you belt out the lyrics like Taylor Swift's breakups are your own."

She scoffs. "Those breakups *are* my own. Don't burn my girl and you won't get a song written about you. Plain and simple."

My grin widens. "Spoken like a true Swiftie."

"The fact that you even know what a Swiftie is…"

"Hey," I say defensively, "I have a sister."

Her arms cross over her chest as she looks me up and down. "Mm-hm. I'm sure you blast "I Knew You Were Trouble" in your truck on the way home from work."

"It's a good song!"

Honestly, I don't even know which song that is. I'm sure I've heard it at one point in time or another, but seeing the way she giggles at my lame joke almost makes me want to listen to it.

Almost.

She walks over to her bed and sits down before slipping her feet into a pair of heels. What I thought was just her being bored and playing dress up to entertain herself is definitely something else.

"What are you doing?" I question hesitantly.

The last thing I want is for her to bite my head off the same way she almost did Cam's.

Laiken looks at me like I've grown a second head. "Going to a party."

"Aren't you supposed to be grounded?" The fact that I sound like a parent isn't lost on me, but I'm not sure I want her going anywhere looking like *that*.

She grunts amusedly. "Okay, first of all, the fact that they even have the ability to ground me when I'm a legal adult is bullshit."

I can't exactly argue with her there, but she isn't done as she continues while walking over and opening her skylight.

"And second, if they didn't want me to sneak out, they shouldn't have given me such easy access. Besides, there's something I need to take care of."

The way she climbs out onto the roof shows that this isn't something new for her. She's too comfortable—not even a bit worried that heels and roofing shingles don't go well together. But me, I don't like the way her shirt reveals a little too much when she moves a certain way.

"I really don't think you should do that," I try telling her when her foot slips.

"Are you going to stop me?"

The question sounds more like a challenge, but if I know anything about this girl, it's that doing so would only push her even more.

My shoulders sag in defeat. "Like I even could."

The corners of her mouth raise as she looks me up and down. "I guess you know me better than I thought."

Before I can even begin to try to unpack that statement, she closes the skylight and the sound of her heels scraping across the roof echoes through the room. I open it back up and stick my head through just in time to see her shimmy down a pole. A few seconds later, she's on the ground and walking down the driveway.

Fucking hell.

Chapter 4

I PUT THE KEY in the ignition and turn it, hearing as my truck roars to life. As I left Laiken's room, I closed the door and locked it in hopes that it will keep her from getting caught. Does it surprise me that she snuck out? Not even a little. We've all done it, especially while our parents *forbid* us from going out. And she had a point—she's a legal adult. However, I don't think her parents will see it that way if they find out.

Pulling out of the driveway, I start heading home when I pass Laiken walking down the side of the road. I thought for sure Mali or another one of her friends would be right around the corner to pick her up, but I guess I was wrong.

My foot hovers over the brake, and I know it's a bad idea. The only thing I should be doing right now is going home to shower and study the new plays for hockey practice tomorrow. And yet, I find myself pulling over to the side of the road and rolling down the window as I wait for Laiken to get up to my truck.

"Get in," I all but demand.

She looks a little confused. "So you can take me home or to the party?"

Ugh.

"The party," I specify, relieved when she opens the door and climbs inside. "Where is it?"

"Heather Fredrick's house."

I nod, not needing any more information, and I'm sure she knows why. Heather has an older sister, Cassie. And let's just say Cass and I aren't exactly strangers. I've been to that house enough to know how to get there.

"You were going to walk that far?"

She shrugs and looks out the window. "I told you. There's something I need to take care of."

Vague, but okay. "And Mali isn't coming with you?"

"She's at work," is the only explanation she offers.

It goes quiet again for a bit, until I let my curiosity get the better of me.

"So, what did you manage to get grounded for anyway?"

She hums, pulling her attention away from the window and over to me. "My dad found out I haven't been getting my oil changed and now my engine is fucked."

That'll do it. "Doesn't he give you the money to get it done?"

"Yes, but no self-respecting woman wants to sit there while a bunch of mechanics stare at our cleavage and offer us things we don't actually need."

I chuckle, having no comeback for that. If I'm honest, I don't want some fucker ogling her while she waits for her car either, but that's just because she's Cam's little sister. She deserves more respect than that shit.

"You could have Cam come with you to get it done," I suggest. "Bet they won't ever do that shit again."

She snorts. "Yeah, well, contrary to popular belief, I don't actually *enjoy* him being as intrusive as he is. He still treats me like I'm twelve."

My jaw drops in mock disbelief. "You mean, you're not? I should've let you walk then."

Using the back of her hand, she smacks my arm. "Shut up."

But I don't miss the way her smile reflects in the window as she turns her attention back to the passing houses.

Chapter 4

WE PULL UP TO find the house packed to the brim. It must be some kind of back-for-the-summer party, because there's people on the lawn that I know for a fact left for college in September. Don't they know it's better if they just stay there? Who would want to come back to this shitty town anyway?

"Thanks for the ride," Laiken tells me as she unbuckles her seatbelt, but she stops as soon as I shut off the truck. "What are you doing?"

I shrug. "I'm already here. Figure I may as well go in and say hi to a few people."

Judging by the look on her face, she'd rather I do anything but that—which is exactly why I'm doing it anyway. There haven't been many times I've seen Laiken so determined to go to a party, and especially not without Mali. Which means the thing she *needs to take care of* is important enough for her to come alone. If I left her here and something happened to her, Cam would never forgive me for it.

I'll just hang out, socialize a little, and keep a subtle eye on her.

No harm, no foul.

The two of us walk into the party, and I don't even get so much as a goodbye before she leaves me to go over to a few friends. But that's okay. It only takes a second before I spot Cassie and a few of the guys hanging out in the kitchen.

"Now there's a face I haven't seen in a while," she says with a smile.

I push my hair out of my face. "What's up, Cass?"

"Not much. Didn't expect to see you here."

"Yeah, well. I was in the area."

It's a blatant lie. Even she knows that. But she's not about to call me out on it, especially because she knows I've never just shown up here *for her*. I was always invited first, and even then, sometimes she had to convince me to come.

I say hello to some of the guys while Cassie goes over to get a beer from the keg. When she gets back, she hands it to me and leans against the counter.

"So, how've you been?" she questions.

As I take a sip, she waits for my answer. "Can't complain. How's university?"

"It's amazing." Her face lights up like it's her favorite thing to talk about. "My roommates are great, and I'm dating this guy. His name is Drew. He was my lab partner."

I smile, even though I genuinely couldn't care less. "That's great. I'm really happy for you."

She runs her fingers through her hair. "Thanks. I'd be lying if I said I didn't wish he was you sometimes, though."

And there it is. The reason I never took her seriously or ever even considered a relationship with her. I've never really done relationships with anyone, but if I was going to, it certainly wouldn't be with her. That girl doesn't have a loyal bone in her body. She always tried to preach that I was that *one guy* for her. The one she's had a crush on for years and can't really find anyone that compares. But I don't buy it.

She just wants to be the girl who can change me.

Not going to happen.

"And on that note," I say, tipping my cup toward her. "I'm going to go see who else is around."

Her smile falls as she realizes whatever she was hoping for isn't going to happen. But I'm not the *cheat on your boyfriend with* kind of guy. I wonder if lab-partner-Drew has any idea she came home with full intentions of hooking up with an old fling if given the chance.

After making rounds and not seeing anyone worth staying for, I'm almost considering leaving. I'm exhausted, and all Laiken seems to be doing is hanging out with a few friends. Nothing out of the usual. But that idea goes right out of my mind when I spot Craig across the room.

He's standing with a bunch of the guys from the football team, both former and current, but every few minutes, he glances in Laiken's direction. And after what happened at breakfast yesterday, you couldn't pay me to leave now.

I'M NOT A CREEP. Or at least that's what I keep telling myself as I pretend to socialize with the sole intention of keeping an eye on Laiken and her douchebag of an ex. Thankfully, other than longing for her attention like a stray puppy, Craig hasn't done anything. I finally convince myself that the two of them can exist in the same room without him being a threat to her, and give myself permission to go to the bathroom.

Big mistake.

I couldn't have been gone any more than five minutes, and yet, when I come back, Craig isn't where he was when I left. Instead, he's standing by the door with Laiken, about fifty feet closer than either of us would like him to be. Her nose scrunches in disgust as he takes a step closer, and she puts a hand on his chest to keep some distance between them. It isn't until he grabs her wrist to keep her from walking away and starts yelling at her that I get involved.

"Hey," I interrupt them, ignoring the way Laiken rolls her eyes. "Everything okay over here?"

Craig grins smugly. "We're fine, Wilder. Isn't that right, Lai?"

She tries to tug her wrist free once more, but fails. Her eyes meet mine, and the message is clear. She may not want to ask for help—she's far too stubborn for that—but she needs it.

"Get your hand off the girl, Craig," I growl.

"Come on, man. I thought we were cool."

Taking a step closer, I nod toward where he's gripping her tightly. "Don't make me say it again."

He lets go and raises his hands in surrender. "All right. Relax."

The second she's free, Laiken storms away, and I don't hesitate to follow her. I put my hand on her shoulder and she flinches, but then exhales when she notices it's just me.

"What's going on?"

She shakes her head and runs her fingers through her hair. "It's nothing."

Yeah, no. "It's not nothing. This is the second time I've seen you arguing with him. So either you tell me, or I'm going to get Cam down here. Regardless, I'm not leaving here until I get to the bottom of this."

Pinching the bridge of her nose, I can tell she's uncomfortable. I wait patiently as she takes a couple breaths and then her shoulders sag as she looks up at me.

"He's mad that I don't want to get back with him, so he's holding some pictures I sent him while we were together over my head like a goddamn guillotine."

She slips her phone out from her back pocket and hands it to me, letting me see all the texts he's been sending her over the past couple days.

Talk to me, baby. You don't want me to share, do you?

You're going to have to answer me at some point.

Babe, I swear. Ben and Tanner went through my phone on their own.

Stop playing so hard to get.

I'm not playing anything. Leave me alone.

Come on. It's not like you'll ever find anyone better than me.

You should be thankful that I'm willing to get back with you.

Now I get it—why she was so quick to cave when I mentioned getting Cam down here. If he knew about this shit, he'd be on the next bus to Neuse Correctional with murder charges pending. Hell, I'm contemplating doing it myself right now.

I don't know what pisses me off more, that he's trying to blackmail her into being with him, or that he's insinuating that he's her only option. As if she should run back to him after everything he did simply because he thinks he's hot shit.

Fucking prick.

"And you don't want to get back with him?" I ask sarcastically as I hand her phone back.

She huffs, a hint of a smile showing through. "It's a wonder, right? He's a real prince charming."

The two of us glance over to see him standing back with his friends. When he notices he has Laiken's attention, he smiles and winks at her, like he's not dangerously close to having my fist embedded into his face.

Yeah, this isn't happening.

I'm not going to sit here and make her feel less than. This

is most likely a horrible idea, even worse than offering to pick her up from the mechanic, or drive her to the party, but the rage running through me blurs my judgment. I place a gentle hand on Laiken's face. Her attention immediately switches from him to me as a mix of fear and confusion fills her eyes.

"I'm going to do something, and I need you to trust me, okay?"

She takes her bottom lip between her teeth and nods. "Okay."

I don't let myself hesitate for a single second as I pull her in and cover her mouth with my own. It's supposed to be quick—soft and simple—but when she wraps her arms around my neck and arches up on her tiptoes to get closer, I can't help myself. The hand that isn't on her cheek moves to her lower back and holds her close as we both deepen the kiss.

The second her tongue tangles with my own, the taste of strawberries and vanilla is all I can focus on. In this moment, we're not in the middle of a party, she's not my best friend's little sister, and I'm not kissing her for the sole purpose of making her ex eat his words.

No.

In this moment, she's mine.

Wait, shit.

The realization of what just went through my mind pours over me like a bucket of ice water, and I force myself to break the kiss. I rest my forehead against hers as the two of us catch our breath, and when I open my eyes, I see Laiken staring back at me.

Taking my keys out of my pocket, I put them in her hand. "Go outside and wait for me at my truck."

She takes a deep breath before nodding and doing as I say. I watch her as she walks right out the front door, and then I turn to Craig. His attention is already on me with his jaw clenched and his eyes narrowed.

"So, tell me," he starts as we meet in the middle of the room. "How are my sloppy seconds?"

I put my tongue in my cheek and chuckle dryly before grabbing him by his jacket and slamming him into the railing of the stairs. Some people gasp while the majority just stop and stare.

"Jesus Christ," Craig says. "Chill the fuck out, bro."

Not your fucking bro. "Hand over your phone, shithead, or this is only going to get worse for you."

"All right, all right," he mutters and takes out his phone.

I rip it out of his hand and instead of going to photos, I go straight into settings. It's bad enough that he's letting his friends get ahold of pictures that were always meant to stay private. I absolutely refuse to betray her by seeing them too, even if it's just to delete them.

Within thirty seconds, his phone is in the process of being factory reset, knowing he hasn't used the cloud since the day he almost got expelled for being caught with the answers to one of his final exams.

"The fuck did you do that for?" he whines, snatching his phone back. "I had shit on there I needed."

"Should've thought about that before you threatened someone I care about," I sneer. "Any other copies of those get out, I'll smash your phone and feed you the pieces. Got it?"

He scoffs, shoving me off him and fixing his jacket. "Whatever, man. She's psychotic anyway. You should see what that bitch did to my fucking car."

I can't help but smirk. Laiken doesn't really do anything small, and I'm sure this is no different. Refusing to dignify him with an answer, I push my way through the shocked party and find Laiken standing by the front door. She looks just as surprised as everyone else, except with a glint of admiration in her eyes that should probably set off alarms in my brain, but I don't miss a beat.

Already gave myself something to explain to Cam, because there's no chance he won't hear about this. I may as well really drive the point home.

Throwing an arm around her, the two of us walk right out the front door and leave everyone behind to question what the fuck just happened.

We both stay quiet as we walk toward my truck, until I see Craig's 1970 Chevelle. The paint is absolutely destroyed across most of the car, and Laiken looks at it like it's her life's work.

"I take it that's *your* artwork?" I ask.

She smiles in a way that's entirely too innocent for the last ten minutes. "I gave it a makeover. He should be thanking me. It has character now."

I laugh, knowing he deserved it. "You're insane."

Her one shoulder raises in a half shrug as she reaches the passenger side of my truck. "I wanted to set it on fire, but Mali said that was a little too much, even for me."

For the love of fuck. "Remind me to thank her."

THE WHOLE WAY BACK to Laiken's house is dead silent. Not even the radio can ease the tension between us. My hand grips the steering wheel tight enough to turn my knuckles white while the other holds a cigarette that is meant to calm me down and failing miserably.

I shouldn't have kissed her. I know that. It was a selfish move on my part, especially knowing how she feels about me. And if Craig's smug attitude hadn't pissed me off, I would've realized that long before it was too late. But in the moment, I wanted nothing more than to wipe that grin off his face—and I did.

And now Cam is going to rip my head straight from my shoulders. At least it will be quick. I might not even feel it.

Not wanting her parents to hear my truck and notice Laiken ever left her room in the first place, I pull over on the side of the road down the street from her house. I can see her turn to face me out of the corner of my eye, but I keep my gaze laser focused on the dashboard.

"I reset his phone," I tell her. "The pictures are gone, and if he has them anywhere else, he knows better than to keep them."

She nods, unbuckling her seatbelt. "Thank you. Seriously."

Her hand rests on my arm, and I hate the way her touch threatens to burn through my skin.

"I really appreciate it."

"We need to talk about tonight," I say before she gets out. "I shouldn't have kissed you. That was wrong of me. I just—"

"H," she interrupts me with a warm smile. "You don't... I know what that kiss was. You were just doing me a favor. It's not like I'm suddenly in love with you or anything."

Except, I can tell by the way she says those words—she is. It's just not suddenly. *God, I'm going to hell.*

"Still. I'm sorry."

"Don't be," she tells me honestly. "I'm not."

With one more grin that does things to me I refuse to

acknowledge, she climbs out of the truck and walks the rest of the way home.

T minus twelve hours until hockey practice, where Cam will inevitably use my head as a puck.

ALL MORNING, I FIND myself mindlessly playing with my bottom lip. I can still feel the softness of her mouth pressed against mine. It's as if kissing her short circuited my brain. It was only meant to be for revenge. In that moment, I wanted nothing more than to see the prick's always cocky attitude falter a bit. And it worked.

Case closed.

Mission accomplished.

But if it served its purpose, why the fuck can't I stop thinking about it?

"Dude," Cam says as he snaps in front of my face. "Did you even hear a word I said?"

I look down at the playbook in his hands. "Sorry, didn't sleep well last night. One more time?"

He starts to go over the play again, but my subconscious keeps repeating *tell him* like a mantra in my head. The problem is, I don't know how.

Hey, I made out with your sister last night.

Shoved my tongue down your sister's throat, but don't worry because it was for revenge against her ex.

Any idea how to get the taste of your little sister off my tongue?

Who am I kidding? No matter how I say it, the outcome will still be the same. He already has to deal with most of his friends hitting on her. Finding out I kissed her the way I did last night...that puts me at the top of his hit list.

Better to rip the bandage off.

"Actually, I have to talk to you about something," I tell him, but before I can say anything else, Isaac comes storming out of the locker room.

"Wilder!" he roars as he steps onto the ice. "What the fuck makes you think you have the right to threaten my brother?"

Cam's brows raise. "You threatened Craig?"

I square my shoulders and direct my attention to Isaac. "If he wasn't being such a piece of shit, I wouldn't have had to. Maybe someone in your family should teach him how to treat a girl."

"Oh, you mean like you know how?" The devious grin on his face tells me I'm fucked. "Yeah, Craig told me all about that kiss. Does Cam know you've been screwing Baby Blanchard?"

"Uh, what?" Cam's jaw ticks as he looks between us, but my attention stays on Isaac.

"You don't know what the fuck you're talking about."

"Sure, I do," he replies. "Tell me, how good is she?"

Cam's head whips toward Isaac. "You'll shut your mouth right now if you know what's good for you."

But his efforts are futile as he smirks. "Come on. I've seen her legs in that leotard. I bet she knows how to ride it just right."

I'm sure I'll add this to the list of bad choices I've made in the last twenty-four hours, but nothing can hold me back as I lunge toward him and bury my fist in his face.

Chapter 4

THE BLEACHERS ARE COLD, which is why the ice pack Cam brings me is almost comical. Why Coach sent us to opposite sides of the place after breaking up the fight is beyond me. He should've just had us lay on the ice to mend our wounds.

"You should get that cut on your lip looked at," Cam tells me as I hiss.

I can already feel it starting to fatten, but at least I'm not thinking about kissing Laiken anymore.

Fuck—scratch that.

"I'll have my mom check it out when I get home," I answer.

I'm almost hopeful he'll walk away, go let off steam or something first after the way he found out about last night, but instead, he sits down beside me.

"So, you kissed my sister?"

Going straight for the kill, I guess. "It's not what you think. I swear, I was just helping her. Craig was being a douchebag, and she needed someone to come to her rescue."

He chuckles. "Clearly you didn't tell *her* that. If you had, you wouldn't be standing there."

Okay, so maybe he has a point. Laiken has never been the kind to need a knight in shining armor. But he didn't see the look on her face last night or the way her ex has the ability to take her mood from sky high to rock bottom in seconds flat.

"Yeah, don't tell her I said that. I've already taken one fist to the face today. I don't need another."

He hums. "Ballsy of you to assume I'm not going to hit you, too."

"I'd deserve it," I answer honestly. "I crossed a line, but just know it was only a kiss. One kiss to get Craig to leave her the hell alone."

"Is that why you hit Isaac?"

The way he's looking at me tells me my next answer will decide where either of us go from here. Luckily for me, I'm used to needing to lie on the spot—the result of trauma from my father leaving and needing to convince everyone I was okay for years.

"What he said was fucked up," I begin. "But if I hadn't punched him, you would've. Your fist was already clenched at your side. Can't have you violating probation on a scumbag like him."

He pulls his gaze away from me and onto the ice, and after the longest second of my life, he nods slowly. "Fair enough."

"So, we're good?"

"Yeah," he confirms. "We're good, but you should know that Coach is pissed."

That's fine. I can handle a pissed-off coach and a few hard practices. Besides, decking Isaac was well worth it. And if I refuse to listen to my conscience when it tells me everything that I just told Cam was a lie, that's worth it, too.

It was just a revenge kiss.

That's all.

Laiken
CHAPTER FIVE

"WHAT DO YOU MEAN, HE KISSED YOU?" MALI ASKS for the fifth time.

I throw my head back against the couch. "Are we in second grade? Do you want me to draw a diagram for you or something? He man, me woman, we pucker and press mouths together."

She scoffs into the phone. "No, I get that, asshole. I just mean, you're telling me this, and you're not freaking out about it. There are no birds singing around your head or fireworks going off in the sky." She pauses to gasp. "Oh my God, is Hayes a bad kisser?"

"No," I answer a little too quickly. "No, it's definitely not that."

And it's not. The feeling of his lips pressed to mine hasn't left me alone all damn day. Honestly, I don't think it will any time soon. Kissing Hayes is something I've dreamed about for years, and it finally happened.

I just wish it was in different circumstances.

"It was a favor," I admit.

She stutters, and I can almost picture the look on her face. "A…favor?"

"Mm-hm. Craig was there, being his typical douchebag self, and Hayes kissed me as a way to get him to leave me alone."

It's quiet for a second, and then she asks the question I should've known was coming.

"Was there tongue?"

I roll my eyes, even though she can't see me. "Does it matter?"

"Of course it matters," she says as if it's obvious. "Because no tongue means it was a pity kiss, but *with tongue* means a part of him wanted it."

This. This right here is why I didn't want to tell her at all. And why I waited until almost noon to answer her texts. I don't need her getting my hopes up about something that is never going to happen again. What happened last night was a one-time thing, and I'm not naive to think otherwise.

"There was tongue, wasn't there?" The excitement in her voice is evident.

I sigh. "Yes, but we're not doing this. It meant nothing. Or at least nothing to him."

Trying to tell her it meant nothing to me would be pointless. There's no way he could kiss me and it *not* mean something. But she doesn't need to know that said kiss caused me to go home and have a depressingly realistic dream that we were happily married with two kids and a house in Barbados.

"Lai," she says, her voice laced with sympathy. "Do you want me to kick his ass?"

"No." Though I'm sure watching her try could be entertaining.

"Key his truck?"

I snort. "He'll murder you and leave a breadcrumb trail with the pieces of your body."

The line goes quiet, almost to the point where I think she hung up, but then she clears her throat. "That's both disturbing and grossly accurate. Well done."

"I try."

"Seriously, though," she continues. "I know he's got his own standards of what's acceptable in your mind, but don't think that just because he hasn't thrown himself at your feet and begged you to be with him, that means you're not the best bitch I know. Hayes Wilder would be fucking lucky to have you on his arm."

Her words make me smile, because I know she's being honest. "Thank you."

Mali may get on my nerves sometimes, and push limits that make me contemplate if twenty to life would be worth it, but when it really matters, she's always there. Always ready to take on the world if that's what I need, but also there to pull me back if I'm about to take things just a little too far.

Like lighting Craig's car on fire.

Would it have been worth it? Absolutely.

Is me getting arrested for arson something my parents can handle so soon after their son almost went to jail for aggravated assault? Probably not.

They're religious and all, but I'm not looking for them to meet God *that* soon. Besides, who would feed Cam? The only reason he's twenty-one and still living at home is because his grocery bill would be through the roof. I don't know where the hell he puts it all.

"So," Mali gets my attention once more. "Was swapping spit with Hayes everything you imagined it would be?"

"How do you do that?"

"Do what?"

I exhale. "Make something so great sound vulgar and disgusting."

She chuckles. "So it was great, huh?"

"I hate you."

"You couldn't even if you tried."

Before I can retort, I'm distracted by Hayes and Cam's muffled voices as they step onto the porch. If I thought I'd have enough time, I'd book it up to my room. Seeing him for the first time since last night is something that I need to prepare for. It can't just be sprung on me. But as the door starts to open, I realize that's my only choice.

"Mal, I'll text you," I tell her.

"Wait! We haven't gone over all the details of you two sucking face!"

I hang up the phone, cutting off Mali's voice just as the guys come in. Cam picks a pillow up off the couch and throws it at me as he passes by, but I barely even notice. I'm too focused on the fresh cut on Hayes's bottom lip. And if that's not bad enough, the knuckles on his hand are a nasty looking mix of purple and blue.

For a second, I wonder if I blacked out and forgot about Hayes getting into an all-out brawl with Craig, but I think I would have remembered that. No girl forgets the vision of a man fighting to defend her honor—and yes, I do consider the way he threw him up against the banister to be defending my honor. I may not ever get to kiss him again, but at least I get that beautiful mental image.

My gaze locks with his as he follows Cam into the kitchen, and the way the corners of his lips twitch upward is enough to tell me things aren't going to be totally awkward now... for him, anyway. I, however, will use muscle memory to reenact that kiss in my mind until I'm old and gray.

Apologies in advance to my future husband.

"Are Mom and Dad home?" Cam shouts.

"No," I answer. "They're at some fundraiser for the church. Why?"

The fridge slams shut, and I hear a mix of footsteps coming toward me and cans cracking open.

"Because we wanted a beer," my brother tells me. "Duh."

I stare back at him, both unamused and mind-boggled.

"You do know you're twenty-one, right? As in the legal drinking age for the state of North Carolina?"

He repeats me in a high-pitched tone, mocking me like a four-year-old. "Obviously, I know that. But my young little baby friend here *is not* twenty-one."

Hayes flips him off while I chuckle. "If you honestly believe Mom and Dad think Hayes, of all people, doesn't drink, you're dumber than I thought you were."

"Hey!" Hayes pouts. "What's that supposed to mean?"

I cock a single brow at him. "You thought it would be a good idea to use jagerbombs in a drinking competition and then vomited in my mom's favorite vase."

"I couldn't make it to the bathroom," he argues. "It's better than puking on the floor."

"You left it there for three days!"

"I didn't remember it happened until then!"

Cam shakes his head and shivers. "And you wonder why we never let people bring Jägermeister and Red Bull anymore. The smell of that shit will forever be burned into my senses."

"Oh, fuck off. Like you haven't done worse," he claps back. "Do you not remember the night you decided to drink a whole bottle of vodka to yourself while chasing it with a container of orange juice?"

"How could I not?" He smiles at the memory. "That was pure brilliance."

Hayes grunts. "Oh yeah. It was also brilliant when you woke up in the middle of the night to throw up over the side of the bed, forgetting I was asleep on the floor."

"Oh my God, I forgot about that." I cringe, still remembering the sound of Hayes's absolute tantrum. "You were literally covered in regurgitated orange juice."

"And vodka," he adds. "Can't forget that. I smelled like the bathroom floor of a frat house for days, and no matter how many showers I took, it wouldn't go away."

Cam tips his beer toward him. "Kept my floor clean, though."

"It won't be when it's covered in your blood," Hayes counters.

As the two of them go back and forth, I notice my phone start to vibrate on my lap and a picture of Mali sticking her tongue out fills the screen. I should've known she wasn't going to let me off the hook that easy.

Rolling my eyes, I hit answer and bring it to my ear. "You know, usually when people hang up on you, you don't call them back."

"Okay, first of all, you're rude. And second, tell me you heard what happened."

I feign surprise with a gasp. "You finally got approved for the sex change you've wanted?"

Both Cam and Hayes stop what they're doing and turn to look at me, confused and concerned, as Mali laughs.

"Please, the world would be a dangerous place if I had a penis."

My jaw drops, and I'm a little speechless for a second. "I'm sorry, what the fuck did you just say to me?"

"Nevermind," she says. "Isaac got the shit beat out of him at hockey practice this morning."

A million different questions run through my mind at once. "What the fuck?"

"That's what I said! I'm surprised Cam didn't tell you about it."

I glance over at my brother as he flicks through channels, beer in his hand and his feet resting on the coffee table. There's only one reason he wouldn't mention something like that.

My attention turns to Hayes, and more specifically, the bruise on his hand and the split in his lip—the one I wish he would stop using his tongue to fuck with. It's bad enough that he manages to look even hotter all roughed up. I don't need to picture what he can do with his tongue, too.

"I'll text you," I tell Mali, and for the second time in a row, I hang up on her.

My blood is boiling as I stand up and level Hayes with a single look.

"Kitchen," I order, like I have any sort of right to. "Now."

He sighs and gets up to follow me, but just as we're walking away from the couch, the sound of Cam's voice stops me dead in my tracks.

"Keep your mouths to yourselves this time, please."

I whip my head around just in time to see Hayes wince. "You told him?"

"We were standing in the middle of a crowded ass party," he points out. "He was going to find out at some point, and it was better that he heard it from me."

I take a deep breath, knowing that it's a totally understandable reason. Still, I was hoping to keep that little event to myself. Well, and Mali. Can't keep anything from her or she'll feed me to a bunch of alligators.

As soon as we get into the kitchen, I lean against the counter and watch as Hayes squirms uncomfortably. His hand rubs the back of his neck, and his eyes seem to look anywhere but at me. It may seem harmless, but it stings a little. It's not like it takes a rocket scientist to figure out why he's all of a sudden uneasy in a room alone with me. But I can't be bothered with that right now.

"What happened to your hand?"

He glances down at the bruise for a second. "Oh, I got hit with a puck at practice."

"Mm-hm." I nod thoughtfully. "And did the puck happen to be Isaac's face?"

The way he smirks, all guilty looking and yet still unfairly gorgeous, tells me I'm right. I press my lips into a line and grab a wooden spoon from behind me, throwing it directly at him.

"Don't lie to me, ass."

He chuckles. "Well, I wasn't aware you already knew!"

Oh, yeah, because that makes it better.

I run my fingers through my hair and sigh heavily. "Please tell me it had nothing to do with last night."

"Okay. Me punching him had nothing to do with last night."

Good. That's good. "Okay, so then why did you punch him?"

"To keep Cam from punching him."

He says it so simply, like it's the obvious answer, and it doesn't even occur to me that it doesn't even make sense as I storm back into the living room and smack Cam over the back of the head.

"Ow," he whines, rubbing his head. "The fuck was that for?"

"You literally *just* got put on probation, and already you're going to risk violating it on someone as worthless as Isaac?" I sneer. "Are you out of your damn mind?"

Hayes leans in the doorway of the kitchen. "Laiken, I wouldn't—"

"Not a word out of you," I tell him, instantly shutting him up. "I'm still not done with you yet."

Cam and Hayes share a look, but I'm not having it.

"Don't look at him," I growl at my brother. "What the fuck were you thinking?"

"Drop it, Lai," he tries.

I cross my arms over my chest. "Absolutely not. Not until you tell me what he could have possibly done that would have been worth risking going to prison over!"

Neither one of them says a thing, but I'm not about to back down.

"I'm waiting."

Cam rolls his eyes and takes another sip of his beer before putting it on the coffee table. "He was talking shit about you."

Oh.

Okay, now I feel a little like a bitch.

Hayes tilts his head to the side. "I mean, *technically,* he was complimenting her."

Cam flips him off, and Hayes chuckles as he sits back down on the couch.

"Craig apparently tattled," he explains. "When he started talking about you, I could see Cam was getting ready to swing, so I beat him to it."

Appearing totally nonchalant over the whole thing, Cam goes back to flipping through channels. "I told you, I wasn't going to hit him."

"You're so full of shit," Hayes argues. "You and I both know he wasn't about to shut his mouth until one of us shut it for him. And *I'm* not at risk for jail time."

He shrugs before turning off the TV. "Whatever. There's nothing good on. Want to go play Call of Duty?"

Hayes agrees and the two of them get up and head toward the stairs, leaving me alone to mentally unpack everything I just learned. Cam defending me is nothing new. He's been doing it since we were kids. But hearing that Hayes beat him to it, that's what shocks me the most.

Maybe he really did do it in order to keep Cam from risking his probation. Isaac has been gunning for one of the captain spots for years, and I wouldn't put it past him to get Cam thrown in jail in order to get it. But there's a small part of me that glimmers with hope that maybe Hayes did it because he wanted to defend me, too.

The same way he did last night.

But even if he was, it's only because I'm Cam's little

sister. Letting myself think any differently is just cruel and unusual punishment.

A LITTLE MORE THAN an hour later, I'm getting a drink when Hayes comes down the stairs. He stops as soon as he sees me and neither of us say anything until I notice a little drip of blood slide from his lip, down over his chin.

"You're bleeding," I tell him.

He instinctively touches the cut. "Yeah, I accidentally bit it and opened the cut back up."

Going over to grab a paper towel, I fold it up and run it under cold water before handing it to him. He thanks me quietly as he puts it on his lip. And I don't miss the way he hisses as it touches the cut.

"Don't be such a baby."

He narrows his eyes at me. "You know, for someone who caused the damage to this beautiful face, you're awfully rude."

I smile involuntarily. "So, you admit it. The fight was because of what happened last night."

"No. It was because of what he said about you. The fact that the events of last night were his motivation for it is irrelevant. It's an entirely different incident."

I don't buy it for a second. The two go hand in hand. But he's obviously not going to change his mind on this, so continuing to go back and forth about it is pointless.

"Fine," I say. "But regardless, like you said, I caused it. So at least let me help you clean it up."

He pulls the paper towel away from his mouth. "Nothing to help with. See?"

The second he smiles to show me he's all good, it starts to bleed again—the stretching of his lip causing it to reopen for the second time. I give him a knowing look and he rolls his eyes. He waves me off, and I go grab the liquid bandage from the medicine cabinet in the downstairs bathroom.

"Here. This will at least keep it closed," I tell him. "Otherwise, it might scar, and you don't want that."

He leans against the counter. "Are you saying I wouldn't look hot with a scar?"

My mouth opens and closes as my brain frantically searches with a way to answer that. If it were before last night, I would've had no problem coming back at him. I'd say something witty that would have him feeling like he just got bitch slapped. But it's not. This is *after* last night, and I can't help but wonder if he's joking around, or flirting.

"Stay still and stop talking," I go with instead. "I can't put this on the cut if your mouth is moving."

He chuckles but says nothing as I come closer and carefully dab the liquid over the damage. I try not to focus on how close to him I am, but as I arch up to make sure I got it all, my foot slips and I fall against him. He catches me with his hands on my hips, and I hate how much I will forever crave this feeling.

"Are you okay?" Hayes asks, his voice nearly a whisper.

I force myself to move, and as I step back, I nod. "Yeah. You should be good now, but promise not to mess with it anymore."

He squints, unsure. "Mmm, I promise I'll make a half-assed effort."

His response doesn't surprise me in the slightest. "You're hopeless, you know that?"

"Yep," he answers proudly. "Thanks for the fix-up, Rochester."

The nickname grinds on my nerves—fucking Mali. Hayes grabs another beer from the fridge, but just as he's about to head back up to Cam's room, I know I can't just let him leave. Not until I say something.

"H?"

He stops and turns to me. "Yeah?"

"Thank you," I murmur. "For defending me…again."

His lips quirk upward. "No problem."

That's the thing; it might not be a problem for him, but it is for me. The events of the last eighteen hours are fucking with my head. And the fact that he ended up injured doesn't sit well with me, even if Isaac ended up worse.

"I'm sorry you hurt your hand," I add.

"Don't be," he replies, using the same words I told him last night. "I'm not."

With a wink that will have me questioning everything all damn night, he goes back upstairs to Cam—completely unaware of the butterflies he just released inside my stomach.

Yeah, I know. I'm a fool.

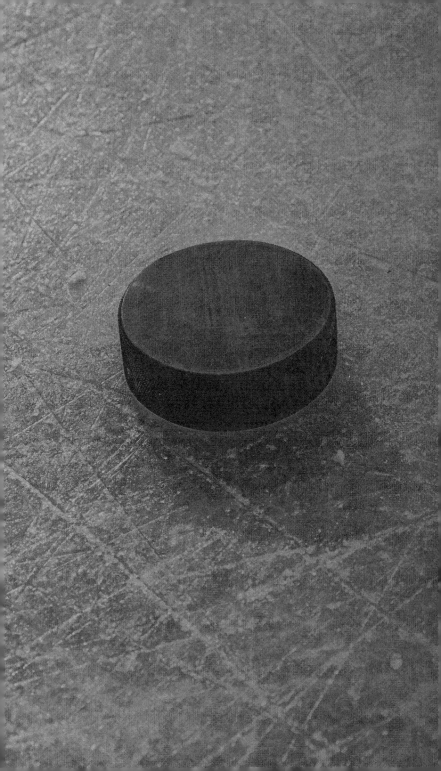

Hayes
CHAPTER SIX

THE DEVIL IS TESTING ME.

I'd blame it on God, but I think he's too holy for the things that have been running through my mind lately.

There isn't a single thing I haven't tried to get my thoughts off Laiken. Dead puppies, naked grandma. I've done it all. And still, I woke up on Cam's floor this morning to find a tent in my pants big enough to fit a family of five.

Let's just say it didn't get any better when Laiken came downstairs wearing only an oversized T-shirt. That's an image that won't be leaving my mind any time soon.

Everything about this is wrong. Wanting your best friend's sister is the easiest way to break bro-code. But just because I can't have her doesn't mean we can't be friends.

The smoke fills my lungs as I take a drag of my cigarette. The roof is a little moist from the early morning dew, but I don't care. I've always loved it up here—a little oasis I can escape to. Cam and I started coming out here a few years ago, and while he stopped doing it after the time he slipped and almost plummeted two stories down, I still can't resist.

It's peaceful up here.

"Hayes Beckett," Cam's mom calls from the ground, and I quickly hide the cigarette. "What on earth are you doing up there?"

I give her my best *I'm a good boy* smile. "Just enjoying the view."

She shakes her head in dismay. "Fine, but be careful."

"Always am, Mrs. B."

Walking over to the car where Cam's dad is waiting for her, she sighs. "I swear, these boys all have a death wish."

I watch as they both get in and drive away, leaving me here.

Alone.

With Laiken.

Cam was gone when I woke up, and I honestly didn't even notice until I saw a text from him telling me that he got called in for an early shift. It's not the first time I've been here when he wasn't, and I'm sure it won't be the last. But there's something different this time—knowing it's just Laiken and me.

I should leave. Get in my truck and drive away. It's what I planned to do anyway after this smoke. But as the sound of Laiken singing meets my ears, a better idea comes to mind.

Climbing up the slope that leads to her skylight is tricky, the dew making it a little more slippery than usual, but I manage. The cigarette hangs out of my mouth as I lie on my stomach. And then it immediately falls out when I realize what I'm looking at.

My plan was to scare her. Swear to God, I thought it would be funny to bang on the glass and make her jump. Bring us both back into safe territory where flirting and kissing at parties isn't a thing. What I didn't plan for, however, was to find her in a towel, fresh out of the shower.

Look away. Fucking look away.

My subconscious is ready to riot, and yet, I can't move. If someone sees me up here, peeking into her skylight like a perverted peeping Tom, I'll lose everything.

My best friend.

The respect of his parents.

My reputation—because getting arrested for something like that is bound to get out.

I know all of this, but as she removes the towel and lets it pool on the floor, it's clear I don't have a say in the matter. My body and my brain are on two totally different circuits. There's nothing I can do.

Her singing dies off as she stands in front of the mirror, running her fingers through her wet hair. The faint sight of a tattoo down the middle of her spine has me more intrigued than I'd like to admit, and it's only getting worse. She drags her fingertips gently down her arm and over her stomach.

No.

Please tell me she's not about to…

But she is.

Of course, she is. Like I said before, the devil is testing me. And by testing, I mean torturing…brutally.

Laiken's head falls back as she slides her hand further south, and I bite my lip in an effort to keep quiet. I wonder if she has any idea how fucking seductive she is. If she knows that she has the power to make a guy fall flat on his face with a single look. But I think that's part of her sex appeal. She knows she's not ugly by any means, but has no idea exactly how fucking gorgeous she is.

Walking over to her bed, she lies down and closes her eyes as she starts to rub circles over her clit. Just the sight of it is enough to have me rock solid against my jeans in seconds. Her movements are slow and deliberate, but as she starts to speed up too soon, they get messy.

Slow down.

You're doing it wrong.

Her head turns from side to side as she chases her own high, but she just can't seem to get there. My fist clenches in frustration as I watch her struggle.

It's not a goddamn scratch off card, Laiken.

Slow the fuck down.

It's painful, literally, to see the frustration on her face and the way she switches hands when her wrist gets sore. And when she finally gives up, without the orgasm she so obviously needs, I can't stop myself from throwing caution to the wind.

I knock on the skylight, smirking when Laiken shrieks. I grin broadly and wiggle my fingers at her, instantly pissing her off. She glares at me and grabs the closest throw blanket to cover herself, but if she doesn't remove that thing soon, I won't apologize for what I do next.

"Unlock it," I demand.

She stares in disbelief for a second before getting up and flicking open the lock.

"You do know this is illegal, right?"

Yeah, I don't give a single fuck right now.

"You're doing it wrong."

"I'm—" she pauses, dumbfounded. "What?"

I push the skylight open further and hop down into her room, staring down at her and the blanket pressed against her chest that only covers the front of her naked body.

"You're. Doing. It. Wrong," I repeat, enunciating each word.

She hesitates for a moment, and then with a sexy sort of confidence I never expected, she squares her shoulders and looks up at me. "Like you could do any better."

Fuck me. "Is that an invitation?"

"Do you want it to be?"

Their mom was right about one thing—I do have a death wish, because if Cam finds out about what I'm about to do, I won't make it out alive. But I can't seem to help myself.

I take a step closer, forcing her to move with me until she can't go any further and falls back onto her bed. "I never turn down a challenge, especially when my skills are in question."

Her breath hitches, but I won't touch her.

Not yet.

"Do it again."

Her eyes widen in surprise, and maybe a hint of embarrassment. "What?"

"You heard me," I growl. "Touch yourself the way you were before."

Her mouth opens and closes as she tries to find the words. "Touch my—no. I can't—"

Lacking patience, I grab her hand and put it there for her. Her jaw clenches, and a moan that has no business being as pornographic as it is comes out of her mouth as I press her own fingers against her clit.

"Fuck," she breathes.

I wish.

Her movements start to speed up entirely way too early again, but this time, I'm there to stop her.

"Shh," I say, slowly shaking my head. "Relax. Stop trying to rush it. Close your eyes and just enjoy the climb."

She exhales, letting her eyes fall shut and pressing her head into the pillow. I keep my fingers on top of hers as I guide her motions. Breathy moans fill the room, and I swear, if my dick doesn't self-combust from this, it'll be a damn miracle. She starts to whimper, losing control by the second, and I know exactly what she needs.

"Slip two fingers inside."

Pulling her bottom lip between her teeth, she lets her eyes flutter open, and her gaze doesn't leave mine. "Show me."

Shots.

Fucking.

Fired.

The way she says it, so innocently, like she has no idea what this is doing to me, I don't stand a chance in hell at denying her. It's so wrong. So damn wrong that I'm drowning in a sea of bad choices. And yet, I need her orgasm just as bad as she does.

I use the heel of my hand to slide hers lower, until her fingertips start to tease her entrance. Grabbing her index finger, I slip it inside to the second knuckle and pull it back out. She presses her lips into a line to muffle the noises she's making, but I won't have it.

Using my free hand, I rub my thumb over her lips. "Don't rob me of those delicious sounds. I want to hear how good you feel."

She smirks and opens her mouth just slightly, covering my thumb and sucking on it in a way that is way too fucking obscene. I instantly picture her hollowing those cheeks around my cock, and if this wasn't about her and her only right now, I'd show her exactly what teasing me like that gets her.

"You're such a fucking cocktease," I growl.

Glancing down at the way I'm still slowly pumping one of her own fingers into her, she purses her lips. "Says the guy who won't actually touch me."

She's calling me out and throwing down the gauntlet all at the same time, and I've never been the type to pussy out. I lay my own finger over hers and press them both in at the same time. If it were my dick, the way she clenches around me would probably make me cum on the spot. She's so fucking tight, and if I didn't know any better, I'd think she's a virgin.

"Use your own cum to lube up your fingers," I instruct her. "It'll feel better on your clit."

An exasperated huff leaves her mouth as I pull our fingers out, but it's quickly replaced by a whine when I go right over her sensitive bundle of nerves. Her own sweet honey makes it so I can slide our touch back and forth with ease. If she thought she was turned on before, it doesn't even begin to compare to the way she starts to lose control. Her moans go up an octave, and her whole body shakes with unmatched need.

"I can't," she whimpers as she gets close. "It's not enough. I need you to do it."

I want to. God, I want nothing more than to be the one to push her over the edge. But I shouldn't. Even what I'm doing now is going to send me to hell. I have no right being anywhere near her. And yet, here I am, my hand pressed over her tight little pussy and licking my lips at the thought of getting my mouth on her.

"You're learning, baby," I say softly. "You're almost there. Just keep going."

She shakes her head and pulls her hand away, leaving nothing between my fingers and her clit, but I follow suit.

"Laiken." Her name weighs heavily on my tongue, reminding me of the severity of what I'm doing. "I can't."

"Can't, or won't?"

I watch as her chest rises and falls with each breath. "Both."

Her eyes soften as she stares up at me. She slowly wraps her fingers around my wrist and pulls my hand back where she wants me.

Where she needs me.

But it's what she does next that tells me I haven't been the one in charge since the second I climbed through her skylight.

She blinks and her tongue darts out to wet her lips. "Please? I want you to," she begs. "Want you to make me cum so bad. I'll be so good for you, I promise."

My jaw drops, and my throat goes bone dry in an instant.

Never in my life did I imagine there would be a point in time where Laiken would be in front of me naked and pleading for me to get her off. Maybe it's the shock of it, or the way her voice already sounds so wrecked from what we've done so far, but before I can tell myself it's a horrible fucking idea, I close the distance and put just the right amount of pressure directly on her clit.

"Is this what you wanted?" I murmur roughly. "Wanted me to make you feel good?"

"Yes. Fuck, yes!"

She keeps a tight grip on my wrist as she arches her hips into my touch, but when her other hand grazes over where my cock is straining against my jeans, I stop her.

"Keep your hands to yourself, or I stop," I warn.

Her bottom lip juts out as she pouts. "But I want to touch you."

"Those are the rules. You said you'd be good for me. Were you lying?"

She pulls her hand back as if she's been burned and shakes her head. Fuck, I could get used to this, and that's what makes it dangerous.

"Look at me," I demand, and she obeys immediately. "Keep your eyes on mine. I want you to see nothing but me as you explode."

The look on her face, so helpless and compliant and desperate for me, it's fucking sinful. And the way her mouth falls open as I push two fingers inside and stretch her open a little more is just another thing I'll remember when I'm in hell for this.

"You going to come on my fingers, Rochester?" I taunt, using my thumb to rub her clit while I bend my two fingers to reach her g-spot.

Her breathing quickens as she nods but doesn't look away from me, being a good girl just like she promised. "Yes."

"Then do it. Clench around them and cover them with your cum." I speed up my motions slightly. "Show me what a good girl you can be."

Any ounce of control she had left vanishes as her movements get frantic. She can't seem to decide whether she wants more pressure or less with the way she starts to ride my hand, treating me like her own personal sex toy.

She looks so fucking good like this.

"Come on, baby," I growl. "I want it, now give it to me. Let go."

"Not yet," she protests.

My brows raise. "Excuse me?"

For the first time since I ordered her to look at me, her eyes flutter closed. She's losing herself in the feel of it all.

The pleasure.

The pain.

I lean down and ghost my lips across hers. "Let me feel you explode. Come for me, Laiken."

Her hips arch once more as she screams out, and I'm right there to take her right over the edge. My fingers don't stop as I ride her through it, sliding them up to her clit then back down inside of her repeatedly. Her whole body shakes as her orgasm takes no prisoners.

The feeling of her nails digging into my wrist is just a taste of how incredible sex with her would be, and in order from taking this from wrong to worse, I bite my lip to keep myself from kissing her. The cut she so kindly closed for me last night splits right back open, but it's the last thing on my mind as she squirms from being oversensitive.

I chuckle, skimming my lips against hers once more before reluctantly pulling my fingers out of her and backing away. Her eyes stay closed as she comes down and slows her breathing. When she finally looks at me again, the fear in her gaze goes hand in hand with the guilt building inside me.

"So, you were saying? Something about I couldn't do any better?"

A smile forces its way through, and she flips me off. "Fuck you."

See, but that's exactly the problem.

I wish she fucking would.

Giving her a cocky grin with my tongue in my cheek, I walk backward toward the door. Just before I leave, I slip the two fingers that were just deep inside of her into my mouth and let the sweet taste of her pussy overtake my senses. Her jaw drops as she watches me, and with a wink, I turn around and leave her to replay everything that just happened on a loop inside her head.

God knows I will.

I'M AN ASSHOLE. THE absolute worst person I know. There is no excuse for what I did this morning. The line I crossed was one I swore I never would. And the more I think about it, the guiltier I feel.

My balls ache as I slam my fists into the punching bag. I considered jerking off when I got home, but I decided against it. There isn't a single part of having blue balls that I don't deserve. Shitheads like me don't get to come, especially not when it means I'd be thinking about her while I do.

The bag swings back and forth with every hit. It's

probably the last thing I should be doing right now, given how bruised my knuckles are from Isaac's face yesterday, but the pain helps. It grounds me. Reminds me of what a fuck-up I am.

Kissing her at the party was a mistake, but at least that I could pass off as a favor, even though it'd be partial bullshit. But this morning was so much worse.

I fingered my best friend's little sister.

And the worst part, the part that scares me the most, is how bad I wanted to do so much more than that. I wanted to stretch her open with my cock and feel her walls quiver around me. Wanted to watch her tits bounce as I slam into her. Wanted to listen to her beg for me to fuck her harder.

Son of a bitch.

I rip one of the gloves off and throw it across the basement.

What happened cannot happen again, no matter how much I may want it or how often the memory haunts my dreams. There's too much at stake. Too much I would be risking.

Sitting on the floor, I pick up my phone and open up a new text with Laiken. It takes a minute to figure out what I want to say, and in the end, I'm not sure any words are good enough, but it needs to be done.

> Please don't hate me. What happened this morning was a bad judgment call. I never should have touched you like that. I promise you that it will never happen again. You have my word.

I press send and lie back on the floor. The coolness of the cement feels good against my skin. My breathing is harsh as I let my eyes fall closed, only to open them again when my phone dings.

The way my dick starts to stir simply by seeing Laiken's name on the screen is just another reason why there can never be a repeat of this morning. She's a fucking temptress. A siren luring me in with the innocent look in her eyes and the sound of her pleas. And she has no idea how lethal she is.

I swipe it open and read the text.

But what if I want it to?

The grip on my phone tightens. It would be so easy, so effortless to just tell her to come over and fuck her into my mattress. But the fallout I'd be risking by doing that would be devastating—the most life changing thing to happen to me since my dad walked out on us all those years ago.

I have no other choice.

I have to stay away from her, no matter how hard that may be.

Laiken

CHAPTER SEVEN

He's avoiding me.

And I'm not entirely sure what hurts more—him doing it, or that I knew he would. His text the other night didn't surprise me. The guilt was written all over his face when he left my room that day. Even if he tried to hide it and distract me with a move I shouldn't have found nearly as hot as I did, I could see it. But he left before I could try talking to him.

My response to him was less of a proposition and more just me trying to say that he shouldn't regret it, because I don't. But he never responded. And by the third day he gave Cam some excuse for why he couldn't come over, I knew.

He won't come anywhere near me.

To say I've been driving myself crazy with this would be an understatement. The kiss was one thing. There was never a point where I didn't know what that was. He was doing me a favor and getting Craig off my back—and while I loved it more than I should have, I didn't let myself get confused by it.

But this time was different.

This time was all him.

There were no ex-boyfriends to ward off. No life-and-death situation forcing us together. Nothing except two people and enough tension to suffocate with. And he can say it was a mistake all he wants, but I could see it in his eyes as we stared at each other.

He wanted it, too.

BY DAY FIVE, THERE'S a shift in my attitude. I'm not confused anymore. That stopped when I finally let myself accept that I didn't force him into anything. Sure, I begged him, but as Mali reminded me, Hayes isn't the kind of guy to get forced into anything.

If he didn't want to do it, he wouldn't have.

It's as simple as that.

There was a point where I was angry. It's a real dick move to avoid me like a coward after everything that happened last weekend. Threatening Craig at the party made it seem like he cares about me, and everything he's done since the morning we spent together has shown the exact opposite.

But time has a way of changing your perspective with everything, and the same is true for this. I'm not angry anymore—I'm just sad. If I had known that *this* would be the aftermath of what we did, I never would have unlocked the skylight.

Hands down the best orgasm of my life, but I would trade it in a second to have him around me again.

"I'm so pathetic," I say, dropping my head into my hands.

Mali sighs. "Being upset over this isn't pathetic. It's human."

"But like, I miss him," I admit. "I miss him so much it

actually hurts. He hit it and quit it, and yet all I want is for him to show up and at least act like I don't exist in person."

She chuckles. "I love you, babe, but he *technically* didn't. Hit it and quit it would entail that he got his rocks off, too. And if he had, I'd make him feel the pain of having his pubes pulled out one at a time until he looks like his balls haven't dropped yet. But that's not the case here."

Groaning, I throw myself backward onto my bed. The same bed I can't lay in anymore without picturing him hovering above me. Is he as hung up on this as I am? Yeah, right. Of course, he's not. If he was, he would be here—instead of giving Cam excuses and showing up late to hockey practice just so he can avoid seeing me.

"I don't think I'll ever wrap my head around this."

Mali lies down beside me. "Me either, but who knows. Maybe he'll show up to the bonfire tonight. Has he ever missed one?"

My lips purse as I try to remember a time he wasn't there, but I come up empty. "I don't think so, but I guess there's a first time for everything."

"Well, if he does show up, I promise to distract Cam and the guys so you can talk to him. Confronting him seems like the only option you have anyway."

She's right, and a part of me considered showing up at the surf shop and talking to him there. But while I may be a total badass when it comes to literally anything else, my brain goes by a different set of rules with him. The fear of rejection is just too strong. I mean, the text he sent still hurts. I can't even begin to imagine what it would feel like to hear him say it to my face.

"Thanks." I roll over and rest my head on her shoulder. "You're the best friend I ever had."

She snorts. "Tell me something I don't know."

Chapter 7

HAVE YOU EVER SEEN a cat in a room full of rocking chairs? The way every little thing has them looking around? That's me. With each car door that shuts, I turn excitedly, hoping to see Hayes walking through the backyard as if nothing happened. And each time, I'm left disappointed.

He's not coming.

Mali seems to be holding out hope, but if he was going to show up, he would be here by now. Instead of filling my head with false hopes, I'd rather face it now.

He's so determined to not come anywhere near me that he's willing to break the one summer tradition he and Cam have kept for the last three years—since the first time my parents let them have a fire without supervision.

I bring my legs up and wrap my arms around them, resting my head on my knees. Mali keeps glancing over at me, a worried look on her face, before she finally decides to put me out of my misery.

"Why do I feel like we're missing someone?" she asks, looking around as if she doesn't already know who isn't here.

"Because we are," Lucas answers. "Hayes and Isaac both didn't come."

"Isaac wasn't fucking invited," Cam sneers.

Mali drops her head as she smiles, then gets back to what her original intention was. "And Hayes? Where's that idiot?"

Cam shrugs. "Not here."

"Well, obviously." She rolls her eyes. "But *why* isn't he here? He's always here."

Owen takes the last sip of his beer and tosses the can onto the pile forming on the ground. "Anyone else think he's been off lately?"

Lucas and Aiden nod, but Cam doesn't seem bothered. He grabs the fire poker and starts to move some of the wood around.

"He's probably hooking up with some new chick," he says simply, with no idea that he just verbally punched me in the stomach. "He usually disappears for a bit when there's someone new. He'll come back around when either he realizes what they're trying to do, or they realize he's never going to settle down."

I know it's not true. Hayes can be a dick, but I don't think he's that cruel to start hooking up with some other girl right after what happened between us. And Cam doesn't know that he's not coming around to avoid me, so of course he would think that way. But that doesn't mean the idea itself doesn't make me feel like I could throw up.

Mali, the goddess she is, is so in tune with my emotions that she gives me an out before I even ask for one. She puts her hands on her lower stomach and winces.

"Lake, can I go lay in your bed?"

I nod. "Yeah. I'll come with you."

Cam's brows furrow as he looks Mali over. "Everything okay?"

"Yeah," she says, waving it off. "Period cramps."

All the guys go dead silent, glancing at each other like it's the most awkward situation they've ever been in.

"What are you, seven?" Mali quips. "I should keep that in mind. Ever want you guys to shut up? Simple. Just mention bleeding out of your vagina."

"If only I knew that while we were still in high school," I chime in.

As we're walking away, the guy talk already begins.

"Have you ever fucked a girl on her period, though?" Owen asks. "Wettest she's ever been. Hands down. No contest."

Aiden sighs. "Yeah, I faint at the sight of blood, so I'll take a pass on that one."

"Let's hope he never has a daughter," I tell Mali.

She glances back at the fire. "Who, Aiden? That would require him getting laid, and he has no game."

Fair enough.

We go into the house and before going up to my room, I gesture toward the fridge. "Should I grab the ice cream and some Midol?"

She shakes her head. "My shark week was two weeks ago. You just looked like you would rather be anywhere but out there."

My shoulders sag as I give her a sad smile. "Thank you."

"You can thank me by letting us watch *Twilight*."

As she rushes up the stairs, I throw my head back and sigh before following her.

I should've known there was a catch.

TUESDAY COMES AND I try to stay at the rink a little longer than necessary after work under the pretenses of doing some registration paperwork. Really, I'm waiting to see if Hayes shows up for practice while I'm still here. But he never does. My guess is that he's somewhere in the area, waiting for my rental car to leave the parking lot before he comes inside.

It's frustrating as hell, but he's definitely determined—I'll give him that.

On Wednesday, I let myself consider showing up at his job for the millionth time, but there's always something that holds me back. A little voice inside telling me that it's a bad idea. That I shouldn't subject myself to the possibility that I'll get my heart stomped on…again.

But as I'm on my way to meet up with Heather and Mali for dinner, I spot his truck out front of the billiards place on Main Street. My thumbs beat against the steering wheel as I keep glancing over at it. And when the light turns green, I finally say fuck it and turn left.

Not doing anything about this is driving me crazy. If he wants nothing to do with me anymore, that's fine. But he'll have to tell me that to my face—potential heartbreak be damned.

Parking my car, I take out my phone and send the girls a text letting them know something came up. Once I press send, I look myself over in the mirror. With one last deep breath, I swallow down the lump in my throat and push away the nausea before going inside.

It only takes me a second before I spot him, standing in the back corner as he drinks a beer and shoots some pool. And the best part of all?

He's alone.

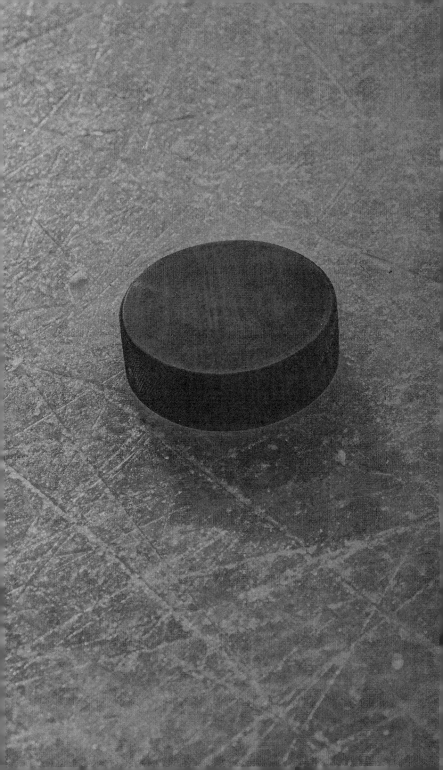

Hayes
CHAPTER EIGHT

There's something relaxing about shooting some pool. There's no timer, no expectations, and when you're playing by yourself, no rules either. The last week and a half hasn't been the most eventful I've ever had. It's mostly consisted of hanging out in my room while listening to music, playing video games, and dodging Cam's invitations to come hang out.

It wasn't until I heard my mom and Devin start to whisper to each other about me, asking if I'm depressed or if I did something to lose all my friends. I realized then it's probably smart to get out of the house for something other than work and hockey practice.

So, pool it is.

I bend over and line up to take my shot when the last voice I expected to hear hits my ears.

"Wow. You still have a pulse after all."

Laiken.

I should've known she was going to confront me at some point. There are plenty of girls who would let me get away with ghosting them after a hookup, but she's not one of them. She has too much self-respect for that. I was just hoping to get a little more time to stop thinking about her before throwing myself into the lion's den.

"What are you doing here, Lai?"

She shrugs and walks around the side of the table,

inspecting the pool cues hanging on the wall. "I've always wanted to take one of these and break it over my knee so I could use it as a weapon like in a Jackie Chan movie."

It sounds threatening, but she doesn't scare me. "Are you saying you want to hurt me? Really living up to that nickname aren't you, Rochester?"

Looking over at me, her eyes rake over my body as if she's sizing me up. "I've considered it."

I huff in amusement. "I guess I deserve that."

"You think?" She turns back to the pool cues and grabs one. "But you've gone to great lengths to not have that conversation, so how about a bet instead?"

My brows raise. "A bet?"

"One game. If I win, you have to stop avoiding me—and don't say you're not because you are." My mouth clamps shut as she takes the words right out of them. "Stop claiming you're too busy to come hang out when you and I both know you're sulking at home with a bag of Doritos."

It's barbecue chips, but whatever. "I don't sulk."

She smirks, knowing she doesn't believe a bit of that. "Sure you don't."

I shouldn't indulge her. Doing exactly that is how I ended up knowing how good her pussy tastes. But a part of me is curious about this bet.

"And what if I win?"

Walking around to the other side of the table, she looks like she's in over her head. "Whatever you want."

I let myself consider it for a moment. It's not like she's asking for anything that wasn't going to happen eventually. I can only get away with not coming around for so long before people start to ask questions, and I have a feeling Cam is getting close to that point anyway.

Glancing down at the pool table and then back up at her, I

can't help but smile. "Have you ever even played pool before?"

She rolls her eyes. "No, but you hit the balls into the pockets. How hard can it be?"

Okay, I'll bite for now. "You have yourself a deal, Rochester."

IT'S A MASSACRE, AND that's putting it nicely. All but two of her striped balls are still on the table while I'm aiming for my last ball before I go for the eight. At first, it was tense and neither of us said much of anything, but the more annoyed she gets when I sink a shot, the more I can't resist teasing her about it.

"You've got to be kidding me," she groans as I make it.

I smile and bounce my brows at her. "Not so easy, is it?"

"No."

Walking around the table, I look for a good angle to get this shot, but it's not possible. Her balls are in my way. I lean over and take a random shot, sending the eight ball into the middle of the table but nowhere near a pocket.

It's her turn.

Her eyes narrow as she tries to focus, but even the way she lines up for the shot, I can tell she's doing it wrong. Her fingers aren't placed right, and she's looking at it from the wrong angle.

"Stop," I say, taking pity on her.

I lean my pool cue against the table and step behind her. It's dangerous, allowing myself to be this close to her. I know that. But when the fuck have I ever been able to follow the rules when it comes to her?

"Relax your shoulders." I gently push them down and then move to fix her hand. "Put it between your fingers and let that guide your shot."

She does as I say, and it's closer, but she still misses. Her head drops in frustration, and I chuckle.

"Try again."

Getting back into position, she does what I showed her, but she still looks uncomfortable. I place my hand on her back and run it down her spine.

"You're too tense," I tell her. "You need to loosen up a little."

She sighs. "I just can't seem to find a way to hold this thing where it's comfortable. And every time I go to shoot, it feels like I don't have enough control over it."

I glance around the room to make sure there's no one we know here, and then give in, stepping up behind her. My chest presses against her back as I put my hands over hers to help her guide the shot.

"Having the proper stance is critical in pool," I murmur, my lips near her ear. "Then, you imagine there being a line pointing exactly where the ball is going to go. You aim, keeping your eye on the ball, and then you shoot."

We shoot the ball together, watching as it hits one right into the corner pocket. Her grin widens excitedly as she glances back at me.

"See? It's not so hard."

She looks proud of herself as she smiles at me. "Show me one more time?"

"This is a bet, Rochester. You want me to make myself lose?"

Like she knows exactly what she's doing, she looks up at me through hooded lashes. "Please?"

That's all it takes. One little word and I'm jolted full force back into the morning we spent in her bedroom—when she begged for me and promised to be a good girl.

"Fine," I agree, trying anything to shake the memory from my mind.

I can't be thinking about that if I have any chance of leaving here the same way I came—by myself. She puts herself in position to take the shot, bent over the table with her ass sticking out. God, it would be so easy to fuck her like that. Watch her grip onto the table for dear life as I thrust into her so hard the balls rattle in the pockets.

I shake the thoughts from my head, trying desperately to focus on anything else.

"Like this?" Laiken asks, but she's holding the stick wrong again.

"No." I lean over her and adjust her hand. "Like this."

"And then I just hit it?"

My hand runs down her arm until it settles on her side. "Aim first. Then hit it."

She looks like she's going to take the shot, but she glances back at me before she does. "What about that one ball? It's in the way."

It's not, but I can see why she would think so from this angle. "You'll clear it. You just have to hit the side of the cue ball instead of the middle."

I move the stick just slightly, but it takes me getting a little closer so I can see exactly where she's aiming. And that's when her ass grinds against me.

It's a slick move, I'm not going to lie. If I was drunk or hadn't spent the last week and a half beating myself up over what happened, it may have worked. But it won't. Not tonight anyway.

A breathy laugh leaves my mouth as I drop my head against her shoulder. "I'm playing right into your hand, aren't I?"

"A little bit. Yeah," she answers proudly.

She takes the shot, but it goes wide, not only missing her ball, but lining my shot up perfectly. I don't move as she spins around, but maybe I should have because she's so close, I can feel the warmth of her breath on my face.

"You don't give up easy, do you?" I question.

"Not really how I was raised."

She's right there. Kissing her could be so fucking effortless. All it would take is moving a couple inches. It would be that simple.

"And what if you got your way? What then?"

Her fingers run up the back of my neck and lace into my hair, massaging gently. "Kiss me and find out."

I smirk, licking my lips as I glance down at hers. And as I start to move in, her eyes flutter closed.

Only to open when she hears the distinct sound of the eight ball going into the side pocket.

"I win."

I step back, putting some much-needed distance between us as Laiken huffs in annoyance. She puts the pool cue back and runs her fingers through her hair.

"Okay," she says. "Fair enough. What do you want?"

Tossing the pool stick onto the table, I keep my eyes on hers as I walk up to her. My hands land on either side of her, and while a part of me thought she would shy away, she keeps her head high and holds my gaze.

"I want..."

I move in closer, toying with her the same way she just

did with me. And when her breath hitches, I know I've succeeded.

"...you to go home."

All the air leaves her lungs as I press a kiss to her forehead and force myself to back away.

I can tell she's not surprised by my answer. Visibly disappointed, yes, but not surprised. She nods slowly and starts to round the table, but just when I think she's going to leave, she grabs the pool cue off the table. As if I was just playing someone else entirely, she lines up and aims the ball like a fucking professional before taking her shot—sinking three balls at once.

Standing up, she puts the cue down, smiles sweetly, and winks at me. And as she walks out the door, all I can do is stare in both amazement and disbelief.

Well played, Rochester.

THERE'S NOTHING MORE BORING than a surf shop on a day where the lifeguards deem the water too unsafe to go in. Sure, you get the occasional thrill seeker who's looking to break the rules, but for the most part—it's a dead zone. The storm brewing out at sea makes for choppy waves and a dangerous current that threatens to pull you under and spit you out.

Honestly, it would be better if we just closed.

But the boss wants us to stay open. His belief is that all the people who come to the beach and learn they can't swim will come in to shop instead. *My belief* is that he should spend a day like today here so he can see how wrong he really is.

I'm staring down at my phone, playing some stupid game Devin got me hooked on, when a text from Cam comes through.

Hey, fucker. You coming to the bonfire tomorrow?

My first instinct is to tell him no. Come up with an excuse or claim I'm not feeling well. Something so I don't see Laiken again. Every time I'm around her, it gets more difficult to control myself. It's pitiful and goes against everything I am, but that's how it is.

For fuck's sake, I even dreamed about fucking her on a pool table last night.

I should stay far away from her, but at the same time, I know I can't do that forever. There's going to be a time where I need to suck it up, control my dick, and spend time around her. I can't avoid my friends forever.

And who knows, maybe seeing her in a group setting will be easier. Less...tempting. After all, it's not like I'm going to pull her into my lap and hump her like a dog in heat with Cam sitting right there.

Not that I would do that even if he *wasn't* there, but I'm learning lately that I have no say in the things I do when she's around.

There are no guarantees, and everything is a risk where she's involved.

But fuck it. If she had actually played pool yesterday instead of playing me, she would have won the bet and I'd be forced to go anyway. I may as well.

Before I can talk myself out of it, I type out a response and press send.

> Yeah, I'll be there. Let me know what beer you want me to grab after work.

His answer comes before I can even put my phone down.

> The kind with the high alcohol percentage.

> Jägermeister it is.

> No! Literally anything but that.

> And vodka. Should probably avoid that too.
> 🤢🤮

Yeah, he has a point.

Laiken

CHAPTER NINE

MOST DAYS, I LOVE MY JOB. WATCHING THE KIDS get so excited about learning something new and seeing themselves improve is so rewarding. But then there are days like today. Days where everyone seems to be in a bad mood. It's full of acting out and temper tantrums galore, and let me tell you—it's not easy picking a screaming, flailing child up off the ice.

All I know is that I'm ready to get my car back from the mechanic and then go home to take a shower that may or may not be hot enough to burn me. It may be a pointless one, being as my hair will smell like smoke after the bonfire tonight, but I don't care. I'm going to do it anyway.

I'm texting Mali as I leave, venting about the day and how a kid's mother asked if she could leave her four kids, including her six month old baby, at the rink while she goes to get her nails done. My thumbs dance across the screen as I type what she will consider to be a novel, but it all comes to a halt when I walk directly into something hard.

The smell of his cologne registers before anything else, and his hands warm my skin as he grabs my waist to steady me. Keeping my eyes closed for a moment, I pretend to need a second to compose myself, but really, I'm just enjoying being this close.

"You okay?" he asks, dipping his head down to look at me.

I force myself to focus. Lord knows I look desperate enough when it comes to him. Mali has always said I should play hard to get, but clearly, my mind goes by its own agenda.

"Yeah," I reply. "Yeah, I'm good."

He releases me and smiles. "Good. Don't want you getting hurt."

Hayes disappears into the rink, and all I can do is wonder if there was some kind of underlying meaning to that statement.

I SHOULD'VE OPENED MY damn mouth. Should've straight up asked him if he was planning on coming tonight or not. Maybe then I wouldn't be torturing myself with the *will he or won't he* game. Sure, I bet I could just go ask Cam, but the last thing I need is to give him any indication that something is going on between Hayes and me.

I can't even figure out what's going on with us for myself.

Sometimes, I feel like I'm crazy. He plays hot and cold so much that I start to think I'm imagining the want in his eyes when he looks at me, or the way it feels like his restraint is hanging by a thread. I thought that after wanting him for so long, my mind was playing tricks on me by showing me something that's not there. A cruel case of wishful thinking, in a way.

But if that were the case, the kiss at the party would have been the beginning and the end to our tragically premature love story.

There has to be something more to it. I just don't know if I'll ever get the chance to find out what it is—especially if he keeps avoiding me like a plague.

THE FIRE CRACKLES IN front of me, mesmerizing as the wood turns to ash. You would think we'd get bored of this at some point, but we don't. Not even a little. I could sit here all night, just watching it burn.

"This is perfect," Mali says happily as she kicks her feet up onto my lap. "We're young, beautiful, and we're sitting around a fire with a glass of wine."

My brows furrow as I look around. "Mal, we don't have glasses of wine."

"We should fix that then, shouldn't we?"

Chuckling, I roll my eyes and push her feet off me. We stand up to go get some wine and are distracted when the guys start to cheer.

"Look who it is!" Owen remarks. "It's Casper the friendly ghost."

"Fuck off. I was busy."

That voice. The one that has me wanting to sigh in relief and stop breathing all at the same time. I look up and sure enough, Hayes walks over and does a bro-handshake with Cam.

"Busy? Is that what we're calling it now?" Lucas asks.

Not going to lie, I hate the way they all seem to think he's been banging some chick. Then again, he could have been. I wouldn't know any different, and even if he was, do I really have the right to be mad about it?

At Lucas's words, Hayes locks eyes with me for a second then forces himself to look away. He laughs, not entertaining him but not denying it either, and I try my best not to let it fuck with my head.

"Guess he's done avoiding you," Mali says quietly.

I exhale slowly. "I wouldn't be too sure."

IT FEELS GOOD TO have everything back to normal. Don't get me wrong, there are subtle differences, like the fact that Hayes has yet to speak directly to me since he got here. But he's here, and my standards may be a bit low right now, because I'll take it.

"Did you guys know they renovated the billiards place over on Main Street?" Hayes questions.

I pretend to chew on my sleeve in order to hide my smile. The shock on his face when I sank three balls at once was priceless. If I had a picture of it, I'd set it as my background.

Cam looks surprised. "That place is still open?"

"Yeah, and they did a damn good job fixing it up."

Owen hums, taking a sip of his beer. "I've always wanted to have sex on a pool table."

The timing is horrible. I'm mid-swallow with wine still in my mouth, when I inhale. Immediately, I start coughing. Mali chuckles as she pats my back like I'm a child.

"Lai, baby," she says with a condescending tone. "We drink the wine, not aspirate it."

But she has no idea that I'm picturing the way my body was pressed between the pool table and Hayes. And judging by the way he plays with his bottom lip as he stares down at his beer makes me think he's picturing it, too.

Note to self: Add sex on a pool table to my Hayes Fuck-It List.

"We should go play one night," Lucas suggests. "But don't be surprised when I kick all of your asses."

The guys exchange a look before busting out into hysterical laughter. Owen's face turns red as he gasps for air, and Cam is almost in tears.

"Dude, every single one of us has beat you at pool before," Hayes tells him.

Lucas scoffs. "That's not true. I know for a fact that I beat Owen."

"The fuck you did," Owen retorts.

"I did!" Lucas argues. He looks over at Cam. "You were there. Don't you remember me beating Owen when I played him at pool?"

Cam squints. "Not quite, but I do remember my sister making you look like an amateur."

Chuckling, I tip my glass of wine toward Lucas. "Cheers."

"That's not fair," he complains. "She can outplay any one of us."

"Can't argue with you there," Owen agrees, and Cam just hums.

But Hayes looks directly at me, talking to me for the first

time all night. "You're just full of surprises, aren't you, Rochester?"

I shrug nonchalantly. "One of these days people will stop underestimating me."

His grin widens, and I'm not sure if it's admiration or fondness in his eyes, but it's definitely something.

THE PROBLEM WITH WINE is that I rarely drink it. Which means, when I do drink it and ingest almost an entire bottle to myself, it hits me hard. And wine drunk Laiken is different from beer drunk Laiken. She's happier. More carefree.

Mali and I dance around while Owen plays the harmonica with the same skill level of a toddler blowing raspberries. She holds my hand and spins me around, and when I fall onto the ground, she lies beside me instead of helping me up.

"Can we just sleep here?" I ask, staring up at the stars. "The sky makes me feel so small."

Mali hums. "I'm down with sleeping out here. It sounds rustic."

"Okay, one, sleeping in the backyard is not *rustic,*" Cam tells her. "And two, you guys do know there are snakes that live in the woods back there, right?"

The two of us screech in unison as we jump up and go sit back down in our seats. Cam and Hayes both chuckle and tap their beer cans together.

Chapter 9

Assholes.

INSOMNIA IS A BITCH. There's really no nicer way to say it. At first I thought I just couldn't sleep because I was drunk, but the room stopped spinning when I sobered up a couple hours ago. And still, I can't seem to shut off my brain.

Mali sleeps soundly beside me as I roll over and check the time on my phone.

Three a.m.

I heave a sigh and rest my arm on my forehead. At this rate, I probably won't fall asleep until sunrise. Thankfully, I don't have work tomorrow morning, so when I do eventually drift off, I'll be able to sleep in.

Maybe I just need some fresh air. Mali's body heat has been making me a little too warm since the second we got into bed—around the same time she drunkenly mumbled something about wanting to buy a porcupine and teach it to stab people that get on her nerves. She's a nut even in her sleep.

Sitting up, I slip out of bed and wrap a throw blanket around me. The lowered part of my ceiling has always been my favorite thing about this room. It's why I wanted the attic in the first place. It makes it so the skylight is low enough for me to be able to stand up through it like my own personal balcony. Plus, it's easy access to the highest part of the roof.

I carefully climb up and out onto the roof. The cool night

air is a little bit of a shock, but as I sit down and snuggle into the blanket, I quickly get used to it. The stars all shine so clearly above my head. The storm that's coming won't be here for another couple of days, so I'm enjoying the view while I can.

Scooting down a little, I lie on my back and take a deep breath. It's so calm out here. So peaceful. I may have been drunk earlier when I told Mali that the sky makes me feel small, but I was serious. There's something relaxing about it.

A few minutes go by and I'm listening to the sounds of the crickets chirping along with a couple owls in the distance when I hear someone climbing up the roof—and I don't need to look to see who it is.

Hayes lies down beside me, but neither of us turn to look at each other.

"Can't sleep?" he questions, right as the silence is starting to be a little too much.

There's something about Hayes awkwardly stating the obvious that has me chuckling. "What was your first clue?"

He nudges me with his elbow. "Don't be a smartass."

"Can't help it," I answer. "It's my default."

Just lying here with him has my emotions going haywire. He didn't have to come up here. I didn't even know he was out here, let alone still awake. It's three in the morning. He could've gone back in through Cam's window and I never would've known any different. But instead, he came up here on his own.

"I'm glad you're back," I tell him softly.

He hums. "Well, I couldn't exactly leave Cam to think I suddenly hate him or something."

"Oh, don't worry. He just assumed you were having a fuck fest."

It's meant to be a joke—an attempt to lighten the mood a little and support the lie that the idea doesn't feel like a blowtorch to the heart. But the sharp look on his face tells me he doesn't find it funny, so I try to distract him.

"Hey, did you know that there's an app you can download on your phone and it uses the camera to show you what stars you're looking at?"

"I wasn't," he tells me, not fooled for a minute. "Sleeping with someone, I mean."

Relief floods through me. "Okay."

It's only quiet for a few seconds before I continue, despite everything in me telling me to shut up.

"Even if you were, though, it's none of my business."

He doesn't answer, and it's so quiet I start to wonder if he fell asleep, but as I turn my head to check, I find him looking back at me. There's an undeniable urge to kiss him coursing through my veins, but I can't.

Not without having some idea of what's going on between us.

I break eye contact and turn back to the night sky. I can't watch his face while I ask the question I'm about to ask. I'm afraid of the answer, but I need to hear it.

"Can you honestly say I'm the only one that feels something here?"

My voice comes out almost broken sounding, and you can hear my confidence starting to falter. But I know he hears me when he sighs.

"Please don't make me answer that."

"Why?" I turn my head to face him. "Because I won't like the answer or because you won't?"

You can see it in his eyes—the way his pupils dilate and how he keeps glancing down at my lips. He's fighting a mental battle in his head, trying to figure out if he should listen to the angel on his right shoulder or the devil on his left. And as he turns on his side and lightly places his hand on my face, I think I can figure out which one is winning.

My heart pounds against my rib cage as I stare back at him. He tucks my hair behind my ear and his jaw ticks.

"Fucking hell," he whispers. "I don't stand a chance when it comes to you, do I?"

I want to ask what he means. Make him expand on that statement and give me something to chew on later when I let my thoughts run wild. But before I can ask, he takes the words right out of my mouth by pressing his lips to mine.

If I thought the kiss at the party was good, this puts that to shame. He pulls me in by the back of my neck and his thumb rubs over my cheekbone as he makes every single part of me come alive. Guiding my mouth open, his tongue meets mine, and the quiet moan he lets out confirms everything for me.

I am definitely not alone in this.

As I throw a leg over him, his hand moves from my face to my side, and he grips my waist to pull me closer. I drag my nails down his back, loving the way his breathing quickens.

Things start to get heated, and I'm sure if we weren't on a roof, clothes would be coming off right now. We grip at every part of each other that we can, and Hayes deepens the kiss like he can't get enough. But soon after we start grinding against each other, he stops everything.

"Fuck," he grumbles, his forehead pressed against mine.

I don't say anything as he sits up and runs his hands over his face. It's overwhelmingly quiet, neither one of us knowing what to say. The one thing I do know is that he won't look at me. I watch him look up at the sky, then in my direction, but never back at me.

He drops his head in defeat. "This is why I was trying to stay away."

I'm sure there's something to be said. Something to stop him from going back into panic mode. And maybe if it wasn't dead ass in the middle of the night, I'd be able to think of it.

But I'm too stunned—just as confused as he is, if not more so.

He stays in place for another couple minutes and then all but whispers "Goodnight, Laiken" before sliding down the roof and slipping back through Cam's window.

And any chance I had of going to sleep tonight disappears along with him.

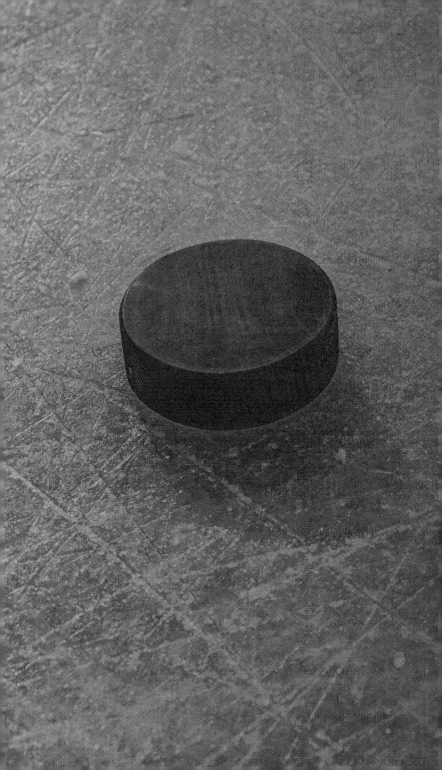

Hayes

CHAPTER TEN

The sandpaper drags across the blank, smoothing it out and helping shape it into the surfboard I've always dreamed of. It's a long process, building your own board, but it's going to be so rewarding when I ride a wave with this baby.

It'll be a little while before that happens, though. After I'm satisfied with the shape, it'll be time to add the fiberglass and resin. I'm also planning on asking Mali to do the artwork for it. I've only seen a couple of her drawings, but Cam constantly raves about how talented she is.

I wanted to mention it last night, but I never got the chance. The only person who knows I'm building my own board is Cam. If the rest of the guys found out, they'd be on my ass about making each of them one, and I don't have time for that shit.

Technically, I could have talked to her about it this morning...if I had stuck around. After going back inside last night, I didn't have a chance in hell at falling asleep. All I could do was lie there and stare at the ceiling while thoughts of Laiken constantly reminded me that I fucked up, again.

As soon as the sun came up, I lied to a still half-asleep Cam and told him that I had to go to work. At least that way I didn't have to see Laiken. It's a dick move, I know, but how could I look at her after last night? I promised I wouldn't touch her again, and then I shot that promise to hell by kissing her on the roof. Yeah, she wanted it too, but only because she doesn't know any better.

If she knew how far out of my league she is, she wouldn't give me a second glance.

Laiken Blanchard is in a category all on her own. Not only is she unfairly gorgeous, but she can insult you and have you apologizing for it later. A lethal mix of beauty and badass. The guy who ends up with her will be a lucky son of a bitch, but it won't be me. Once she gets past this image of me that she has in her head, she'll move on and end up marrying some rock star or billionaire.

But that doesn't mean it won't grind on my nerves.

I tug on my bottom lip mindlessly, still able to feel her there. It's fucking torture. I wish I could blame last night on being drunk, but I was stone cold sober. The only reason I went out on the roof was to smoke a cigarette after I woke up to piss, and I should have left it at that. When I first heard her climb out of her skylight, I thought she was sneaking out again. It's not like she can just walk out the front door at three in the morning. And honestly, with Mali asleep in her room, I wondered who she could be sneaking out *for.* But instead, she went up to the peak and laid there, gazing at the stars.

I should've pretended not to notice her—gone back inside and forced myself back to sleep—but when have I ever done the right thing when it comes to her lately? Just like last time, I was drawn to her like a moth to a flame. And just like last time, I couldn't help myself.

Now I don't know where to go from here.

Taking a break, I leave the garage and head into the house in search of a drink. I take a beer from the fridge and crack it open. The ice-cold liquid is refreshing as it slides down my throat. I lean against the counter and use the bottom of my shirt to wipe the sweat from my forehead.

"What the fuck do you think you're doing?" Devin questions accusingly.

My brows furrow. "Taking a break?"

"Not that, asshat," she barks. "You kissed Laiken? You know how she feels about you. What the hell were you thinking?"

Well, fuck. "I wasn't thinking," I admit with a sigh. "It was late and we were on the roof, looking at the stars, and it just happened."

"What roof?"

"Laiken's roof."

We stand completely still, both looking confused, until it clicks.

I cringe as I exhale. "You were talking about the party, weren't you?"

Pursing her lips, she comes beside me and hops up onto the counter. "So, you've kissed her twice then."

"Yeah."

It's not a lie. I *have* only kissed her twice. She just doesn't know what *else* we've done, and I plan on keeping it that way. The less people that know, the better.

"So, are you into her or something?" Dev questions, lightly kicking her feet against the cabinet.

I drop my head. "It doesn't matter. Cam would slit my throat just for looking at her that way."

She chuckles. "Okay, one, that's not an answer. And two, you don't know that for sure. He could surprise you."

"He could also tell me he's changing his name to Edgar and becoming a Vegan Buddhist, but the chances of it happening are low."

Rolling her eyes, she leans over to nudge me with her

shoulder. "I'm serious. Would you kill *him* if he wanted to date me?"

Like a total hypocrite, my head whips toward my sister. "You better start fucking talking, and now."

Her hands raise in defense. "Easy, Cujo. It was just a hypothetical question. And you answered it wrong, so forget I said anything."

See? This is what I mean. I'm a douchebag. A hypocritical piece of shit that has no business being anywhere near her, let alone in her bed. If Cam ever finds out what we've done, I won't blame him for tearing me limb from limb and using the pieces of my body as Halloween decor.

"You don't even want to try talking to him about it?" Dev asks after a few minutes.

I look at her like she's lost her mind. "Are you *trying* to be an only child?"

She chuckles. "No, but Laiken doesn't deserve to be played with, so either man up or fuck off, because if you hurt her, I'll be forced to punch you."

Hopping down, she walks back to her room, but her words replay in my mind long after she's gone.

My annoying little sister has a point—Laiken *doesn't* deserve to be played with. She doesn't deserve any of the shit I've been putting her through lately.

Like I said, she's way out of my league.

THE SUN IS STARTING to set as I add the last little details to the shape of the board. A cool breeze is blowing in through the open garage door, but it doesn't stop the sweat from dripping off my forehead. If I can manage to get Marc to keep the surf shop closed tomorrow, I may be able to get the resin on the one side by tomorrow night.

Looking up from the board, I see Cam's Jeep pulling into the driveway. He hops out and slams the door, and my life starts to flash before my eyes.

"I have a bone to pick with you," he says as he walks toward me.

Yep, this is it.

This is when I die.

It's fine, I guess. Not exactly how I saw myself going, but I've lived a somewhat decent life. Wish I got to turn twenty-one, but it is what it is.

I put down the sanding block, so I don't instinctively try to defend myself, and hold my head high. Whatever he's about to do to me, I deserve it.

But when Cam gets close enough, all he does is hand me next week's game schedule and a list of things we need to practice before then.

This is about hockey?

"Could've given me the heads up that you were going to skip practice," he growls. "Coach made us all skate suicides. Said we haven't been working hard enough lately. And your ass got to miss it."

Oh, thank God.

I thought for sure I was a dead man standing.

"Shit, sorry," I tell him. "Been working on this thing all day. I guess I just spaced out. Though, I'm not sorry I missed practice, because that sounds brutal."

He flips me off. "Dick."

I watch as he walks up to the board, inspecting it in a way

only an experienced surfer would. He squats down to look at the subtle curve and runs his hand over it.

"This is going to come out so sick."

A proud grin appears on my face. "I know. I'm excited about it. Pain in the ass, though."

He grunts. "No shit. Why do you think I've never tried building my own?"

"Because you're too busy refurbishing Mali's dream car."

"Oh, ouch," he hisses. "If I knew I was going to get called out, I wouldn't have come over. And besides, it's just a coincidence that we both love that car."

I give him a sarcastic look that tells him I don't believe a word of it. "Okay."

Walking over to the secondhand sofa we put in here last summer, he lies down and takes out his phone. "My parents are cleaning the house and asked Laiken and me to help. I got out of it by telling them I have a date, but she canceled, so I'm just going to chill here."

"Suit yourself," I say. "Or, hear me out, you could always take out the one girl you really want."

He snickers. "Better idea! You could fuck all the way off."

"Pussy," I murmur, and my conscience glares at me.

Yeah, yeah. I know.

Pot, meet Kettle.

Laiken
CHAPTER ELEVEN

There's something wrong with me.

I mean, there has to be, right? Why else would I be sitting here, staring at my phone and waiting for a text I know is never going to come?

Waking up the next morning to find out Hayes had already left was a blow to my ego. It's not that I thought I would wake up to cuddles, forehead kisses, and breakfast in bed. But I had mistakenly let myself hope that we would at least talk about it the next morning.

And you know what they say about hope—it breeds eternal misery.

After I interrupted his game of pool and all but handed myself over on a silver platter, I made a promise to myself that I would never look so damn desperate again. So, I gave Mali my phone for the day and told her not to let me text him for at least the next twenty-four hours.

She did great. I'll give her that. She forwarded all my calls to her phone, and then locked my phone in her car. No amount of begging and/or threatening was enough to convince her to give it back.

Seriously, if anyone ever tries torturing information out of her, they're going to be left disappointed. The girl just doesn't crack.

I swear, there was a method to my madness. Not saying anything to him for at least a day accomplishes three things.

First, it gives him the opportunity to reach out first. Second, it keeps me from looking desperate for his attention. And third, it forces me through the part where the urge to text him is the worst, which makes it easier to not text him after that.

Except, scratch that last part, because after Mali gave me my phone back, I didn't last more than twenty minutes before I texted him, asking to talk.

"Ugh," I groan, throwing myself down onto Mali's bed. "I'm so fucking sick of the hot and cold."

She doesn't look up from her phone. "So you've said."

"I mean, seriously. How can he kiss me and then go right back to acting like I don't exist?"

"The damn nerve," she mumbles, and I smack the phone out of her hand. "Okay, rude. I'm not the one who left you with metaphorical blue balls."

"Does the offer to kick his ass still stand?" I question.

She tilts her head from side to side. "If you catch me in a shitty enough mood, I'm sure you could get me to knock him around a little. But I don't think you honestly want me to do it."

Tossing my phone to the end of the bed, I sigh heavily. "I might if he doesn't at least have the common courtesy of answering my text."

"How do you know he saw it?"

I let my head flop toward her side of the bed. "He has read receipts on."

"Oh," she says, her lips staying in a puckered circle for a moment. "Maybe he's still trying to figure out what to say."

"Stop doing that."

"Doing what?"

"That." My finger gestures at her face. "Telling me what I want to hear instead of being honest and risking hurting my feelings."

She smiles and reaches over to play with my hair. "But you're my little baby princess. When you're sad, I'm sad."

"Mali," I warn.

Her nose scrunches in disgust. "Ew, don't say my name like I'm in trouble."

"Stop trying to change the subject."

"Stop trying to get me to crush your hopes and dreams," she counters.

As if I lack even a minimal amount of self-control, I sit up and grab my phone to see if he answered.

NO NEW NOTIFICATIONS.

I drop my phone into my lap and rub my hands over my face. Things were better before—when I had myself convinced that shit with him was just an unrealistic fantasy inside my head. That there was no chance in hell of it ever actually happening.

Taking a deep breath, I crack my neck and then look at Mali. "Okay. Lay it on me."

Mali whines. "Lai."

"Please? I know it's going to hurt, but I need to hear it."

She thinks about it for a second before rolling her eyes and putting her phone down. Her bed moves as she sits up and holds my hands. The way she looks into my eyes tells me that everything she's about to say is meant to help me, not hurt me—even if the latter is inevitable.

"I think he's no good for you," she says bluntly. "I'm sorry. I know he's your first love and, in your eyes, he can do no wrong, but he doesn't deserve you. The way he's been acting lately only proves as much."

A single tear slips out and slides down my face. "It's all been a game to him, hasn't it?"

Wiping my face with her sleeve, she shakes her head. "I wouldn't say that. I think Hayes clearly feels something for you. I don't know how strong those feelings are, but I don't think the last couple weeks would have happened if he didn't feel some kind of way."

Her words make me feel a little better, knowing I'm not completely delusional.

"But," she continues, and my stomach churns, "that doesn't mean he plans on ever acting on those feelings. At least not without running away immediately after like he still believes girls have cooties. And if he's not willing to talk about it, I'm not really sure there's anything you can do about it."

I know she has a point. Guys have a tendency of being stubborn as hell when it comes to avoiding things they don't want to deal with, and Hayes is even worse, but it still stings. Maybe it was wishful thinking, but I had hoped he'd at least agree to talk—even if it was always going to end with my heart in pieces.

I'm not even sure what to do here. Do I try to move on and get over him, as impossible as that might be? And if so, do I let him get away with ignoring me, like what happened meant nothing to either of us?

No.

He doesn't get to treat me like a plaything. Other girls might let him get away with his hot and cold behavior, but I'm not other girls. And I'm sure as fuck not going to let him off the hook without at least getting to say my piece.

"Screw that," I tell her, getting off the bed and grabbing my keys. "He's going to listen to what I have to say whether he likes it or not."

Mali's brows raise, and I can't tell if she's nervous or impressed.

It's probably both.

"What are you going to do?" she questions.

The one thing I've been avoiding.

The thing I couldn't build up enough courage to do until now.

"The only thing I can do," I tell her as I tie my hair up. "I'm going to confront him at the one place he can't leave."

THE WAVES CRASH AGAINST the shore while the wind whips the red flag around. It's meant to ward off anyone looking to take a dip in the ocean, but the irony of it being right in front of the surf shop is comical. Maybe someone should make Hayes carry one of those around all the time.

It might save a few hearts.

Not mine, though. Mine's already fucked.

His truck sits in the parking lot, letting me know he's inside. And the fact that we're the only two cars here says that he's by himself. I take a deep breath.

"You can do this," I tell myself. "He doesn't get to treat you like your feelings don't matter and get away with it."

Finishing my pep talk, I muster up all the confidence I can manage in the time it takes to cross the parking lot, and push the door open.

Here goes nothing.

Hayes has his back to me as I walk in, but the bell tells him that someone is here. "Hey. Welcome to Wax and Waves."

I stay quiet. The anger I had driving over here must have

flown out the window on the way, because now I'm standing here, all I want to do is cry.

Quick, WWMD? *What would Mali do?*

Well, for starters, she would tell me that I'm not a doormat for him to walk all over. And she would be right. If the shit with Craig taught me anything, it's that if I don't want to be treated like shit, I must refuse to accept shitty treatment. I may not be able to control what someone does, but I can control how I respond to it.

When he realizes no one answered, Hayes turns around and his eyes meet mine.

"Laiken." He says my name like it's a sigh, which steels my backbone.

"You can't keep doing this," I tell him. "You can't kiss me and then refuse to talk to me after. I don't care if you regret it or not. I deserve better than that."

As if he's completely aware how in the wrong he is, he drops his head and nods. "I know."

His answer catches me off guard. More specifically, it's the sadness in his voice. It fucks me up, making my anger dissipate—which sucks because that was my driving force. At least if I'm pissed off, I'm not upset. And I refuse to let him see me upset.

We're going for *less* pathetic, remember?

I walk deeper into the store and start looking through the shell necklaces on one of the tables. They're beautiful, but they're not why I'm here.

"What are we doing?" I force out, spinning around to face him.

He looks caught off guard by the question. "What do you mean?"

"Don't play stupid. What is going on with us?"

If he's going to put an end to whatever the hell this is,

he's going to do it to my face. Not through a text he'll inevitably send later.

I watch as he struggles to find an answer, waiting patiently until he settles on one.

"We're friends."

A dry laugh echoes out of my mouth as I take a couple steps toward him. "Yeah, I don't buy it."

"There's nothing to buy," he says, but I don't think even he believes what he's saying.

I cross my arms over my chest. "Mm-hm. So, I take it you kiss all your friends the way you kissed me the other night?"

He looks away from me and runs his fingers through his hair. "I don't know what you want me to say."

Of course, he doesn't.

Even I don't know what I want him to say. I know what I'd *like* him to say, but we're not going there. Not when I have zero confidence that he wouldn't take it back the next morning.

Leaning against the counter, I throw out a theory I've been tossing around my head. "You heard me that night when I was in the kitchen with Mali and Devin. You heard the conversation and then played it off like you didn't."

His eyes fall closed as he sighs. "I told Devin not to tell you that."

"She didn't. You just did."

He exhales, muttering *fuck* under his breath. "Look, I didn't want you to feel awkward or weird around me."

I scoff. "So instead, you decided to fuck with me? You're right, that's much better."

"No, Laiken." He shakes his head. "That's not it at all."

"Then what is it?" With every second, I start to lose my patience. "Tell me, because from where I stand, that's exactly what it looks like."

His fingers lace into his hair and he pulls at it, groaning in frustration.

"What do you want me to say?" The defeated look on his face threatens to disarm me, but I didn't come this far to back down now.

"The truth! What you're thinking. What you're feeling."

He turns around and grips the back counter, though it does nothing to calm him down. His back moves with every breath he takes, and his tight grasp on the counter turns his knuckles white.

I do my best to remove the venom from my tone. "I'm in the dark here, H."

Throwing his hands in the air, he looks me in the eyes. "I want you, okay? When you're around, I can't seem to keep my eyes off you. And when we're alone together, I lack even the most basic fundamentals of self-control." He takes a step closer and puts his hands on the counter in front of me. "But no matter how crazy you make me, at the end of the day, you're still my best friend's little sister. We can't cross that line."

Forcing myself to look away from him, I roll my eyes. "Oh, fuck off."

His brows raise in surprise as an involuntary laugh slips from his mouth. "Excuse me?"

"No. You're *not* excused," I sneer. "You can take your moral compass and your shitty excuses and shove them up your ass because that *line* you claim we can't cross? You obliterated it the moment you sucked my cum off your fingers."

Not giving him a chance to respond, I leave him and his shell-shocked expression behind me and march my ass right out of the shop.

My heart is racing. The adrenaline coursing through me makes it hard to catch my breath, but I'm thankful for it.

Because I know that the second it's no longer there, I'm going to cry.

I climb into my car and peel out of the parking lot. For the first time since my heart decided to latch itself to the seventeen-year-old boy with an intoxicating smile and a tattoo on his bicep, I don't want Hayes anywhere near me.

Driving down the street, I swat away a few tears that manage to escape. I'm not just hurt—I'm aggravated, and I'm annoyed. He knew this whole time that he was never going to let anything become of us, and he did it anyway.

It was selfish, and inconsiderate, and everything I convinced myself he wasn't, despite all the red flags that told me otherwise.

Mali is just about to get in her car when she sees me pull into her driveway, and that's when I lose it. I scramble to get my seatbelt off and jump out of the car.

"Mal," I hiccup.

She sighs and opens her arms just in time for me to crash into her. Sobs rack through me without mercy. They rip me to shreds and all I can do is let it happen.

"Come on, babe," Mali says softly. "Let's go inside."

I sniffle and try to dry my eyes but it's no use. "Weren't you about to go somewhere?"

Holding me close, she starts leading me into the house. "It doesn't matter. You come first."

Chapter 11

I LIE WITH MY head on Mali's lap as she plays with my hair in the way she knows I love. It's not something I can explain. It's just one of those things that always manages to calm me down.

My eyes burn from crying, and even a few tears still manage to leak out, but thankfully, it's nothing like before. At least for now, anyway.

"So, what are you going to do?" she asks after I was finally able to explain what happened. "You can't keep putting yourself through this back and forth."

"I know I can't. It's not fair to me. Which leaves me with only one option." I grab my phone and delete his number. "I think it's time he gets a taste of his own medicine. He's had hot. Now let's see how he likes the cold."

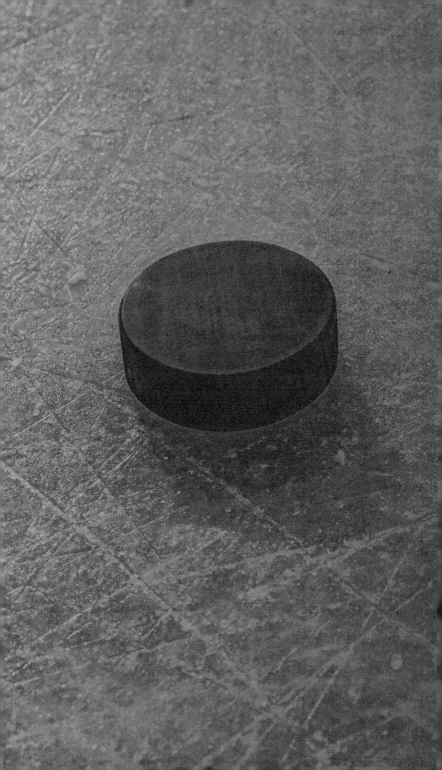

Hayes
CHAPTER TWELVE

TWO WORDS FOR YOU: RADIO SILENCE.

It's been three days since Laiken stormed into my job, laid into me the way no other girl ever has, and walked out with my dignity in her hands. I've always known that Laiken was the no-bullshit type. It's one of the things most guys find so attractive about her. But I don't think I ever expected what happened.

As she stood there, giving me the verbal ass kicking I rightfully deserved, I knew there was nothing I could say. There was no excuse I could give her. Nothing that would justify the things I've done and the way I've treated her.

I've been an asshole, and messing with her when I knew about her feelings for me was fucked up. There's nothing else to it.

And now I'm forced to deal with the consequences—which are all apparently in the form of Laiken's silence.

OKAY, I'LL ADMIT, THIS is bothering me more than I thought it would. This is what I wanted, right? For her to realize she doesn't want a going-nowhere guy like me? So then why is it that I still can't go an hour without thinking about her?

I get to the rink a half hour before I usually would. Coach asked me to come early to show him the new plays I came up with. The sight of Laiken's car in the parking lot tells me she's inside, and I'm not entirely sure how I feel about it.

Classical music plays through the speakers as I walk through the front door, telling me that Laiken is most likely on the ice. The urge to watch her is strong, but I know I have no right to be anywhere near her. Not after everything. So, I turn into the locker room instead and drop my bag on the bench.

"Hey, Coach," I say, popping my head into his office.

He looks up from his playbook. "Hey. Thanks for coming in early. Our upcoming game against Beaufort is an important one. While they may not be our biggest rivals, they've been making a lot of waves lately."

I scoff. "And talking a bunch of shit while they're at it."

"Exactly," he agrees. "So, I'm making it our mission to humble them a little."

"Sounds good to me. I'd love nothing more than to knock them down a peg."

The grin that stretches across his face makes me a little uneasy. "I'm glad to hear you say that. Come with me."

Getting up from his desk, he leads me out of the locker room and over to the rink. Laiken has the whole thing to herself and she's gliding around the ice with her usual unmatched skill. She has a way of making it look easy, and the only thing I can do is watch in awe.

Coach crosses his arms over his chest. "She's good, isn't she?"

"She's amazing," I all but whisper.

Her whole body launches in the air, and she spins quickly, making two rotations and landing a double axel like it's the simplest thing in the world to do. Honestly, if she tried, she could probably master the triple, but then Mr. Zimmerman would never leave her alone about going pro.

Seeing her all in her element is mesmerizing. She's confident off the ice—especially when she's standing in the middle of the surf shop, laying into me and making me regret every wrong thing I've ever done. But *on* the ice? It's like she's the only one that exists.

There's nothing she can't do.

No one she can't be.

Her whole world is inside that rink, and she owns every inch of it.

"She's also going to be our secret weapon," Coach says.

My gaze is ripped away from Laiken and over to him. "She's *what*?"

He chuckles, as if this is exactly what he expected from me. "Laiken is going to teach you and the rest of the team skills that will make you better on your skates. Today, you're all taking lessons…from her."

Fate has always had a way of laughing in my face, and it must have teamed up with Karma for this one. The timing of this couldn't be worse. Laiken hates my guts—rightfully so—and now I have to spend the next three hours with her.

Oh, *and* her brother, who can't know there is anything off between us.

This should be a blast.

"You're wasting your skills on the tiny tikes," Coach tells Laiken as the music stops.

She comes over to the gate and uses her skates to stop short, spraying snow onto the floor, but all I can see are her legs. Isaac was right. They're fucking perfect. And it pisses me off that he's noticed it, too.

"You don't know that," she counters. "One of those kids could be the next Ilia Malinin."

He chuckles. "It's going to be the one who was picking his nose and wiping it on the ice, isn't it?"

"Gross," I chime in, using it as an excuse to talk to her. "Which one was doing that?"

It suddenly gets frigid in here, and it has nothing to do with the ice. She glances over at me, barely even acknowledging my existence before she turns back to Coach.

"I'm going to get a drink. Let me know when you're ready for me."

He nods in response. "Will do. Thanks, Laiken."

She gets off the ice and removes her skates before walking away in her socks. Once she's gone, Coach looks in the direction she disappeared to and then at me, letting out a long whistle.

"What'd you do to piss off Baby Blanchard?"

I cringe, rubbing the side of my head. "It's a long story."

His hand comes up to pat me on the shoulder as he snickers. "Oh, today is going to be fun for you."

Hypothetically, if I were to punch him in the face, would I be removed from the team? I mean, at the very least it would probably get me out of the cruel torture he has planned. Maybe the risk would be worth the reward.

"I thought we were going over new plays today." I groan. "If this was your plan, why did you have me come in early?"

He gives me a onceover. "Because the other guys follow your example, and I knew you would be the one to give me the most crap about this."

"Well, you clearly didn't think *that one* through," I tell him. "What do you think Cam is going to do when you tell him?"

"You don't think he'll be okay with it?"

It takes everything in me to hold back a laugh. "Taking skating lessons from his little sister? Oh, yeah. I'm sure he'll be thrilled."

ALL OF US GATHER around on the rink, with Coach and Laiken in front of us. Half the guys are annoyed, while the other half are too busy checking her out—something I'm struggling to ignore. And then there's Cam.

"You're fucking with me," he says with a shake of his head, in total denial.

Coach looks over at me and I smile, mentally telling him *I told you so.* I can see why he thought I would be his biggest problem when it comes to this. There is nothing about me that screams *ballet on ice,* and I've never had a problem refusing to do something.

For example, the practice I missed. When I came in next, Coach told me I would have to make up the suicides I missed. The last thing he probably expected was me to tell him he had a better chance of me smoothing out the rink with my tongue, and that he can fuck off and find a new co-captain if he doesn't like it, but that's exactly what he got.

This, however, is different.

Cam and Laiken are really close. They have a bond that most siblings don't. But there's always been a dynamic between them. Cam is the typical big brother—intimidating and protective to a fault when it comes to her. Laiken, on the other hand, is the princess in the tower. Don't get me wrong, she can knock someone out without putting so much as a finger on them. If anyone else were to try to treat her like she needs them, they'd regret their words before they even finished saying them. But with Cam, she allows it.

Which is exactly why having to learn from her is a blow to Cam's ego.

"I'm not," Coach tells him. "You all have a lot of potential, but the place you need the most improvement is in the basics. Being able to control the puck will get you nowhere if you aren't skilled on your skates."

Isaac grunts. "She's a glorified dancer on ice. There's nothing she can teach me that I don't already know." He looks her up and down and smirks. "Unless she wants to take this somewhere more private."

My jaw locks as Laiken rolls her eyes.

Cam turns to glare at Isaac. "Shut your damn mouth before I shut it for you."

"Not this again," Coach huffs. "Listen up. This is nonnegotiable. If you don't like it, go ahead and sit out. But if you're on the bench during this, you can expect to be on the bench during the game, too."

Everyone groans, clearly not liking the idea of having to learn from a figure skater. Some of them are even taking issue with the fact that it's Laiken. And as I stand here, knowing how much she would rather be anywhere else right now than in the same room as me, I can't watch this.

"All right. That's enough," I say loud enough for everyone to hear me. "What's wrong? Afraid of being shown up by a girl?" Looking at Isaac specifically, my brows raise. "What about you? Cause personally, I think she can skate circles around your ass."

"Fuck off, Wilder," he spits.

I shrug. "Prove me wrong then."

Coach nods a silent thank you at me and then turns to Laiken. "They're all yours. Good luck."

"Thanks." Her eyes meet mine for a second, but she quickly tears them away and addresses the team. "All right. In hockey, your most important tool is your stick, but in figure skating, it's all about your body. Knowing where to place your balance is an underestimated skill set. For me, it means landing a double axel. For you, it means being able to skate faster than your opponent. And they can't stop you from scoring if they can't get to you in time."

SPOILER ALERT: I SHOULD'VE sat the fuck out. Screw Beaufort getting their asses handed to them. It's not worth it when I have to stand in the middle of the rink with a bunch of dudes, practicing a goddamn demi plié.

Where is the button to abort fucking mission?

"This is ridiculous," Owen whines. "What in the world does ballet have to do with hockey?"

A devilish smirk appears on her face. "Good question. Let me show you."

She skates over to the bench and grabs two broken hockey sticks and a roll of duct tape. Owen stays completely still with his eyes pinched shut as she tapes the wood to the back of his legs. When she's done, she stands back up and looks at Cam.

"You two are going to race," she tells them. "First one to the other side of the rink wins."

Owen doesn't look happy about it, but he walked himself into this bear trap. He and Cam line up beside each other, and when Coach blows the whistle, Cam takes off, but Owen is having a little trouble.

And by a little trouble, I mean he's waddling like a fucking penguin.

He doesn't even reach the middle of the rink by the time Cam crosses the finish line. Laiken giggles at his frustration, having proved her point.

"Bending your knees the right way is crucial to your speed." She looks at Cam and nods toward the starting line.

The idea of racing Laiken doesn't intimidate him at all. His cocky attitude comes out as he lines up next to her. But he should know that she never puts herself in a situation that isn't going to go in her favor.

The whistle blows once more, and they're off. You can tell Cam is pushing himself more than he was before, but he doesn't stand a chance. Laiken crosses the finish line a full three seconds before he does, and she barely even breaks a sweat while doing it.

"Dude," Aiden laughs. "You just got your ass handed to you by your sister."

Cam flips him off. "I've never claimed to be the fastest on the team. If she beats H, then I'll be impressed."

Laiken looks away at the mention of me, but she mumbles a quiet *fine* and skates over to the goal line. I follow suit, spraying a little snow her way in an effort to lighten the mood, but it doesn't work.

"You two ready?" Coach asks. "Laiken, you need a minute? You just got done racing Cam."

"Nope," she answers confidently. "Let's get this over with so they can apologize and we can get back to ballet."

Chuckling, he blows the whistle, and we push off the ice at the same time.

I have to win this. Not that I don't respect Laiken. I do. But I have a reputation to uphold. And yet, even with pushing my absolute hardest, it's not enough. She's at least a foot in front of me as we cross the line.

Both our skates turn to the side and snow sprays the wall.

I drop my head and laugh quietly to myself.

That's twice in one week that I've gotten my ass handed to me by her.

With a hand on her hip, she turns to the rest of the team. "Anyone else?"

All knowing they don't stand a chance; they shake their heads.

"Great." She gestures for them to continue. "Now that we've settled that, let's get back to demi pliés."

"Wait!" someone shouts, and Cam looks like he's in his own personal hell as Mali runs up onto the bleachers with her phone tightly in hand. "Oh, thank fuck. I thought I missed the good part."

"Amalia!" Coach shouts. "There's no recording practice. You know this."

She grins widely but doesn't put down the phone. "Don't worry, Coach! This video is for blackmail purposes only. I promise."

Lucas stops and tilts his head at Mali. "Your name is Amalia?"

"Watch it," she growls. "You're looking less like a Lucas and more like a Lucy in this video. You do *not* want to be on my bad side."

His eyes widen in fear.

It's no secret that Mali doesn't bluff.

Chapter 12

If she doesn't like you, you're pretty much fucked.

BY THE END OF practice, I'm spent. Exhausted doesn't even begin to explain it. My legs ache in places I didn't know *could* ache. But just by executing some of the things she showed us, I can see how they'll be beneficial. We've got the basics down. It'll just take some time to perfect it all.

"Mali, come on," Cam begs.

She shakes her head, smiling like the cat that caught the canary. "No way. You couldn't pay me to delete that video."

"Hey, just be glad she didn't get one of Laiken beating you in a race," I tell him.

Mali's jaw drops as she turns to look at Cam, and he sighs.

"Thank you so much for that," he grits through his teeth.

Laiken comes over with her bag on her shoulder. "If he hadn't told her, I would've."

Her hair is thrown into a messy bun on the top of her head, and she's wearing a pair of shorts and a hoodie, but fuck, she looks so good. Maybe it's the way she keeps putting me in my place, or that I've been desperate to see her since the moment she stormed out of the shop, but it's so easy to get lost in everything she is.

I let myself look at her for a moment and then tear my

eyes away, not wanting Cam to catch on. Although, he seems to be leaving.

"Okay, well, before you give her even more ammunition, I'm going to go." He walks backward to the door and then he's gone. Only Mali, Laiken and I remain—except for Aiden, who hasn't gotten his ass off the ice yet.

"If only his trial hadn't happened yet," Mali says. "We could have shown that video to the judge. 'Your honor, does this pointed toes princess look like a threat to you?'"

Laiken chuckles and shakes her head. "You're fucked up."

"I know," she answers proudly.

"Look, guys!" Aiden yells.

We all turn to see him gliding around with one leg lifted behind him. When he realizes he has our attention, he stands up straight and raises his arms above his head like in ballet.

"I'm feeling fabulous," he calls, but as he goes to do a trick, he wipes out like a freshly born baby gazelle.

Mali shakes her head slowly. "How does Coach not make him wear a helmet at all times?"

"I feel like the damage is already done at this point," Laiken replies. "Are you ready to go?"

"Yeah. Are you going to follow me?"

She nods, and just before they go to leave, I can't hold myself back. My hand moves before I can think it through, and Laiken stops when she feels my fingers lightly grabbing her hand.

"Can I talk to you for a minute?" I ask, hating the way she actually manages to make me nervous.

Glancing down at our hands, she looks like she might agree, but then she pulls herself out of my grasp.

"No." My hand falls to my side as she takes a step back. "The time to talk was around the same time you ignored me and made me feel like I was just a game to you. It's too late for that now."

Mali looks impressed as Laiken grabs her arm and walks out of the rink, leaving me feeling like I may have fucked up even more than I thought.

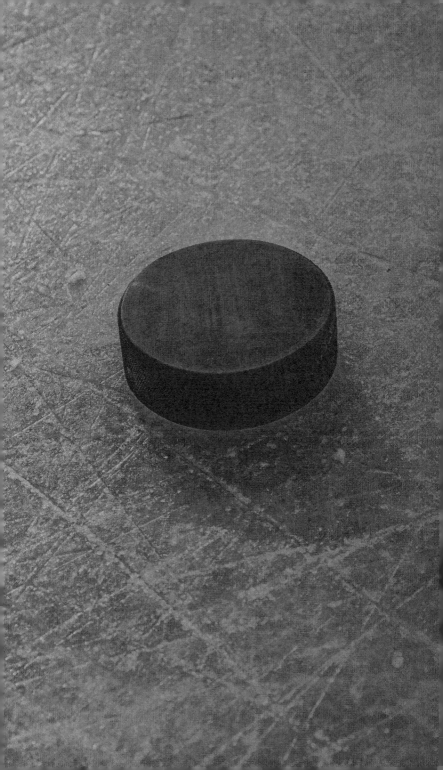

Hayes
CHAPTER THIRTEEN

WHAT DO YOU DO WHEN ANOTHER TEAM DOES AN interview and talks shit about yours? When their recent luck goes to their head, making them obnoxiously cocky, and you're determined to make them regret it? That's simple. You all agree to come in for a couple extra practices.

Coach stands at one end of the ice with a stopwatch in his hand, timing each of our speeds. He's been writing them down to compare where we were when we started to how we are now, and I don't think there's a single one of us who hasn't improved.

Well, except maybe Aiden, but he's basically a glorified water boy anyway. Still a valued member of the team, just not someone we'd put in at the final hour of a timed game. Or even the final hour of a game we're winning by three points.

"All right," Coach says. "I'm definitely happy with these results. Cam, you upped your speed to what Hayes's was originally."

Cam purses his lips and nods. Attaining my speed has always been one of his goals. He's just never figured out how to do it—until Laiken.

"H!" Coach barks. "You're hitting times a whole three seconds faster. If you were to race Laiken now, I think you'd give her a run for her money."

Yeah, fat chance of ever getting her to go near me willingly again.

He goes over the results for each of the guys. Some are doing great; others could use some more improvement. They probably spent the time during Laiken's lesson following along but believing they didn't actually need to know any of it.

Fucking idiots.

"Lucas." Coach stops and shakes his head. "Somehow, you managed to get slower. How the fuck did that happen?"

The rest of us chuckle while he rubs the back of his neck. "I don't know, Coach. Maybe I need some one-on-one lessons from Baby Blanchard. I'm sure that'll teach me."

My whole body tenses at the thought of what he's insinuating. Lucas hitting on Laiken is nothing new. He's been doing it for years. But now, I want nothing more than to check him into the boards hard enough to cause whiplash.

Cam rolls his eyes. "One of these days I'm going to convince her to get a restraining order on you."

Now *that's* an idea I could get on board with.

"Aw, come on," Lucas argues. "Are you saying you don't want me to be your brother-in-law one day?"

This motherfucker is going to get *me* on probation for aggravated assault if he keeps it up. Then again, I probably wouldn't be as lucky as Cam. I'd end up in prison—spending my nights dreaming of conjugal visits with the girl I can't have.

A bark of laughter shoots out Cam's mouth. "Dude, I wouldn't even let you marry my fourth cousin twice removed."

Lucas looks offended. "Now that's just mean. You're fucking with my destiny."

"Don't hold it against him," Owen chimes in. "Cam not wanting you in his family has nothing to do with why you won't be marrying Laiken."

"What's that supposed to mean?" he demands.

Coach pinches the bridge of his nose. "It means *Laiken* wouldn't have you, especially if you keep referring to her as

Baby Blanchard like some kind of pedophile. Can we get back to business now?"

The look on Lucas's face is priceless—like he just had all his hopes and dreams stomped and spat on. Owen puts a hand on his shoulder and smiles.

"It's all right, dude," he says. "She's just out of your league."

Cam snorts. "She's out of all your fucking leagues. None of you stand a chance with her, and even if you did, I'd never let it happen. My sister is off limits to every single one of you dipshits."

If that's not a sign from the damn universe, I don't know what is. Over the years, Cam has gotten increasingly annoyed with the guys hitting on her. Once, when she was the subject of locker-room talk, he damn near put Owen through the wall. Looks like Lucas might be next—unless Cam finds out what *I've* done.

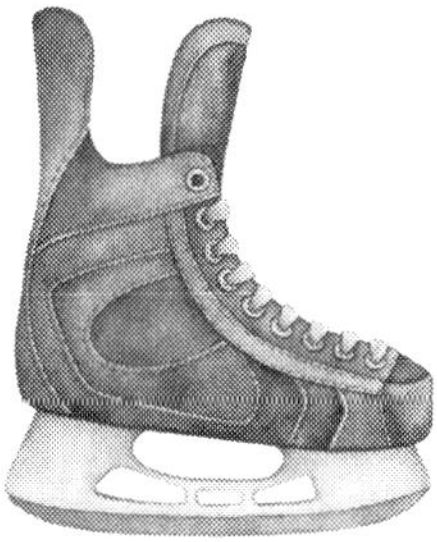

I NEVER IMAGINED THERE would be a time I would even feel slightly uncomfortable at Cam's house. Not after the years I've spent here. The last thing I want to do is disrespect Laiken, and being here when I know I'm on her shit list feels like disrespect. But when Cam asked if I was coming back to his place for video games like we normally do, I couldn't think of an excuse quick enough.

So, now I'm sitting on the couch, playing video games.

Their parents left shortly after we got here to go have dinner with a couple friends. They tossed Cam some money for pizza and told him to tell Laiken when he orders it, and out the door they went. That and the fact that her car is in the driveway is the only reason I know she's in the house.

Maybe she came downstairs and when she realized I was here, took off back upstairs. I mean, if she hates me to the point where she never wants to be around me again, I can't say I'd blame her. But damn, it would suck.

"I'm going to grab another beer," I tell Cam. "You want one?"

He picks up his can off the coffee table and shakes it. "Yeah, I'm low. Thanks man."

"No problem."

I go into the kitchen and open the fridge, looking for where Cam put the beer. Just as I spot them, tucked away on the back of the second shelf, I hear a cough and a sniffle coming down the stairs. My head whips around, and when Laiken's eyes meet mine, she freezes.

Her nose is red and irritated, and the blanket that's wrapped around her is a clear indication that she's sick. It looks like she tied her hair up yesterday and never fixed it after she woke up, with the way the bun hangs to the side of her head. And the most infuriating part is how fucking gorgeous she still manages to look.

Congested and miserable should never look that damn good.

"Can, uh..." She pauses to cough. "Can you hand me a bottle of water?"

I nod and grab one, putting it on the island for her to grab.

"Thanks."

It's the first time we've talked in three days, and it feels like getting to take a quick breath after nearly drowning. But knowing it'll be short lived is like being shoved right back under.

"Are you okay?" I ask.

She waves it off as she takes a sip of water. "I'm fine. It's just a cold."

My brows raise. "It's almost June."

"It's probably from the weather changes." She stops and then hums. "You should know all about that, being an expert on bouncing between hot and cold."

Her words hit dead in the middle of their target, and I wince at the way they hurt. My intention was never to hurt her or play with her feelings, but that doesn't change the fact that it happened. And all I want to do is make up for it.

"Lai," I breathe, but anything else I was going to say is gone as Cam comes into the room.

"Are you hungry? I think I'm going to order pizza." He stops and looks at Laiken just as she tears her eyes away from me. "Oh, hey sicky."

"Careful," she taunts him. "I'll go upstairs right now and cough on your pillow."

He grabs a menu out of the drawer and puts it on the counter. "Does Mom know she gave birth to a demon?"

Laiken smirks. "Yeah. She talks about your labor all the time."

There's no way I could fight off the smile that comes. Even while she feels like shit, she's a total spitfire—making you regret every word that leaves your mouth.

It would just be nicer if I wasn't also on the receiving end of it.

Chapter 13

THE RINK IS PACKED with fans. It's usually a full house, but this is next level. There aren't enough places for everyone to sit. After Beaufort's interview, the whole town wants to see us show them who's boss.

We're all in the locker room, getting ready and making sure our mindset is on point. If there's anything we do best, it's this. We might not always get along, but when it comes to proving that we're the best team around, we band together. That's what happens when you've all been playing together for years.

I look around for the playbook, wanting to go over it one more time, but it's nowhere to be found. And neither is Cam for that matter.

"Owen," I get his attention. "You seen Cam?"

He nods toward the door. "He stepped out for a minute."

"Did he have the playbook with him?"

"Sure did."

Ugh. "Thanks, man."

Every single game, Cam leaves the locker room for a minute to see his family. His parents wish him luck, and Laiken makes a comment about how she hopes he falls on his face. It's basically become a tradition at this point.

I grab the handle and pull the door open to go find him, but all the air is instantly sucked out of my lungs the second I step out.

Holy. Fucking. Shit.

Laiken is standing there with Mali and Cam, looking every bit like regret personified. Her hair is curled, and the light dusting of makeup Mali must have done for her accents her already breathtaking features.

I let my eyes move lower, and I bite my lip when I see the way her white top stops just beneath her tits, leaving her stomach exposed. The belly button ring shines in the light just above where her jeans hug her body in all the right places. The whole thing put together makes my damn mouth water.

The locker room door begins to open behind me, but when I notice it's Lucas, I quickly slam it shut again. If he sees her looking like that, he'll pop a boner, and then I'll be forced to slaughter him and paint the ice red with his blood.

It takes everything I have to keep my eyes off her and my jaw off the floor as I approach Cam.

"Hey," I say, clearing my throat. "Can I have the playbook? I just want to go over a couple things before we head out there."

He nods. "Hold up. I'll join you."

As he turns back to the girls, they each give him a hug and Laiken does her typical thing of backhandedly wishing him luck. And then she's gone, without saying a single word to me. Thankfully, Cam doesn't even notice and heads back into the locker room while I watch her walk away.

She has me eating my words like a five-course meal.

Chapter 13

HOCKEY IS ONE OF the few things I pride myself on. After using it as an outlet when my dad walked out on us, it became the most important thing in my life. It's the one thing I've always been good at, and there's never been a time where my head wasn't in the game—until tonight.

We all filter back into the locker room after the first period, every one of us needing the break that the intermission provides us. We may be winning by two, but it's not nearly the massacre I was hoping it would be. Every person on the ice has been giving it their all.

"What's up, man?" Cam asks as he fucks with something in his locker.

I shake my head and exhale. "I don't know. It's just not my night, but I'm trying."

It's a much safer option than the truth. *I'm distracted by your sister looking like sex on legs* is not something that would go over well.

He takes his phone out and hands it to me, the interview on the screen. We both watch the video we've seen over twenty times and listen to the way they talk their shit—acting like we're just a speedbump on their way to the championship.

"Imagine what they'll say if they actually beat us," Owen says.

And he has a point.

Under no circumstances can we lose this game, no matter how hard it is to stop picturing kicking everyone out of here and fucking Laiken on every surface of the place.

Standing up, I hand Cam back his phone and grab my helmet. Luckily, everyone else is pumped up. We're winning, and as long as we can keep this momentum, their undefeated streak will end tonight.

But as I walk out the door, the sight in front of me has a better idea—murdering their fucking captain.

Laiken has her back against the wall and a flirty look on her face while he leans over her. My teeth grind together, and the only thing I want to do right now is rip him away from her and knock him the fuck out, but I can't.

What right do I have to do that? *She's not mine.*

Forcing myself to keep my eyes straight, I let my stick take the brunt of my anger and walk past them. But that doesn't mean I don't put my eyes on her the second I get back on the ice.

I hate every goddamn thing about this.

The way he has all her attention locked on him.

The way he plays with a strand of her hair.

The way her whole face brightens as she laughs at something he said.

I'm not a possessive person. A girl once tried to hook up with Cam to make me jealous, and all it got her was me tossing him a condom and telling him to have at it. But watching her with him feels like I'm living in my own personal hell.

Mali goes over to get Laiken, and for a second, I'm relieved, but when he hands her a small piece of paper, all I can see is red.

Both teams get back on the ice, and everyone takes their seats again as it's time to face off—and I'm up against none other than Mr. Flirt himself. We stand across from each other with the ref to the side of us, and my rage twitches at the way he looks over to smile at Laiken.

"Hey," I growl. "Keep your eyes on the ice."

He scoffs. "The fuck is your problem?"

"As long as you stay the fuck away from her, I won't have a problem."

The sarcastic chuckle that leaves his mouth is the last thing he should do, and when the puck drops, only for him to immediately shove me, all bets are off.

My stick falls to the ground as I come back swinging. Usually fights in hockey have at least a few seconds of dancing around each other, but not this one. I rip his helmet off his head and toss away one glove to make sure he feels every bit of my fist slamming into his face.

He tries to fight back, landing a few punches, but it's nothing compared to the beating he's getting. And when I grip his jersey and take him down to the ice, the ref just blowing a whistle isn't enough. He has to pull me off him.

The two of us skate off to our respective penalty boxes, and it isn't until I sit down that I see her. Mali looks impressed, but Laiken is far from it as she rolls her eyes and shakes her head.

Whatever. Add it to the fucking list of things I've done wrong.

I don't care.

Chapter 13

I THOUGHT THAT WAS it. That I'd get my anger out by bloodying him up a little. But I was wrong. So drastically wrong.

Shit hits the fan after the second intermission. I should feel great. They may have managed to get another goal in, but we raised our lead by two more points, making the score 7 to 3. If we can't win by a shutout, this is the closest thing to second best. But when we all head back out to the ice, the rage that explodes inside of me is enough to light the whole fucking world on fire.

Laiken is sitting in the bleachers with Mali and her parents, but she's no longer freezing her ass off in the white top she was wearing before.

It's so much worse than that.

She's wearing his fucking jersey.

Every rule I have of giving her space and keeping myself away to respect her boundaries goes right out the window as I skate over to her and bang on the glass. Mali laughs as Laiken's gaze locks with mine, watching me wave her toward me. She steps down off the bleachers and stands on the other side of the glass.

"Take that shit off," I roar.

She's anything but impressed. "No."

Wrong answer. "I mean it, Laiken. Take it the fuck off or I'll cut it off you."

The corner of her mouth raises slightly, and she crosses her arms over her chest. "My drink spilled, meaning if I take this off, I'll literally be sitting here in my bra. Is that really what you want?"

Fuck. She has a point. But that doesn't mean I'm just going to stand around and let her look like she belongs to him. That will happen over my dead body.

Getting off the ice, I go into my locker and grab the backup jersey I have hanging in there. I grip it tightly as I throw the door open again and bring it over to Laiken, passing it to her as I stand off to the side of the bleachers.

Her brows furrow as she holds it up and looks at the back. "No. Absolutely not. You're not staking a claim on me or whatever it is you're trying to do. Go get me one of Cam's."

Yeah, that's not happening. "It's that or the bra, and you may be ballsy, but you're not the type for self-humiliation."

She gives me a look that rivals the one she had in surf shop. "You're an asshole, you know that?"

"Yep," I answer. "And I'm glad you've figured that out. Now, hate me all you want, but *take off his fucking jersey*."

There's no chance for her to argue it further as I walk away and get back on the ice. And when I glance over at her again, she may be pissed off, but she's doing it while sporting *my* number on her back.

THE THIRD PERIOD STARTS up, and it's not long until I'm back up against the dude who must be looking to die today if the smirk on his face is anything to go by. We're in their zone, with the chance to score again if this play goes the way we'd like. But as we wait for the puck to drop, he just can't help himself.

"You think I won't still fuck her while she's wearing your

jersey?" he asks, his grin turning smug. "Don't worry. I'll make sure to let you know how her pussy feels."

It's not my fault.

My actions are not my own.

And the way my stick flies into his face, slicing through the flesh near the corner of his eye, is not something anyone will ever get an apology from me for. Honestly, he's lucky that's all I did.

His glove instantly covers his eye, and before I can go after him further, the ref gets in between us and holds me back.

"Go get that checked out," the ref shouts to him and then turns back to me. "Good job, tough guy. You just got yourself thrown out of the game."

Maybe that was his plan. After all, the only chance they have at winning against us is to get rid of one of our best players. It wouldn't surprise me if after the last period, they decided to play dirty. I may have played right into his hand but fuck it.

It was worth it.

I shove the ref's hands off me and skate off the ice. Coach shakes his head as I pass but he does nothing to stop me from going into the locker room. Every single person on my team knows that now is not the time to try talking to me.

My blood is still boiling as the door shuts behind me. I rip off my helmet and throw it across the room, no doubt scratching it up and making me need a new one. Fuck staying for the rest of the game. The guys have it under control. The best thing I can do for everyone right now is get the hell out of here.

I sit on the bench and rip off my skates, low-key wondering if the blades are sharp enough to slit the guy's throat.

Yeah, like I said...

I need to get far away from this place.

I manage to get my uniform off, and I'm pulling up my jeans when I hear the door open. My whole body goes still, not even having to look to know who it is.

The tension that vibrates between us is enough to know.

"You want to tell me what that was about?" she asks.

I refuse to look at her. "It's hockey. Fighting happens all the time."

The only way I'm making it out of this room without doing something else I'll inevitably regret later is by acting like it wasn't about her, even though we both know that's not the case. Call it plausible deniability.

"And the jersey?"

I scoff. "You can't wear the opposing team's jersey at one of *our* games. Don't let it go to your head."

She huffs out a laugh, not believing a word coming out of my mouth. "And what about this?"

Finally turning around, I see her holding up the same small piece of paper from earlier, with his phone number scrawled across it.

"You mean to tell me it had nothing to do with this?"

I drop my head as I chuckle, knowing there's not a damn thing I can do now. The moral compass she told me to shove up my ass goes right out the window, and not a single ounce of self-control is anywhere to be found.

There's no stopping me anymore.

"You really think he's what you want?" I question, my voice low as I walk slowly toward her. "You think he can make you feel the way I did? Make your whole body shake when you cum?"

Her throat bobs as she swallows, but she doesn't dare say a word. All she can do is stare back at me as I reach her. Slipping the lighter out of my pocket, I don't look away from her for a second as I light the paper on fire.

As the heat reaches her fingers, she lets it go and watches it fall to the floor—turning to ash as it burns on the tile. I take her chin between my thumb and the knuckle of my index finger and turn her gaze back to mine.

"He can't, and I won't even let him try." I keep her in place as I move in until my lips are right against hers, feeling the heat of our breath mixing together. "Because you're fucking mine."

And the small space between us disappears as I kiss her in a way that throws us both into the abyss.

Laiken
CHAPTER FOURTEEN

I WASN'T GOING TO BE THE ONE TO DO IT, BUT THE second he crosses the line he's blurred so many times before, there's nothing holding either of us back. My arms wrap around his neck, my fingers sliding into his hair. The way he wastes no time in forcing my mouth open and tangling his tongue with mine… It's all got my senses on overload.

The only thing I can focus on, the only thing I can *think* about, is him.

His hands grip my waist as he lifts me with ease and pins me up against the wall. I wrap my legs around him, and the moment I feel his hard cock rub against my pussy, I moan into his mouth.

Dragging my nails up his back, I revel in the way he arches into me, but it's not enough. There are too many layers between us. Too much keeping him from exactly where I want him.

Where I *need* him.

He breaks the kiss, only to move his lips to my neck. I gasp at the sensation and turn my head to give him more access. He could mark up every inch of my skin and I don't think he'd get a single complaint out of me right now.

"God, you look so fucking good in my jersey," he murmurs against my skin. "Such a little temptress. You love testing my limits, don't you?"

I let my head hit the wall, breathing heavily, but he's not

having that. His hand comes up to wrap around my throat, and his eyes glare into mine.

"Answer me, Laiken."

Fuck me. "Yes."

"Yes what?"

"I love testing your limits," I admit. "Wanted to see you break."

The sexiest smirk I've ever seen appears on his face. "Mission fucking accomplished."

With his fingers wrapped around my neck, he covers my mouth with his own once more. The way his tongue moves with mine, like I don't stand a chance in having any kind of dominance, it's intoxicating. I could quite literally get drunk on only him.

The buzzer sounds and cheers erupt, telling us both that the home team scored, and Hayes reluctantly pulls away. His eyes move across my face, looking for something unbeknownst to me, and then he exhales.

"As much as I want to take you right here, the last thing we want is someone from the team walking in on us," he says.

I nod, still trying to catch my breath. "Right. You're right."

He gently puts my feet back on the ground and takes a step back. For a moment, a pit settles in my stomach, thinking it's over and this is when he goes back into his usual spiral of regret, but that's wiped from my mind the minute he speaks.

"Can you think of an excuse to tell your parents?"

I nod and run my fingers through my hair in an attempt to fix it.

"Good." He grabs the shirt out of his locker and throws it on. "Go take care of that and then meet me at my truck."

"Okay."

I turn around to do just that, but before I can reach the door, he pulls me back. His thumb rubs against my cheek as he kisses me once more—softly this time.

"You're going to be the death of me," he all but whispers.

Smiling, I arch up on my tiptoes to kiss his cheek, and then I'm out the door.

I wrap my arms around myself as I go back into the stands. Everyone is still pumped up from the goal that was recently scored, but I have a job to do.

"There you are," my mom greets me happily. "You okay?"

"No," I lie. "I think I may have overdone it. I'm still not feeling one hundred percent yet, so I'm just going to go home and rest."

Her brows furrow, but as my dad yells about something in the game, her attention is pulled elsewhere. "Okay, sweetie. Well, I hope you feel better."

"Do you need me to drive you home?" Mali asks, reminding me I rode with her.

I shake my head. "That's okay. I have an Uber waiting outside."

"How convenient." The sarcasm that laces her tone goes unnoticed by my parents but I hear it loud and clear.

I subtly flip her off, making her chuckle. Picking up Greg's jersey, I hand it to Mali.

"Make sure he gets this back."

Her brows raise. "You don't want to hold onto it?"

Oh yeah. I'm sure that would go over so well. "No. I have no use for it."

Before she can say anything else my parents may catch onto, I wave to the three of them and walk away—eagerly heading for the door.

Hayes's truck is running in the parking lot when I get outside. I keep my head down and go climb into the passenger side. He glances over as I buckle my seatbelt, and once I'm done, he puts the truck into drive.

Neither one of us says a word as he pulls out of the parking lot. I don't think the reality has set in that this is actually happening. He's driving us to God knows where with the sole intention of touching me in all the ways I've dreamed he would.

Pulling up to a red light, he looks over at me and chuckles, shaking his head as he focuses back on the road.

"What?" I ask curiously.

"You play dirty."

My grin widens, but I admit nothing. "I don't know what you're talking about."

Humming amusedly, he puts his foot on the gas as the light turns green. "Every game I've seen you come to, you're in jeans or sweatpants, with your hair tied back like you couldn't be bothered. But tonight, you show up looking like you're ready for a night on the town."

To be honest, the outfit was Mali's idea, and a brilliant one at that. It may have been a little cold in there, but what's that saying? No pain, no gain? Clearly, it was worth it.

"And then you had the nerve to put on someone else's jersey."

I can't help but laugh. "In my defense, my shirt was ruined, and I needed something else to wear."

"So, you go into the locker room and take one of mine," he growls. "But the only goddamn number that goes on that body of yours is mine. The fact that you even gave that shithead the time of day pisses me off."

Good. That was the point. "Maybe I just wanted to feel good."

He chuckles, turning the steering wheel to the left. "Oh, trust me, baby. You're going to."

Baby. God, I have such a love hate relationship with the

way that makes my heart race.

HAYES PARKS THE TRUCK and turns his headlights off, leaving the moonlight to be the only thing illuminating the empty parking lot. The beach in front of us isn't a popular one, mainly only used by local surfers and fishermen. He knew exactly where to go to make sure we don't get caught.

As he turns to face me, my breathing stutters a little.

"If we do this, neither one of us can take it back. You know that, right?"

I press my tongue to my cheek. "I was never the one taking anything back."

Closing his eyes for a second, he lets out a breathy laugh. "Hard to know who's going to kill me first, you or Cam."

"It's probably fifty-fifty," I admit.

"Of course it is." He smiles fondly, but it fades as he turns serious. "Not being straight with you before was a dick move. I should've talked to you, and I'm not making that mistake again, so I'm talking to you now."

He pauses for a moment to be absolutely certain he has my attention.

"If you're looking for a relationship, you won't find one here. Tell me that's a deal breaker, and I'll take you home right now. No hard feelings."

Hearing those words isn't a shock. I've always known the

kind of guy he is, and I never thought we'd do the things we've done, so it's no surprise that we won't be riding off into the sunset together or some romantic shit. But that doesn't mean the part of me that longs for that isn't a little let down.

Still, I'm not about to back out now over a small technicality.

If I get my heart broken, well, at least I got a few orgasms out of it.

"And what if I don't care about that?"

His tongue darts out to moisten his lips. "I just want you to be sure this is what you want."

"It is," I say with zero hesitation.

He smirks and leans on the center console. "Then come here."

I meet him in the middle. He tucks a strand of hair behind my ear and moves his hand to the back of my neck to pull me in. The kiss is patient. Soft and intentional. He moves his mouth against mine like we have all the time in the world. But when I take his bottom lip between my teeth, he doesn't hold back anymore.

Everything goes from light and delicate to a fiery inferno of want and need. He pulls on the lever to lay his seat back, tugging me on top of him.

"Fuck," he groans.

I grind down against him, feeling how hard he is inside his jeans. "Need this. Need you."

Letting out a light moan, he undoes his jeans and arches up enough to take them off. His cock lies against his stomach, looking like it may actually rip me in half. And the angry shade of red shows just how turned on he is. If any part of me still thought I was the only one who wants this, it's quickly reassured.

His fingers move to the button of my pants. It's tricky,

getting them off in this position, but we manage. As my panties land on the floor of his truck, he runs his thumb over my clit—sending a shot of pleasure straight into my core.

"I can't wait to be inside of you," he tells me as he plays with my pussy. "Gonna feel so fucking good."

The anticipation is going to kill me. I grab the bottom of his jersey and go to pull it over my head when he stops me and lowers it again.

"Oh no, baby," he growls. "Leave it on. Want to fuck you while you're wearing it."

Let me tell you, for a guy who doesn't do relationships, he's awfully possessive. But mentioning that right now would bring this to a screeching halt, so instead, I lean forward and kiss him.

Feeling his two fingers dip inside of me, I moan in relief. I've needed him like this since the last time he did it. Nothing I've done, not even the vibrator Mali insisted I buy, would do the job. None of it made me feel anything close to the way he does.

"H," I plead. "God, H."

He smirks into the kiss. "Tell me what you want, Rochester."

Under any other circumstances, I'd be blushing and shying away from his request, but right now? Screw it.

Pulling away, I look him straight in the eyes. "I want you to fuck me."

"Good girl."

I preen at the compliment as he reaches into the center console and pulls out a condom. He takes his dick in his hands and jerks it a couple times, keeping his gaze on me. I look away to watch him slide the condom over himself.

"Last chance to back out, baby," he tells me, but I shake my head.

"Never going to happen."

Gripping my hips, he positions me over his cock. "Thank fuck."

Everything in me feels like it's on fire as he rubs against my entrance, teasing and torturing. And as he starts to lower me onto him, the stretch stings and burns all at the same time. I do my best to hide the pain, but he's paying too much attention. Before he even gets the whole tip inside, he watches as I wince slightly, and he freezes.

I look away, hoping it'll make him keep going, but he's not about to allow that.

"Look at me."

I'd really rather not right now.

"Laiken," he says, and it's not a request. "Look at me."

Taking a deep breath, I do as he says. He stares into my eyes. There's a whole range of emotions on his face, but the biggest one is concern.

"Are you…"

He doesn't finish the question, and I use that to my advantage.

"Gay?" I finish for him. "No, clearly not. Mali is attractive and all, but she's lacking the necessary parts."

It's meant to be a joke, but he's not amused.

"Are you a virgin?"

Shit. I roll my eyes like the idea is outrageous. "Psht, no. I've had sex plenty of times."

Yeah, he doesn't buy it for a second. Not that I thought he would. I'm a horrible liar, and that was the furthest thing from my best performance.

He exhales like he's ashamed of himself and pulls out of me immediately. I throw my head back and groan as he lowers me back down, this time with his dick lying beneath my pussy instead of pulsing inside of it.

"This is so fucked up," he says, struggling with himself.

"It's not. I told you." I put my forehead against his. "I

want this. I want *you*."

Kissing him slowly, I feel him hold back a bit and then he starts moving his mouth with mine. I move against him and let out a breathy moan when his dick twitches. I'm starting to think he's back to being on board with this, but when I try to put him inside me again, he stops me.

"Lai," he says, and I'm afraid of what's going to come next. "This isn't some random fuck we're talking about here. It's your *first time*. You deserve so much fucking more than this."

He looks around the truck to emphasize his point.

My shoulders sag as I realize this isn't going to happen—disappointment filling the void I would much rather fill with him. But when he notices my expression fall, he softens just a little.

"Hey." He puts his hand on my face to make me look at him. "Just because we can't have sex doesn't mean I can't still make you feel good."

Pulling me into him, he kisses me again, this time while rubbing circles against my clit. It's not nearly as good as I imagine fucking him would be, but God, it feels amazing. He knows exactly how to touch me, exactly how to move, to make me want to scream out.

As I start to grind against his dick, his hands slide up my stomach and underneath my bra. He grabs both my tits, toying with my nipples. When he sees the way my body reacts to his touch, he grins deviously. Pushing his jersey and my bra up just enough to leave me exposed, he covers one breast with his mouth.

And *holy fucking shit*.

Don't get me wrong, I've messed around with guys. At one point, when I thought I actually wanted to be with Craig, I jerked him off and let him feel me up. But it didn't feel anything even remotely close to this.

This is everything.

I throw my head back, letting out sounds I have no business making. Hayes's cheeks hollow around my nipple as he sucks on it and teases it with his tongue. Lacing my fingers into his hair, I pull him closer and grind myself harder against him.

The pressure starts to build inside me, but it's not enough.

I need more than this.

More than his fingers.

I need *him*.

"Yes, baby," he moans as he lies back. "Grind against my cock. Use me to get you off. Take what you want."

I bite my lip in frustration. "What I *want* is for you to fuck me."

His eyes narrow as he stares at me, and I know he's thinking about it. I can feel him beneath me—feel how hard he is and how his dick is begging for release. In a last-ditch effort to push him over the edge, I look at him with nothing but pure desire in my eyes.

"Please?" I beg. "I need it. Need to feel you inside me."

"Laiken," he warns.

I roll my eyes. "I know, I know. I deserve better. I heard you. But that doesn't change the fact that this is what I want. So, if you don't want to fuck me because you genuinely just don't want this, or because you have some weird complex about taking my virginity, that's fine. I'll find someone else to pop my cherry and then we can revisit this. But if you're only doing it because you have some notion in your head that I—"

My words are cut off as he kisses me…hard. His tongue dances with mine as he lifts me up and lines himself up against me once more. And this time, as he starts to lower me onto him, he doesn't stop.

He doesn't pause.

He slides himself into me and kisses me through the pain.

And fuck, it hurts so good.

The feeling of his cock stretching me open is everything, and when he bottoms out, the sounds that fill the truck are straight up pornographic.

"You're so goddamn tight," he groans.

"I'm not hurting you, am I?" I ask, feeling a little insecure.

He chuckles breathlessly. "No, baby. You're perfect. I'm going to move, okay?"

I nod and he uses his hold on my waist to start lifting me up and lowering me back down. For the first few times, it hurts just as much as the first, but as he quickens his pace with each thrust, the pain morphs into pleasure.

"Oh God," I moan, feeling so good. So full of him.

He's right along with me as he presses his head back against the headrest. "That's it. Just like that. Fuck, Laiken. You're so good for me."

His words spark something inside of me, the same way they did in my bedroom. My only goal, my only care in the world, is being everything he wants me to be. And right now, all I want is to give him what he wants.

I pull his hands off me and pin them beside his head as I start to bounce on his cock. His fingers lace with mine, and his teeth sink into his lip as he watches me chase both our highs.

"I love seeing you like this," he tells me. "Seeing you in my jersey, feeling your pussy wrapped around my dick. Can't wait to feel you come all over me."

A small whimper falls from my lips, and he smirks.

"Is that what you want, baby? Want to come all over my cock?"

"Yes," I breathe. "I want to make you feel so good."

He arches up into me. "You are. You're making me feel so fucking good."

Increasing my speed, I realize I'm so close. It's right there, ready to explode like a bomb inside of me. I just need him deeper.

I need every last inch of him deep inside my pussy.

The second I release his hands he grips my waist again and pulls me down onto him—hard and rough. I drop my head onto his shoulder as I start to lose control. In this moment, nothing else exists. It's just him and me and the way he's fucking himself up into me while pulling me down onto him.

"Fuck, Laiken," he moans. "I'm gonna come. Need you to come with me."

My fingers dig into his arms, and as he reaches between us and starts to play with my clit, I'm thrown into the deep end. Hayes turns his head and kisses me, swallowing down my moans as my whole body clenches and quivers around him.

"Yes," he pants. "Fuck, yes. Such a good girl for me."

He thrusts a few more times, dragging out my orgasm before he follows me right off the edge. His cock pulses inside me as he empties everything he has into the condom.

My head stays rested on his shoulder as the two of us try to regain our breathing. All the windows are fogged up, like something you see out of a movie, and I smile as I lift my hand up and put it on the window, sliding it down until I reach the door.

Hayes snickers as he watches me. "*Titanic*, really?"

"What?" I argue. "It's a classic."

He may act like I'm ridiculous, but the grin on his face says otherwise—as do the circles he's mindlessly rubbing against my back.

We stay like that for a few more minutes, until it starts to get uncomfortable. With a soft kiss pressed to my head, he lifts me off him and places me back in the passenger seat.

"I didn't hurt you, did I?" he questions as he takes the condom off and hands me my clothes.

I shake my head with a smile. "No. Not at all."

"Good."

He's almost fully dressed while I'm still trying to find my panties. When he notices, he smirks and holds them up.

"Looking for these?"

I nod, but when I go to grab them, he pulls them away and shoves them into his pocket.

"I'm keeping them," he tells me. "Get dressed."

That shouldn't be nearly as hot as it is. But yet, even as I pull my jeans on and feel how uncomfortable they are without underwear on, I can't stop thinking about it.

"Wait." I narrow my eyes at him. "That's not some weird fetish of yours, is it? Do you have a whole stash of women's panties in your room?"

He snorts. "So glad you think I'm such a man-whore, Rochester."

"That's not what I—" I clamp my mouth shut and huff.

Could he have a whole drawer in his dresser filled with tokens of the girls he's fucked? Sure. Will he tell me if he does or not? Not a chance in hell. There's no way to answer the question without making him look a way he doesn't want to look.

If he tells me he does, it looks like I'm just another number. Another random fuck to him.

And if he tells me he doesn't, he's admitting that I mean more to him than any of the women he's slept with before me.

It's essentially a trick question. There's no winning for him.

Chapter 14

HALFWAY BACK TO MY house, we're listening to the radio and my hand is hanging out the window—feeling the breeze between my fingers. I sing along with the music as I lay my head back. Hayes looks over at me and smiles before resting his hand on my leg.

It's such a small gesture, and to anyone else it might be insignificant, but butterflies take over my stomach because of it. The possibility of what could come next weighs heavily in the back of my mind, but I push it away. I refuse to ruin this by overthinking. I can worry about it later.

Right now, I just want to enjoy this.

We pull up to my house ten minutes later, and thankfully, no one is home yet. There's no telling what any of my family would say if they saw Hayes dropping me off. Cam, especially.

I unbuckle my seatbelt, but he doesn't move his hand from my thigh.

"You sure you're okay?" he asks, sounding genuinely worried about it.

It's cute, really. "Yeah, I'm good. I promise."

Satisfied with my answer, he glances at the house and then leans over to kiss me once more. It's not a pity kiss, or an obligational one, it's just...nice. He pulls away and looks at me with something unexplainable in his eyes.

"Goodnight, beautiful."

My breathing stutters. "Goodnight."

Climbing out of the truck, I'm about to shut the door when he stops me.

"Oh, and Laiken?"

"Yeah?"

"You're enough of a distraction at our games," he tells me. "If you expect us to win, I'd consider not dressing like that again."

My grin widens as I giggle. "Got it. Next time, I'll wear a trench coat."

His eyes narrow. "With clothes under it?"

I shrug. "We'll see."

His head falls back, and he whines as I close the door and head inside. He can enjoy picturing that mental image for the rest of the night. Meanwhile, I go straight up to my room and change into something more comfortable.

With every move I make, I can feel it.

The way he stretched me open.

The soreness he left behind.

I throw myself backward onto my bed and bite my lip. It may not have been the way I pictured losing my virginity, but I wouldn't change a thing.

I'M LYING IN BED, reading a book, but I can barely get through a couple paragraphs without my mind wandering. It's been a few hours since Hayes dropped me off, and it only took about twenty minutes before the anxiety started to set in.

If past experiences are anything to go by, this is when he goes into retreat mode. When he regrets every single thing that just happened and texts me to let me know it was a mistake.

That he's sorry.

That it won't happen again.

I thought about texting him, but as hard as it may be, I'm trying to refrain from doing that tonight. If he were to leave me on read again, the perfect little bubble I'm living in right now will pop and I'll be forced to deal with the pain of him going cold again.

Forcing myself to go back to reading, I finally manage to make it through a page and a half, when my phone dings. Both excitement and fear rush through me, but they both die down as I see it's just Mali.

Okay, spill. How big is it?

A bark of laughter shoots out of me as I text back.

You're crude.

After a second, I send another.

At least a solid eight, maybe nine. And thick.

Well damn, go Wilder. Be careful, though.
That thing could rip your cockhole.

My cockhole? 🤣

Well, it's either that or a tamponhole, and
that's not nearly as fun.

Seriously, sometimes I wonder what is wrong with her.

🙄 And on that note, goodnight Mal.

Her responses come one right after another, as if she has no problem blowing up my phone if that's what it takes.

Wait!

I need details!

You can't leave me hanging like this. It's just wrong.

Laiken Rose!

Don't you dare go to sleep on me. I did not stick around through all of this to not find out if my sexpectations were met or not!

Ugh. You're a bitch. I love you.

I chuckle and put down my phone. She can wait until tomorrow morning. Besides, this is a conversation I'd much rather have in person. I don't need my parents or Cam overhearing me, or getting ahold of my phone.

Rule number one of keeping something a secret: never put it in writing.

My phone dings again and I sigh, picking it up and expecting it to be Mali, but when I see a number that I recognize but don't have saved in my phone, my heart sinks.

Hayes.

I take a deep breath, holding it for five seconds before letting it out. It's supposed to help with my nerves, but it does fuck all right now. There's no telling what could be in that message.

All I know is if it's another apology text, I'm going to

shove his phone so far up his ass, he'll need to have it surgically removed.

I give myself another minute to compose myself, and then silently count to three before swiping it open.

What are you up to?

Okay. That's definitely not the worst.

Unless he's leading up to it…

Lying in bed and reading a book. You?

It goes from delivered to read instantly, and the three dots that appear have more of an effect on me than they should.

Imagining you in a trench coat.

My face hurts from the smile that stretches across it.

Hidden fantasy of yours or something?

You are the hidden fantasy. Just you.

I grab my pillow and squeal into it, realizing how ridiculous it is but not caring in the slightest. I'm not thinking about how this may end, or how it could all go wrong. I'm not anticipating getting my heart broken or thinking about ways I could try to get him to want a relationship. I'm simply living in the moment.

I send back a kissy face emoji and a heart and put my phone down as I cuddle into my pillow, smiling from ear to ear.

He's not taking it back this time.

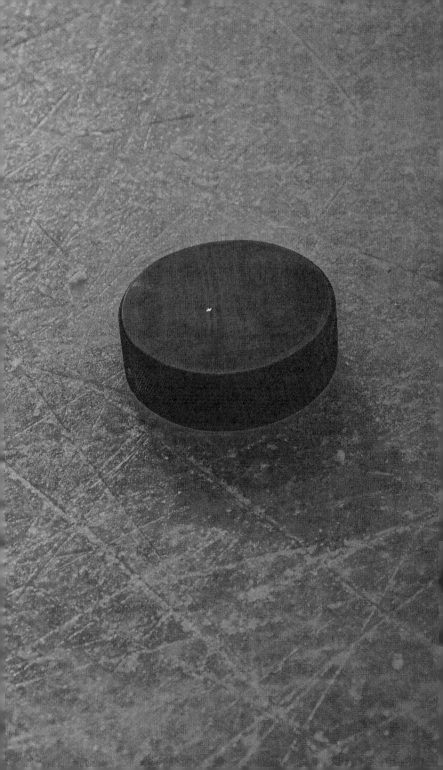

Hayes
CHAPTER FIFTEEN

I SHOULDN'T BE HERE.

Every part of me knows I should just sit in my truck and wait for the guys to get here for practice. But as I stare at Laiken's car sitting across the parking lot, I can't be bothered with what I *should* do.

Screw it. I've already fucked everything to hell a few days ago. It's not like making the right choices now is going to change my fate.

As I walk in, the music Laiken skates to plays on blast through the speakers. I quickly drop my bag off in the locker room and then head over to the rink. I'm expecting to see her on the ice, making spins and turns look like magic, but when I get there, it's completely empty.

Where the fuck is she?

First, I wonder if Mali picked her up or something. It wouldn't be the first time she left her car at the rink. We all do it. But then I think about how the music is still playing, and a part of me worries something might have happened to her.

My eyes search the rink, trying to see any sign of her, and just when my stress level starts to rise, it falls right back down again.

"Looking for someone?"

I spin around to see Laiken standing there, skates still on her feet as she drinks from a water bottle.

"Yeah, actually."

Without hesitation, I step closer and pull her in for a kiss. She drops her water bottle on the floor and immediately melts into me. Her arms wrap around my neck and I lift her up, carrying her behind the bleachers, where we aren't so out in the open.

Hooking up isn't something new to me. What *is* new, however, is the way I fucking crave her. I've never found myself going out of my way to see a girl until Laiken.

I'm not sure I like it, but if I've learned anything over the last month, it's that I don't have a single say in the matter.

Moving my hands to her ass, I press her against the wall and grind into her. She reacts exactly how I thought she would—moaning into my mouth like the needy little thing she is. Between that, and her tugging on my hair, all the blood goes straight to my cock.

Fucking hell, I'm like a goddamn preteen who just discovered porn.

I allow myself to kiss her once more before reluctantly pulling away and putting her down.

"If we keep going, I won't be able to get my cup on," I explain when I see the look on her face.

She scrunches her nose. "Those things do not sound comfortable."

"They're not, but it's better than taking a puck to the balls, so we deal with it." I pause as I think of how Isaac refuses to wear one during practice. *Idiot.* "Well, most of us anyway."

She pulls the hair tie out, letting her hair down and running her fingers through it. And while I should probably be a little less eager, I can't help myself. Leaning in to kiss her one more time, I feel her smile against my mouth.

"I'll be right back," she tells me. "I just have to go turn off the music."

As soon as she's gone, I reach down and fix myself in my jeans. It would be so much easier if I could just wear sweatpants or basketball shorts, but they provide nothing in terms of being discreet if someone catches us together. They'd see the tent in my pants and there would be nothing we could say to deny what's going on between us.

I sit on the bench and look around. The last time I was here, I walked in with only two goals in mind. One, make Beaufort regret everything they said about our team. And two, keep my mind on the game and off Laiken.

Only one of those were accomplished, and it wasn't because of me.

The moment she stepped into the locker room and held up that phone number like some kind of trophy, I knew I couldn't push her away anymore. It would have sent her straight into his arms. And after finally having her attention again, I wasn't about to let that happen.

Although, I didn't know that she was a virgin. That one was a shock. If I had any idea, I never would've brought her to that beach. And even once I knew, I had no intentions of fucking her. I meant it when I said that she deserves more than losing her v-card in the front seat of my truck near a public beach.

She needed some relief, and I was going to give it to her, but I was never going to let it go that far. But watching her grind herself up and down my dick, chasing her own high, I needed it. I needed to feel her clench around me as she explodes. And once she mentioned the possibility of giving that part of her to someone else, that was it.

I could no longer deny her of what we both wanted.

And now that I've had her, I can't get enough. She's got her claws in deep, and it drives me nuts. We haven't been able to have sex again, because apparently sneaking around isn't the easiest thing in the world, but we have been able to slip in a few make-out sessions that leave me with blue balls for the rest of the day.

Laiken comes back and smiles as she sits beside me, untying her skates and taking them off.

"So, how was work?" I ask.

She hums, giggling slightly. "It's always interesting, to say the least. The girls are great, and some of the boys have a lot of focus and determination. It's the ones that are being forced to come by their parents that give me the most issue."

"Using you as a daycare service?"

"Pretty much," she answers. "I was thinking about telling the parents I need them to come on the ice and help with them in order to lessen the chance of injury. I figure they'll either do as I ask or stop bringing their kids to lessons. Regardless, I win."

I chuckle and nudge her with my elbow. "You've just got everything all figured out, don't you?"

"For the most part." She winks at me. "Oh! There is this one little girl. She's only six, but I've had to move her up to the class with the eleven-year-olds because she catches on so quickly. She's just so determined for being so young, and she listens really well."

Her voice trails off as she turns to see me already smiling back at her.

"Sorry, I'm sharing too much," she says.

"No," I tell her, grabbing her hand with mine. "I like hearing you talk about things that are important to you."

She looks down at where I'm holding her hand, and I know I probably shouldn't have done it. The last thing I'm trying to do is give her things to read into. But the way she smiles up at me and leans in for a kiss, I can't find a bit of regret in me.

Owen's voice bounces off the walls, followed by Isaac

telling him to shut up, and I know our time is up. I drop my head and sigh heavily.

"That's my cue."

She chuckles at my disappointment. "I could always ask Coach if I can give you guys another ballet lesson."

My eyes widen. "For the love of God, no."

It was bad enough that I had to do that shit once, and in front of Laiken, for that matter. It was solid proof that Karma has a sense of humor. But having to do it now, after we've had sex, that's a whole new level of humiliation.

Knowing they've probably already seen my truck in the parking lot, it's only a matter of time before one of the guys comes looking for me. So, in the interest of not getting caught, I give Laiken a quick kiss goodbye and squeeze her hand before letting go and heading into the locker room.

"Hey, Mayweather," Owen jokes, getting his cracks in now since he hasn't seen me since the game. "How was your early night?"

I roll my eyes and flip him off. "That shithead deserved every bit of what he got."

"What he *got* was three stitches near his left eye," Isaac informs me. "Since when do you play dirty like that?"

"Since people don't know when to shut their fucking mouths. You want to be next?"

Isaac and I tolerate each other for the sake of the team, but we're not friends by any means. He's a prick. A pompous, arrogant, pain in my ass who thinks he's the best at everything because his parents spoiled him as a child. Even in high school, he thought that he was hot shit simply because his family is wealthier than most.

It's probably why he's yet to leave home even though he has the trust fund to do so.

He's completely content living off Mommy and Daddy's

money, only doing something somewhat productive when he comes to hockey practice.

"Dude, did you see someone tried to burn the place down?" Lucas questions, pointing to the black mark on the tile.

My brows furrow. "What the fuck? Who would do that?"

"I thought it was you," Owen tells me.

"Me?"

He shrugs. "You were the last one in here."

I chuckle in disbelief. "What part of me screams arsonist to you?"

"All of it," Owen and Lucas answer in unison.

"Fuck you both."

Cam walks in as Owen is trying to rub the spot away with his shoe with no luck. "I'm just saying, you were pretty pissed when you got thrown out of the game."

Looking at the mark and then back at me, Cam's brows raise. "You trying to burn the whole world to the ground, pyro?"

There is no believable excuse for lighting that asshole's phone number on fire, so my only option is to deny it.

"That shit wasn't me," I tell him. "If I wanted to set the place on fire, I'd have done a lot better job than *that*."

The guys all exchange a look and Cam purses his lips as he nods. "Fair point."

Everyone goes back to getting ready for practice while Cam places his stuff on the bench beside me. I try to read him, to see if he has any idea of what went on the other night, but there's nothing off about him.

"Wilder," Coach says as he walks out of his office. "Give me one good reason why I shouldn't bench you for the stunt you pulled the other night."

I can think of plenty.

He's an asshole who fucked with the wrong guy.

He doesn't know when to shut his mouth.

He was hitting on my girl.

But none of those are the answers he wants to hear, and the last one isn't an option. The only thing I can do is drop my head and swallow my pride.

"He got under my skin," I tell him. "It won't happen again."

"Not good enough. You're one of my best players. I can't have you getting thrown out of games, especially ones where we have something to prove."

I nod, accepting that I'm going to be forced to sit out the next game, but Cam shuts his locker and spins around.

"Coach, with all due respect, I'm on H's side here," he says.

Coach looks anything but amused. "No shit, Sherlock. He's your best friend."

Cam shakes his head. "It's not that. Some of the guys on the Mariners were trying to use Laiken to fuck with us. I heard them talking about it after the game."

The possibility passed through my mind at one point, but hearing I was right pisses me off. I hate knowing I played right into their hand. But what I hate even more is that they tried to use Laiken as a pawn.

"Is that true, H?"

I nod. "He said some pretty disrespectful things about her, and I lost my temper."

Coach glances between Cam and me, then sighs heavily. "Fine, but if it happens again, I'm benching you. No exceptions."

He disappears back into his office as Cam sits down to pull on his skates. "What did that guy say to you, anyway?"

I'm not surprised Cam didn't hear it. Ever since he got arrested, he's been keeping earplugs in during games. At first it was so he didn't hear things people were saying about him, but after he got used to it, he realized that it helps him focus.

As far as I know, the only person that heard what was said is the ref.

"Just called her a couple inappropriate names and made Laiken spill her drink all over herself so she would have to wear his jersey."

"Ahh." He nods. "I was wondering why she was wearing that, but before I could ask her, she changed into yours."

Huffing, I lace up my skates. "Yeah, there was no way I was letting them get away with that shit. They want girls in their jerseys, they can bring their own puck bunnies with them."

We all finish getting ready and some of the guys start to leave the locker room. Cam and I stand up to follow and he pats me on the shoulder.

"Coach may disagree with it, but I appreciate you having my back," he says, making the guilt in me intensify. "Thanks, man."

I watch as he gets on the ice and all I can think about is how fucked up this all is. He thinks I'm this great friend, and meanwhile I'm lying to him and sneaking around with his little sister—betraying him in a way that's bound to ruin our friendship.

But I've tried to stop.

I've tried to stay away from her.

It's just not something I have the ability to do.

I want her too much.

Chapter 15

WALKING THROUGH THE FRONT door, Cam is going on and on about some new play he figured out and how it's going to be a game changer. Honestly, he's probably right, if we can get the guys to figure it out. It's complicated, and it'll take a lot of practice before we can use it in a game.

As he does every time he comes home from practice, Cam heads straight to the kitchen to refuel. I'm looking down at my phone, smiling at a text Laiken sent me, when his words catch my attention.

"Hey, traitor," he quips.

Looking up, I see Laiken standing there. She's leaning against the counter and peeling open a banana.

She scoffs. "Traitor? I wore the thing for all of like two seconds before Hayes got me one from the locker room."

It's smart thinking on her part, making it seem like she asked me to grab her something else to put on. Not only does it make her look less guilty, but it makes *me* look less like the possessive fuck I was being.

"Doesn't matter. You wore another team's colors."

Putting the banana down for a second, she hops up to sit on the counter. "Fine, next time I'll just walk around in my bra."

Thank God Cam has his head shoved in the fridge as he grabs everything somewhat appetizing in the fridge, because if it wasn't, he would see the way my jaw locks and I glare at her.

Don't you dare, I mouth at her.

She smiles, winking at me before going back to taking all the "stringy things" as she calls them, off the banana. If she was considerate, she would break off a piece and eat it that way. Everyone knows that eating it the regular way looks erotic as hell. But as the devious little smirk appears on her face, I realize that may be her plan.

She's not.

She wouldn't.

Oh, who am I kidding? Of course, she would.

And she does, making eye contact with me and everything as she wraps her mouth around the banana like she's imagining it's my dick.

I try to look away, to focus on literally anything else, but she's still there in my peripheral vision, blowing the goddamn banana. There's no way I can stand here while she does that and look completely unaffected.

"I'll be back," I tell Cam. "I need to use the bathroom."

He waves me off as he opens and shuts another drawer of the fridge. I shoot Laiken a dark look as I pass her, and she chuckles quietly. As soon as I'm safely behind the bathroom door, where my hard-on can go unnoticed until it goes away, I take out my phone and send her a text.

You're going to pay for that later.

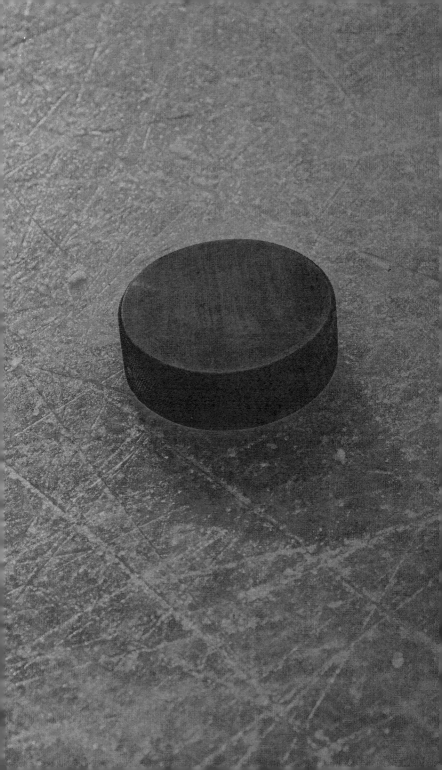

Hayes
CHAPTER SIXTEEN

The fact that it's a Friday night and I'm sitting at home is pathetic. Normally, I would be sitting at a bonfire at Cam's right now—drinking a beer and trying not to make it obvious that I would rather be fucking his sister. But Mother Nature apparently had different plans, and you can't exactly have a bonfire in the pouring rain.

So instead, I'm sitting on my couch. The TV is on, but I'm not paying much attention. Texting Laiken is a much more appealing option.

> Do you think if I leave my skylight open during the storm, that it'll fill my room like a pool?

I snort and shake my head. Only she would even think to do something like that.

> I think you should try it and find out. I'm sure your parents will love the idea.

> Hmm, fair point, but your sarcasm is noted.

> I don't know who you think you're with, but sarcasm is all you're going to get out of me.

The response she sends shouldn't get the reaction out of me that it does, but the grip on my phone tightens.

Technically, I'm not WITH anyone. I'm single as a Pringle and ready to mingle. Ooh, I should try speed dating.

My thumbs hit the screen a little harder than necessary. I know she's only kidding, but the mere thought of someone else's hands on her is enough to make me stabby. Relationships may not be my thing, but that doesn't mean I'll ever be okay with her dating someone else.

Toxic as fuck? Sure.

Give a fuck? Nope.

You try that and let me know how it works out for you. 😈

The three little dots appear, and I sit there watching it, anticipating her answer.

You failed sharing in kindergarten, didn't you?

God, she's such a brat. It's like she knows exactly how to get under my skin, and then make me smile so I think it's okay. No wonder she works with kids. This gaslighting probably works wonders on them.

I hate you.

You don't. You're just still mad that I beat you in a race.

I knew she was never going to let me live that down.

Hey! I'll have you know that Coach said if we were to race again, I'd give you a run for your money.

I bet he told you you're good at hockey, too. 😏

Laughter booms through the room as my head falls back against the cushion. There's nothing I can say to her that she doesn't have a comeback for. People think Mali is bad, but that's just because Laiken's sass only comes out when she's comfortable with you. When the two of them are in rare form at the same time, look out. You'll learn that death by insults is an actual thing.

"Who has you smiling like an idiot?" Devin asks as she comes in from the kitchen.

I drop my phone face down on my lap. "Oh, I was just watching a funny video."

Her brows furrow. "Without sound?"

Shit. "Yeah. It, uh, was muted, but it was still funny."

She watches me intently before calling my bluff. "Okay. Show me."

"What?"

"Show me the video," she says, leaning on the back of the couch to get a good view of my phone.

I look over at her, rolling my eyes as she waits expectantly. "You know, I begged Mom to return you to the hospital and bring home a boy instead."

"You were three and didn't know any better." She tries to grab my phone for herself. "Now let me see the video, you weirdo."

I grab it just as she gets her hands on it, and the two of us start to fight over my phone. The problem is, she has a much better hold on it than I do, and the fact that she's standing works to her advantage. Just as she starts to slip it from my grasp, I panic.

"I was watching porn," I blurt out.

Devin drops my phone like it's diseased and holds her

hands up with a disgusted look on her face. "Wait, you were laughing at porn?"

Well, we've come this far. May as well really mortify her.

"Yeah, he slapped her in the face with his dick and left a mark."

She stares back at me completely dumbfounded. "I swear, I will never understand what girls see in you."

Taking a pillow from the couch, I toss it at her and chuckle as it hits her in the face.

If it wasn't for our dad leaving, I don't think we would be as close as we are. But she was only twelve when he walked out and never came back. I was hurt, as any kid would be from something like that, but Dev took it hard.

Almost as hard as Mom did.

I quickly fell into the man-of-the-house roll, and one of those things entailed being there for my sister. It made us closer, in a way. Maybe not as close as Cam and Laiken are, but I can definitely understand Cam's protective nature when it comes to her.

If anyone were to hurt Dev, I'd skin the fucker alive.

"I'm surprised you're not hanging out with your friends," I tell her.

She shrugs. "I was going to see a movie with Paisley, but I have to pack."

"Pack?"

"Yeah. I leave tomorrow morning," she replies. "Valerie, Quinn, and I are going to Myrtle Beach for a night. We'll be back Sunday, probably late morning."

I hum, trying to recall those names. "Do I know them?"

"No. We met at the new gymnastics place I'm assistant coaching at. And don't even let the thought go through your head. I refuse to bring them here."

Yeah, definitely not where my mind was going. Not when all my thoughts seem to be glued on Laiken.

"Jeez," I mock. "I hook up with one of your friends *one time* during a sleepover and suddenly I want them all."

She crosses her arms over her chest. "It's not *you* wanting *them* that I'm worried about. Do you know how annoying it is for your friends to constantly talk about how hot your brother is?"

"Can't say I do," I answer. "I don't have a brother, and if any of my friends called you hot, I'd elbow them in the face."

My subconscious glares at the screaming hypocrisy that just came out of my mouth, and I get it. I'm a walking double standard. Add it to the list of things that are damning me to hell.

"Good thing I don't think any of your friends are attractive." She pauses. "Except maybe Isaac. He's got that rich guy vibe."

I narrow my eyes to slits. "First of all, not considered one of my friends, and second, if he even so much as says your name, I'll make him regret the day he was ever born."

"I'm telling Mom how deranged you are."

"Where do you think I got it from?"

She chuckles as the microwave goes off and grabs her food before taking it to her room. Meanwhile, the gears in my head are already turning.

If Devin isn't going to be here tomorrow night, that means I'll have the house to myself. Mom works overnights at the hospital—the glorious life of a nurse—and since it's an hour away, she sleeps there after a shift, so she doesn't risk falling asleep at the wheel. Sometimes, depending on how busy they are, she doesn't come home at all until she has a day off.

It's a shitty schedule, and I can tell it takes a toll on her, but that's what happens when your husband walks out and leaves you to support your two kids on your own. She may have let it knock her down for a while, but once she picked herself back up, she became determined to still give us the best lives she could. And she succeeded.

I glance down at my phone, see a waiting text from Laiken, and I smile at the idea that comes to mind.

Aw, did I hurt your big man ego?

Devin almost saw my phone. I'm changing your contact in my phone to a guy's name.

That's going to make for such awkward sexting. I can't wait.

SATURDAY MORNINGS ARE THE only day where hockey practice is earlier than Laiken's shift. The practices usually suck when we're all hungover after Friday night bonfires. But since none of us were drinking last night, we're unusually lively for ten in the morning.

Except Owen. He's still hung over.

Laiken sits in the stands, waiting for her shift to start while we run some drills. She alternates between writing in a notebook and scrolling through her phone. Regardless, her attention isn't on me, and I don't fucking like it.

Lining the puck up just right, I push it off my stick and send it flying into the glass. The loud bang that echoes through the rink startles everyone around, but especially

Laiken. Her eyes widen as she jumps, notebook falling on the floor and her hand going to her chest.

It wasn't supposed to be funny. It was meant to get her attention. But from her reaction, I can't seem to stop laughing, and neither can Cam. Laiken flips me off, and once I'm sure no one is paying attention, I bounce my eyebrows a couple times—silently saying *yes please.*

Skating past her during the next drill, I wink. She rolls her eyes, but I see the way she smiles as she looks down at her phone.

All I want is to get my hands on her again. To lay her down on my bed and feel her beneath me as I slide my cock into her. I may be the furthest thing from desperate, but I'm fucking starving for her.

If I don't get her alone soon for longer than a few minutes, I'm pretty sure my balls are going to shrivel up and die. They've been through enough lately with the constant teasing.

It's like the world's longest edging, and I don't even get my name in the Guinness Book of World Records.

IF IT DIDN'T MEAN no more Friday night bonfires, I'd highly consider staying sober the night before every morning practice. Sure, I guess I could not drink, but what's the fun in that? Sitting around the fire with a beer in my hand is my own personal heaven. Well, one of them.

I walk out of the rink with the guys, watching as Owen nearly runs a kid down by not paying attention.

"Shit, sorry," he says, then winces. "And sorry for saying shit!"

Lucas chuckles. "Such a role model you are."

"Fuck off."

I shake my head as I see the two other kids within earshot of him. "Batting a thousand, dude."

He waves it off. "Like they don't hear worse from their parents."

Okay, he kind of has a point.

"Meeting me at my place?" Cam asks.

"I wish," I answer. "Instead, my lucky ass gets to sit at the surf shop for the next eight hours and tend to the morons who buy a board under the assumption that surfing is easy."

At least once a week, someone will come in who clearly has no idea what they're doing and buy a surfboard based on how it looks alone. And when I tell them about the lessons we offer, they practically laugh in my face.

It's standing on a board, not rocket science.

Okay, well, don't come crying to me when you break the board and nearly drown because you thought you knew everything.

"I'd rather do that than carpentry," Cam counters. "There's nothing fun about your constantly drunk boss making you run the company for only a small percentage of the profits."

"So, quit. Find another," I suggest.

He shakes his head. "Just because I'm only making a small percentage, doesn't mean it's not a bigger percentage than I would get anywhere else. And besides, maybe if he drinks himself to death, I'll get the company."

"Doesn't his son work with you?"

"Yep. Useless little twit."

I snort, and just as we start to reach where his Jeep is parked beside my truck, I feel my empty pockets.

"Motherfucker," I grumble. "I forgot my keys inside."

He opens the door to his Jeep and climbs in the driver's seat. "Better be sneaky. I forgot something once and Laiken roped me into helping tie kids' skates before I left."

"I'll keep that in mind," I tell him. "Later, man."

I start walking back toward the ice rink and watch as Cam drives out of the parking lot, with the rest of the guys following suit.

Perfect.

Kids run around in circles, hyped up on an unfair amount of natural caffeine. Seriously, where does that all go when you get older? Because if I did even half of the shit they do, I'd need a damn nap.

Dodging a few NHL-not-so-hopefuls, I glance around for Laiken and when I don't see her, I head straight for the girl's locker room. She's just coming out the door, and she squeals as I grab her.

I spin us around and press her up against the wall, out of view from any innocent eyes. "What are you doing tonight?"

She hums, only to giggle when I kiss her quickly, just because it's been too long since I was able to. "I have a hot date, actually. It's a menage a trois."

The smile drops off my face, until I see the way she's trying her absolute hardest not to laugh. "It's you and ice cream, isn't it?"

"Don't say it like that. My relationship with Ben and Jerry is sacred."

"Mm-hm." I pinch her side. "I think you just like getting a rise out of me."

Her grin widens. "I mean, it's pretty amusing."

"So glad I could entertain you, princess." I kiss her again, and she melts into it. "For real, though. Plans tonight?"

"No. Why?"

"Well, my mom has work, and Devin is away for the night with some friends, so my house is going to be empty." I slide my hands down her body to her waist. "I was thinking maybe you'd want to come over."

Her brows furrow, and she presses her hands against my chest, gently pushing me away. "That sounds a lot like a booty call. What kind of girl do you think I am?"

Okay, that's not at all how I thought this would go. "N-no, that's not...I didn't..."

She puts her fist to her mouth as a laugh forces its way through, and I close my eyes as I exhale.

"Do you get off on fucking with me?" I ask.

"A little bit. Yeah."

The smile on her face could rival even the most loved views in the world. And if I was the romantic kind, I'd tell her as much. That won't happen, of course, but damn. Happiness looks so fucking good on her.

"That's all right," I tell her, bringing my lips to her ear. "Now you have two things to pay for, and I always collect."

She moans quietly and leans into me. "That's just mean."

"Oh, you haven't seen anything yet." I kiss the top of her head and then her lips as she looks up at me. "I'll text you and let you know when I get out of work."

"Okay," she agrees.

I walk backward as I check her out one more time, and then I spin around and head out—refusing to admit how excited I am for tonight.

Not to myself, and sure as fuck not to her.

Chapter 16

THERE AREN'T MANY DAYS when I wish it was busy in here, but today is definitely one of them. If I was constantly dealing with customers, the hours might not feel like they're standing still. I swear, I thought it was almost time for closing, only to look at the clock and realize it was three hours past the time I got here.

So, I started to busy myself with taking the inventory I've been putting off for a while.

Picking up my phone, I see a new message from Laiken. It's a video of the little girl she was telling me about the other day. She's tiny—small enough to where you can't see what she's doing when she gets too far away. Honestly, she reminds me of Laiken.

The first time I ever laid eyes on her, she was on the ice. I remember watching her and wondering why someone would waste their time skating around like that when they could be playing hockey, but I was still impressed by her. She may not have skated anywhere near as gracefully then as she does now, but she's always had a natural skill that other people would kill for.

Reminds me of someone else I know. 😘

She's going to be better.

Somehow, I doubt that.

The thing about Laiken is that she has the tendency to not acknowledge how good she really is at something. She's been doing it for as long as I've known her. Ice skating? Calls it a hobby. Singing? Claims she doesn't have what it takes. Cheerleading? Takes her team to Nationals as captain and says she wasn't good, everyone else just sucked worse.

It's like she can't wrap her mind around the fact that she's talented at so many things—so she tells herself she's mediocre.

The store phone rings and snaps me out of my thoughts.

"Wax and Waves," I answer.

"Hey H," Marc says. "How's it going?"

Looking up, I notice a few people in the store, but I'd be an idiot not to take the opportunity that's in front of me. "Eh, it's dead in here."

He hums. "Really? No one at all?"

"Nope. Haven't seen anyone for hours."

"Mm-hm," he says, and I chuckle as I hear his voice through the phone and outside the door. "So, the people in the back are what? Ghosts?"

Marc walks in and I smile guiltily as I hang up the phone.

"In my defense, we haven't sold a single board all day," I tell him.

"Excuse me?" a customer asks. "Could I have some help in the back? There's a longboard I'm interested in."

Oh, sure. Just make a fucking liar out of me.

"Don't look at me like that," I tell Marc as I see him smirking. "You don't have to sit here for eight hours at a time. It's brutal."

He laughs as I follow the customer back and help him bring the board to the front. Usually, I'd help measure him and make sure it's the right size, but with the way he was talking about the different specs, there's no point. He knows what he's doing. Once he swipes his card, I hand him the receipt and hold the door open for him as he leaves and heads for the beach.

"Okay, so we sold *one* board today," I correct myself to Marc.

He snorts as he looks over some of the reports from the last month. "Who is she?"

Nope. Not doing *that.* "Who is who?"

"The girl you're trying to get out of here to see."

I should deny it. The more people who know about us, the higher the risk of it getting out. It's the epitome of the saying *two can keep a secret if one of them is dead.* But if there's a chance of him letting me leave a couple hours early, it may be worth telling him there's *someone.*

Pushing my hair out of my face, I exhale. "It's not serious."

"It never is," he shoots back. "Do you like her?"

Ugh. "She's all right."

The little voice inside of me telling me I'm a fucking liar is a nuisance I have to mentally swat away like a bug.

My phone vibrates on the counter, and I grab it before Marc sees the name. I really do need to change her name in my phone. God forbid Cam was here and saw her texting me. There's no way that would go over well.

"That her?" Marc questions.

Not going to lie, I wasn't in the best place when Marc came into my life. I was fighting a lot at school, acting out at home. It was a year after my dad left, and I blamed every single person in the world for it. And when he gave me a job as a favor to my mom, I felt like I was being punished.

Little did I know, he wasn't punishing me at all.

He was saving me.

Having me here every day after school meant I wasn't getting into trouble. It meant I wasn't hanging out with the wrong crowd, or getting offered drugs I probably would have tried just for the sake of teenage rebellion. It kept me on the right track, and in a way, he became the dad I always needed.

"Yeah," I say as I swipe open my phone.

> So, what's the attire for tonight? Trench coat chic?

I start texting her back, not even aware I'm smiling until Marc says something about it.

"Get out of here, H."

My brows raise as my head snaps up to him. "Seriously?"

"Yeah, I can handle the rest of the day," he says with a shrug. "Any girl who has the ability to make you that happy just with a simple text is pretty special."

"Wait, no. We're not—"

He snickers. "You're not dating. Right. Got it."

If he wasn't letting me leave right now, I'd probably flip him off. But in the interest of *not* making him change his mind, I decide against it. I grab my keys off the back counter and thank him as I leave.

Now to get home and make sure my room doesn't look like a bomb went off in it before Laiken gets there.

IT TAKES ME FIFTEEN minutes to clean my room, and by clean, I obviously mean shove everything scattered on the floor into my closet. I'm getting laid tonight, you really think I have the patience to do this shit the right way? Come on.

Thankfully, my mom keeps the rest of the house pretty tidy, so the only other thing I need to do is get rid of the dishes I left in the sink. I turn on the sink and grab the sponge like I know what I'm doing, but I quickly realize I'm a little more spoiled than I thought.

Fuck it. Why do we need twelve plates anyway? There's only three of us. One won't be missed.

Tossing it into the trash can, along with the fork I used, I close the lid and walk away.

Problem solved.

As I start pacing around the room, waiting for her to get here, it dawns on me that this is the first time I'm having a girl in my bed. *Wait, what the fuck?* I rack my brain, trying to think of any time where I hooked up with a girl here, and there was one of Devin's friends once, but that was in the living room. Anyone else, I've always gone to their place or met them somewhere.

It's not that Laiken means more to me or anything. It's just that we don't have many places we can go to hook up. Can't go to her place because Cam can't find out. Public places are tricky because we risk getting caught by someone we know. After the game was a one off. If I didn't get my hands on her that very second, I was going to self-destruct.

Yeah, it's simply the circumstances. She's not...This isn't...

Fuck.

A car pulls into the driveway, and I force myself to stop overthinking as I step onto the porch. Laiken gets out the passenger side as Mali rolls her window down.

"Excuse me, Mr. Wilder. What are your intentions with my Laiken?"

Lai's face turns beet red as she turns to glare at her. "Mali."

"What? I need to know he's not trying to steal your virtue," she argues then focuses back on me. "Well? I'm waiting."

"Hi, *Amalia*," I say, knowing she cannot stand when people use her whole first name.

Her lips press into a thin line. "Wrong answer. Laiken, get back in the car. We're going home."

Laiken sighs and stares up at the sky. "What did I do to deserve this?"

"Get back in the car and I'll take you to the strip club!" Mali shouts. "We can make it rain on dem big booty hoes!"

My brows raise and I chuckle as Laiken mutters *for the love of fuck* under her breath. She turns to me and smiles.

"Do you have a hockey stick I can borrow?"

I nod toward my truck. "Check the bed."

Walking over, her grin widens and she grabs a hockey stick—holding it like a baseball bat. Mali shrieks and curses as she throws the car in reverse and floors it into the street.

"Don't do anything I wouldn't do!" she yells and quickly drives away.

Once she's gone, Laiken sighs in relief. "Any ideas on where to bury a body?"

I snicker and open the door for her to come inside. "I'd offer to figure it out, but I'm not sure I want her haunting my ass."

She purses her lips. "Okay, good point. I guess she gets to live, for today."

"Mm-hm."

Wrapping my arms around her, I bend down and kiss her softly. She takes a deep breath and exhales, like the entire day was spent waiting for this moment.

Fucking same.

"How was work?" she asks as we pull away.

"Boring, but Marc showed up and let me leave early."

"That was nice of him." She holds up her empty Starbucks cup. "Garbage?"

I nod toward the corner of the room. "On the other side of the fridge."

She walks over to it, going to throw away the cup, when it occurs to me at the last minute. *The fucking plate.* But it's too late. She presses her foot on the lever and it pops open, revealing the perfectly fine dish I threw away.

Staring at it for a second, she tilts her head to the side and starts to giggle. "Did…did you?"

"You know what, maybe Mali should have taken you home with her," I say, only half joking because I'd very much like to avoid *this* situation.

She narrows her eyes for a second, but she's obviously not about to let this topic slide. "Why'd you throw away the plate, H?"

I look up at the ceiling, then over at the wall, then at the floor—anywhere but at her. "Because I didn't want it in the sink."

"And you didn't think just washing it was an option?"

Fucking fucker fuck. "I don't know how, okay?"

Her jaw drops and I can tell by the look on her face, she's loving this. "You're twenty! How do you not know how to do the dishes?"

"Because I've always just gotten takeout or ordered a pizza," I explain. "And if I needed a dish, I just left it in the sink and my mom or Devin always did it."

She bites her lip in an effort to keep from smiling too much. "You're adorable."

My eyes roll. "Yeah, yeah. Can we drop it now?"

"No." Taking the plate and fork out of the trash, she puts

them back in the sink and comes over to me. "Come on. I'm going to teach you."

"What? No. We don't—"

She grabs my hand and pulls me toward the sink. "We do."

I huff and stand in front of the plate that I'd like nothing more than to shatter into pieces. I should've just broken it before I threw it away. Could've avoided this whole thing. But no.

"Okay, take the sponge," she says, and I grab it with my right hand. "Now put some of that dish soap on it, but not too much."

"How do I know if it's too much?"

"You'll know."

Turning the bottle upside down, I squeeze it and it squirts out, covering the sponge with the blue liquid. Laiken's eyes widen as she laughs and grabs the bottle from me.

"Okay," she says. "Maybe you won't know."

I drop the sponge in the sink and go to walk away, but she stops me.

"I'm sorry, I'm sorry." Her laughter is still dying down. "All right, turn on the water and run the plate under it."

"This is stupid," I grumble.

She kisses my shoulder. "No, you not knowing how to clean a plate is stupid. *This* is necessary."

I do as she says and look to her for the next part.

"Now use the sponge to scrub it." As I drag the sponge around the plate, not a lot seems to be happening. "No, like you need to apply pressure."

"I'm going to break it," I tell her.

She shakes her head. "You're not. Imagine it's a clit."

I stop what I'm doing as laughter booms out of me. "What am I going to do with you?"

"With me?" she asks, surprised. "You're the one who

doesn't know how to do the dishes. I can only imagine what else you don't know."

Looking over at her, I smirk. "I've spent my time mastering other skills. And if you weren't forcing me to do this, you'd be on the receiving end of those skills right now."

She licks her lips as she stares up at me, but then she turns back to the sink. "Nice try. Come on, time to rinse."

My jaw clenches as I run the plate under the water and watch as all the soap washes away, leaving nothing but a clean surface. Laiken smiles proudly and takes it from me to put in the drying rack.

"See? That wasn't so hard." She picks up the fork and hands it to me. "Now this."

I mutter a few choice words under my breath as I follow the same steps with the fork, and hand it to her once I'm done.

"Thank fuck that's over," I say, but she scrunches her nose.

"Now the sink."

"The sink?" I balk. "Why the fuck do you need to scrub the sink?"

"Because." She gestures toward pieces of food inside it. "You don't want all that sitting there. It'll harden and get gross."

Motherfucker.

You know, when I invited her over, this was not even a possibility on the list of things I thought we would be doing. And if I had any idea this would turn into a lesson in domestication, I would've eaten over the sink instead of using a damn plate in the first place.

I finish scrubbing the sink and rinse it away, when an idea comes to mind. Turning off the water, I turn to her and she smiles back at me.

"You did it," she says. "I'm so proud of you."

"Thank you for teaching me."

Her eyes are locked on mine, so she doesn't even see it coming, but she feels it the moment my hands touch her cheeks, covering them in suds as I bend down and kiss her hard. And when I pull away, she presses her lips together firmly and exhales.

"You did not just do that."

"I did," I admit, taking a step back.

It's as if I can see the idea pop into her mind as she looks away for a second and her brows raise. Her hands reach down and she pulls her shirt over her head, using it to wipe the bubbles off her face. But it's the lace bra she's left in that has me struggling to remember how to breathe.

"Now that's just cruel," I growl, letting my eyes graze over her.

"Is it?" she teases. "Are you going to do something about it?"

"You're damn fucking right I am."

Within seconds, I lift her up and sit her on the counter, slotting myself between her legs. I start kissing her neck while my hands slide up her back until they reach her bra clasp. Breathy moans leave her mouth as I nip and suck on her skin, careful not to leave a mark even though it's so tempting.

Her bra pops open and I drag it down her arms, letting it fall on the floor next to her shirt. Her tits are perfect, and I immediately cover one with my hand while taking the other into my mouth. Laiken leans back to give me some more room. Her head rests against the cabinet as she laces her fingers into my hair.

"God, you do that so well," she breathes.

I lightly bite down and she flinches, showing me just how sensitive she is. And her reaction is even better than I was hoping. Releasing her with a pop, I smirk.

"Oh, this is going to be fun."

Lifting her up, she squeals, but I swallow it down as I cover her mouth with my own. I walk down the hall to my room, and she holds onto me tightly, licking into my mouth as she kisses me. Once I lay her on my bed, I stand up to admire how fucking perfect she looks—all wanting and needy for me.

"You're stunning," I murmur.

The compliment catches her off guard, but before she can think too far into it, I lean down and lightly drag the tip of my tongue from her belly button, up to the center of her chest, and then to her neck. She squirms, arching her hips up to seek the friction I won't give her yet.

We're all over each other, hands gripping wherever possible to pull each other closer. But when she starts to undo my jeans, I stop her.

Her brows furrow. "Do you not want to?"

What? "That's crazy talk. Of course, I want to," I tell her. "The other night was amazing, but I took your virginity in the front seat of my truck. I wasn't lying when I said you deserve better than that shit."

"Well, we're in a bed now. So why aren't you fucking me into the mattress right now?"

God, she's a dream. A whole ass fantasy come to life and put in mine just to test the shit out of me.

"I'm going to, but there's no rush this time." I connect our lips once more. "I'm going to enjoy every fucking inch of you, and if you don't leave here without feeling me every time you move, I didn't do my damn job."

Grabbing her hips, I roll her over so she's on top of me and slide my hands down to her ass. I pull her down as I arch up into her. It's exactly the friction she was craving, and she whimpers into my mouth.

"Too many clothes," she pants. "Please. I need to feel you."

"Oh, you're going to feel a lot, baby," I growl.

She continues to grind against me, and it's embarrassing how easily I could come in my pants right now. My balls ache and my cock is hard as steel, desperate for release, but I refuse to make this another quick fuck.

Sitting up, I take her with me and spin around to put her on her back again. My fingers undo her jeans, pulling them down along with the lace panties that match her bra. I make a mental note to have her put just those two articles of clothing back on after this.

Her pussy is so wet, glistening in the light. I run my hand over it and bask in the way her whole body tenses up. I lick my lips as I tease her entrance. I've wanted to get my mouth on her since the first time I watched her come apart on my fingers.

"Tell me, Rochester." I look her in the eyes. "Has anyone ever put their mouth on your pussy? Made you scream out as you ride their face?"

She swallows and shakes her head. "No."

"Good," I tell her as I drop down. "Fucking keep it that way."

The moment I drag my tongue up her slit, I know I'll never be able to get enough. Her sweet taste coats my tongue, and the way she presses her head back into my pillow as the sounds of her moans fill the room—it's everything.

I wanted to tease her for a bit. To make her pay for the banana stunt and for torturing me with endless blue balls the last few days. But that would take a level of self-control that I clearly don't have.

My tongue dips into her pussy just before I slide it back up. I pucker my lips and suck her clit into my mouth, and her whole body convulses. Smirking, I slip two fingers into her and feel the way she clenches around them.

"Holy shit," she breathes. "Holy fucking shit."

The faster I pump my fingers in and out of her, the faster I lick and suck at her clit. She can't stay still, no matter how much I try pushing her hips into the mattress. And when she reaches down to grab a handful of my hair, I groan against her.

"Don't be shy, baby," I mutter, my tongue still darting out to taste her some more. "Go ahead. Grind on my face."

She starts out slow, barely pulling me down as she arches up against me. But after a minute, she starts getting more comfortable. More desperate. She fucks herself against my mouth, and I shove my fingers deep inside of her, curling them upward to hit the little bundle of nerves inside of her.

"I need you," she begs. "Please, Hayes. Need you inside me."

"No fucking way," I murmur against her. "You're going to be a good girl and come on my tongue. I want to taste every ounce of your pleasure. Make me fucking drown in it."

She whimpers, and her breathing quickens as she chases her orgasm. All my senses are overtaken with her. Her taste. Her smell. It's all so goddamn intoxicating. Each time she pulls me closer, I have trouble breathing, but I'd gladly suffocate for this.

"That's it," I hum. "Come all over my face, baby. Such a good little princess for me."

The way she instantly explodes the minute that last line leaves my mouth has me more shocked than ever, but right now, I have a job to do. Her pussy tightens as she clenches around my fingers, and the grip she has on my hair doesn't loosen as she pulls me into her. I suck on her clit, circling it with my tongue and making her orgasm last as long as possible, until her whole body relaxes.

"That's not a skill," she says through labored breaths. "That's pure witchcraft."

I lick my lips and suck her cum off my fingers. "You're fucking delicious."

Standing up, I commit the look of her lying naked on my bed to memory as I pull my shirt over my head. Laiken bites her bottom lip as her eyes rake over my abs. And when I drop my pants and boxers in one swift move, she looks at my cock like it's her favorite toy.

It fucking better be.

I take it into my hand, jerking it slowly as I walk over to the nightstand and pull out a condom. Ripping it open with my teeth, I go to slip it on but she sits up and looks at me through hooded lashes.

"Can I?" she asks, and it looks every bit like innocence and sin wrapped into one.

Not trusting my voice to answer right now, I hand her the condom, but she has other plans first. She wraps her hand around my cock, making me hiss at the contact. Pumping it a couple times, her tongue darts out and she licks the tip like it's a lollipop then moans quietly as she tastes the precum that lingers there.

"Teach me."

All the air is instantly expelled from my lungs. "Lai."

She licks from halfway down my shaft to the tip. "Like that? Does that feel good?"

"Does that..."

I can't even finish repeating her question because she opens her mouth and wraps her lips around my dick. The muscles of my ass tighten as I do my best not to come, and my hand rests on her head, gently pulling her off.

"Baby," I say softly.

There's hesitation in her eyes as she looks up at me. "Did I do it wrong?"

I'm shaking my head before the question is even fully out of her mouth. "No. No, you're perfect." I rub my thumb over her lips. "Such a talented little mouth. I just know that if I don't get inside of you soon, there's a strong chance I'll lose my mind."

Her mood shifts and she slides the condom down my length. Once it's securely in place, I push her backward and place one knee on the bed. Lining myself up, I press into her slowly. The way she stretches around me is the same as the other night, and she tries to hide it, but I see the way she winces at the pain.

I go slow, but I don't stop until I'm fully bottomed out inside her. My head falls back as I tell myself not to come. We rarely get the chance to do this, and I'm not about to waste it by only lasting two seconds. I focus on my breathing, and as soon as I feel like I've stepped back from the edge, I pull almost all the way out, just to slide back in.

"I love the way you make me feel so full," she moans. "Want to spend every second with you inside me like this."

Leaning over her, I wrap my hand around her throat. "You'd like that, wouldn't you?" She nods, and my eyes narrow as I watch her intently. "You're such a good girl, aren't you?"

Her eyelids flutter closed, and she moans, wrapping her fingers around my wrist.

I pull out, flipping her over and lifting her ass in the air, only to thrust back into her pussy again. The angle is so much better, my cock rubbing against her walls and feeling the way she's getting close again already.

I wrap her hair around my hand and use it to pull her head back as I start to thrust in harder. "Look at you, taking my cock so well. My good girl."

The sound of my skin slapping against hers mixes with our moans. And the higher pitched hers get, the closer I know she is. I slap her ass, hard enough to leave a mark, and she screams out.

Her breathing slows, and I wait for her reaction. If I wasn't paying so much attention, I may have missed it. But the way she whispers *do it again* burns itself into my brain and takes up permanent residence.

"Fucking hell," I groan, slapping her again and watching the way her ass cheek jiggles.

The fact that my handprint lingers on her skin speaks to the part of me that wants to claim every inch of her. Lock her away where only I can ever reach her. The only part of me that has ever even considered more than just mutual sexual gratification.

I move my grip from her hair to her neck and pull her toward me, until my chest is pressed against her back. Grazing my lips against her ear, I nip at the lobe.

"So proud of you, baby," I murmur into her ear. "You make me feel so good."

Her head falls back against my shoulder as she gives in to the pleasure. I take my hand off her hip and move it to her pussy, putting pressure exactly where she needs it.

"Give me it, Laiken." I rub circles right over her clit, and she shudders from how sensitive she is. "I know it's there, and I want it. Come all over my cock. Show me how good you are."

Only a few more seconds of rubbing and a tightened grip on her throat and she loses it. The second I feel her pussy squeeze my dick, I let go of her throat and bend her forward—slamming into her with everything I have as I shoot everything I have into the condom.

She pushes back against me and moans at how deep I am, and I chuckle. Second time having sex and she's already a rock star, just like every other thing she tries in life.

With one last slap to her ass, I pull out and crash onto the bed beside her. She rolls over to face me as the two of us wait for our breathing to calm.

"You are every guy's wildest dream, you know that?"

She blinks back at me, her head resting on her forearm. "Even yours?"

I know I shouldn't, but there's no stopping myself as I roll over and kiss her lightly. "Especially mine."

The smug grin on her face is one I should regret, but I don't. Not when she looks as happy as she does. And definitely not when we're both in post-sex bliss.

Speaking of… "So, any other…*interests* you want to share with me?"

Her cheeks pink, and she looks away. "I don't know what you're talking about."

"Mm-hm. So, if I were to wrap my hand around your throat and call you my good g—"

She covers my mouth with her hand, stopping me from finishing what I was saying. She sighs and looks up at the ceiling, and I can tell she's nervous.

"I don't know what it is," she admits. "There's just something encouraging about it, and I like it."

I roll onto my side and put my hand on her face, turning her head until she's looking at me. "Hey, you don't need to be embarrassed. Not for that. It's sexy as hell."

She smiles and leans in to kiss me, slowly and lazily. When she pulls away, she presses a quick peck to the tip of my nose and sits up, throwing her legs off the edge of the bed. My gaze immediately locks on the tattoo she has going down her spine.

It's subtle, a light gray ink against her skin, but it looks so good on her.

I sit up and ghost my lips over it. "Do your parents know you have this?"

She looks back at me over her shoulder, exhaling as I

press a few light kisses up her spine. "No. They would kill me. That's why it's in a place I can hide it."

"From everyone but me," I specify.

Her eyes roll as she giggles. "Can't hide anything from you."

"Glad you're catching on."

I'VE NEVER BEEN ONE for cuddling. The whole concept of lying together, not knowing where one of you ends and the other begins just for the sake of being close, it always felt like more of a romance thing to me. I had no interest in it. But as Laiken laid her head on my chest as I started the movie, I couldn't find it in me to stop her.

I couldn't find it in me to *want* to stop her.

My fingertips graze her back as she sleeps. She passed out a little over an hour ago, and I've just been lying here, replaying the last few days in my head.

I know I should wake her. Get her back to her car so she can get home. But I don't want to.

Not yet.

I just want to lie here, where there's no judgment, no fear, no second guessing. Just let me feel the weight of her head on my chest as the smell of her hair relaxes me in ways that beer never has.

Let me have this, before I can't anymore.

Laiken

CHAPTER SEVENTEEN

The sound of birds chirping meets my ears as I start to wake, but something is off. My body sinks into the bed too much, and I'm warmer than I would be in my room. As my brain starts to realize its surroundings, it all hits me.

I'm still at Hayes's house.

His arms are wrapped around me as he sleeps, pressed against my back. It reminds me of last night—the way he pulled me against him as he fucked into me. I'm so ridiculously sore, the feeling of him lingering with every move I make, but I already crave it again.

"H," I whisper, hoping he's not mad.

We never discussed me sleeping over. As far as I knew, I was meant to go back to Mali's at some point last night. Thank God I told my parents I was sleeping there so they didn't expect me home at a certain time. Otherwise they'd probably be filing a missing person's report right about now.

I try to wake him again, this time a little louder. "Hayes."

He groans, removing one arm from around me as he rolls onto his back. Blindly reaching for his phone, he presses the button to see the time, and grumbles.

"Too early. Need sleep."

His arm drapes back over me, and I spin around to face him. His eyes are closed, and he looks so peaceful, but when he peels one open, I can't help but smile.

"Hi," I say softly.

He hums. "Hi, creep."

The way the corners of his mouth turn upward involuntarily tells me he's not mad. A little cranky, maybe, but definitely not mad.

"I guess it's a good thing I didn't drive here yesterday," I tell him. "My car would have been outside your house all night."

He lets his eyes fall closed again, clearly too exhausted to wake up right now, and I almost follow suit, but when I hear the front door open and shut, my heart damn near stops as panic starts to run through me.

"Uh, H?"

He hums in response.

"Did someone just get home?" I glance at the bedroom door, but thankfully it's shut.

He takes a deep breath and then exhales. "Relax. It's probably just Devin."

I prop myself up with my elbow, resting my head on my hand. Hayes must feel my stare because his eyes peek open once more.

"What?"

My brows raise. "You're just not even a bit concerned about Devin finding out about us?"

He sighs and stretches his back out before cracking his neck. "No. Devin is one of like four people in the world that I trust."

"Oh yeah?" I ask. "And who are the other three?"

"My mom, Cam..."—he pauses and smirks at me—"...and Barney the Dinosaur."

I collapse back down onto the bed as I giggle. "Solid third choice."

"Hey, he's been around without fail since I was three, okay?"

"Mm-hm."

Of course, there's a part of me that hoped he would say I'm the third, but thinking like that is just setting myself up for heartbreak. I've known exactly what this is since the moment it started. Just because we spent the night wrapped up in each other doesn't mean anything has suddenly changed.

"What time is it?" I question.

"A little after nine," he answers. "You have work at noon, right?"

I nod. "We should probably get dressed."

He whines, clearly wanting to lie in bed some more, and I don't blame him. I would like nothing more than to spend all day here, lying with him like this, but that's not an option I have.

Probably won't be an option I *ever* have.

"Okay, fine," he grumbles, kicking off the blanket.

I stand up and look around for my clothes, and when I spot them on the chair, I turn around to toss them onto the bed. Hayes is looking me up and down with a glint in his eyes.

"What would it take for you to wear only *that* every time we're alone together?"

Glancing down at my bra and panties, I remember how he handed me only these two things back last night and refused to let me have the rest of my clothes. Not that I minded. He stayed in his boxers. If I got completely redressed, I would've felt weird.

And besides, the way he couldn't keep his eyes off me was worth it.

Mali and the lingerie store for the win.

I hum and put my finger to my lips. "Do that thing with your mouth again and you can have anything you want."

"Fucking deal," he agrees, and tries to pull me back to bed, but I stop him reluctantly.

"We don't have time," I tell him sadly. "And besides, Devin would hear us."

"Let her. I don't give a fuck."

Chuckling, I grab his hand and pull him until he's sitting up. "Next time."

He looks down at the way his boner tents his boxers. "Look what you did."

"*That* was not me. That was all you," I say. "No one told you to check me out."

Hayes scoffs. "Oh, yeah. I'm just supposed to have a gorgeous, half-naked girl in my room and *not* look. Sure."

I shake my head as I chuckle. "You're insatiable."

"I know. I blame you."

"Me?"

He nods. "I was perfectly fine before you started masturbating in front of me."

A bark of laughter shoots out and I slap my hand over my mouth. "You mean when you were peeping through my skylight like a total fucking creep? I'd hardly classify that as masturbating in front of you."

"You see it your way, and I'll see it mine," he says, kissing my forehead and getting out of bed.

My eyes roll playfully. "Do you always create your own reality?"

He tilts his head from side to side. "Pretty much, yeah."

I pull my pants up and button them before slipping my shirt over my head. Hayes grabs a couple things out of his dresser and tugs them on before heading into the bathroom.

While I'm alone, I think about how incredible last night was. I mean, I knew he was good in bed, especially after what happened in his truck, but I had no idea he was *that* good. There's no way sex could be that enjoyable with anyone, all the time. No one would ever get anything done.

No. That was all him.

He's ruined me for everyone else before anyone even got to try.

Coming out of the bathroom, he holds out a tin. "Mint?"

I cross my arms over my chest. "Are you saying my morning breath smells?"

Instead of thinking I'm actually offended like I had hoped, he rolls his eyes and grabs the back of my neck, pulling me in and kissing me deeply. He forces my mouth open and tangles his tongue with mine, only to slip the mint he must have just put in his mouth, into mine instead.

With one more peck, he pulls away and grabs another mint, popping it between his lips with a wink.

I look down and smile to myself as I follow him out of his bedroom and down the hallway. But just as we get into the living room, his mom's voice calls out.

"Honey, is that you?"

My eyes widen and I turn to look at Hayes, but before we can even turn around, his mom comes around the corner. She seems pleasantly surprised to see me.

"Oh, Laiken. I didn't expect to see you," she says. "How have you been?"

"Really good," I answer honestly. "How are you?"

"Oh, you know. Just spending three-quarters of my life at work as always." She pauses and looks at Hayes. "That and trying to keep this idiot in line."

I look up at Hayes, and it takes every ounce of self-control I have not to smile like an idiot. "Well, whatever you're doing, I think it's working."

"That's good to hear, because sometimes I wonder."

Hayes sighs exasperatedly as he rolls his eyes and looks away, making his mom and I laugh.

"So, did you come by with Cam?" she questions, and starts looking past us. "Where is he? I feel like I haven't seen him in ages."

Ugh. This is not what I expected when I woke up this morning. Not with the way Hayes didn't seem to care when I heard the door shut.

Hayes coughs. "He's not here, Mom. I was just about to bring Laiken home."

I pinch my lips together and look anywhere but at her as she catches on.

"Oh. Okay. Well, I guess I'll see you when you get home." She steps backward toward the kitchen again. "It was nice seeing you again, Laiken."

"You, too!" I answer kindly.

With a hand on my lower back, Hayes leads me out the front door and we climb into his truck.

There are so many emotions running through me, but the biggest one is dread. His mom catching us so soon into this is bound to scare him away. He's going to call it off, once again telling me he can't risk it. Or Hayes's mom could let it slip to Cam.

Or even worse—to my parents.

I'm biting my nails anxiously and staring out the window when Hayes reaches over and pulls my hand away from my mouth.

"Relax," he tells me.

I turn to look at him, and he glances over at me for a second but stays focused on the road.

"Don't act like you're not freaking out," he says. "I can see it all over your face."

It's honestly a surprise, how calm he's being, but it helps me breathe a little.

"I was not *freaking out*," I specify. "I've just never been caught with a guy that I'm secretly sleeping with *by his mother*."

He smirks in a way that threatens to melt me on the spot. "Look at me, stealing all your firsts."

I scoff, rolling my eyes, but I feel better knowing he's not mad. A weight lifts off my chest. If he's not panicking, there's no reason I should be right?

Everything goes quiet for a minute before he breaks the silence again.

"You were *so* freaking out."

And I can't even deny it as I huff.

MY CAR SITS AT the end of Mali's driveway. Hayes parks in the street in front of her house and takes off his seatbelt. My brows furrow as he turns to face me.

"I, uh..." He rubs the back of his neck. "I want to give you your birthday present."

Wait, what? "You're not coming to the party?"

Mine and Mali's annual birthday party is even more of a tradition than our summer bonfires. It's the biggest party of the summer at my house, and I don't think Hayes has missed a single one in six or seven years.

"No, I'll be there," he assures me. "But I didn't get Mali anything, and I don't want Cam to think too much into me only giving you a present."

Reaching into the glove compartment, he pulls out an envelope, and I've never been more confused. At first, I hopelessly think it's a love letter—handwritten and telling me everything he said about not wanting a relationship is a lie. But as I open it, what I find inside is surprisingly better.

My eyes widen as I gasp. "You got me tickets to a Thomas Rhett concert?"

Thomas Rhett is my favorite singer, only second to Kurt Cobain, but obviously I can't see him in concert. I had no idea he was even putting on a concert anywhere near here. And the seats are incredible.

"Holy shit," I say in disbelief. "Thank you. You didn't have to do this."

He smiles as I kiss him. "Now that I think about it, I could've just given you one and Mali the other."

I freeze, thinking of an idea that may be crazy, but it's worth a shot.

Nibbling on the inside of my cheek nervously, I force myself to ask. "What if I want you to come with me?"

He instantly looks unsure, telling me he never even considered the idea when he bought the tickets. "I don't know, Lai. It's in public."

"Yeah, but it's over an hour away," I point out. "The chances of seeing anyone we know there are low. And besides, Cam doesn't even like Thomas Rhett."

"Neither do I."

"Yeah, but you like me." The words spew out of my mouth before I have the chance to stop myself.

His brows raise, and I'm about to take it back or apologize, but I decide against it. He *has* to like me, whether he wants to admit it or not. You don't sleep with someone you don't like at least a little bit.

Instead, I take a different approach.

Puffing my bottom lip out, I pout just slightly. "Please?"

He exhales all the air in his lungs. "Now that's just unfair."

I smile and lean across the center console, putting my lips next to his ear.

"Please?" I say again, lower this time.

Repeating the word like a prayer, I nip at his earlobe and his breathing starts to get heavier. Just as I slide my hand over his leg and toward his dick, he grabs my wrist to stop me.

"Don't start something you can't finish," he warns.

I back away just enough to look at him. "Say you'll come with me."

He narrows his eyes at me and we stare at each other for a moment before he sighs. "Okay. I'll come."

Beaming happily, I thank him and kiss him once more. I open the truck door and climb out, but when I go to close it, I see him glaring at me playfully.

"You play dirty," he says.

I chuckle. "I know."

And with that, I shut the truck door and head into Mali's to get my keys—only looking back once to watch Hayes as he drives away.

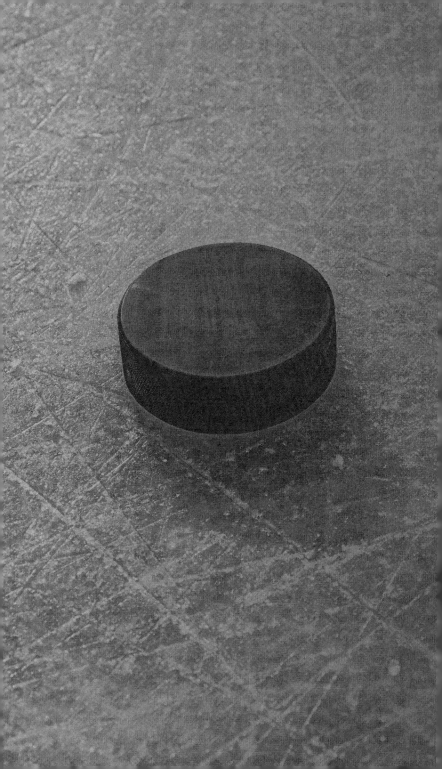

Hayes
CHAPTER EIGHTEEN

DRIVING BACK TO MY HOUSE, I KNOW I'M IN FOR IT. I played it off like my mom catching us was no big deal, but that's only because Laiken looked like she was on the verge of a damn breakdown. I couldn't leave her like that for the rest of the day.

Her sleeping over was not in the plans. I had every intention of waking her up when the movie was over. But then I fell asleep. And as much as I hate to admit it—it was one of the best nights of sleep I've ever had.

I pull into my driveway and climb out of my truck, taking a deep breath to prepare for the impending interrogation. If I had known it was her that came home, I would've snuck Laiken out my window. But hindsight is 20/20, and all I can do now is rip the Band-Aid off.

Walking into the house, I find my mom sitting at the kitchen table, a cup of coffee clutched in her hands. I go over to the fridge and grab a beer, knowing I'll need it for this conversation, but I should've known she would never allow that.

"Boy, it is ten in the morning," she says with an incredulous look.

"Which makes it five o'clock in Italy," I joke, but her pressed-together lips tells me she's not amused.

She cocks a single brow at me. "Put it back."

Thank God Laiken isn't here to see this. Watching me get bossed around by my mother is something she would never let me live down. I can only imagine the commentary she would provide to the situation.

Note to self: don't let them in the same room for longer than a few minutes.

I put the beer back and switch it out with a Red Bull, which still doesn't make her happy, but she knows to pick her battles. As I crack it open and bring it to my lips, she sighs.

"Do you know what you're doing?"

I act coy. "Destroying my insides?"

My mom stares back at me, her eyes like laser beams. "Hayes Beckett."

I cringe at the way she uses my middle name. Putting the Red Bull on the counter behind me, I sigh heavily.

"We're just having fun, Mom."

"Does she know that?"

My first instinct is to say yes. I told her as much the first night I threw caution to the wind. But something holds me back. I clamp my mouth shut as last night replays in my mind, followed by this morning, when she was able to convince me to go with her to the concert.

Fuck. That's a date, isn't it?

When I don't respond, my mom stands up and brings her empty mug over to the sink. "Don't play with her feelings, H. That girl deserves more than that."

I hum, knowing she's right. The topic of what Laiken deserves is one I think about often. She may want me, but that doesn't mean that she doesn't deserve a whole hell of a lot better. She does. But for her to realize that I would have to resist her, and I can't do that.

I've tried.

"What are you doing home, anyway?" I ask. "You always sleep at the hospital before driving."

She chuckles. "I was able to nap for a few hours during

my shift. But I'll give you the heads up next time so you can sneak Laiken out *before* I get home."

"You're fucking Laiken?" Devin's voice booms through the room.

Motherfucker! "A little louder, Dev. I don't think the entire town heard you."

"You know, I should," she claps back. "Maybe one of them can smack some sense into you."

I roll my eyes. "Oh, fuck off. What are you even doing here, anyway? I thought you weren't coming home until later."

"Plans change," she says as she waves off the topic. "But forget about that. Laiken? Seriously?"

"Leave it alone, Dev," I growl, clenching my jaw.

She clearly doesn't want to, but she agrees anyway. "Fine, but promise me one thing."

"What?"

A devious smirk crosses her face. "You'll let me watch when Cam kills you."

"Ooh," Mom chimes in. "Record it."

This little comedy duo is getting old. "Ay!"

"What?" she asks innocently. "I'll need something to remember you by."

Flipping them both off, I walk away and head straight for my room. I fully intend to go back to bed until I have to wake up for work. Early mornings are just not my thing, especially when they're filled with Mom and Devin getting on my case.

I shut the door behind me and flop face first onto my bed. But as I get comfortable and breathe in, I realize the smell of Laiken's shampoo still lingers on my pillow.

It relaxes me more than I'd like to admit.

Chapter 18

TRESPASSING IS NEVER A good idea. It's illegal. No joke—there's actually a law on being somewhere without permission, even if all you did was drive past a few signs that warn you not to. But when Laiken showed up at my job and told me she wanted to take me somewhere after work, I didn't hesitate.

We lie on the grassy hill at the end of the runway, watching as the planes take off and land, flying right above us. The sun starts to set in the distance, but as sappy as it may be, the view beside me is better.

"Okay, I've got one," she chuckles. "Would you rather surf naked with a shark, or have all your fingers get frostbite?"

Easy. "Frostbite."

Her eyes widen. "It's *surfing* with a shark, not getting eaten by one."

"I don't care," I reply, not changing my mind. "I'd rather lose my fingers than risk losing my dick. It's more important."

She smirks. "Clearly you haven't felt what your fingers can do."

"You'd be fine. My tongue isn't in jeopardy."

Her head falls to the side, and she whines. "That's just cruel. You can't remind me of that when we can't do anything."

Right. *Her period.* The tangent she went on this morning

about how only she would end up getting it the day before her birthday, taking away her right to birthday sex, was adorable. The texts kept pouring in, and every time I went to respond to one, there would be another.

I ended up just waiting until she was done before answering.

"Who says we can't do anything?" I question, rolling onto my side to face her.

"Oh, I don't know. The fact that we're out in the open, and already trespassing."

Leaning down, I suck on her bottom lip. "Exactly. We're already breaking the rules. What's one more?"

I slide my hand down her stomach and dip the tip of my pinky beneath the waistband of her shorts. The look in her eyes tells me she's considering it. I kiss her slowly and she breathes out a moan.

"What about the passengers on the planes?" she questions. "They'll see us."

Humming against her mouth, I slide my hand further south. "Then let's give them a show."

The moment my fingers graze her clit, she exhales and arches against me. I press my lips to hers as I rub her in a circular motion, slow and with just the right amount of pressure—exactly how she likes it. Her period must make her more sensitive, because with each second that passes, she starts to get more vocal.

She reaches down and grabs my wrist, holding it in place as if I'm going to take it away at the last minute. It's so fucking hot, the way she grinds herself against my hand, using me to get herself off.

It's so goddamn hot.

The sound of sticks cracking catches my attention, and I break the kiss for a second. Laiken whimpers, lifting her head to try to reconnect our mouths, but that's not going to happen.

Not when there are two cops standing ten feet away from us.

"All right," the one says. "Show us your hands."

Laiken whines, not thinking clearly from being wrapped up in her impending orgasm. "Does he have to? It's a little occupied at the moment."

Unable to help myself, I drop my head onto her shoulder and laugh. "Babe, it's the cops."

"Oh," she says, her mouth forming into a circle. "Well, shit."

Slowly and carefully, I slip my hand from her shorts and the two of us stand up. Laiken looks away as she spots the two officers, but I have nothing to be ashamed of.

If they had someone who looks like her, they wouldn't be able to get enough either.

She's the best kind of drug.

"What can we do for you, officers?"

They share a glance at each other. "Well, for starters, you're on private property."

Laiken feigns innocence. "Are we really? Wow. I'm so sorry about that. We'll see ourselves out right now."

She starts walking toward my truck when one of the cops stops her with his hand on her arm. "Not so fast. Let me see your ID." He nods toward me. "You too, son."

I pull my wallet out of my back pocket and hand over my license, while Laiken puts her hands on her hips. "Look at me. What makes you think I have my ID on me?"

Smirking, my eyes rake over her, and I realize she has a point. The girl is in a crop top and a pair of tiny shorts. Unless he thought she was hiding it in her bra, it's clear the only thing on her is her phone.

"Ma'am, the attitude is unnecessary."

"You interrupting my orgasm was unnecessary, *sir,*" she spits back.

Her being a bitch in the name of sexual gratification should not be nearly as attractive as it is. I know we haven't been able to get enough of each other lately, but goddamn. I created a monster, and I fucking love it.

Officer Oblivious, on the other hand, is *not* impressed.

"All right," he says, taking out his handcuffs. "Turn around and put your hands behind your back."

"I haven't done anything wrong," she argues.

"You're trespassing. That alone is enough for me to detain you until we figure out what's going on here."

He grabs her arm and turns her around, taking out his handcuffs. I take a step toward them. I want to be close enough to help her if needed, but getting in a fight with the police is something I'd like to avoid if possible.

Laiken scoffs and lets him handcuff her without issue, but that doesn't mean she's going easy on him.

"Oh," she squeals as he starts to pat her down. "I wouldn't do that if I were you. My boyfriend's name is Bubba, and he tends to get a little possessive."

The officer glances at me. "I take it you're Bubba?"

"No," I answer through a laugh.

Every time she opens her mouth, the guy seems to turn a little more red in the face. Meanwhile, his partner is trying not to laugh.

"You're the risk-taking type," Laiken says when she continues to be searched. "I like it."

"Ma'am," he growls, exasperated. "Please just let me do my job."

She smirks. "Okay, but you should know, my safe word is prune juice."

Yeah, nope. No way I can hold back from laughing at that one. And apparently, neither can the other cop—though he does make a solid effort. When it forces its way through, his partner glares at him.

"What are you doing?" He nods his head over toward me. "Cuff him, too."

Laiken's grin widens. "Aw, you get a pair of bracelets too!" She focuses on the cop again. "Do we get to keep these? A little souvenir, maybe?"

"What do you—" he starts, but then he sees the way she bounces her eyebrows. "On second thought, how about you just give me your name since you don't have your ID? And before you answer, you should know that giving a false name to the police is a crime."

Her bottom lip juts out as she pouts. "Fine. Laiken Blanchard."

He writes that down, along with her date of birth. Though, he doesn't seem to care for the way his partner wishes her a happy early birthday. Once he has all the information, they walk us over and sit us in the back of the car.

"Wait here while we run your information," he tells us. "Make sure you are who you say you are, and that neither of you have any outstanding warrants."

Just as he goes to shut the door, Laiken stops him. "Wait!"

He huffs and looks at her expectantly. "Could you uncuff him so he can finish what you fine gentleman interrupted?"

My head falls back against the seat as I laugh loudly, but he doesn't find it so funny. His jaw tenses and he slams the door shut, muttering to himself as he walks away.

"He secretly loves me," she says. "It may not seem like it now, but we're going to be the best of friends."

"Oh are you now?"

Her head tilts from side to side. "It's either that, or we get arrested and Cam slaughters us both."

"We won't get arrested," I say, certain of it.

"How do you know?"

"Because we didn't do anything except trespass. It's not an arrestable offense," I explain. "And even if it was, he would let us go simply because he doesn't want to deal with *you* for as long as it would take to book us."

She squints and hums. "I don't know. We're in handcuffs in the back of a cop car. That qualifies as being arrested."

"It doesn't."

"It does!" She frowns. "Stop taking away my ability to say that I've been arrested. It's such a buzzkill."

I bark out a laugh. "Why do you want to be able to say you've been arrested?"

"It sounds badass," she answers, *DUH* written all over her face. "Anyway, it's your turn."

My turn?

Oh! Right. We were playing a game that seems to blur the lines between would you rather, truth or dare, and marry fuck kill. Basically, just shoot questions and scenarios at each other.

"Okay, I've got one," I begin. "Marry, fuck, kill. Owen, Isaac, and Aiden."

I considered making Lucas an option, but there's no chance of her killing him off, and I don't want to hear her say that she would marry or fuck him. Not when he's so eager to do either.

She snorts. "That's easy. Marry Aiden. Fuck Owen. Kill Isaac."

My jaw drops. "Aiden? Seriously?"

"Yeah. He's a few fries short of a happy meal. I could use that to my advantage." Damn, she thought that through fast. "Plus, the alternative was marrying Owen. I'd sooner marry *you*."

The way she says it, as if marrying me is an outrageous

thought—it hits me in all the wrong places. Not that it would ever happen. The whole white-picket-fence lifestyle isn't in the cards for me. But goddamn, I didn't know bullets flew *inside* of police cars.

"Go ahead, Rochester," I tell her. "Sound a little more repulsed at that idea."

She giggles, looking away as she tries moving to get more comfortable. "You're so easy to fuck with sometimes."

I don't know what's worse—that I just played right into her hand, or the relief that floods through me when I realize she was kidding. Meanwhile, Laiken smiles like the cat that caught the fucking canary.

"Whatever," I grumble. "It's your turn."

Her nose scrunches as she thinks. "Truth or dare?"

I cock a brow at her. "Uh, being as we're locked in the back of a car with handcuffs on, I think dares will be a little difficult. Nor do I trust you enough to pick it right now. So, truth."

"You're no fun."

Ha. "Even you know that's a lie."

She looks as if she wants to argue it, but she knows better. It would most likely end up with the two of us getting sexually frustrated back here.

Thinking hard about it, she finally comes up with a question. "What's your dream job?"

I have to say, I thought it was going to be a lot more X-rated than that. Or a smart ass question. That would have been on par too. But not this.

Still, the answer has been the same since I was fourteen years old. "I want to own a bar."

"Really?"

"Yeah," I shrug, as much as I can while handcuffed. "Not like one of the places drunks hang out at all day instead of taking care of their shit. More like the kind of bar people our age would want to hang out at, with surfer decor and live music."

She sits there patiently, listening as I talk with a small smile splayed across her face. "That's amazing. Have you looked into the semantics of it all?"

"On and off," I reply. "But it's all not cheap, so for now, it stays a dream."

It goes quiet for a moment, but it's my turn to go anyway.

"What about you? What's *your* dream?"

Laiken doesn't miss a beat. "Rob a bank."

I choke on air, needing to clear my throat. "Well damn, Shawshank. Get borderline arrested one time and you suddenly become a career criminal?"

She hums. "On second thought, I don't like pussy enough for prison."

What she doesn't know is that she's too pretty. She would most likely be the one *getting* instead of giving, but there's no way I'm telling her that. She doesn't need to be enticed to go to jail.

Before I can come up with a response, Pissy the Po-Po opens the door to let us out.

"All right," he says curtly. "You're free to go. But if we ever find you here again, you *will* be arrested."

Laiken turns to me with wide eyes, and I shake my head.

"You don't like pussy enough, remember?" I tell her.

She sighs, pouting like a child. "Fine."

My cuffs are removed first, but when he goes to take off Laiken's, she spins to face him so he can't.

"Any chance I can keep them on?" He stares back at her blankly. "What? It's on my fuck-it list."

Fuck-it list?

"Fine," he agrees. "You can keep them on."

"Really?"

"Yeah. It's policy to stay handcuffed while we take you down to the station and get you processed."

Her brows raise and she spins once more so he can reach the cuffs. "On second thought, they're hurting my wrists. Better take them off."

He grins smugly, finally getting one over on her. Once he removes them, he slips them back into their holster. The other officer comes over and hands each of us our belongings.

"Oh, Mali texted me," she exclaims, then straightens up. "Hey, Copper Dude. Are you single? Because my friend Mali would be *perfect* for you."

"Ignore her. We're going." I put my arm around her and start leading her to my truck. "Are you crazy? Mali would kill you."

She smiles giddily. "I know, but imagine how funny it would be to watch."

A breathy laugh leaves my mouth as I shake my head. "It's all fun and games until Mali gets arrested."

We both climb into the truck, and I put the key into the ignition. As it roars to life—clearly with an exhaust that is louder than allowed—I check the rearview mirror to see the officers' reactions. They share a glance, but as the one goes to step toward my truck, Pissy stops him.

Good job, Shawshank.

I put it in drive and pull away, looking over at Laiken just as we turn onto the road.

"So, about that fuck-it list..."

Chapter 18

DROPPING HER OFF AT her house is risky. All it would take is Cam deciding to go somewhere and—depending on which way he turns—he would see us together. But Mali had plans tonight, and if Laiken's car was at her house, Mali's parents would have questions.

Questions we don't really know how to answer.

So, the best thing to do was to have Laiken drive home so she could leave her car there. Mali picked her up and dropped her back off at the surf shop just as I was getting off work.

It's a good thing she knows about us, because this would all be much more difficult without her.

I pull over a couple houses down, knowing her best bet is to walk the rest of the way. Both her parents and her brother would recognize the sound of my truck if I turned into their driveway. And again—questions we don't have answers to.

"Today was fun," she says. "You know, other than getting arrested."

I try to look annoyed, but I fail, miserably. "Yes, Rochester. You're such a badass."

The smug grin on her face and the way she leans over to kiss me goodbye shouldn't have the effect on me that it does. It shouldn't make my heart jump, wanting to break through my rib cage and throw itself at her feet. It shouldn't make my stomach hurt knowing I won't see her until her party tomorrow, and even then, we have to play it safe.

And yet, here we are.

"Text me when you get home," she tells me, and it's not up for debate.

Thing is, I don't need to be told. I would've done it anyway; I can't help myself. Not when it comes to her.

"I will," I promise.

She opens the door but turns around to kiss me once more. I wrap my hand around the back of her neck to keep her there just a little longer. It's soft. Slow. The epitome of a kiss a couple would share before one of them is gone for a while, even though neither of us is going anywhere. And when she pulls away, I feel it throughout my entire body.

"Night, H," she says, climbing out of the truck.

"Goodnight, baby."

But the last part comes out silently, my voice cracking to keep from giving myself away, because nothing has changed. This—the sneaking around and the stolen kisses when no one is watching—is all this can ever be.

I know this more than I know anything else.

It's just…for the first time, I'm starting to realize I won't make it out of this unscathed.

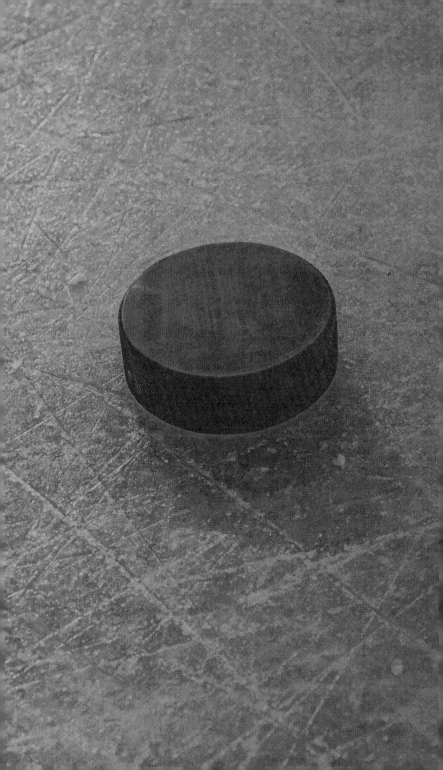

Hayes

CHAPTER NINETEEN

The backyard is covered in decorations, and I'm guessing the massive one and nine balloons that are tied to the mailbox were not Laiken's idea. Usually, I come hang out with Cam while they're setting up. And by *they,* I mean Mali. Last year, Laiken laid on a hammock they tied between two trees and drank wine straight out of the box.

I wish I was kidding.

Their attitudes may be the same, but their personalities couldn't be more different. Laiken would rather have a few people over, light a fire, and spend the night cracking jokes at everyone else's expense because *"it's my birthday and you can't insult me on my birthday."*

Mali, however, loves to make a show of everything. So, all the decor, the three-tiered cake they have every year, and the tiaras sitting on both of their heads—yeah, all Mali. It's like every year is as big as their Sweet Sixteen.

And every year, Laiken just wants to get drunk and have fun.

I hop out of my truck and head toward the back to get Cam. I may be strong, but not *carry a whole keg across the yard* strong. He's over by the fire pit, arranging the wood for later tonight.

"Yo!" I call.

He looks back at me and nods, but his attention isn't the only one I got. Laiken's eyes meet mine, and she smiles. Mali smacks her arm to make her focus while glaring at me for the distraction.

Oops.

"The keg?" Cam asks as he approaches.

"Yeah," I answer. "Brandon wasn't there, and the other guy could tell my ID was fake. He almost didn't give it to me."

He shakes his head. "You would think he would know to make sure he's on shift. We do this every year."

"And every year you don't invite him."

Pausing for a second, he hums. "Okay, fair point. But I don't control the guest list. That's Drill Sergeant Hughes over there."

I chuckle. "She already glared at me once. Maybe this will be the year she kills me."

"If you stick your finger in the cake again, I can almost guarantee it."

We grab the keg out of the back of my truck and carry it into the backyard. There's a table set up with cups, and every year the keg goes right next to it, but Cam has to be a smartass about it.

"Where do you want this, boss?" he asks Mali.

She crosses her arms over her chest. "Really, Cameron? Really?"

His lips purse at the sound of his full name. "So, right here then? You've got it."

He puts his side down in the middle of the yard, forcing me to do the same. Mali looks anything but impressed.

"Fine. I'll just move it myself." But as she tries to pick it up, it doesn't even budge. "Laiken! Come help me."

Looking over at her, Laiken scrunches her nose. "Yeah, no. I make it a rule not to do manual labor on my birthday."

Cam grins smugly as Mali pouts. After a couple more

useless attempts at lifting the thing, she rolls her eyes and sighs as she gives in.

"Okay, I'm sorry," she tells him. "You're so helpful. My own personal hero with abs of steel. Can you *please* put it over by the tables?"

"Now was that so hard?" he teases as he nods at me, giving me the go ahead to move it.

Her eyes narrow as she glares at him. "It killed me inside, slowly and painfully."

We carry the keg over to its proper place and set it down. Cam goes inside to grab the tap from his room, while I take the opportunity that's given to me. I still need to be careful. There are other people around. But there's no law about greeting my best friend's sister on her birthday.

Still, I hug Mali first for extra measure.

"Happy Birthday," I tell her.

"Thanks!" she says loudly then murmurs, "but let's not pretend you're here for me."

I snicker and turn to Laiken. She looks gorgeous. She's wearing a dress I know she had to be strong-armed into and a tiara she would like to use as a Frisbee, but as she smiles back at me, she's glowing. Radiating happiness like the damn sun.

Nineteen looks so good on her.

Wrapping my arms around her, I hold her close and breathe in the smell of her perfume. My lips move to her ear, and I speak low enough for only her to hear.

"Happy Birthday, baby."

She lets out a breathy giggle. "Thank you."

The term of endearment may be one I save for bedroom talk to keep from blurring the lines, but seeing how happy it makes her, I don't regret it.

Not even a little.

"All right!" Cam shouts as he comes out the back door,

and I release Laiken as she steps back. "Let's get this bitch ready to go."

We stand around and watch Cam tap the keg. Once he's done, he pours four glasses and hands us each one, taking the last for himself. It's something we started doing two years ago, when the keg was flat and nasty and we didn't know it until Owen accidentally spit it out all over Isaac.

Personally, I liked that better, but I won't turn down a beer.

"So, where'd you send your parents this time?" I question.

Cam and Laiken both start to laugh, so Mali answers for them. "Amish Country. Lancaster, Pennsylvania."

"Oh God," I cringe. "Your dad is going to hate both of you."

It was Laiken's idea, sending them away for the weekend the party is planned for, and after it worked the first year, they've repeated it every year since. Cam and Laiken put away some money all year, and then they book a trip that's non-refundable. They even get in touch with their jobs to make sure they have the Friday before and the Monday after, off work—eliminating all their potential excuses before they're even used.

"No," Cam corrects me. "He's going to hate *her*."

Laiken shrugs. "I was all for sending them on that weekend fishing trip he's been wanting to go on, but then he grounded me. Churning butter will give him plenty of time to consider the error of his ways."

I chuckle as I look over at her. "Is there any part of you that's *not* evil?"

"No," she answers promptly.

Yeah, I already knew that.

Chapter 19

PEOPLE BEGIN TO ARRIVE just as darkness starts to fill the night sky. Mali plugs in the lights she spent the last two days stringing throughout the yard. The whole backyard becomes illuminated just enough—but not too much. She and Laiken look around, taking everything in, and fist bump when they see the outcome.

It's perfect.

I grab a beer and go sit by the fire, only for everyone else to join me. It's no surprise the guys are here before everyone else. In another hour or so, this yard will be filled, but no one shows up to a party before ten p.m. anymore.

It's a concept Cam and Laiken's parents never really understood when they tried putting a midnight end time on the party—hence the weekend trips. They solve the problem *and* make it so we can have a keg.

"God, I missed this," Owen says. "The rain last Friday threw off my whole damn weekend."

"It almost stormed this weekend, too," Mali informs him. "Thank God it didn't."

Cam snorts. "He probably didn't want the hellfire you'd bring if it had."

She cocks a brow at him. "Watch it, Blanchard. You're already on my shit list tonight."

Laiken, not paying attention, picks her head up. "What did I do?"

"Not you, princess," she assures her, tapping her leg. "The *other* Blanchard."

"Technically, Laiken is the other Blanchard," Cam argues. "I was born first."

"So, what I'm hearing is you want to be on *both* our shit lists," Laiken shoots back. "It's my birthday. You can't insult me on my birthday."

I chuckle as I look down at my beer. She may like to think she's a wildcard, but I predicted that word for word. Either she's easy to read, or I've been spending a little too much time around her.

I'd go with the latter, but there's no such thing as *too much time* when it comes to Laiken.

"Aid," Cam says, getting Aiden's attention. "Stop checking out Hayes. It's creepy."

I lift my head in time to see Aiden flip Cam off before he turns back to me.

"I'm just trying to figure out what's up with him lately," he says, squinting like it'll help him see into my soul.

Shit. Leave it to the team moron to notice a shift in my attitude. Can't shoot the puck into an empty net but can spot the second I'm in a slightly better mood than normal.

"Fuck off," I tell him. "There's nothing up with me."

"No, no," Owen agrees. "He's right. You're different."

I roll my eyes, trying to play it off. "All of you fuckers are delusional."

After a moment of feeling like I'm in a damn fishbowl surrounded by people staring at me, Aiden snaps.

"I know what it is," he says confidently. "He got laid."

Jesus Christ.

Cam scoffs. "When doesn't he?"

"Thank you," I reply, putting out my fist to bump his.

That should be the end of it, but while Aiden figured out

the start of it, Owen fills in the rest. He smirks as he tips his cup at me.

"But this one he actually likes."

Motherfucker.

My heart starts to race, even as I will it to slow the fuck down. I spare a quick glance over at Laiken. She's looking down at her phone, trying to make it seem like she's not paying attention, but the small smile playing on her face tells me she's listening to every word.

"Is that true?" Cam questions.

I chuckle, lifting my beer to my lips. "I have no idea what you dipshits are talking about."

"Good for you, man," Cam tells me, seeing right through my act. "Good pussy is hard to find these days."

I'm mid-sip as the words leave his mouth, and the sharp breath I suck in has more beer than air. I cough violently as I try to expel the beer I just sucked into my lungs. Everyone's eyes are on me, which is good. That way they're not paying attention to Miss Fit-of-Giggles Mali over there.

And Laiken? Well, she looks like a cross between smug and grossed out. But if Devin unknowingly referred to me as *good dick,* I'd feel the same way.

THERE'S NO REASON FOR me to feel the way I do right now. Absolutely none. And yet, every single time I see a guy pull Laiken into his arms to wish her a happy birthday, I want to bounce their head off a curb.

It makes no sense.

I've had plenty of female friends, a decent amount of them that I've hooked up with, and never once did I feel the least bit possessive. Then again, I never craved their touch when I couldn't have it, either. I was around for a good time, not a long time.

And that's the same way I should be with Laiken, but things with her never seem to go the way I planned.

She stands beside me as we play a game of cornhole—her and Mali on one team, Cam and me on the other. Thankfully, she's not nearly as good at this as she is at beer pong. But it's still cute how she gets mad every time she misses.

She's so close that all it would take to touch her is putting my arm out. And yet, she might as well be across town.

I start to wonder what the likelihood of me being able to sneak into her room later is. After Cam passes out from drinking too much, there's no chance of him waking up. But like she is with everything else, Laiken is loud in bed. If anything was going to manage to do the impossible, the sound of his sister screaming in straight pleasure would do it.

"Hey," Laiken says, pulling me from my thoughts. "It's your turn."

Whoops. I focus on the hole and aim as I toss the bag, watching it go right in. Cam grins triumphantly while Laiken groans.

We're now up by seven.

"What were you thinking about?" she asks quietly, waiting for Cam and Mali to gather the bags for their turn.

"Nothing," I lie.

She snorts. "Bullshit. You were doing that thing where you chew on the inside of your cheek."

My brows raise as I smirk. "Paying close attention to me, Rochester?"

Her gaze turns to Mali and Cam, but her words are meant for me as she drops her voice a little lower. "Better than picturing you above me in bed while we're in the middle of a party."

I let my jaw fall open just slightly as I chuckle in disbelief.

"You do it when you're turned on," she explains.

The fact she knows that does not bode well for me. Devin may be able to tell when I'm full of shit, but Laiken's ability to read me goes so much further than that. If she sees that I'm more invested in this than I should be, I'm fucked.

Then again…I'm fucked anyway.

"Oh!" Mali squeals, dropping the bags in her hands. "Laiken, come with me. Monty is here."

Without so much as a glance in my direction, Laiken walks away and the two of them excitedly head toward the front of the house. I take a sip of my beer, using it to disguise the rage that's building inside of me, as Cam and I meet in the middle.

"Who the fuck is Monty?" I growl, a little too obviously.

"Montgomery Rollins," he says.

Rollins. The name rings a bell, but I can't put my finger on it. "Where have I heard that name before?"

"Because his dad is Jeremiah Rollins."

"The senator?" *Son of a bitch.*

He nods. "That's the one. Apparently, they met him at a club one night a few weeks ago and hit it off. You would've heard all about it if you didn't skip the bonfire."

Ugh, great. So the fact that Laiken is now besties with who the media calls one of North Carolina's Most Eligible Bachelors is my fault. Jeremiah Rollins is on track to be the next president, and if his son is anything like him, he's exactly the kind of guy I picture Laiken ending up with.

"I met him when he picked them up for lunch one day," Cam continues. "They think he's great, but if you ask me, he's a fucking douche."

His words resonate as Laiken comes back into view with Monty's arm draped over her shoulders. It doesn't matter that he's just as physical with Mali—that's Cam's problem to deal with.

He needs to get his fucking hands off my girl.

Laiken

CHAPTER TWENTY

THE THING ABOUT BIRTHDAYS IS THAT EVERYONE'S attention is on you. And normally, that would be great. My enjoyment being the goal of everyone's night? Sounds amazing. Except…it's not.

Because the only thing I want right now is to find a way to be alone with Hayes. And when it's a party about *you,* that becomes even harder to do. Even being absent for a half hour could make someone wonder where I am.

Mali comes up and sits beside me. "It's our party and you can cry if you want to?"

I hum, only half amused. "I'm having fun. It's a great party."

"It is a great party," she agrees. "But the other part was a damn lie."

Looking over at her, I sigh. "It just sucks. That's all."

Cam and Hayes always being by each other's side is nothing new. They've been close for so long, they naturally sort of gravitate to each other. It's the same way for Mali and me. But right now, I just want him to gravitate toward *me.*

Oh, God. I'm jealous of my brother.

Mali watches me pick at my shorts. I changed out of that hideous dress right after everyone got here. And when she tried to fight me on it, I used the excuse I had in my back pocket since I put the thing on.

I don't want to risk someone seeing my tampon string.

She couldn't argue it and I won, getting to change into a tank-top and a pair of jean shorts.

"Hey," she nudges me. "I have an idea."

My brows furrow as she hops off the picnic table and goes over to where the guys are setting up beer pong. I don't know what the hell she has up her sleeve, but being anywhere but right beside her is stupid.

It's not *my* mouth that'll get me into trouble. It's *hers*.

I'm up and on my way toward her in seconds. She crosses her arms over her chest as she stands in front of Cam. Honestly, for a second, I wonder if she's going to attempt to hurt him.

Sending him to the hospital would be a Mali way to get Hayes and me alone.

Instead, she smiles. "Okay, we're picking new teams."

"What?" Cam argues. "You can't do that. We always have the same teams."

"I know, and I don't feel like losing beer pong at my own party because you and Hayes are some kind of power couple. It's not fair." She keeps her head high, showing she's not backing down.

My brother rolls his eyes as he groans. "Fine, but that's not why you're going to lose. You're going to lose because you can't make a shot to save your life."

Her mouth opens to retort, but then she smiles deviously. "For that comment, I'm picking you."

"Shit."

"Yeah," Mali teases. "Walked yourself right into that one."

He drops his head. "I know."

Turning to me, Mali winks, and I swear, I love her so hard right now. "Lai, it's your turn."

I look at her like she's crazy. "Hayes, obviously. I want to *win*."

Cam scoffs in disbelief. "Now *that's* unfair. None of us stand a damn chance."

"Not with that attitude we don't," Mali chastises him. "Damn, Other Blanchard. You're really batting a thousand tonight."

His eyes narrow at her. "When we're not celebrating your birthday, you're going down."

"Maybe when it's your birthday," she quips, then moves on like she didn't just allude to a blowjob in front of everyone. "All right, everyone else's partners will be decided the same way we decide everything. H?"

Hayes pulls the switchblade out of his pocket and hands it to her.

"Uh, what are you doing with that?" Monty questions.

Mali, being the little shit she is, smiles like a psycho. "Testing everyone's blood types. Those that match will be partners."

Horror fills Monty's face as we all stay silent, until Owen breaks it by laughing. From there, it becomes contagious—all of us chuckling at the way he thought she was serious. Mali, however, is disappointed.

"Owen!" she whines. "I could've lasted for at least another minute."

"The poor guy looked like he was about to stroke out," he protests.

She rolls her eyes but doesn't even make an effort to explain anything to Monty. So, I do it for her.

"Whenever we can't decide something, we spin the switchblade. Whoever it lands on normally has to do the thing that none of us want to do," I tell him. "In this case, it'll work more like a spin the bottle. The person who spins and the person it lands on will be partners. But it really doesn't matter, because Hayes and I are going to win the whole thing anyway."

"Fuck yeah, we are!" Hayes says, going for a high five.

The minute my hand touches his, I realize how much I'm craving being alone with him—where we can be all over each other and speak without censoring ourselves. That little bit of contact is nowhere near enough.

THERE ARE FOUR TABLES set up, making the back yard look like a makeshift beer pong competition. We had to spread them out so balls didn't get mixed up as they bounce off cups. Though, that's a problem for everyone else.

I don't miss.

Owen is teamed up with Aiden, but we're all pretty sure they cheated. Monty ended up with Liam, a guy we went to high school with that Mali invited. But my favorite part of the pair up was when Devin's spin landed on a guy she's been crushing on for the better part of two years. *Tommy Valentine.*

Yes, he's as cheesy as his name is.

The two of them have been playing cat and mouse forever. Either he likes her or she likes him, but it never happens at the same time. Until now. And big brother seems anything but happy about it.

"Leave her alone," I tell him as he cranes his neck to watch her.

He shushes me. "I'm not doing anything. I'm simply keeping an eye on her."

Looking across the table, I make sure our opponents

aren't paying attention. "Could you imagine how things would be if Cam was always *keeping an eye on me?*"

"That's exactly *why* I'm keeping an eye on her."

"Oh, that's right," I say sarcastically. "A brother's only job is to cockblock their sisters."

Hayes gets the point, sighing and finally looking away from them. "If he hurts her—"

"You'll kill him," I say with a sigh. "I know. Just don't get blood on the switch blade. They'll take it for evidence and then we can't use it anymore."

"Noted."

The first few games are easy. Hayes and I make every shot, getting the balls back until there are no cups left. They get the chance for redemption, of course, but it's useless. They miss, and we're left waiting twenty more minutes until the next round.

I glance over at Devin just in time to see her hug Tommy as she makes her shot, winning them their game. I smile, just happy to see her enjoying herself, but I'm not the only one who sees it.

"They allow conjugal visits in prison, right?" Hayes asks.

Looking up at him, I smirk. "I think so. But if you don't tell my soulmate I said hi when you see him, we're done."

"Now he's your soulmate? I thought he was your best friend."

"Position's taken, and Mali is even worse at sharing than you."

WITH EACH GAME WE play, the more comfortable we get around each other. Maybe a little *too* comfortable, if I'm honest. Hayes high fives me every time we win, which is literally every game, and when we start to get a little bored, we up the stakes.

"You know, neither of us has missed a single shot," I tell him. "It would be such a shame if you fucked up now."

It's along the same lines as what he told me during our first bonfire of the summer. He chuckles as he takes his shot, but the damage is done. I jinxed him. It hits the rim and flies to the right, off the table.

"Why'd you have to fuck with me like that?" He pouts.

I smile innocently. "Who, me? I would never."

"Mm-hm."

It's my turn to shoot. I step up to the table, but the angle is off. When I go to take a step to the left, the side of my body bumps into Hayes.

"Excuse me," I sass. "I need you to move."

He snickers as he raises his hands and takes a step back.

"God," I grumble. "Gotta carry the whole team by myself over here."

The sound of Hayes laughing almost fucks me up, but thankfully, I shoot the ball before second guessing myself too much. It sinks directly into the cup, making a splash sound as it goes in.

"See how that's done?" I tease.

His eyes darken, almost like he's picturing all the ways he can make me pay for this later, and I can't fucking wait.

Chapter 20

THE LAST GAME BEFORE we face Cam and Mali is against Monty and Brandon. Honestly, I'm a little surprised that Monty is good enough to make it this far. I thought he was too high-class for this sort of thing. But it turns out, rich kids can party like the best of them.

Once Hayes missed the one shot, he's missed a few since then. I, however, have only missed one—and that was because I went a little too far with telling him he's useless at this game. He walked behind me just as I was taking my shot, and the way his hand lightly brushed against my lower back made me flinch.

It's not fair. He shouldn't be allowed to touch me when I'm *this* high strung.

This game is a close one, and that's saying a lot, being as we won almost every game by a landslide. We may be down to our last cup, but they're down to three. I don't think anyone has made it that far against us yet.

While Monty lines up to take his shot, I pull my phone and type a message into it. Once I'm done, I place it on the table in front of us so Hayes has a chance to read it without looking obvious.

Sink this next shot and I'll blow you.

I know the second he reads it because his head falls back as he groans. His eyes meet mine, and I can tell he's struggling to keep his hands off me.

"Seriously?" he asks.

Monty's shot goes wide, still leaving them with three cups.

"Do you really think I would joke about that?" I tease. "Aren't those things like sacred to guys?"

His smile brightens. "Yes, and if you could experience one, you'd agree."

"Mmm, I've experienced something else. I'm sure I can imagine."

Impulsively, as if he's remembering the taste of me, he licks his lips—just in time for Mali to interrupt. She stands in front of the beer pong table, leaning back against it with a glass of wine in her hand.

She's definitely tipsy.

"No joke, your fuck-me eyes are even turning *me* on," she tells us, but keeps her voice low. "I'd cool it if you don't want Cam to realize what's going on."

Ugh, I fucking hate this. But what I hate even more is when Brandon uses Mali as a backboard, bouncing the ball off her back and getting it in the cup. Monty and Brandon high five, while Mali grins in a way that begs me not to hurt her.

"Oops?"

"Mali," I warn.

She quickly moves away from the table. "I'm going, I'm going."

But before I can even drink the beer from the cup they made, I hear the distinct sound of the ball being sunk into the last cup. Looking up at Hayes, he winks.

He made the damn shot and won the blowjob.

And with them failing to get the last two cups, the game is ours.

"Can we do that for every game cup?" Hayes asks as we move all the cups back into place.

My brows furrow as I look at his smug yet eager grin. "My

jaw would never close again."

He stares back at me, chuckling for a second. "I'm not seeing an issue here."

If I pretend to have a muscle spasm and bite him when he cashes in later, is there any way Cam wouldn't find out what we were doing?

OKAY, SOMEHOW MALI GOT better at beer pong, and I have to say—I'm not really happy about it right now. Cam is good. On some days, he's even better than me. But I was counting on the fact that Mali makes one shot for every three she takes on a *good* day. Right now, she's sinking more shots than she's missing.

"Mali, I swear to God," I growl. "You're somewhat decent as my partner, but as Cam's, you start knowing how to play?"

Mali shrugs as Cam makes me want to slap the smirk off his face.

"I saw the mistakes she was making and corrected them," my brother explains. "You've got to work with the cards you've been dealt."

I glare at the two of them. Here I was thinking that Mali took Cam as her partner so I could have Hayes, but she must have really meant it when she said she didn't want to lose at her own party.

But it's *our* party, and one of us is going to lose.

"Relax," Hayes tells me. "It's just a game."

I sigh heavily. "It's not. If we lose against them, Cam will always insist he's the best. That I lost with Mali as my partner, but he didn't. And it's not just me. He'll never let you hear the end of it either."

Hayes takes his shot and makes it with ease. "You're forgetting something."

"What's that?"

"I know his weak spots."

He steps off to the side of the table and nods for me to do the same. Cam sends Hayes a dirty look before aiming the ball. The second it leaves his fingers, my jaw drops. We watch as it flies right over the table and lands in the grass.

He missed.

"Fucking asshole," Cam growls.

But Hayes has never looked hotter to me than he does right now.

MALI AND I WALK Monty out to his car—a blacked-out Range Rover with a sound system that could blow out your eardrums. He wanted to stay later, but he has a breakfast date planned with his mom. Honestly, I was surprised he came at all. I thought he would still be on vacation in Barcelona, but he flew back a day early and came here straight from the airport.

"I had a lot of fun tonight," he tells us. "And now that I'm back, we can hang out more."

"You mean you're not jet setting around the world all summer?" Mali teases.

He snickers and shakes his head. "Nah. I'll be around."

Giving Mali a hug first, he says goodbye to her and then turns to me. I step closer and his arms wrap tightly around me.

"Happy Birthday, Laiken," he says softly. "I'm glad I was able to celebrate it with you."

"Yeah, me too." I step out of his hold, feeling like I'm being watched. "I'll see you later."

He looks me up and down and smiles. "Count on it."

As he drives away, Mali leans into my side. "Does he have a thing for you?"

"I don't think so," I tell her. "I'm pretty sure he's gay."

She snorts, turning around to head back to the party, but we both stop short when we see Hayes standing there, watching us. Watching me. And he does *not* look happy. He starts walking toward the front door of the house, and I know I'm supposed to follow him.

"Have fun with that," Mali says. "I'll try to make sure Cam doesn't come looking for you two."

"Thanks."

She heads for the backyard, and I take a deep breath before walking over to Hayes. The whole way, I rack my brain trying to think of anything that could have irritated him, but I come up empty.

"You okay?" I ask the second I'm close enough.

Instead of answering, he grabs my wrist and pulls me inside. He knows we can't go to my room; that's the first place someone would look for me. So, we end up in the guest room. It's downstairs, tucked in a hallway off the living room. Most days, I forget it's even here.

The moment the door shuts behind us, he presses me up against it and his mouth meets mine in a bruising kiss. It's desperate, like he was going to self-destruct any moment without it. But then he forces himself to back away by pushing off the door.

He's taking a deep breath, almost as if he's trying to calm himself, but it doesn't seem to be working.

"What's it going to take for you to never let another guy put their hands on you again?" he growls.

My brows furrow. "What are you talking about?"

"Out there!" he shouts, pointing toward the window that faces the front yard. "That's what I'm talking about!"

He can't be serious right now. "With Monty? It was a goodbye hug."

Scoffing, he rolls his eyes. "Maybe to you, but I saw him all fucking night, watching you like you were the only thing in the damn room. He wants you!"

"He does not."

"He does," he argues. "And all I wanted to do is rip his hands right off your body. To see him hug you like that...God. I almost lost it. If you hadn't backed away when you did, I may have." He pauses to tug at his hair. "You can't. You can't let him touch you again. I can't handle it."

"Funny, that sounds a lot like boyfriend talk," I say, only a bit sarcastic.

He turns to glare at me. "Is that what this is about? I won't give you a title, so you let some rich douchebag think he can try to get with you?"

"I'm not letting anyone think anything!" I yell, not giving a fuck anymore if someone can hear me. "It was a fucking hug! I hugged half the guys here tonight!"

"Yeah, I know," he sneers. "And watching it was my own personal form of torture. But Moneybags plans on sticking around more than a few pricks you see once a year, and I'm letting you know now, I don't fucking like it."

It's so not the place to be smiling, but I can't help it—and biting my lip does nothing to stifle it. Hayes's chest moves with each heavy breath he takes, but when he sees it, he expels all the air in his lungs.

"What?"

"Nothing," I try.

He takes a step closer. "Nuh-uh. What are you looking at me like that for?"

I shrug and shake my head. "No, it's nothing. I just never took you for the jealous type."

His eyes darken as he comes toward me, putting his hands on the door on either side of me. "I'm not jealous—I'm possessive. There's a difference. And I've told you before. You. Are. Mine."

Smirking, I keep my gaze locked with his while my hands start to undo the button on his jeans. "Well, Mr. Possessive, let me show you just how little you have to worry about."

I arch up and kiss him softly as my hand slides into his boxers. He's already hard and waiting for me. The moment I wrap my fingers around him, he hisses against my mouth.

"Someone's needy," I tease.

But he isn't having it. He grabs the back of my neck and pulls me in, forcing my mouth open and tangling his tongue with mine. I start to slide my hand up and down his shaft, slowly at first, and then speeding up as he moans.

"Laiken," he groans.

I bat my lashes as I look up at him. "What? Is this not how you do it?"

His jaw locks, and he presses his forehead to mine. "You do not want to do that right now, baby. I'm already going to have to stop myself from fucking your mouth."

"Don't," I say simply. "I don't want you to hold yourself back from anything."

He stops breathing for a second, then exhales. "You

don't... You've never done this before. I don't want to hurt you."

"You won't." I drop down to my knees, pooling his pants and boxers around his ankles. "I trust you."

Hayes watches me as I bring his cock to my lips, carefully sucking on the tip and swirling my tongue around it. I'm not a pro by any means; I'm just doing what I saw in the couple porn videos I watched for tutoring. And by the way his eyes fall closed as I take him into my mouth and hollow my cheeks around him, I'd say I'm doing a semi-decent job.

"Fuck," He moans. "That's my good girl."

The praise has me taking him deeper, wanting nothing more than to please him. It's something I never knew I was into until the morning he fingered me in my bedroom. But there's something about him telling me I'm doing a good job that spurs me on.

My hand moves with my mouth, sliding up and down his cock in all the places I'm not currently sucking on. Each time I take him into the back of my throat, his whole body clenches. And when his hand comes down to rest on the top of my head, lacing his fingers into my hair, I know what he wants.

Pulling him out of my mouth with a pop, I lick my lips and look up at him. "Do it."

He looks conflicted as he bites his lip. "If I start to hurt you, you have to tell me."

"Yeah, yeah. Whatever," I say, waving him off. "I just want you to do it. Use my mouth for your pleasure."

Before he can argue it further, I wrap my lips around him once more and swallow around him. Whatever restraints he still had snap in that moment, and he grips my hair tightly, thrusting into my mouth.

It takes a minute to adjust as he drives himself into the back of my throat, but there's something about it that's so fucking hot. I make sure my lips are covering my teeth—thank you, *Cosmopolitan*—and let his dick slide back and forth over my tongue.

"God," he murmurs. "You're fucking perfect, taking all of me in your mouth. You're amazing, baby."

I moan, vibrating my mouth around him, and he reacts by slamming himself into the back of my throat. I choke and gag on his cock, making him freeze.

"Shit, I hurt you, didn't I?"

His dick slips out of my mouth, pulling some saliva with it. "No. Now stop worrying. I want it. Want to choke on your cock."

He smiles lazily as I immediately go back to bobbing my head on him. "You are going to be the death of me, aren't you?"

Instead of answering, I move my hands to the backs of his legs and pull him closer. Without my hold on his dick, he goes even deeper. His head falls forward like he's not even trying to hold it up anymore, and his breathing stutters.

"Touch yourself, baby," he orders as he uses both his hands to control my head. "Let me see how you play with yourself while I fuck your mouth."

I do as I'm told, sliding one hand into my shorts while the other stays on the side of his leg. My finger brushes over my clit, and I jump from the sensitivity. I've wanted him so badly all night that just this has the ability to send me over the edge.

"Good girl," he purrs. "Now, if you want me to stop, tap on my leg three times. Understood?"

I nod in confirmation, and he doesn't waste any time as he pulls my head onto his cock completely. My nose brushes his skin as he buries himself in my throat. It cuts off my air supply, but only for a moment before he pulls back out again.

My fingers move in circles, trying to imitate the way

Hayes does it, and while it feels nothing like him, seeing him using me for his pleasure is enough to make up for it. He fucks my mouth like he's been dying for it. And the way I choke on him is everything—for both of us.

His legs start to shake as he gets close, and the faster he moves, my fingers match his pace. I moan around him as water fills my eyes from gagging on his cock. And when I look up at him, completely wrecked and wanting nothing more than for him to fill my mouth with his cum, his mouth falls open.

He looks so fucking hot as we stare at each other, and when he finally explodes, shooting everything he has down my throat, my orgasm follows—taking me with him right over the edge. I rub myself through it as I swallow every drop he gives me, only letting him slip from my mouth when I know I got it all.

"Holy fuck," he breathes. "Holy fucking fuck."

I take my hand out of my shorts and sit on my heels, looking up at him through hooded lashes. "Did I do okay?"

"Did you..."

He stops and puts his hand out to help me up. I take it and as soon as I stand, he runs his thumb over my cheek.

"You were phenomenal," he tells me. "I'm starting to think there isn't anything you're *not* amazing at."

"I just want to be good for you."

"You are," he says, pressing a kiss to my forehead. "So fucking good for me, all the time."

But the double meaning lingers in the air.

Maybe if I'm good enough, our inevitable end will never come.

Maybe if I'm good enough, he'll choose me.

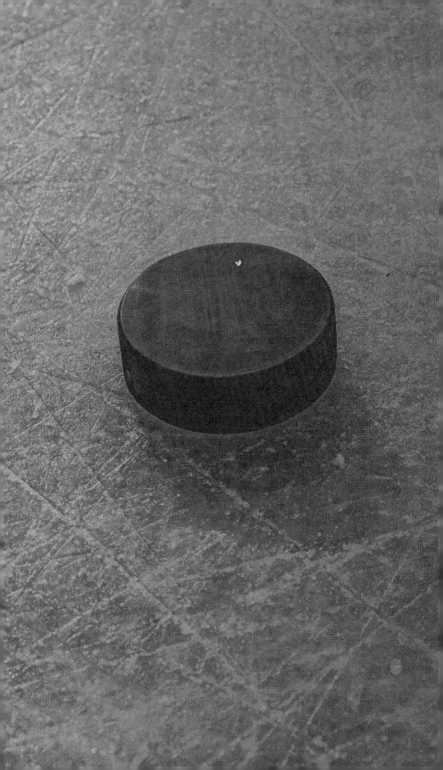

Hayes
CHAPTER TWENTY ONE

I HAVE TO ADMIT, I'M A FUCKING ASSHOLE.

It could have been the alcohol. The age-old saying about a drunk mind speaking a sober heart or whatever the damn thing is. But that's not an excuse. Arguing with Laiken, on her birthday of all days, was uncalled for.

The next day, when I found her in the kitchen before Cam woke up, I apologized for it. She didn't seem to mind, but I did. She deserves so much better than a prick like me. And if she knew that, she would run.

But she stays—and I'm too selfish to tell her to leave.

Pulling up to Mali's house, I check to make sure I have everything we need. The concert is an hour and a half away, and if we have to turn around for any reason, we risk missing it.

Tickets? In the glovebox.

ID? In my wallet.

Bottles of water in the cooler for the drive home, when her throat hurts from singing along? In the back seat.

The front door opens, and Laiken comes out. She looks amazing, but that's nothing new. She's wearing a pair of jeans and a crop top, with some boho jewelry on her head. The flip flops aren't exactly what I'd recommend for a concert, but if it becomes a problem, I'll just let her jump on my back.

"Hey, you," I greet her, kissing her the moment she's close enough.

She melts into me and smiles as I pull away. "Hey."

The lip gloss she has on brings all my attention to her mouth—instantly catapulting me into the other night. Honestly, I thought I was going to have to walk her through it. After all, the last time she tried, she told me to teach her, but I was too eager to be inside of her.

She proved me wrong though, sucking me off and choking on me like she needed it as much as I did. I'm never going to settle down, but fuck. The way she wrapped her lips around my cock had me mentally writing my damn vows.

"Wait!" Mali calls, flying out the front door.

Laiken cringes. "Shit. Run!"

My brows furrow as Laiken goes around me and tries jumping into my truck, but Mali catches up before I can even process what's going on.

"Laiken Rose, you get out here and let me take your picture!" Mali demands, like a soccer mom on the first day of practice.

Laiken's eyes close as she exhales. She climbs out of the truck, grumbling under her breath the whole time. Meanwhile, Mali looks like she enjoys nothing more than embarrassing the shit out of her.

"Last time you ever try trapping me in my closet," Mali tells her with a dark look.

A bark of laughter shoots out of me. "You did what?"

Laiken sighs. "You'll see why."

"What?" Mali asks. "It's just one picture. It's your first date together. It needs to be memorialized."

My lips press into a line, and Laiken gives me an *I told you so* look.

"Mali, I don't—"

"Yeah, I know," she interrupts, waving me off. "This isn't a date. You two are just messing around. It's not serious. Blah, blah blah. I know all the lies you're telling yourself. But

I'm just going to take the picture, and you can thank me for it later, 'kay?"

Laiken grinds her teeth together. "Mali!"

"Smile pretty, darling," Mali coos, holding up her phone.

If I know anything, it's that fighting with Mali is pointless. It's only going to delay us. She's still going to get her way, so we may as well give it to her.

I put my arm around Laiken and pull her in next to me.

"You don't have to—" she starts, but I don't let her continue.

"Just smile."

We both grin, letting Mali take pictures until she feels satisfied. When she's done, Laiken glares at her then climbs back into the truck and shuts the door.

I, on the other hand, step closer to Mali. It may be stupid, showing my cards to the one person who would use them against me if it meant making her best friend happy, but right now I can't find it in me to care.

"Let me see them."

She hands me her phone, and I scroll through the pictures. Once I pick out the best one, I send it to myself. The vibration in my pocket tells me I received it.

"Thanks," I tell her, handing her phone back.

A smug grin appears on her face. "Nice. Very *messing around* of you."

I flip her off as I walk away and over to the driver's side of my truck. When I get in, Laiken is looking at me curiously.

"What was that about?" she asks.

Leaning over, I kiss her just because I can. "Don't worry your pretty little head about it. You have your ID?"

"Yes," she answers. "We should stop by the police department. My cop friend would be so proud of me."

I chuckle. "Maybe next time."

As I put the truck in drive, my phone vibrates once more.

I pull it out of my pocket to see a second message from Mali. And when I open it, it's a picture of the kiss I just gave her with a small note underneath.

Thought you might want this one too. 😘

I roll my eyes and save both photos, then type out my response.

Thanks. Now delete them all from your phone.

Ugh. I don't know what she sees in you.

Join the club.

"Everything okay?" Laiken questions.

I nod, slipping my phone back into my pocket. "Yep. Ready to go see Thomas Rhett?"

"Yes," she says, beaming. "I have a playlist made for the ride there and everything."

It takes everything I have not to cringe. Nothing against him. I'm sure he's great. Country music just isn't my thing. But it makes Laiken happy, and that *is* my thing, so I smile happily and pull out onto the road.

"Sounds great, babe."

Chapter 21

THE WHOLE HOUR AND a half ride is spent in the best way possible—listening to Laiken sing along to the music, cracking jokes with each other, and laughing. I think that's part of why I can't seem to get enough, no matter how much I'm around her. She has this way of making me feel like I'm hanging out with one of my best friends. There's no judgment, no anxiety. It's just us, enjoying our time together.

The only lull in the drive is when she starts talking about what her, Mali, and Monty got up to yesterday. Apparently, Mr. Moneybags had the brilliant idea of bringing them to lunch at one of the most expensive places in town, followed by a shopping spree where Laiken bought the outfit she's wearing. I have half a mind to ask if she's the one that paid, or if he did, but the last thing I want right now is to start an argument.

We pull into the parking lot, and I show my pass to the gate attendant. She scans it, telling me which way to go. The whole place is swarmed with people decked out in country attire. Seriously, if you're looking for a guy in a cowboy hat or a girl in boots, just come to one of these things. You're practically guaranteed to leave happy.

We're directed into a parking spot, and I put the truck in park, turning to Laiken. The smile on her face almost makes me second guess what I'm about to say, but I have to. She's not going to like it, and I will hate to wipe that smile off her face, but just being here is a risk in itself.

"Listen," I tell her softly. "We have to be careful. And by careful, I mean no PDA."

Sure enough, she stops smiling to roll her eyes and sigh. "We're literally over an hour and a half away, and Cam is all the way back in Calder Bay."

"I know, but someone else might be here. He's a popular performer."

Leaning over the center console, she kisses me softly and

then grabs the door handle. "There are so many points I could make right now, but fine. No PDA."

"Thank you," I say, but what she doesn't know is that there's a part of me that hates the idea too.

THE SEATS ARE AMAZING, right in the middle of center stage and as close as we can be without being in the pit. Laiken looks around in awe as she takes everything in. Watching her and seeing the wonder in her eyes, I'm already mentally kicking myself for the no PDA rule.

I bought the tickets thinking she would take Mali with her. The two of them are constantly blasting his music in Mali's car. I pictured them both driving here, all dolled up, and having the time of their lives as they jumped around and sang along. But as much as I may have fought against coming with her, I'm really glad I'm here to see this.

No matter what show is put on that stage tonight, it won't even compare to the view beside me.

Chapter 21

OKAY, I HAVE A confession.

I don't completely hate the concert.

The crowd goes wild when he comes out, and they only seem to get louder as they sing along to every song. Laiken sways with the music, her mouth moving with each word. And as he starts singing "Craving You," I feel her hand brush against mine.

It's not completely breaking the rules, but it's walking the line. Still, I can't find it in me to stop her, even as her fingers tangle with mine. Since the second we left my truck, I've wanted to touch her again. To feel her body pressed against mine.

As I listen to the lyrics, I realize exactly why she chose this song to test my limits. Every single word is spot on—hitting its mark dead in the center. It's exactly how I feel about her.

I make a mental note to add it to my playlist later.

The playlist she'll never know exists if I have anything to say about it.

While the concert goes on and he moves into another song, I notice the guys on the other side of Laiken keep looking over at her. If the way they glance between the two of us is anything to go by, they're trying to find out if we're together or not.

And if there's anything that will get me to break all my damn rules, it's a couple pricks checking out my girl.

Without second guessing myself, I slip my hand into her back pocket—pressing a kiss to the top of her head and glaring at the guys who can't seem to realize the stage is in front of them. Laiken is too into the concert to know anything is going on, or that I'm staking a claim I don't actually have, but I feel much better as they realize she's not free game and take their attention off her.

And since I've already damned my own rule to hell, I may as well enjoy it.

I move her so she's standing in front of me and wrap my arms around her waist. She leans back against me, acting like it's no big deal, but the pink tint to her cheeks tells a different story.

OUT OF ALL THE things I expected tonight, getting metaphorically punched in the chest by another one of his songs was not on the list. But as he starts singing "Marry Me," that's exactly what happens.

The whole time, I can't stop picturing it.

Laiken in a white dress, clutching a bouquet with one hand and her dad's arm with the other.

Her hair done all nice with a veil placed perfectly on top.

And her walking down the aisle to someone who isn't me.

Just the thought alone puts a pit in the middle of my stomach. It's not like I wouldn't be there. Her brother is my best friend. Even if she tried not to invite me, there would be no excuse she could give him.

I'd have no choice but to stand there and watch as she promises to spend the rest of her life with someone who probably won't even realize just how lucky he is.

And it would absolutely fucking destroy me.

The song comes to an end, and I find myself pulling Laiken in impossibly closer. I know there may be a time where that becomes my reality. I'd be naive to think she'll just be happy with our *situationship* forever. But that doesn't mean I'm not going to take advantage of the time when she *is* mine.

It's everything I'm going to hold onto when she goes off and finds her prince charming, and I'm left remembering the girl who made me feel things I didn't know existed.

THE CONCERT COMES TO an end, and it's all going too smoothly. I've said it before and I'll say it again, good luck is not something I have. It's never on my side, like the universe enjoys laughing at my misfortune. So, it's no surprise when Laiken wants to stop at the merch stand before we leave and the girl beside me starts crossing boundaries she should really avoid.

"You should get that hat," she says, pointing to a gray and blue snapback. "It would look really good on you."

"Thanks," I say dismissively. "I'll think about it."

Hints must not be her strong suit, because she giggles and grabs my arm. "I'm serious. How about this, we'll trade. I'll do the world a favor and buy you the hat, and you give me your phone number in return."

There is literally no part of me that's interested. Don't get me wrong, she's attractive, but she's not my focus right now. And the one who is looks ready to level this chick.

"Thank you," I tell her, trying not to be rude. "But I'll pass."

Removing my arm from her grip, I walk away and pull Laiken with me before she really *does* get arrested this time. There's an obvious shift in her mood, and maybe I shouldn't ask her about it, but it's a long ride home—one that will only be longer if it's spent in silence.

Besides, we've had a good night. Why let something as small as this ruin it?

Laiken is walking a couple steps ahead of me when I stop her by grabbing her hand. She turns around, looking at me expectantly but saying nothing.

"What's wrong?" I question, even though I know the answer.

I need to hear it from her, but she's not going to make it easy on me.

"Nothing," she lies.

"Come on," I plead, pulling her closer. "Just talk to me."

She shakes her head and looks anywhere but at me, and it strikes a nerve. If it were her asking me, she would press until she got the answer. So that's exactly what I plan on doing.

"I'd really rather not spend the entire drive home with you pissed at me."

Her eyes roll as she scoffs. "Fine. I'll take an Uber then."

Spinning on her heels, she takes out her phone and goes to walk away but I stop her. No way in hell is she getting in a car with some random ass driver and expecting them to take her the hour and a half home instead of to some abandoned building they run a sex trafficking ring out of.

Plucking her phone out of her grasp only angers her more, but I don't care. She's going to talk to me whether she likes it or not.

"Give me my phone," she demands.

"No. Not until you tell me what's wrong."

"You know what's wrong!" Her voice carries enough for people to look over at us, but that's not my concern right now.

Feeling embarrassed, she turns to walk away, but I didn't let her before and I'm still not going to now.

"Stop," I growl. "Just tell me what the hell I did that has you all pissed off."

"I don't know, H," she snaps. "Maybe it has to do with the girl that was just all over you."

I snort at her choice of words. "She touched my arm. That hardly qualifies as all over me."

But she's not amused. "Whatever. Call it what you want. I didn't like her hitting on you."

Smiling the same way she did the night of her birthday, I raisc my brows at her. "Now who's the jealous one?"

"Says the guy who literally set another guy's number on fire," she counters.

"That was different. I didn't like him."

"Well, I don't like her."

What? "Why not?"

She throws her hands in the air. "Because she hit on you! Keep up!"

Laughter bubbles out of me, but Laiken clearly doesn't

find it funny. She turns away from me, and when I try to come closer, she pushes me away from her. It's the first time she's ever done that, and I hope it's the last, because I don't like it.

There are enough people telling me I shouldn't be anywhere near her, me included. I don't need her saying it, too.

"Come on," I say hopelessly. "What did you want me to say? *Sorry, don't touch me because my secret girlfriend is right there mentally burning you alive?*"

She tries to hold onto her bad mood, but it quickly dissipates as she smirks. It's such a fast shift that it threatens to give me whiplash. And the way she looks at me has me questioning what the hell changed in the last three seconds.

"What?" I ask.

Taking her bottom lip between her teeth, she can't seem to contain herself. "You just called me your girlfriend."

Of course she caught that.

I don't even think it's the first time I've done it, but it *is* the first time I've done it out loud. By all definitions of the word, she is my girlfriend. It's not like I've even thought about hooking up with someone else from the moment we started blurring the lines between us. But even with as happy as it makes her, I can't help it.

I need to fuck with her about it, especially after the argument we just had.

"Yeah," I say, pretending to be confused. "You're a girl who is my friend."

The smile drops right off her face, and she goes to storm away, but I expected it. Hell, she's done it enough in the last five minutes alone.

Not giving a shit anymore, I grab her wrist and pull her back. She spins around and crashes into my chest, looking up just in time for me to kiss her in the middle of the crowd.

She gasps against my mouth, but I use it as an opportunity to deepen the kiss. Her tongue moves against mine as my fingers lace into her hair to hold her in place. It's everything I need after that argument. Even as short as it was, every single second was miserable.

I can add *her not wanting to be around me* to the list of things I can't seem to handle.

As we break the kiss to catch our breath, I keep my forehead against hers.

"You may not have the title, but that doesn't change the fact that you're the only one who has my attention."

She smiles and goes to kiss me again, but just as her lips brush against mine, someone clears their throat.

My first thought is Cam, and I mentally ask God for forgiveness. If I'm about to die, now's the time to do it. But as we look over at the culprit, we find Monty standing there, looking disapproving and heartbroken all at the same time.

Something tells me this isn't going to go over well.

Laiken

CHAPTER TWENTY TWO

The moment was perfect. Not that I thought Hayes was hooking up with anyone other than me. Every chance we get, we seem to be together. But there was always that thought in the back of my mind. So, hearing him confirm that I'm the only one, it made me come alive in more ways than I thought it would.

We were in our own little bubble, and the crowd of people walking all around us didn't exist.

And then Monty popped the bubble.

He stands there, looking at us like he just cracked the case. I'm half expecting Hayes to back away—not wanting us to get caught and all that. But instead, he puts his arm around my waist and pulls me into him.

"Can we help you, Rollins?" he asks.

Monty snickers. "You know, I thought there was something up between you two at the party, but I wasn't sure until now."

"That's why you couldn't stop checking her out, right?" Hayes counters.

I turn to glare at him. The attitude is uncalled for. But what Monty says next catches me even more off guard.

"Does Cam know you're stabbing him in the back?" he spits. "I'm guessing not, since you keep your hands to yourself while he's around. Though that's probably better for her sake. Wouldn't want people to find out she's slumming it with you."

Hayes releases me and takes a step toward him. "What the fuck did you just say to me?"

I jump into action, getting myself in front of Hayes before he gets to Monty. Right now, it's a situation I can control. Monty is my friend, and I can try talking some sense into him. But if Hayes gets his hands on him, we're going to have a lot worse things to deal with than my brother finding out.

"Stop," I tell him. "You don't want to do this."

"You should listen to her," Monty sneers.

Hayes goes to move toward him again as I whip my head around. "Will you shut the fuck up?"

Monty rolls his eyes and looks away, but my attention is on Hayes. I move my hands to his face in an attempt to calm him down.

"Let me handle this," I say softly. "Go. I'll meet you in the truck. Okay?"

The expression on his face and the death glare he's shooting in Monty's direction tells me he wants to argue it. He'd love nothing more than to rough him up a bit. But he knows he can't.

There would be no probation for him like Cam got. Monty's dad wouldn't stop until Hayes was behind bars.

Without saying anything, he bends down and presses his lips to mine. I know better to think this kiss has anything to do with me. It's all for Monty's benefit. But no good will come from me pushing him away right now.

Not when he's all enraged and full of possessive testosterone.

Breaking the kiss, he gives Monty one more dark look and then heads toward the parking lot. I watch as he pushes his way through the crowd, and once I know it's not just a way for him to get to Monty without risking hurting me in the process, I exhale.

"Let's go," I growl at Monty, grabbing his wrist and pulling him with me over to a spot less busy than the exit.

He may be my friend, but no part of what just happened was acceptable. And if it came down to a choice, between him and Hayes, it would be Hayes. Hands down. Every single day.

"Well, that explains why *he* hates me," he jokes.

I run my fingers through my hair as I scoff. "Can you blame him? What the fuck was that?"

"Oh, come on," Monty argues. "He started that shit. And I wasn't checking you out. When you grow up the way I have, you learn to watch everyone around you. It's a way of keeping my guard up."

"Even so, the remark you made about Cam was not fucking cool! You have no idea what's going on between us."

He snorts. "Yeah, I do. Laiken, he treats you like you're his property. Why else would he murder me with his eyes every time I'm around? He genuinely believes no other guy is even allowed to look at you."

"You've been around him all of like twice," I sass. "That's hardly enough to judge, so don't talk about him like you know him."

Seeing how worked up I am, he sighs. "Okay, fine. But what's the plan here? You're just going to stay in Calder Bay? Be Hayes's dirty little secret for the rest of your life? That's never going to be enough for you, and it shouldn't be. You're so much better than that."

It's not something I haven't thought of before. Hell, sometimes it keeps me up at night. The more I fall for him, the more I know it'll hurt when it ends. But that doesn't mean a part of me isn't holding out hope that he'll change his mind and want to be with me like I want to be with him.

Out in the open, not hiding in the shadows.

Kissing me as we pass each other in between work and

hockey practice, without worrying about who might be able to see us.

Just him wanting me to be his, no matter what it takes.

"I know," I agree. "But I need you to trust me and stay out of this. I know what I'm doing."

"Do you, though? Do you really?" he presses. "What happens if this doesn't go the way you want? What if it ends badly? Are you going to be able to handle seeing him all the time after he breaks your heart?"

"I don't know!" I snap. "I don't know what will happen or how I will feel if or when this ends. What I *do* know is that he makes me happy. Now you can either accept that and keep what you saw today to yourself, or you can tell Cam and we'll deny it." His face drops, but I'm not done. "I'll have Mali back me up, and Cam will think you're just a bored rich kid who wanted to cause some drama."

"Laiken," he breathes.

I shrug. "Go ahead. But if you tell him, just know that I will *never* speak to you again."

The pain in his eyes is evident, but I'm not about to back down. And the second he realizes that, he softens. He drops his head and nods.

"Okay, I'm sorry," he says. "I didn't realize things were that serious. I thought he was just someone who was taking advantage of you. But you're right. You know what you're doing, and if you say you have a handle on this, I believe you. Your secret is safe with me."

Relief floods through me. "Thank you."

I wasn't bluffing. If he had told Cam, we would instantly go into damage control mode. And chances are, we would get away with it. But it would effectively end things between Hayes and me. Cam would start paying too much attention and Hayes wouldn't refuse to risk it.

"Should I, uh..." He winces. "Should I go apologize to Hayes?"

"Not unless you want to become roadkill," I tell him, only half kidding. "If I know him like I think I do, he'll run you over before you even open your mouth."

Monty chuckles nervously. "Fair enough. I guess I deserve that."

"You think?"

A smile forces its way through, and the two of us laugh—lightening the mood. I'm sure Monty has taken self-defense classes his entire life, but I've seen Hayes get into fights during hockey games. And that's on skates.

I can only imagine the damage he would do without having to worry about the ice beneath his feet.

"I hope he's good to you," Monty tells me.

My grin widens as I nod, thinking about how much I loved having his arms wrapped around me as we watched Thomas Rhett perform. "He is. He really is."

"Good," he says happily, but there's a hint of sadness there. "That's really good."

As we head toward the exit, I nudge him with my elbow. "Don't worry. There's a guy out there for you, too."

His brows furrow, and I realize I probably shouldn't have said anything until he came out to me. For all I know, he hasn't come out to anyone yet. But at least this way, he knows I'm not judging him for it.

"I'll see you tomorrow?" I ask as it comes time to head in different directions.

He nods. "You bet. You're going to love this place. It has the best mimosas."

"Sweet. I'll make sure to bring my fake ID."

"Don't bother. No one is going to card you when you're with me."

I chuckle. "Lifestyle of the rich and the famous, right?"

He pulls his sunglasses off his head and puts them on his face. "You know it."

Just like that, he's gone—walking over to the blacked-out SUV that has been waiting for him in a VIP area. I take a deep breath and head over to Hayes's truck. He's sitting on the tailgate when I get there, smoking a cigarette.

"It's all good," I tell him. "He isn't going to say anything."

He hops down and drops the cigarette, putting it out with his foot. As he exhales the smoke into the air, he pulls me in and kisses me in a way that takes my breath away.

Maybe he was just as nervous as I was—knowing this could be the end of us and not wanting it to end. Maybe there's really a part of him that wants me just as much as I want him.

I break the kiss and pull my head back to look at him. "You're such a caveman."

"You know it, baby," he says, pecking my lips once more. "Me, Tarzan. You, Jane."

Snorting, I scrunch my nose. "I'm not sure if being the king of the jungle makes him a caveman."

"Wouldn't know. I never watched it."

My jaw drops as he kisses the tip of my nose and releases me, closing the tailgate.

"Okay," I say decisively. "I know what we're doing the next chance we get."

We climb into the truck, and he turns the key in the ignition. "You mean, as long as Moneybags keeps his mouth shut."

"He will," I assure him, but he doesn't look convinced.

As he pulls out into the traffic all waiting to leave, he looks over at me. "He still wants you."

I can't help the laugh that bubbles out of me. "He's gay!"

"Yeah, okay," he says sarcastically. "And I'm becoming a monk."

"Are you?" I tease. "That's great. I'm sure your mom will be really proud of you." Turning to look at him, I smirk deviously. "Though, I guess that means I can't give you road head on the way home."

And the way his head whips over in my direction and he almost rear-ends the car in front of us has me laughing until my stomach hurts.

HAYES DROPS ME OFF at Mali's so I can get my car, but I decide to go inside first. She may have pissed me off earlier, with her whole *I need to get a picture* bullshit, but she also spent the whole day cooped up inside so no one knew she wasn't with me at the concert.

Besides, now I have a picture of Hayes and me.

Walking through the door, I say hello to Mali's mom and head upstairs. Mali is in her room, lying on her bed and scrolling on her computer. She looks up and smiles as I come in.

"You're back. How was the concert?"

"Amazing," I grumble, falling face first onto her bed.

She snorts. "Well damn, babe. Try not to sound too thrilled. I may get jealous."

I roll over and rest my arm on my forehead. "No, the concert was great. It was *after* the concert that sucked."

Her brows furrow as she stops what she's doing to look at me. "Do I need to hurt him?"

"If the *him* you're referring to is Hayes, then no."

"Who else would I be referring to?"

"Montgomery." I sigh heavily. "He caught us kissing at the concert and threatened to tell Cam."

"No!" she gasps. "Did Hayes slaughter him? Did anyone see him do it? Hold on, let me change and I'll help you hide the body."

I giggle as she actually starts to get up from her bed. "Mal, stop. No one died. Though, I can't promise someone won't if he outs us to Cam."

"Do you think he will?"

"I don't know," I shrug. "He said he won't, but I don't really know him well enough to trust him."

She hums as she thinks about it. "You should be fine. He's from the high society world. They don't care about the bullshit we deal with."

I nod, knowing she's right, but he really seemed to care while we were standing there. It was wrong of me to threaten him the way I did. He was only trying to look out for me. But when it comes to what I have with Hayes, there are no lengths I won't go to in order to protect it.

Besides, Monty hasn't been in my life long enough to *talk some sense into me* or whatever he was attempting to do.

"Yeah," I exhale. "You're right. I'm sure there's nothing to worry about."

Mali shuts her laptop and rolls over, resting her head on my shoulder. "And if there is, I have your back. I don't care how much money he has. You're my girl."

"Way to not sound like a total gold-digger," I tease.

She groans and pushes herself away from me. "It's not like I'm dating him. And if spoiling his friends is his idea of a good time, who am I to stop him?"

Chuckling, I grab the nearest pillow and hit her with it.

Lord help the man that ends up with her.

Laiken

CHAPTER TWENTY THREE

THINGS ARE TENSE FOR A COUPLE OF DAYS. IT'S like every time Cam's phone goes off, I wonder if it's Monty. Even as Mali and I went to brunch with Monty, I sat there the whole time, wondering if he was going to spill my secret. But so far, nothing has changed.

Cam still doesn't know.

Monty is acting like everything is normal.

And I'm still falling deeper in love with Hayes, even if it means my heart could get shattered into a million tiny pieces.

It's not like I can help it. I've known that from the start. When it comes to him, I'm hopeless. All I can do is hope that he doesn't end up breaking my heart after all.

I WALK INTO THE surf shop, holding an ice cream cone I bought before I came in. Hayes looks up from the counter and he smiles when he sees me.

"Hey," he greets me, glancing at the time. "You know I don't get off work for another hour, right?"

"Yeah, I know," I tell him. "But Mali couldn't drop me off later, so I had to come a bit early."

His brows raise as he sees right through my bullshit, and after only a few seconds, I cave and roll my eyes.

"Fine. I missed you," I grumble. "Sue me."

He chuckles, leaning over the counter to kiss me before going back to what he was doing. Meanwhile, I sit on the stool beside him.

It only takes a few minutes before I start to realize that getting this on a cone was probably a bad idea. It's melting faster than I can eat it, and every time it drips, I have to catch it with my tongue to keep from making a mess.

All the licking and slurping I'm doing must go straight to Hayes's dick because he drops his head and laughs quietly. He turns to look back at me, but that was probably a bad idea on his part. Sticking my tongue out, I drag it up the ice cream and wrap my mouth around the tip.

"What?" I ask him innocently.

He narrows his eyes at me. "You're cruel, did you know that?"

The corner of my lips raises as I smirk. "And you have a one-track mind. Did *you* know *that*?"

Shaking his head, he goes back to focusing on the computer. "Sure, I'm the problem here. Has nothing to do with you blowing an ice cream cone like it's your favorite cock or anything."

"I mean, I'd much rather do the real thing," I tease. "But he's busy being a working man and all."

He closes his eyes and whines. "That's not fair. Why do you have to torture me like that?"

"Because it's fun," I quip.

"Mm-hm," he says as he gets up and starts walking toward the back. "We'll see how *fun* you think it is later."

Chapter 23

WITH THE SHOP CLOSED up and two surfboards lying in the bed of Hayes's truck, the two of us head off to a remote beach. It's the same one we came to the night we finally had sex for the first time. And it's just as empty now as it was then.

It's not like there is anything wrong with this beach. For a while, it's where all the locals would come when the tourists would take over the main ones. But when the seabed shifted one year after a rough storm, the waves made it more worth it for the surfers to deal with the crowds.

Fortunately for us, this empty beach is exactly what we're looking for.

We carry the surfboards across the sand, setting them down so Hayes can wax them up. Meanwhile, I pull a towel out of my bag and spread it out for somewhere to sit. Removing my shirt and shorts, I start to apply sunscreen, when I realize Mali isn't here to do my back.

"Babe?" He looks up from the board at the sound of my voice. "Mind putting this on my back for me?"

Smirking, he comes over and takes the sunscreen from me. "Rubbing my hands all over you? How could I ever say no to that?"

At first touch, it's cold against my skin, but the more he rubs it in, the better it feels. He starts massaging my back, and his lips move to my neck—kissing the spots he knows I'm the most sensitive in.

"One-track mind," I remind him.

He hums, moving his hands to my stomach and pulling me back against him. "Are you sure that's a bad thing?"

No, because it's never a bad thing. But I've heard enough horror stories from Mali about having sex on the beach. The sand gets in places you never want it to be, and it's just not all it's cracked up to be.

But God, it's so tempting to just fall right into him when he's touching me like this.

Forcing myself to move, I pull his hands away and stand up. "Come swimming with me."

He lets out a mix between a laugh and a groan as I start to walk down toward the water, but when I turn around, he's still in the place I left him.

"Are you coming?" I call.

He forces himself up and grumbles under his breath. "I fucking hope so soon."

"I heard that," I say through a chuckle, and the determined look in his eyes tells me I should run.

Hayes takes off, starting to chase me as I run into the water, and I make the rookie mistake of looking behind me. His arms wrap around my waist, lifting me up as I squeal. The water is cold on my feet, and as he tosses me into the air, I prepare myself for the blow.

If anyone saw us splashing each other and playing around, they would probably think we're just some loved up couple. Because when we're alone, there's no reason to assume anything different.

He holds me the way a boyfriend would.

Kisses me the way a boyfriend would.

And sometimes, I let myself pretend that there aren't a million obstacles in the way of us being that couple.

We stop to catch our breath as Hayes dives under the water. When he comes up, he moves his head in a way that moves his hair to one side and sends water flying. It really shouldn't look as hot as it does, but when he smirks and comes toward me, my heart feels like it does a flip.

"Hey," he says as he wraps his arms around me.

I stare up at him, unable to keep from smiling if I tried. "Hi."

Bending down, he covers my mouth with his own—completely unaware of what he does to me. I arch up on my tiptoes and revel in the feel of his hands on my back, pulling me into him as closely as possible.

"Are there any sharks in this water?" I ask, suddenly remembering the *would you rather* question I gave him at the airfield.

He hums and looks around. "I don't think so, no. Just really big crabs."

Okay, there is no greater fear I have than my feet being attacked by something I can't see. Have you ever been pinched by one of those things? I have, and it fucking hurts. So, it's no surprise when I yelp, jumping up and wrapping my legs around Hayes's waist.

It isn't until I feel his hard cock pressing against me that I realize what just happened.

"I just played right into your hand, didn't I?"

He chuckles. "You're not the only one who can use tricks to get what you want."

I know what he's referring to—the night at billiards when I had him thinking I had no idea how to play pool. Not going to lie, I had every intention of kicking his ass that night, but the way it played out was so much better. And I still got him to come around again.

It was a win-win. But I'm not so sure I love my own tactics being used against me.

"You're mean," I tell him.

He chuckles, ghosting his lips across mine. "Should I remind you of the ice cream cone from earlier?"

Instead of answering, I close the gap between us and let my tongue dance with his. He groans into it, and his hands on my ass hold me up as I use my legs to pull him closer. I grind against his dick, and the more I do, the more turned on I get.

"Fuck me," I breathe. "I want you to fuck me. Right here. Just like this."

The corners of his lips raise as they're still pressed against mine. "Gladly."

He unties half of my bathing suit, making it fall out of the way and hang on my one leg, and the thought of a condom doesn't even cross my mind until he's slipping inside of me.

Our grip on each other tightens. It feels so much better like this, with nothing in between us. I can feel every inch, every ridge. And if it feels this good for me, I can only imagine how much better it feels for him.

His breathing stutters and his whole body jerks as he bottoms out. He sucks my bottom lip into his mouth and groans. And when he releases it, I throw my head back and start to bounce on his cock.

"Goddamn," he moans against my skin. "You feel fucking incredible like this. Always take me so well."

His fingers dig into the flesh of my ass, gripping and kneading as I slide myself on and off his cock. With each movement, his hands slide closer to the center. And when his finger presses against my hole there, I feel every part of me tense up.

"Relax, baby," he says softly. "Keep your attention on me. On the way my cock feels, completely raw inside your pussy."

I do as he says, and as he starts to push his finger in, I didn't anticipate how good it feels. It's just one finger, but somehow, it's so much more intense. Between his dick being deep inside of me and the way he slowly moves his finger in and out, I feel so fucking full of him.

"Holy shit," I moan.

"Fuck. I can feel myself inside of you," he tells me, his voice cracking. "I can't wait until the day I claim this hole, too." I whimper slightly, and he smirks. "Yeah, you'd like that, wouldn't you? Being such a good girl for me as I fill your ass with my cum."

"Yeah," I pant, pressing a kiss to his shoulder. "It scares me, but I want it. I want all of it with you."

"Oh, don't worry. You're going to get it all. There's not an inch of your body I won't claim," he growls. "Going to make you wish every guy you ever fuck is me."

"There is never going to be anyone else. No one can make me feel the way you do. I'm ruined. You've ruined me. Nothing will ever feel as good as this." I may be rambling, but not a thing coming out of my mouth is a lie. "I'm yours. Only yours."

He starts to take over, slamming me onto his cock as he fingers my ass. "You're damn right you are, baby. All fucking mine."

The pressure builds in my core, growing faster with every time I feel him deep inside of me. All I can hear is the sound of the water sloshing, mixing with his heavy breathing and my quiet moans. And as my orgasm rips straight through me, I bite down on his shoulder.

"Yes," he growls, removing his finger for a better grip on my waist. "Fuck, yes."

With a few more harsh thrusts into me, he pulls me off him at the last second, letting his cum spill into the water around us. I kiss his neck and taste the salt on his skin as we both calm down.

"What if a fish gets pregnant with your baby?" I ask, thinking about the millions of sperm that are in one drop of cum. “Wait, they can’t like swim back up me or anything, can they?”

He snorts and starts to fix my bathing suit for me. “If they can, that is one determined sperm. We’d be the parents of the next Bill Gates.”

It’s a joke. I know that. There’s no confusion there. But even the simple thought of us being parents together, raising a kid with him by my side, it releases butterflies in my stomach—fluttering around with their false hope and pointless dreams.

Standing up, I force myself to think of anything else. “Okay, I’m ready to try surfing now.”

“I don’t know, Lai,” he says, looking unsure. “There’s a pretty strong current, and the water is crashing pretty hard against the rocks. Maybe we should go surfing another day.”

I cross my arms over my chest. “Are you underestimating me?”

“No,” he shakes his head. “I know better than that. I’m just not sure it’s the best idea.”

“Nuh-uh.” I walk backward, still facing him but moving toward the shore. “You promised me surfing. We’re going surfing.”

He exhales, giving in and coming with me to get the boards, and I start to wonder what else he would be willing to do for me.

SPOILER ALERT: I SHOULD have listened.

We should've laid on the beach, talking about anything we wanted and sharing lazy kisses. But I insisted on going surfing. And to make matters worse, I was so determined to impress him, so focused on looking good, that I put myself in danger.

I realize all this as I hear Hayes scream my name, just in time for me to see the rocks before I fall off the board. The water tosses me around without mercy. I can't even tell which way the surface is. And when I feel something slice into my side, all the air I had left leaves my lungs.

The likelihood that I could die right now passes through my mind. I wonder what Hayes would tell Cam. Would he be honest and tell him what was going on between us? Would he lie and just say he was giving me surfing lessons? Would Mali kill him before he would tell him anything? There's so many questions I don't know the answers to.

Time moves so slowly as my panic settles. It's not that I *want* to die. It's more accepting my fate. Just as I start to feel like I'm losing consciousness, I feel two arms wrapping around me and pulling me to the surface.

I inhale deeply the second I reach the air, only to break into a coughing fit. Hayes carries me to the shoreline, and I collapse onto my hands and knees. Every breath hurts my chest, but it doesn't compare to the pain on my side.

"Are you okay?" Hayes asks, still trying to catch his breath.

I nod. "I think so."

But as I turn to look at the damage, I hiss. The gash that goes from my back toward my side is probably four inches long, and it looks nasty. Blood drips down my body and Hayes's eyes widen as I turn to show him.

He stands up and extends his hand toward me. "I have a first aid kit in the truck. Let's go."

I'm a little lightheaded, feeling everything spin as I stand, but Hayes holds on to me as we walk across the beach. He puts down the tailgate and grabs the first aid kit from the back.

"You're bleeding, too," I tell him, seeing the cut on his leg.

He shakes his head. "I'm not concerned with that right now."

"I am!"

But he doesn't listen. Instead, he takes extra time cleaning me up and closing it with butterfly strips before covering the whole thing with gauze. Then and only then does he work on his own.

"How did you get that, anyway?" I ask.

He answers like it's no big deal. "I dove into the water the second I saw you go under."

It shouldn't surprise me. Of course, he would risk his life to save mine. That's just how he is. But the fact that he tried to talk me out of surfing and I pushed the issue makes me feel bad.

We both got hurt, and it's no one's fault but my own.

Before I can think up a way to apologize, he closes the first aid kit and opens the passenger side door.

"Get in," he tells me. "I'll go get our stuff."

I do as he says, sitting in the truck and watching as Hayes goes down to grab my bag, the towel, and the wax he brought. As far as the surfboards go, though, they're currently floating out to sea. The cord ripped off my ankle at some point while I was flipping around like I was in a washing machine. And I'm guessing Hayes took his off so it didn't keep him from getting to me.

He comes back and tosses everything into the back seat before climbing into the truck.

"Are you okay?" he asks me again.

I nod. "Are you?"

Starting the truck, he puts it into reverse to pull out of the space. "I am now."

My mind runs wild with all the things he could mean by that, but I don't think I'm in the place to ask him about it. Not right now, anyway. So, I lean my head against the window and watch all of the boats out in the distance.

THANKFULLY, HE ISN'T MAD. I did, however, have to hear him lecture me on how he knows the ocean a lot better than I do, and how next time I should listen when he tells me something is a bad idea. He's not wrong, either. But ultimately, he's just glad I'm okay.

Now if this cut could heal, that would be great.

The first time I showered hurt like a bitch. The warm water getting in and cleansing it was necessary, but fuck. It burned so bad. It also wasn't easy to apply new butterfly strips and a big Band-Aid the way Hayes did it, but I managed.

It's been three days and I've managed to keep it a secret from everyone by wearing t-shirts bigger than I usually opt for. It works pretty well…until I move a certain way at Mali's without thinking.

"What the fuck is that?" she says. "Please don't tell me you got Hayes's name tattooed on you."

Monty scoffs. "Jesus Christ. You let him brand you?"

"Would that surprise you?" Mali asks him. "Because it wouldn't surprise me."

I roll my eyes and wince as I pull the bandage half off. "I didn't let anyone brand me. It was a surfing accident."

They both cringe as they look at it, and I realize it's not nearly as healed as I hoped it would be by now. Covering it back up, I drop my shirt and sigh.

"I fell off the board and got tossed around," I explain. "Hayes got the same kind of cut on his leg jumping in to save me. There must have been a sharp rock beneath the water or something."

Mali smirks. "Was this before or after you had sex?"

We haven't talked about that day, but she knows me well. "After."

Monty snorts as Mali rolls her eyes. "I swear, you two must have some sort of exhibitionist kink or something with the amount you two fuck in public places."

"We do not," I scoff. "First of all, we were in the water and no one else was around. And second, we have to work with the opportunities we have. It's not like we can just fuck like rabbits at my house."

"You could if he just told your brother about you two," Monty says.

I turn to glare at him, and he puts his hands up in surrender. But while he may be afraid of my wrath, Mali isn't.

"He does have a point, you know," she says.

But honestly, it's not something I'm willing to hear right now. The way things are right now—it's working for us. There isn't the pressure of everyone knowing our business or cracking on us for it. I'm not fighting with my brother or worrying that he's going to get pissed at Hayes every time I'm not in the best mood.

Don't get me wrong, I would love nothing more than to be an actual couple, but it's not as important to me as it once was. Not when he treats me like I'm the only one that matters when we're together.

Judge me for being okay with the circumstances, I don't care.

I'm happy.

I go to answer Mali when my phone vibrates in front of me, and I see it's from Hayes. A smile makes its way to my face as I open it.

How's your day going, baby?

The giddiness I feel from something so simple must be written all over my face, because Mali leans over to read the text before I have a chance to stop her.

"Baby?" she asks. "That doesn't sound very casual of you."

I shrug, playing with the string hanging from my shorts. "It doesn't *feel* casual. Not anymore, at least. Not since he told me that I'm the only one who has his attention."

Mali hums, an impressed look on her face. "Hmm, Hayes might not be the lost cause I thought he was after all. But if I see another cut like that on you again, I'm going after him."

"I told you," I whine. "It wasn't his fault."

She rolls her eyes and focuses back on her computer. "Yeah, yeah. You got hurt surfing after going to the beach to have sex."

The way she explains it makes me laugh, because she's not exactly wrong. Almost every time we're together, we end up messing around in some way. But it's not like he's only hanging out with me to hook up. We just have a problem with keeping our hands to ourselves.

"Here's an idea," Mali exclaims, like she just cured cancer. "Stop fucking in public!"

"Victims of circumstance!" I shout back, smiling when she flips me off.

"Actually," Monty chimes in. "I may be able to help with that."

My brows furrow, wondering what on earth *he* could do to help—except pay for a hotel room, but that would be weird. "I'm listening."

"I have a boat," he tells me. "And if Hayes has a license for it, I wouldn't be opposed to letting you two take it out for the day. Maybe then he won't hate me so much."

That's unlikely, but I'm not about to turn down the offer as I lunge off the bed and jump into his arms. "Thank you! You're the best!"

As I grab my phone to text Hayes about it, I can't stop myself from imagining spending a whole day with him, out on the water where there is no risk of getting caught.

A whole day of just being us.

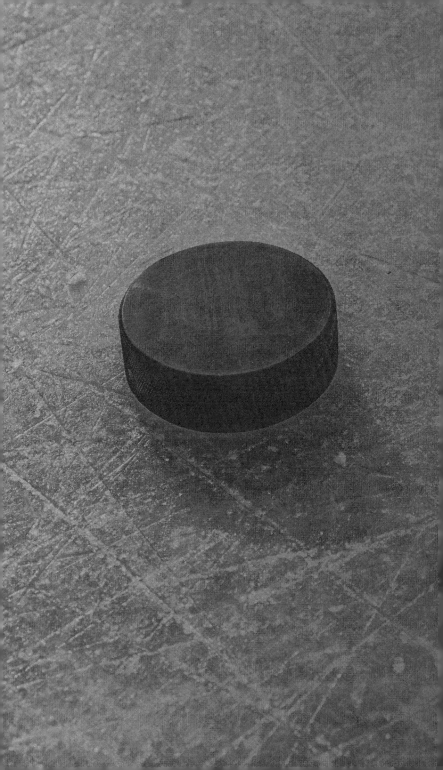

Hayes

CHAPTER TWENTY FOUR

Before my father left, he taught me one important lesson—nothing in life comes for free, and most of the time, people have an ulterior motive. And as I walk down the docks with Laiken, heading for Monty's boat, I'm starting to think this is one of those moments. There's no way the guy who practically drooled on Laiken at her birthday is giving us his boat out of the goodness of his heart.

But the opportunity to spend the day alone with her is too good to pass up.

Is he probably just trying to win her over and make her believe he's a good guy? I'd bet money on it, but that doesn't mean I'm not going to take advantage of it and fuck her on every surface of his boat.

He can lust after her all he wants—she's always going to be mine.

"There you are," Monty greets us. "She's all ready to go for you. Gas tank is full of fuel and I had it detailed yesterday."

"Thanks, Monty," Laiken says. "We really appreciate it."

I look him up and down, sizing him up. "I'm still wondering what the catch is."

"H!" Laiken chastises me.

But Monty just shakes his head. "No, it's okay. There is no catch. I'm just trying to help out a friend." He shrugs and tilts his head to the side. "And maybe get in her boyfriend's good graces so she doesn't feel like she needs to choose between us."

There's a little voice in the back of my head, telling me that I should correct the boyfriend term he used, but I'm thinking that's what he wants. He wants Laiken to be reminded that we're not official, and he wants me to be the one to do it. Instead of playing his little game, I focus on the last part.

"Oh, rest assured. Any choice between the two of us would not go in your favor."

Laiken sighs, no doubt rolling her eyes, but Monty takes it like a man, chuckling as he nods.

"Understood." He takes the keys out of his pocket and hangs them in front of me, dropping them into my hand when I put it out. "You two have fun, and I'll meet you back here around nine."

"Thanks again, Monty," Laiken shouts as he walks away.

He turns around and smiles as he answers. "No problem!"

Once he's gone, she focuses her attention on me, completely unamused.

"What?" I play innocent.

She cocks a single brow. "Did you have to be an asshole, or is that just part of your personality?"

"It's who I am, baby," I tell her as I kiss her cheek. "Now, let's see how this beauty does on the water."

Her eyes roll, but as I step onto the boat and turn around to help her, she leaves her anger on the docks.

THIS THING RIDES LIKE a dream. It's not as big as I thought it would be. I expected a yacht, though I'm sure he has one of those, too. But driving this thing, feeling it glide across the water, I'm in my element out here.

And watching Laiken sunbathe in front of me is the icing on the cake.

Beautiful boat, beautiful girl.

She must feel me looking at her, because she lifts her head and smiles as her gaze meets mine. Getting up, she comes over and gets behind me, draping her arms over my shoulders.

"You look happy," she says.

I turn my head to glance behind me. "How could I not be with you all half naked and gorgeous?"

She giggles. "I meant driving the boat."

"Oh," I downplay my excitement. "It's all right."

"Mm-hm." She presses her lips to my cheek. "So, you can see how Monty isn't all that bad?"

"And now you ruined it," I groan. "I was enjoying the little fantasy I had going in my head, and you just brought Moneybags into it."

"Fantasy, huh? Tell me about it."

I shake my head. "Can't. It's gone now. You killed it."

She chuckles, coming around to sit on my lap. "In that case, let me give you another one."

Holding the steering wheel with one hand, I wrap my other arm around her. Her palm rests on my face as she presses her lips to mine—soft, but just enough to tease. I hum against her mouth, letting her deepen the kiss and take control for once.

When it starts to get a little heated, I lift the throttle until the boat comes to a stop. My hand moves from the steering wheel to her waist, sliding up her skin until I cup her breast over her bikini top. The way she arches into my touch, pushing herself further against my hand, it's fucking sinful.

"I am never going to get enough of you," I murmur, feeling her smile into the kiss.

"Good," she says, an evil hint to her tone. "That's my plan."

WE SPEND THE DAY in the most laidback way possible. Laiken is perfectly happy just lying in the sun, while I take advantage of the fishing poles and bait Monty stocked for us. But no matter what we're doing, we always stay close to each other.

If I moved to the back of the boat, it wasn't long before she would come over to me.

If she went to go lay back down, I'd feel off until I went up there to be near her.

And when the sun starts to set, I sit on the bow with her in my arms, watching as it dips beneath land. LED lights around the boat light up once they no longer detect the sun, illuminating the inside. But Laiken doesn't make an attempt to move, and neither do I.

It's so innocent how I run my fingers through her hair and she gently rubs her thumb across my knee, but somehow, it's everything. I don't think it's a coincidence that this is the best day I've had in a while—spent with her and not having to worry about a damn thing.

"Lai," I all but whisper. She turns her head to look up at me, and I tuck a strand of hair behind her ear. "You're so beautiful."

She exhales, smiling as I gently take her chin and kiss her. This one feels different than all the ones before it. It's softer, lazier, like we have all the time in the world. But most importantly, the part that scares the shit out of me, is that there's more meaning to this one.

For both of us.

Even if neither of us will say it out loud, we feel it.

Laiken turns and straddles my lap, deepening the kiss, but still not rushing it. I slide my hands up her back and untie her bikini top. The fabric falls and gets discarded beside us as I cover her nipple with my mouth. She throws her head back, letting out breathy moans as I pay special attention to each one.

Worshipping them.

Worshipping *her*, because dammit, she deserves to be worshipped.

I lift her up and move onto my knees, gently laying her down before hovering above her. Her hair splays out on the boat, and the light reflects in her eyes. She's so gorgeous it's hard to believe she exists, and that she's beneath me, looking at me in a way that silently tells me everything I'm terrified of hearing. It all seems more dream than reality.

"You have no idea how perfect you are," I tell her.

Smirking, she reaches up and pulls my head down. Our mouths move together as she drags her nails down my back. I graze my fingers over her skin until I reach her bathing suit bottoms. The moment I untie each side, it falls apart beneath her, leaving her completely naked and withering for me.

"Hayes," she begs as I skim my touch over her clit.

"Shh, baby," I whisper. "I've got you."

Slowly, I make my way down her body, taking my time as I kiss her skin the whole way down. She squirms and whimpers and I know exactly where she wants me, but I'm not going to rush this.

I can't.

I need it.

Moving my mouth to the inside of her thigh, I suck on her skin, leaving a mark behind when I'm done. Then, and only then, do I finally lick right across her pussy. She mewls as my tongue goes back and forth across her clit. When she tries to speed things up by arching her hips, I press down on her lower stomach to keep her in place.

"Always so needy," I murmur against her.

I slide two fingers inside her as I suck on her clit just the way I know she likes it. Because that's the thing—with every time we've been together, I've started to memorize her body.

Her sensitive spots.

The way she moves.

How her voice changes when she's about to come.

They're all burned into my mind, in a compartment reserved just for her.

My cock is straining against my bathing suit as she's starting to get close, but while normally I'd get her off before fucking her into oblivion, that's not what I'm looking for tonight.

I slip the condom out of my pocket and ditch my trunks before sliding it on. Sucking on her clit once more, I kiss my way back up her body. When I reach her head, I kiss her deeply, letting her taste herself on my tongue as I press into her.

Her legs wrap around my waist, and she pulls me in deeper. I want to feel her raw again, like the other day on the beach. Being inside her without anything between us was a religious experience. And I know if I were to ask, she would let me, but I've heard all about how sick the plan B pill can make someone.

I won't do that to her.

Our fingers tangle as I hold her hand, and her breath hitches as I bend down to kiss her. There's no rush. No slamming roughly into her because I want to get off. It's just her and me, and a moment I don't think either one of us will ever forget.

And as we come together, moaning in unison, our gazes stay locked on each other—like we're the only things that matter in the world.

I want to be the only thing that matters in her world.

A LITTLE PAST NINE, we pull the boat back into its slip. Monty is waiting for us and ties the boat up so it doesn't go anywhere. I hop off first, turning around and picking Laiken up by the waist to make sure she gets onto the dock safely.

"The boat behave okay for you?" Monty asks.

I nod. "It's a great boat. You take good care of it."

"Can't take the credit for that," he says with a smile. "My father has a whole team of people who do it for us."

Figures. Still, I extend my hand to shake his. He looks at it for a second, then takes it.

"Well, regardless. Thanks for letting us take it out," I tell him.

"No problem at all."

Throwing my arm around Laiken, we say goodbye to Monty and head back to my truck. *Maybe Moneybags isn't so bad after all.*

LAIKEN SLEEPS AT MY house again, but this time, it's intentional. After spending the whole day with her, I'm still not ready for it to end. So, we spend the night lying in bed together, sharing lazy kisses and keeping a part of us touching at all times.

When the morning comes, I don't want to move. She's sound asleep, with her head resting on my chest. But if I don't wake her, she'll be late to work. And there's nothing she hates more than to leave the kids waiting.

I bring her to her car, kiss her goodbye, and head home to go back to sleep for a few hours—only to wake up to my mom knocking on my door. It creaks as it opens, and I need to blink to adjust to the light.

"Laiken forgot her sweatshirt," she tells me, coming in and draping it over the back of my chair. "So, is this a thing now?"

I don't even know how to answer that, if I'm honest. But as the memory of last night plays through my head, I know there's a part of me that would be completely content if she never left my side. Though I'm not about to admit that to my mom.

"How do you know she wasn't here for Dev?"

"Because I have a brain, and you're smiling."

I don't answer that, and she doesn't say anything else as she leaves the room. It's almost as if she's letting me off the hook for now, and I'm grateful for it. Because I may not know what's going on with us, or with me, but I do know that Laiken does something to me that I don't fully understand.

Laiken

CHAPTER TWENTY FIVE

The beach is crowded, filled with surfers, sponsors, and a whole boatload of girls who are only here for an excuse to wear their bikinis in front of a bunch of guys. It's the annual Wax and Waves Surf Competition—the biggest event of the summer in Calder Bay.

It's the one day of the year Hayes isn't allowed to take off work. It's all hands on deck, and this year, his job is to help size people for surfboards, telling them which he thinks would work best for their body type and skill level.

So of course, that means the line is a mile long, and more than half are girls with no interest in learning how to surf and *all* the interest in getting in his pants. We may all be here to watch Cam surf in the competition, but I can't seem to take my eyes off Hayes.

"I'm so glad the booth is in the same direction as the ocean so your staring isn't obvious," Mali quips. "Oh…wait."

I force myself to look away and flip her off, but I find myself glancing over there within seconds anyway.

"Ugh, would you just look at them?" I snarl in disgust. "I'm pretty sure that girl's tits are going to fall out of her bathing suit if she pulls it down any lower."

Mali sighs and turns toward the booth. "Well, if it makes you feel any better, it doesn't seem like he's enjoying himself."

She's right, he doesn't. Every time a girl twirls her hair or puts her hand on his arm, he couldn't look any less interested. And when one girl hands him her phone number, he doesn't even wait for her to walk away before he crumples it up and throws it in the trash.

Still, I hate the way they're all treating him like a piece of meat. And I hate it even more that I can't go over there and tell them to back off.

"Look at the way she's looking at him," I scoff. "Could her fuck-me eyes be any more obvious?"

Both Mali and Devin glance in that direction, then share a look as they laugh. Dev shakes her head, as if saying she's not touching this one, while Mali smiles at me lovingly.

"Lai," she says. "*You* look at him like that."

"You look at him like that," I mock her like a child. "Seriously, feel free to fuck off anytime now."

If there's one thing Mali knows best about me, it's when to try to talk some sense into me, and when to just let me bitch, moan, and pout. And this is a time to do the latter.

ONE THING MY PARENTS never understood is why Cam has his heart so set on hockey, when he's such a talented surfer. They offered once to move somewhere warmer, where he could practice all the time and enter bigger competitions than this small town one, but he turned it down. He told them that this is our home, and he has no interest in leaving it.

I've always wondered what things would be like if he had

taken them up on that offer. Trust me, the idea of possibly having to leave Mali was devastating. I cried for days simply because they were considering it. But now, the thought of leaving Hayes hurts just as much, if not worse.

The announcer calls for the final run over the loudspeaker, and we all turn our attention to the water. The waves could be better, but as Cam paddles out, I know he's got this. It's between him and two other guys. The winner gets a trophy and a year's sponsorship from Wax and Waves. But honestly, I think Cam just tries to win for the bragging rights.

The one guy goes too soon, in too much of a rush to get some early points in. If he had taken his time to read the swell, he would've seen that it was going to break early. But he didn't, and he wiped out—hard.

As the next set of waves come, Cam and the other guy start to go for it together, but the moment he notices his opponent isn't going to back down, Cam holds back. It's a decent wave, and he manages to land a couple tricks which scores him some points, but his score isn't impossible to beat.

Especially not for Cam.

The timer starts to tick down, and we're all waiting with bated breath for the next swell. As the water starts to build, everyone gets on their feet. It's the best wave they've had all day, and I can practically feel the happiness radiating off my brother as he starts to paddle into it.

He takes advantage of the opportunity, doing tricks he knows will score the most points, as well as a couple more just to show off. And when the timer buzzes and his score is announced, my chest swells with pride.

Cam Blanchard has taken the championship title for the third year in a row!

Mali and I cheer the loudest, just like we do every year. And when I glance over at Hayes, I see him clapping proudly for his best friend. He turns to look at me, our eyes meeting for the first time since I got here. We smile at each other, and for a moment I feel better, but when he pulls his attention away a little quicker than normal, it stings.

It's not like I'm expecting him to come over and kiss me in front of everyone. Hell, I'm not even looking for a hug. But when he won't even look at me for longer than a couple seconds, I start to wonder if we're ever going to be anything more than a secret.

The other day, when we spent the entire day on Monty's boat, it felt too good to be true. Like he somehow knew about my little game of pretending we're actually a couple and he was playing along. Though I don't think there was anything fake about that night, when he held me close and stared into my eyes as he fucked me.

It felt like more than just sex, and I almost asked him about it that night at his place. The only reason I didn't was because I didn't want to ruin the moment. If the answer wasn't what I hoped it would be, it would've popped the fantasy bubble I put us inside of in my mind. Even without hearing it spill from his lips, however, I know what I saw.

He definitely felt something, the same way I did.

But all of that means nothing if he's always going to tuck the truth about us into the darkest corners of his closet.

AS THE EVENT ENDS and the prizes are given to the

first, second, and third place winners, I go over to the booth. Hayes is just starting to clean up, taking everything down and putting it away, and I start to help him without saying a word.

"You okay?" he asks as his coworker goes to bring one of the boxes back to the shop. "You seem off today."

I shrug. "I don't really want to talk about it."

It's not a lie. I *don't* want to talk about it, because it sounds stupid. And there is nothing I hate more than sounding stupid.

But he's not about to let it go that easily.

"Please?" He frowns. "I just want to know what's bothering you so I can fix it."

I shouldn't tell him. The smartest thing to do would be to keep it to myself. It's not like I won't get over it later. But if he's just going to keep asking me, then fine.

Running my fingers through my hair, I glance around to make sure no one is close enough to hear me. "It's just not fun to see you get hit on all day when all I want to do is tell them you're mine, and I can't."

He doesn't respond at first, and when I finally get the nerve to look at him, I want to kiss him and smack the smirk off his face all at the same time.

"Anyone ever tell you you're cute when you're jealous?" he teases.

I roll my eyes as I pass him the cash box to pack away. "Whatever, at least I'm not lighting shit on fire."

He throws his head back as he laughs. "I'm never going to live that down, am I?"

"No. No, you're not."

"Guess you get to deal with my ass for another year!" Cam says as he comes over, effectively ending our conversation.

Hayes chuckles, giving him an aggressive bro-hug,

complete with back pounding. "Congrats, man. You killed it out there."

When they separate, Cam turns to me and I willingly go into his arms. "Proud of you, big brother."

"Thanks," he tells us both. "Now I'm ready to party."

"What were you thinking?" Hayes questions as he gets the last of the stuff packed away, moving for the tent itself.

Cam goes to the other side to help him. "Well, there's a girl I've been talking to for a bit, Layla. She's already having a party, so I figure we'll just go there."

"Sweet," Hayes answers. "Count me in."

"Lai?" My brother turns to me. "You coming?"

I shake my head. "I think I'm going to pass. The sun wore me out, and I'm exhausted."

It's a total lie—one Hayes can see right through. I just figure I already tortured myself all day, watching girls hang all over Hayes like they have some sort of right to. There's no part of me that wants to deal with that tonight, too.

"Suit yourself," Cam says.

He goes on to talk to Hayes about something with hockey, but I don't really care to listen to what it is. All I can focus on is the way Hayes keeps glancing over at me every chance he gets. There's a worried look on his face, as if he's silently wondering if I'm okay. But he can't ask me about it with Cam standing there, and I have to admit, I'm grateful for it.

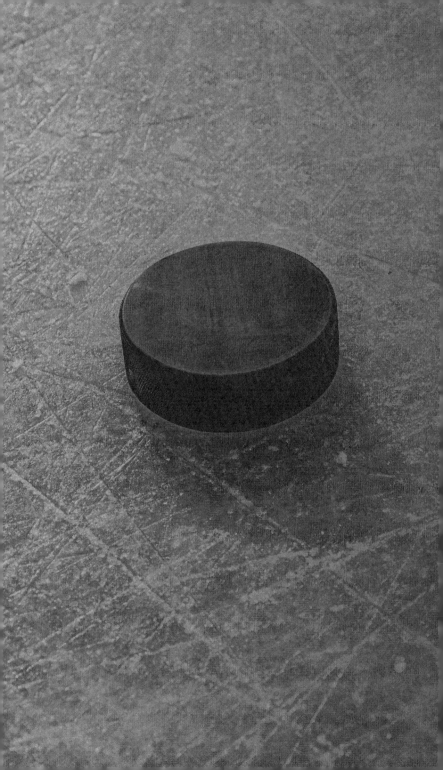

Hayes
CHAPTER TWENTY SIX

The house party that Cam brings us to is insane. It's crowded, but not overcrowded, and everyone is in a good mood. Usually, I'd be all about it—cracking a beer and celebrating Cam's win. But right now, all I can think about is the look on Laiken's face as she walked away from the beach.

She looked genuinely upset, and if I hadn't already told Cam I would come tonight before she said she wasn't going, I would've made an excuse to get out of it. I just assumed that she would come too, and we'd have a chance to sneak off together once Cam got a good buzz going. But she decided to go home instead, and I can't help thinking it's because of me.

I tried texting her a couple times, but she hasn't answered. Even though I know she was lying when she told Cam that the sun wore her out, a part of me still hopes she's sleeping and not just ignoring me intentionally.

"This is a good party," Cam shouts to me over the music, looking around. "I might disappear in a bit with Layla, just so you know. But there are plenty of hot girls here. You should have no issue finding someone to entertain you tonight."

I force a chuckle as I take a sip of my beer. "No thanks, man. I'm good."

His brows raise in surprise. "No way! You're still sleeping with that same girl? Damn! When's the last time someone was able to hold your attention like that?"

This conversation is awkward, and I hate it. I feel like an

asshole. Lying to Cam isn't something I enjoy, which is why I try to avoid it. Everything with Laiken hasn't been blatant lies to his face; they've been more of omissions of truth. I'm not telling him that we're not hooking up, but I'm not giving him a reason to think we are, either.

"This would be the first," I say, looking around the party to avoid looking at him.

"Well, good for you, man," he tells me. "I guess the saying is true. There really is someone for everyone."

A few minutes later, he ends up spotting Layla heading up the stairs, and he tells me he'll be back down in a bit. But I'm still stuck on his earlier words.

Since the day my dad left, I convinced myself that it was all a lie. The whole notion that you could find someone, fall in love, and spend the rest of your lives together—it was all just a hoax. A bunch of chemicals in your brain, tricking you into giving over parts of yourself that you should never trust anyone else with.

But as his words circulate in my mind, I can't help wondering if he's right. And if he is, if there *really is* someone for everyone, there's not a doubt in my mind that my person is Laiken.

THE NEXT MORNING, I wake up an hour earlier than I usually would, which is surprising since it took me forever to fall asleep last night. I kept tossing and turning, trying to think of something sweet to do for Laiken. After the way she looked yesterday, so genuinely upset, I just want to put the smile back on her face.

After finally accepting that I'm not exactly the most experienced person when it comes to romance, I resorted to the knower of all things—Google. I found all sorts of ideas, from as extravagant as taking her on a surprise getaway trip, to things as small as sending her a cute good morning text. I opted for something in the middle, which is why I'm on my way to the store to buy some flowers so that I can sneak into the rink while she's working and leave them next to her bag in the locker room.

I get to the store just after they open, and it only takes a few minutes for me to find the perfect bouquet of pink roses. They're freshly picked, and the florist, an old lady named Mrs. Garrison, even offers to add a couple more and some baby's breath for me.

"Here," she says, handing me a blank card and a pen. "You fill this out while I spruce up this bouquet for you."

I thank her and watch as she slowly makes her way to the back room. I've been coming here for years to get my mom something for Mother's Day and her birthday, and every time I come, it's Mrs. Garrison who's here. She has to be approaching ninety at this point, but ever since her husband passed, this place has become her entire life.

She says it's the only thing to bring her joy anymore, and she just wants to help people show their love the way Mr. Garrison always showed her.

Picking up the pen, I rack my brain on what to put. I don't want it to be too cheesy, nor do I want to tell her something I don't fully mean. I just want something to put a smile on her face.

Something that at least hints at the fact that I may not

have it all figured out right now, but she means more to me than just a good time.

The words she said yesterday while we were cleaning up run through my mind, and just like that, I know exactly what to put.

BY THE TIME THAT Mrs. Garrison finishes with the flowers and I pay for them, I only have forty-five minutes to get to the rink, sneak into the locker room, and leave before she sees me. It should be plenty of time. But as I start walking toward my truck, my steps slow as I see Monty leaning against it.

I fucking knew it.

"Hey, Monty," I greet him, trying to hide the venom in my tone. "What's up?"

He looks at the bouquet in my hand. "Those are pretty. It's a shame she'll never see them."

"What the fuck are you talking about?" I spit.

"You know exactly what I'm talking about." He places his hands in his pockets and takes a step toward me. "You're going to end things with Laiken, or you're not going to like the consequences."

I laugh dryly, wanting nothing more than to knock this fucker on his ass. "I'm not sure how you were raised,

Moneybags, but around here, you don't threaten someone without being prepared to back it up."

"Okay, let me be a little clearer then," he says. "Break up with Laiken and tell her you don't want to do whatever it is you've been doing anymore, or I'm going to tell Cam all about how you've been fucking his sister behind his back."

"And he's going to believe you over his best friend and his sister? You have no proof."

"Don't I?"

He takes out his phone and turns it toward me as he presses play. I recognize it immediately. The memory of that day we spent on his boat plays on a constant loop in my mind. I watch as I eat her out before sliding inside of her.

"H," she moans.

"Shh, baby," I respond. "I've got you."

My fist clenches and I go to lunge for his phone when he jumps back. "Ah, ah, ah. Careful. I'm not stupid enough to show you my only copy, and one wrong move from you will get this sent straight to Cam."

He smiles like he's got it all figured out, and that only enrages me even more. But I still have one other option.

"What if I tell Cam myself?" I ask.

Monty doesn't look the slightest bit concerned. "You won't, because you know as well as I do that you can't give her everything she deserves. You're selfish, but you're not heartless. Not where she's concerned, anyway. You'll never risk putting her through what your mother went through when your father would treat her like shit." His brows raise. "Correct me if I'm wrong, but that's why you won't commit to her, isn't it? Too afraid that you and daddy dearest are cut from the same cloth?"

He walks around me, and I turn around to watch him.

"Do her a favor, Wilder," he yells as he stops to look back at me. "She'll be better off and you know it."

"You know she thinks you're gay, right?" I call back, but it has no effect.

He simply smiles at my pitiful attempt to get under his skin and turns the corner. My jaw clenches as I climb into my truck.

There wasn't a word he just said that didn't strike a nerve. And the worst part is, all of them were spot on. I've known from the beginning of all this that Laiken deserves someone steady, someone she can count on. Someone who isn't practically guaranteed to fuck it up. And as much as I'd love to be that person for her, I'm just not.

I'm my father's son—a fuck-up who's only good for getting drunk and letting people down.

Gripping the flowers tightly in my hand, I throw them across the truck. It bangs into the door, landing on the passenger seat. And I watch as petals and the handwritten card fall out onto the floor.

I am yours.
I hope you know that.
- H.

I SIT AT THE kitchen table, barely even blinking as I try to figure out how everything all went wrong. The minute Laiken brought up the idea of borrowing Monty's boat, I had a feeling it was a trap. No one goes from hating someone's guts to letting them borrow their boat within the same few days. But she insisted that he was just trying to be nice, and I chopped it up to him having enough money to not care if anything happened to the boat.

The worst part is, if I could go back, I don't think I'd change anything—except maybe finding the hidden cameras and tossing them into the ocean. That whole day we spent together, and the night that followed after it, was one of the best of my life. The kind of memory you think about when you're in a bad mood and need something to cheer you up. There isn't a damn thing anyone could say to me that would make me regret it.

And now it's going to be all I have to hold onto.

Devin comes in and stops when she sees me. "Damn, H. Who pissed in your cheerios?"

"A rich prick with entitlement issues," I growl.

She snorts. "You mean Monty? Yeah, I figured he was going to be a problem. No one flies back a day early from Barcelona to come to a birthday party in someone's yard unless there's an ulterior motive."

Taking a beer out of the fridge, she ignores the *only after three p.m.* rule that Mom set after my recent breakfast beer attempt and places it down in front of me.

"Thanks," I tell her, cracking it open and chugging the whole thing in one go.

Her eyes widen and she smiles hesitantly, but goes to get me another one. "Try sipping it this time. If Mom gets home to find you drunk before noon, the rich prick will be the least of your worries."

I wish that were true. To be honest, I would trade my mother's wrath for what I'm going to have to do, any day of the week.

"He's threatening me," I admit. "He said that if I don't

end shit with Laiken, he's going to tell Cam. He even has proof on his phone."

"That's vindictive. What did Laiken say about it?"

Dropping my head, I know what's coming. "I haven't told her about it."

Grabbing the empty beer can, she throws it at my head. "Are you really that fucking stupid? She deserves to know!"

"Why?" I snap. "So she can yell at him? Piss him off by telling him she never wants to speak to him again? I may as well send Cam the proof myself."

She goes quiet for a moment, softening her voice when she speaks next. "Or you could just tell him. Be honest and own up to what's been going on, and then actually try having something real with Laiken."

I laugh dryly, taking a sip of my new beer to settle the burning in my throat.

"What?" Devin argues. "You obviously like her enough to risk sneaking around."

Shaking my head, I look anywhere but at her. "It's not like that."

She scoffs. "Okay, Mr. Denial. Go ahead and keep your head up your ass."

I don't even know why I try. She's been able to tell when I'm lying for years, and I brought Laiken back here the other night while she was home. I'm sure she could hear us laughing and joking around.

I swallow down the lump in my throat as I stare back at my sister. "I'm going to fuck it up."

"You don't know that."

Rolling my eyes, I throw my hands in the air. "Look at our parents, Dev. Should I destroy her now by leaving, or wait until after we have a couple kids together like Dad did?"

The thing is, Dev and I haven't talked about our Dad in

years. I think she prefers to convince herself that it's always just been the three of us. We've always been close, holding onto the family we have left with a tight grip. But the way she's glaring at me right now has to be the angriest I've ever seen her.

"You are *nothing* like him," she roars. "Do you hear me? The only goddamn thing that man gave you of his was a little bit of DNA."

"Devin—" I begin, but she's not about to let me get a word in.

"No, fuck that! You don't get to throw away what's most likely the best thing to ever happen to you because of him! If you don't want to be with her because she's not your type, or because you just don't feel the connection, that's one thing. But he doesn't get to take this away from you, too. I won't allow it."

"You were twelve. You don't remember."

She narrows her eyes at me. "Yeah, I was twelve. And I may not remember everything, but do you know what I do remember?"

"I'm sure you're going to tell me," I grumble.

"I remember my fifteen-year-old brother coming into my room and giving me his headphones so I didn't have to hear Mom crying at night. And I remember you walking me to school, even if it meant you were late, so I didn't have to walk alone. And I remember the time I broke down after school one day because I didn't know who was going to walk me down the aisle at my wedding—a problem that was so small to anyone else at the time, but you didn't care. You wiped my tears and promised that you would be the one to give me away. So don't you dare act like you haven't been ten times the man that Dad was since the day he walked out. You're talking about the *absolute best man in my life*."

Getting up, I go over to give her a hug, the same way I used to when we were kids. "I get what you're saying, but you and I both know she deserves better, whether I'm like Dad or not."

"No offense, bro, but I don't think that's your decision to make." She lets go and starts to leave the room, stopping at the doorway. "I've seen you two together, and I may have thought you were crazy at first, but I don't think there's anyone better for her than you."

"But what if there is?" I counter. "What if by being with her, I'm holding her back from having the life she's always dreamed of?"

"Then one day, she'll leave and find someone else. But at least you'll know instead of always wondering *what if*."

The sound of her footsteps fade as she retreats to her bedroom. I know she has a point. She *always* has a point, as annoying as it is. But this is a bigger risk than I've ever taken —not just with Cam, but with Laiken's heart.

I sit there in silence, letting everything run through my mind. Thinking about everything Monty said, voicing every insecurity I've ever had, and then thinking about the way Devin contradicted all of it by nearly ripping my head off for even suggesting I'm like our father. I picture Laiken and the way she smiles at me, like I hung the moon and the stars all for her. I may not have realized it until just now, but she always looks the happiest when we're together.

And finally, I remember what Cam said last night—that he's happy for me and how there's someone for everyone. There's not a chance in hell he was referring to his sister when he said it, but maybe, after seeing how happy I've been the last few weeks, it's enough to keep him from murdering me in cold blood.

Before I can talk myself out of it, I grab my keys and head out the door.

Chapter 26

I PULL INTO THE driveway that I know so well, parking in my usual spot before heading inside. Cam's parents are in the living room, and they smile warmly when they see me. I wonder if they'll still do the same after they find out I've been sneaking around with their daughter.

"Hey, Hayes," Cam's dad greets me. "How's everything going?"

"Pretty good," I tell him, leaving out the part of Laiken having everything to do with anything good in my life. "Cam's home, right?"

Someone from the opposite team hits a home run, ripping his attention away from me and over to the game as he yells at the TV. Cam's mom rolls her eyes fondly before nodding toward upstairs.

"He's in his room, sweetie," she tells me.

"Thanks, Mrs. B."

My heart is racing with every step I take, and I can't believe I'm about to do this. Hopefully with his parents' home, he'll be less likely to kick my ass. But then again, if he tells them what's been going on, they might hold me down while he does.

I stand in the hallway and take a deep breath before opening the door. Cam is sitting on his bed, playing Call of Duty.

"Oh, hey," he says. "Didn't know you were coming over."

Shrugging, I walk around to sit on the bed. "My plans got canceled."

He gets up and switches the game to NHL Center Ice, handing me the other controller. It's something we've been doing for years, playing video games together. And sure, maybe it's supposed to fade a little as you get older, but we still take care of all our responsibilities, so I don't see the harm in it.

The words sit on my tongue as we both choose our teams, and as the game starts, I force them out.

"I actually wanted to talk to you about something," I tell him. "It's about Laiken."

He sighs. "I had a feeling this was coming."

My brows furrow as I glance at him. "You did?"

He chuckles, managing to steal the puck from me while we talk. "Yeah. It's pretty damn obvious."

There's no way to explain how confused I am. I thought we were hiding it well, but I guess he was able to see right through it. What gets me the most though, is how he doesn't seem even the slightest bit mad about it. But as he continues, it all becomes clear.

"I'm sure she'll get over it soon, but I get that it's awkward. Her having a crush on you and everything."

Oh. *Ohh.* He thinks it's all one sided.

"That is what you wanted to talk about, right?" He asks. "Laiken's newfound tendency to want to be around you all the time?"

"Y-yeah," I answer, not exactly lying but choking on the whole truth.

He presses a few buttons, and I'm so distracted that the puck flies into the net, making the score 1-0.

"Honestly, I'm glad it's you and not one of the other guys."

My brows raise. "You are?"

"Fuck yeah," he replies. "At least with you I know I have nothing to worry about. Those assholes would try to sleep with her just for the bragging rights. You'd never even think about touching her."

Well, fuck. Any chance of me telling him goes right out the window. If I do, I risk losing the closest friendship I've ever had. There's no way he'll ever forgive me for betraying him like I have.

"Right," I murmur.

He snickers and nudges me with his elbow. "Just ride it out. Like I said, she'll get over it. But I appreciate you being a man and coming to talk to me about it. You're a good friend."

Correction: *Now* I feel like an asshole.

THERE'S NOTHING I CAN do. I've racked my brain trying to figure out a way that I can keep my best friend and not lose Laiken. I even tried to find a hacker on the internet who could erase the video off all Monty's electronics. But it all keeps coming back to the same answer.

I can't have them both.

My phone vibrates in front of me—another text from Laiken. I haven't answered in a few hours and I feel bad because she actually seems like she's starting to worry about me. I just needed some time to myself, to really think things over and figure out what I'm going to do. But as a call comes through from her phone, I know I can't avoid it anymore.

"Hello?" I answer.

"Oh, thank God," Laiken breathes. "I thought you were dead in a ditch somewhere."

Doesn't sound like the worst thing right now. "Sorry. I got in late last night and woke up with a killer hangover, so I slept most of the day."

"As long as you're all right," she says warmly. "I miss you."

Hearing those words sends a pain right through my chest, knowing it's probably the last time I'll ever hear them.

"I miss you, too," I reply, meaning every word. "I meant to come by the rink earlier, but I didn't wake up until after you already left."

"Well, what are you doing now? Do you want to hang out for a bit?"

Devin walks in the door and sees me on the phone, but before she says anything, I hold up my hand to stop her.

"Yeah, actually. Can you meet me by the lake where the statue is?"

I can practically hear her smile through the phone. "Sure. Give me about fifteen minutes and I'll be on my way."

"Sounds good, baby." The last word burns as it rolls off my tongue.

We hang up the phone, and I instantly feel like I'm going to be sick. I'm about to break her heart, and she has no idea. Devin, however, obviously doesn't know how to read the damn room.

"So, you're seeing Laiken tonight?" she asks with an excited clap of her hands. "I take it your talk with Cam went well?"

I don't have to say a word. All it takes is lifting my head from my lap so she can see the look on my face, and the single tear that escapes. I watch in slow motion as all the pieces fall into place for her.

Her smile fades as she stares back at me. "No."

Laiken

CHAPTER TWENTY SEVEN

I DRIVE DOWN THE STREET, WINDOWS OPEN, WITH the wind flowing through my hair. Today was amazing. I watched my favorite student land a trick that took me years to attempt. And I know you're not supposed to have favorites, but she's incredible. You can't be around her and *not* love her.

I was hoping Hayes would stop by the rink like he usually does. He acts like a hardass, but really, I think he's just as proud of her as I am. Though he keeps saying she reminds him of me. Personally, I think she's better.

When she wins the Olympics one day, I'll be smiling and telling people that I called it before anyone else.

It's silly, really, how worried I felt when he wasn't answering my texts. Normally I would at least know he saw them, but they weren't even being opened. If my call went to voicemail, I was going to try getting ahold of Devin next.

I pull up to the lake, finding Hayes already waiting for me. He's standing outside of his truck and leaning against it. It should be illegal, the things he does to me. Even seeing him right now, with a pair of sunglasses on to help with his hangover, he's unfairly hot, and all I want is to feel his arms around me.

Getting to spend some time with him, no matter how little, is the perfect end to my day. I let my mind wander, picturing what it would be like if we were together and didn't have to hide. If he could come over after work and lie in bed with me, watching a movie while we talk about how our days went.

Maybe it's wrong to have hope, but I can't help it.

As I turn off my car and get out, I smile at him. He pushes off his truck, walking right for me. The second he's close enough, he grabs my face with both hands and presses his lips to mine. It's so needy, so desperate, that it takes my breath away.

And that's when he lights the fuse.

Breaking the kiss, he rests his forehead against mine with his hands everywhere. On my face. In my hair. Sliding down my back to pull me just a little bit closer. He pulls away, kissing my forehead, and warmth spreads through my whole body.

"Fuck, please don't hate me for this."

My heart leaps in my chest and the smile falls off my face. "Hate you for what?"

But he doesn't respond. And with every second of silence, I can feel the fire getting closer to the bomb—ready to shatter my heart into so many pieces that it'll never go back together the same.

I push myself out of his hold, feeling the tears pool in my eyes. "Hate you for what, Hayes?"

"Lai," he says as he tries to reach for my hand, but I yank it away like I've been burned.

"Don't!"

Throughout my life, I've broken bones, lost loved ones, and been betrayed—but none of that even begins to compare to the pain in my chest. It's tight, unforgiving as it rips me to shreds. For a second, I even consider breaking open my ribcage and tearing out the culprit.

I'm sure it would hurt less.

My breakdown is right on the surface, threatening to take me down without an ounce of mercy. And the longer I stand here with him, the worse it gets. He's looking at me, like this hurts him as much as it does me, but if that were the case, he wouldn't be doing it.

"I'm so sorry," he tells me. "We just…We're not meant to be together."

The knife twists inside my chest, and I don't think there's anything he could have said that would hurt me more. Every last part of me that held onto the idea of him and me disintegrates right in front of my eyes.

"Please don't go," he says as he watches me step backward. "I don't want this to be how we leave things."

I shake my head, continuing to distance myself from him. "I have to. I can't—"

A hiccup interrupts my words, and I throw my hand over my mouth as the bomb explodes inside of me, destroying every single thing in its path. Hayes takes a step toward me, but for the first time in my life, that's the last thing I want right now.

I may not have much resistance when it comes to him, and I may cave before I should at times, but as I stand here, feeling the pain of my heart breaking, I refuse to let him see me cry. I will not be the pathetic little girl who sobs in his arms, begging him to change his mind—even if it's the only thing that could make me feel better right now.

Sparing one last agonizing look at him, I turn around and walk to my car. I can feel his gaze on me as I back out of the parking space, and one last call of my name meets my ears, but I won't stop.

I can't.

The moment I get far enough away, the dam breaks, and there's no stopping the tears from falling. I try to keep driving, to get home where I can crawl into my bed and never leave, but as my eyes start to blur, I'm forced to pull over.

I thought we were getting somewhere. Yeah, I knew what

this was when we started. He told me as much before anything happened. But that was when we were just hooking up—sneaking around with the sole intention of sexual gratification.

Somewhere along the way, things changed. He looked at me differently. Like I mattered. Like he cared. And the part of me I had locked into a box, the part of me that dreamed of a life with him, broke out and fed on the hope that swelled inside my chest.

Now all that's left are the broken pieces, and there's no one to blame but myself.

I knew better than to get involved with him. I knew the chances of me coming out of this undamaged were slim. But I thought I could handle it.

And then I let myself get too comfortable.

I stupidly thought he was actually starting to feel something for me. That the night we laid in his bed, kissing with no intentions other than being close, meant something. But I should've known better.

I was never anything but a good time to him.

Barely able to see the screen, I try calling Mali, but it goes to voicemail. My hand grips at my chest, pressing to try to relieve the pain. It's no use. I'm going to feel every moment of this until there's nothing left of me. And to make matters worse, I can't even see to get home.

The thought of calling Devin passes through my mind, but it's her brother. She might be my friend, but she's naturally going to be biased. And besides, I don't want him knowing how he broke me.

How he single handedly tore me apart.

But I can't stay here, pulled over on the side of the road where Hayes can find me and see the damage he caused. I need to get home, but I can barely see my phone, let alone out the windshield. While I might not care about a car accident at the moment, I'm not trying to take someone else with me for my stupidity.

There's only one other person I can call, and he answers on the second ring.

I CAN'T BREATHE. OR at the very least, I can't breathe enough. Each inhale feels too shallow, and the tightness in my chest doesn't seem to be going anywhere. I'm stuck in pure agony, like my own personal hell made just for me.

A knock on the window spurs hope inside my chest, as if it hasn't learned any better yet. I turn my head and there's a part of me that wants to see Hayes standing there, ready to say that he didn't mean it.

That he doesn't want to lose me.

That he loves me the same way I love him.

And when I see Monty staring back at me, I somehow break a little more.

I open the door and he wraps his arms around me, holding me close as I cry violently on his shoulder.

"You were right," I sob. "I should've listened to you."

"No. Shh," he tells me. "You were blinded by your feelings for him. But you deserve so much better. You're going to find someone better."

"I don't want to," I answer through my tears. "I don't want anyone."

His fingers run through my hair, but it's not the same as

when Hayes did it. Because when he did it, I felt warm. All I feel as I stand here now is empty.

"You're going to be okay," Monty whispers. "I promise. You're going to be alright."

IT TAKES THREE HOURS, a whole box of tissues, and four rounds of vomiting my entire stomach into Mali's toilet, but she finally manages to get me somewhat calmed down. The second Monty got ahold of her, she immediately left work and told him to bring me to her house. And my breakdown started all over again in her arms.

"Can I fight him?" she asks. "Or at the very least, we can go all Carrie Underwood on his truck."

Normally, I would find her excitement comical, but right now, all I feel is numb. There's no color left in my world. All that remains are shades of black and gray.

I force a smile to appease her, but judging by the way she frowns, it wasn't even close to believable. She lies down beside me and moves the pillow I was holding so she can snuggle against me.

"It hurts, Mal."

She sighs, rubbing my back. "I know it does, babe. I know it does."

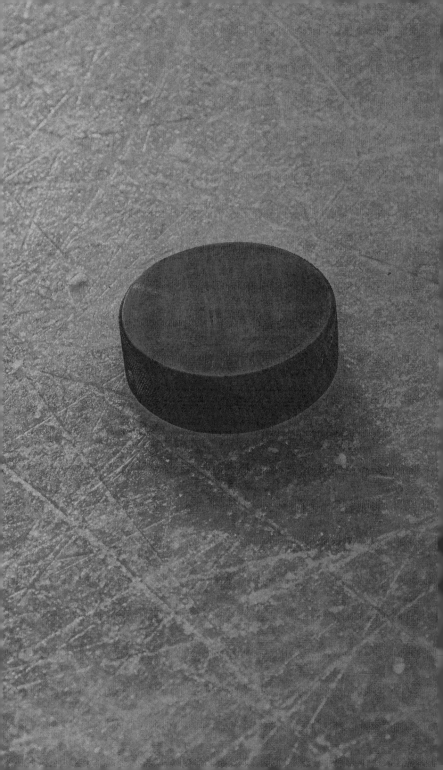

Hayes

CHAPTER TWENTY EIGHT

I used to think heartbreak was a myth. That it was just intense sadness, comparative to depression. But as I watched her drive away that day, leaving me behind in her rearview mirror, I was proven wrong. I felt every last excruciating second of it.

I almost changed my mind. At the very last second, as she drove herself right out of my life, I called her name with every intention of taking it back. But the brake lights never came on, and not a single part of me blamed her for it.

The first few days are excruciating. I force myself through the motions, going to work and hockey practice, but I'm miserable. I try to make it look like everything is okay. I'm sure Laiken is anything but fine, and if Cam sees the same on me, he'll put the pieces together. Especially since I had talked to him about her the same day.

With only one of us being allowed to show emotion, it goes to her.

After all, I'm the one that did this.

I should regret getting involved with her. It's not like I didn't know everything was going to end up this way. I may not have known I'd be *this* torn up over it, or that it would end prematurely because of some pompous ass with a death wish—but I knew I was going to break her heart.

And yet, I can't seem to regret the time we spent together. She taught me that I'm not some hopeless piece of shit. That it's possible for me to feel something real for someone. I wouldn't trade the time we spent wrapped up in each other for anything.

EACH SECOND FEELS LIKE an eternity as I sit at work. It seems like every single thing I do has a way of reminding me of Laiken. If I sit at the computer, I remember her licking and slurping that ice cream cone, just to torture me. If I see the nautical mural that's painted on the wall, it reminds us of the time we spent on the beach. And If I look out the window, I see the ocean and remember when we went from here to the beach.

That day, I got the scare of a lifetime. The moment I noticed she wasn't paying attention to where she was going, I knew it was bad. And when she went under, a part of me died inside. The whole time I swam toward her, I thought about how people drown all the time. I never would have forgiven myself if something happened to her that day.

I never would have been the same.

For the hundredth time today alone, I grab my phone and go to text her—like a bad habit I can't seem to quit. I'm so used to her filling my day with random commentary that its absence feels isolating. But as I open our message, I see the last two texts and feel the ache all over again.

A few hours after she left me standing by the statue, I tried texting her, telling her I was really sorry and that I never meant to hurt her. But all I got back was a thumbs up. No words. No real response. Just a thumbs up. And somehow, that stung worse than no reply at all.

If she hadn't responded, I could at least pretend she never saw it. Convince myself that she turned her phone off when she left or something. But I can't, because the single emoji she sent back basically glares at me from the screen.

Having to guess, I'd bet that was Mali's doing. Laiken would refuse to even open the text, the same way she refused to stop when I called her name. So, it wouldn't surprise me if Mali saw my messages and responded so I would stop texting her. It doesn't matter that I consider her a friend. Her priority will always be Laiken, and I respect it, but that doesn't make it easy.

None of this is easy.

IT'S SELFISH, I KNOW, but I need to get my eyes on her. Even if it's just a glimpse. Even if it's just in passing. I need to see that she's okay. That she's breathing. That I didn't destroy her the way I always knew I would.

It's been a week and a half since I broke both of our hearts. I thought at some point I would see her at the rink, as she ended work and hockey practice began. But not only have I not seen her—there's no trace of her being there at all.

I even went early one day, when she should have been

right in the middle of her shift. I planned on going in and staying out of sight while she worked, just so I could see her smile once more. But she wasn't there, and when I asked one of the parents Devin babysits for, she said that Laiken hasn't been there in a week.

That was a few days ago, which lines up directly with when I ended things between us.

She's avoiding me, the same way I avoided her when I was trying to do the right thing. Only, instead of coming to work late or leaving early to dodge a run in, she's not going to work at all. It's a surefire way to make sure we don't cross paths, and the message is clear—she doesn't want to see me.

So tell me why I'm pulling up to the Blanchard's, feeling more relieved than I should that Laiken's car is parked in the same spot it always is. It's not like I'm showing up unexpectedly. Cam invited me over, the same way he does all the time. And I could easily use the excuse that I couldn't turn him down any longer without something seeming off. But as I walk in the front door, it doesn't look like she's here at all.

There's no laptop set up on the kitchen island.

No music blasting from her bedroom.

The only sound I hear is Cam's voice as he yells obscenities at whatever video game he's currently playing.

As I make my way up to his room, I glance up the second set of steps that leads to Laiken's. At the top, I see her door wide open, which can only mean one thing—she's not home.

My heart sinks. Why is it that when I try to avoid her, she manages to track my ass down at a place I hadn't gone to in years, but when she avoids me, she's nowhere to be found?

Because you don't deserve to see her, my subconscious tells me.

I drop my head because it's true. I don't even deserve to breathe the same damn air as her right now. But I can't help it. I'm drawn to her—like a force pulling me toward her—and I'm not strong enough to stay away.

I never have been.

"Hey shithead," Cam greets me as I walk in.

Intentionally leaving his bedroom door open, I go over to sit on his bed. "Are the insults really necessary?"

He chuckles. "Does it help if you're my favorite shithead?"

"Not really, no," I say, faking a smile.

I get up and grab the other controller, while Cam nods toward the door. "Can you shut that?"

Shit. "No. It's fucking hot in here. Besides, it doesn't seem like anyone else is home anyway."

"Oh, okay." He puts the controller down and stands up. "I didn't realize they left already. In that case, let's go use the better TV downstairs."

They. It's so vague, and I can't resist the urge to dig deeper as I follow him downstairs. "Where'd they go?"

"My parents?" He shrugs. "Out to dinner with a few friends, I think. I don't really pay attention when they tell me things about their social life."

Well, that attempt was a bust. And I'm not ballsy enough to ask him where she is. So instead, I sit on the couch, take the controller Cam passes me, and hope she walks through the door at some point.

I RUB MY HANDS over my face as Cam wins the fifth game in a row. On a normal day, I would be kicking his ass. But I'm too distracted. Too busy anticipating the front door opening and Laiken walking through it.

"You good, dude?" Cam asks.

I nod, stretching my arms above my head. "Yeah, just tired. I've been sleeping like shit lately."

I don't tell him that it's because his sister haunts me at night, or that I wake up in the middle of dreaming about her, only to be slapped in the face by reality.

He hums. "Sounds like you need a beer."

More like a shot. "Actually, I think I'm going to get going."

"Well, do you mind getting *me* a beer before you go?" he asks.

I chuckle genuinely for the first time in a week and a half. "Oh, so that was your motive. You were using me as a gopher."

"I was going to let you have one."

Flipping him off, I get up and grab a beer out of the fridge, but on my way back from the kitchen, my angle provides me with a clear view out the window. My breath hitches as I see Laiken standing there, talking to Mali…and fucking Monty.

Son of a bitch.

"Is that the same dude from Laiken and Mali's party?" I question, handing Cam his beer.

He glances out the window as he cracks it open. "Yep. Looks like it."

"I didn't realize he was still coming around." I watch her out the window, but she has her back to me, so I can't see her face.

"They've been hanging out a decent bit the last week or so."

Of course they have. That was his goal, wasn't it? To force me right out of the picture so he could take my place?

I snort. "I'm sure *that's* been fun. That guy seems like a tool."

Cam nods in agreement as he puts the can on the coffee table. "He is. He even tried asking me about joining the hockey team, but I told him we're full."

Damn, he really does have a death wish. Thankfully, Cam dislikes him almost as much as I do. And without either of our approval, he'll never see the inside of the locker room, let alone put on a uniform.

"What's up with the rich kids and thinking they're skilled at everything? Does he even know how to skate?"

"Who knows," he says then shrugs. "I didn't care to ask."

The fact that he's been hanging around Laiken grinds on my nerves. I've been doing nothing but missing her, thinking about her constantly and wishing she were with me, and he's been basking in the destruction he made. If I don't get the fuck out of here, I'm going to end up in jail.

My mugshot on the front page while the headline reads *Man Arrested For Hospitalizing Senator's Son*.

The media would spin it into something political. My hockey coach would lecture me on my anger issues. And Monty would get Laiken to come to visit him in the hospital, playing the victim card before they ride off into the sunset together.

It's just best if I leave.

Saying goodbye to Cam, I head out the front door and Mali's eyes immediately land on me. Laiken must notice she's looking past her, because she turns around and her gaze locks with mine. I walk toward my truck as her breath hitches.

She looks good. A lot better than I feel. And I realize that seeing her when I can't pull her into my arms is like putting a

Band-Aid over a bullet wound. Only an idiot would think it's a good idea.

After a second, Laiken's shoulders sag, and she forces herself to look away. I clench my jaw as I watch Monty put his hand on her arm, rubbing his thumb over her skin and quietly asking if she's okay. As if he wasn't the one who did this.

If he hadn't blackmailed me, we'd still be together.

We'd still be happy.

Fucking piece of shit.

Hopping into my truck, I grip the steering wheel tightly before peeling out of there. My tires screech on the pavement as I pull away, and Cam probably notices, but right now I simply don't give a shit.

If I don't get out of here, I'm going to run him the fuck over.

I PULL UP TO the place that could very easily become my funeral. All night, the image of Monty with his hand on Laiken was in my head. Every time I close my eyes, it's right there—taunting me with the fact that he gets to spend time with her while I don't. He gets to see the way her eyes light up when she laughs and listen to her talk about all the kids in her skating lesson.

He gets all the parts of her that were mine not too long

ago, but I need to know how deep it runs. And there's only one person who can tell me the answer.

I open the door to Wrapped in Lace, a little boutique downtown. Honestly, I've never been in here, but I don't get a chance to look around before I hear the voice of the person I'm looking for.

And she does *not* sound happy.

"Oh, *hell no,*" Mali growls.

Whipping my head toward her, I can confidently say that judging by the look on her face, I'm the furthest thing from her favorite person right now.

"You need to leave," she demands as she stomps closer.

I raise my hands in defense. "I just want to talk."

"About what?" She cocks a brow at me. "About how you're an asshole? About how you broke my best friend's heart? About how you play games without taking other people's feelings into consideration?"

Yikes. "All of the above?"

She crosses her arms over her chest. "No. I am not discussing Laiken with you."

"That's fine," I tell her, expecting that answer. "I'm talking about Monty. What's up with him lately? Is he seeing anyone?"

A smirk appears on her face. "He's hardly your type."

"Mali."

She shakes her head. "You don't get to be jealous when you're the one that ended things. It's not fair to her."

For the first time, I let a little bit of vulnerability show. "You know I wouldn't be here if I wasn't desperate."

Her gaze bores into me, like it's trying to see into my soul. It's intense and unwavering, until finally, she sighs.

"Fine. You get three questions."

Thank God. "Is she okay?"

Her lips purse as she raises her brows. "Wow. That's not what I thought it would be."

It's honestly the only thing I care about. I've been walking around blind lately. She doesn't come anywhere near me so I can't read her emotions on her face. I can't ask Cam about it, and even if I did, he probably wouldn't know. And when I asked Devin, she gave me some lecture about how I'm an idiot and she's Switzerland—a neutral party or some shit.

Running her fingers through her hair, she thinks about it for a second. "Honestly? No. She's existing, and she's trying to be okay, but she's not. She had her heart broken by the guy she's liked for years. It's going to take a little longer than a couple weeks to recover from that."

It hurts, knowing she's struggling the same way I am, if not more. And it hurts even more knowing I caused it.

"Next question," she tells me.

"Is she dating and/or hooking up with Monty?" It's the one question I'm afraid of the answer to, but I know I need to ask it.

Mali chuckles, looking so smug. "Not knowing that is killing you, isn't it? Your possessiveness knows no bounds, Wilder."

"Please," I press.

"No," she answers. "They're just friends. Last question."

I swallow, realizing there's another one that scares me even more. "Does she hate me?"

She hums, looking to the side for a second as if it's comical in the fucked-up kind of way. "She should." She pauses, and her eyes meet mine again. "But no, she doesn't. I'm not really sure she's even capable of hating you."

That's a relief. I mean, if she did, I wouldn't blame her. She has every right to hate me. But it's still nice to know she doesn't.

"That doesn't mean I can't hate you, though," she continues. "Now get out of my store before I call security."

I smile sadly, thanking her as I turn around, but just as my hand reaches the doorknob, I see a mannequin wearing the same lace bra and panty set that Laiken wore our first night together. I spin back around, a newfound supply of hope rushing through me.

"One more," I request.

"No."

I ask it anyway. "Is it fixable?"

Her eyes close for a second as she exhales. "I don't know. But I *do* know that she deserves a lot better than being played with and strung along, so if you're just going to treat her like your personal sex toy and make me want to kick your ass *even more*, I'd strongly advise against it."

"And if I'm not?" I press her further. "If I'm serious that she's what I want?"

She shrugs, letting her shoulders sag. "That's not for me to answer."

I nod slowly and drop my head as I go to leave.

"And H?" I stop. "If you really think she would move on that quickly, you need to pay closer attention."

I'm not sure what it is about that statement, but it breathes life into me. There are a lot of things I don't know, one of those being if I'm good enough for her, or if I even *can* be. But I do know that the moment she drove away, she took a part of me with her.

I walk out of Wrapped in Lace and take out my phone, typing out the first text I've sent her in over a week.

> I know I don't deserve another second of your time, but if you could meet me tomorrow morning at our beach, I'd really appreciate it.

Pressing send, I feel like I might vomit all over the sidewalk, but I can't just stand around and watch Monty try to steal my girl. If he wants her like I think he does, he won't do anything to piss her off—which includes telling Cam about us. But even if he does, if this idea backfires in my face, it'll be worth it because I'll have her.

It's time to lay my feelings on the line.

It's time to win back my girl.

Laiken
CHAPTER TWENTY NINE

Seeing the notification that I got a text from Hayes causes a whole whirlwind of emotions. At first, I think it's a mistake. That my phone is glitching or I'm seeing things. But as I open it, I realize that he did, in fact, text me.

The shadow that's been hanging over me the last week lifts slightly. But with that comes acknowledging how pathetic that is. How I'm still allowing him to be the key to my happiness.

The first few days after he ended things were spent comatose, taking Tylenol PM just to avoid the world. At least when I was asleep, the pain in my chest wasn't as excruciating. Was that a healthy way to go about it? Definitely not. But no one ever makes the best choices right after a breakup. And it was better than going the other direction and taking a hockey stick to his truck.

Reading over the text for the seventh time, I choose not to answer it. Not because my fingers aren't itching at the chance to text him back, but because I want to be able to change my mind and turn around—if I even go in the first place. Honestly, it could go either way.

Chapter 29

I SIT ON MY roof, looking up at the stars. It was about an hour ago that I finally gave up on the idea of sleep. Not that I've been getting much lately anyway. The only thing that helps are pills, which I'm not allowed to take anymore because they make Mali worry about me, and booze. But hangovers the next day aren't fun, and I refuse to be drunk all the time. I don't care how much it hurts.

The last time I was up here was the night of Cam's most recent bonfire. I had decided it was best to stay in my room, but halfway through the night, curiosity got the better of me. I tried to look out my window, but there's a tree that sits right in my way. So, the roof was the only option.

And he wasn't there.

A part of me thought he was avoiding me again. That he didn't want to deal with the damage he caused. And a part of me was okay with it because the thought of seeing him was too painful anyway. But even knowing he wasn't there, I didn't go down to the fire.

I didn't want to be around anyone.

It wasn't until Mali and Monty stormed into my room one morning and forced me out of bed that I actually started functioning again. Personally, I was content lying in my bed and crying over romcoms all day, but they weren't having it. Monty arranged a whole day of pampering for Mali and me, and she knew exactly where to go for lunch to get me to eat something.

They helped pull me out of the darkness, and I'm grateful for it—which is why I'm not sure if I'm going tomorrow.

I'm not over him by any means. I still tear up when certain memories play in my mind. I still listen for his voice when Cam comes home from hockey practice, wondering if he's with him. Hell, my heart nearly cracked wide open when I saw him leaving my house yesterday.

I know I'm not exactly ready to see him again—not yet, anyway. But I'm not sure I'm ready to ignore this chance to hear what he has to say.

And that's where my hesitation lies.

THE SUN PEEKS THROUGH the blinds as it starts to rise, and I know that time is ticking for me to make a decision. I tried calling Mali and asking her what I should do, but she said she couldn't help me. That it's a decision I have to make on my own, and she'll support me regardless.

It was sweet, but holy fuck. All the times she's intrusive and overbearing, and she chooses *now* to mind her own business? Unbelievable.

My phone vibrates against my nightstand, and my heart stutters when I see that it's another text from Hayes. Honestly, it's a little surprising he's even awake right now.

> I'm on my way to our beach now, and I'll wait there until noon. I hope you come, but I'll understand if you don't.

God, I don't know what's worse. The fact that he's willing to wait around for six hours to see if I show, or that he's being so selfless about it. The thing about Hayes is that he doesn't put himself out there much. I think it's a defense mechanism. He's like a brick wall in that way. But over the time we spent together, I like to think I learned to read him pretty well. And the amount of vulnerability in that message is enough to make me get out of bed and start getting ready.

I don't know how this is going to go. There's a good chance I could end up even more broken than I was before. But I owe it to myself to eliminate another *what if*.

PULLING INTO THE PARKING lot, I see his truck already there and waiting. I park my car and take a deep breath, willing myself to calm down, but all that is shot to hell when I see him get out of his truck holding a bouquet of roses.

My heart begins to ache the second I lay eyes on him, and I hate it. I hate the way he can still make every part of my body react to him like a goddamn puppet master. It wasn't even two whole weeks ago that he spoke the six words that shattered every hope I ever had for us, and yet my heart thinks it's all just water under the bridge.

I'm not sure I'm strong enough to get out of the car, but if I don't, he's going to try to get in. And I know I can't handle being that close to him.

With one last deep breath, I open my door and get out, moving my sunglasses to the top of my head. I walk around to the front of my car and lean against it in an attempt to keep some distance between us.

He goes to open his mouth, but nothing comes out, so he clamps it shut again. I watch as he presses his lips into a line, almost as if he's mentally giving himself a pep talk, and then tries again.

"I'm sorry, it's just…you look really good," he says once he gets his voice to work.

My head drops, because hearing that is like heaven and hell all mixed into one. But I can't let him sweet talk me back into his arms, and with more comments like that, that's exactly what will happen.

"What did you want to talk about?" I ask.

A hint of a smile pushes its way through. "Straight to the point?"

I shrug but say nothing.

"Okay," he says, pausing to take a deep breath. "I like you."

Fuck me. My heart damn near leaps right out of my throat, and it takes everything I have not to react as I wait for him to continue.

"A lot," he adds. "I don't know if I ever told you that. I mean, I think I showed it in certain ways, or at least I tried to, but I never said it. And you deserve to hear it."

I exhale. "You didn't have to. I got the message. But then you ended things between us and I convinced myself that I imagined it."

"You didn't," he assures me, and the vulnerability in his eyes is evident. "Laiken, I fucked up. There's nothing I can say that will erase the pain I caused you, but I need you to know that the time we've spent apart has been hell for me, too.

"I have hated every last second of not having you in my life. The only thing I've been able to think about is holding you in my arms again, and the fact that I can't is devastating."

He pauses, and I can tell this is hard for him, but he's doing it anyway.

"I know that I don't deserve a second chance," he admits. "Hurting you the way I did is unforgivable. But if you give me one, I promise you that I will do everything I can to make up for it. Take me back. Please."

I stand there in silence, trying to remind myself how to breathe. Everything that just came out of his mouth is everything I've been dying to hear. And all I want to do is say yes. To jump back into his arms and let him love me the best way he knows how.

But I can't.

"No," I say sadly.

The smile falls right off his face and is replaced by hurt. "Oh."

"It's just..." Running my fingers through my hair, I know I need to explain. He needs to hear it, and I need to get it off my chest. "It wouldn't be a second chance, Hayes. The thing is that you keep pushing and pulling at me, and I keep letting you. But I can't anymore."

"I don't want to push you away anymore," he tells me. "I just want to be with you."

My brows raise. "And what about Cam? Do you think we'll just be able to stay a secret forever? Have babies and tell him that the father is the milkman?"

Judging by the look on his face, he didn't come here with the intention of changing that stipulation. The terms are clear—my brother still can't know. Hide and seek may have been my favorite game when I was a kid, but it's not anymore.

"All I need is some time to figure things out," he says. "But I *want* to figure them out, because you're worth it to me."

"And I appreciate that. I really do. But do you have any idea how much you hurt me? I was willing to do just about anything for you, and you were able to just throw me away like it was nothing. Another random Sunday." I give him a sad smile and shrug. "I'm sorry, but I have to love myself more than to risk that again."

He looks down at the ground, nodding but not saying anything, and the silence is too overwhelming. We both said what we had to say, and as much as it hurts, I have to get in my car and drive away—for good this time.

But just as my hand grabs the door handle, his voice stops me.

"I didn't *want* to end it, you know."

I let my eyes meet his once more. "And yet, you're the one that did it."

He shakes his head. "I had to."

"Care to tell me why?" I ask, but my question is met with nothing but silence.

"That's what I thought."

The moment I pull open the car door, his admission comes out in a panic. "Monty threatened me."

My blood starts to boil as what he just said sets in. Why would he go as low as to try to pin this on Monty when he's been nothing but good to me lately?

"You are something else," I growl. "I know you've got

your jealousy issues, and I'm no angel either, but I didn't think you'd actually try to lie and blame this on him."

"I'm not lying," he says, and there's nothing but honesty in his tone. "The morning after the competition, I went to get you flowers. I was going to sneak them into the locker room because you seemed like you needed something to make you smile. But Monty approached me in the parking lot in front of the florist.

"He said that if I didn't end it with you, he was going to tell Cam everything. And this time, he had proof on his phone. There was no way around it. I had no choice."

I press my lips together and cross my arms over my chest as I focus on the ground. There are a million different things coursing through me right now. Rage. Betrayal. Exasperation. And each one of them will need to be dealt with, but hearing his words, I suddenly know exactly where I stand with him, and it hurts.

A humorless laugh bubbles out of me, and I shake my head as I look up at him again. "Sounds to me like you had a choice, H. And when push came to shove, you decided that telling Cam about us was a worse option than not being with me. You had a choice, but you chose him."

He takes a step toward me. "Laiken, I—"

"No," I say, stopping him. "I don't want to hear it anymore. You don't want me. Not really, anyway. You want something easy. Less messy and complicated."

The two of us stand there, staring at each other as both are hearts are breaking all over again, but this time, he tosses the flowers onto the hood of my car and closes the gap between us.

"You're right. I don't want you." He pushes my car door shut and places his hands on either side of me. "I fucking need you."

His lips press against mine in a way that makes all the

pain go away. It takes away the doubt in my mind and the fear of getting hurt again. And for a second, I allow myself to melt into it—loving the way his mouth moves against mine. But I know that it's all just a facade. When he's not kissing me like I'm the only thing that matters in the world, all of it is going to come creeping back in.

With a hand on his chest, I gently push him away, forcing him to break the kiss. And I know I can't look him in the eyes as I compose myself. But when I do, I see a man who figured out what he wants a little too late.

"I can't," I murmur. "I'm sorry."

He doesn't try to stop me while I get into my car, and as I back out of the parking space, the roses roll off the hood and land on the ground. I spare one last look at him as the pieces of my heart that I had taped back together fall apart once more.

"Bye, H."

HAVE YOU EVER BEEN so frustrated that you can't help but cry? And then the fact that you're crying about it pisses you off even more? That's about where I'm at. I swat each tear away as it slides down my face, cursing at myself about how I shouldn't be crying.

Yeah, it hurts, but this time, I know that this is necessary. Everything with him has been such a mindfuck from the start. And the truth is I want him, but not in the way he's willing to have me. I can't be his dirty little secret anymore. I need more than that.

I *deserve* more than that.

And I sure as fuck deserve more than a friend who thinks he can insert himself into my relationship after I already told him to mind his own damn business.

I pull up to Monty's oversized mansion—I mean, really, does a family of three actually need a house this big? I've only been here a couple times, and I thought it was beautiful, but right now, everything about him is pissing me off.

I ring the doorbell and hear the sound of footsteps approaching. When the door opens, Monty's mom stands on the other side of it. At first, I wonder if she even remembers who I am, but I'm quickly corrected as she smiles.

"Laiken," she greets me. "It's so good to see you again. Monty is up in his room. Do you want me to get him for you?"

"No, that's okay," I tell her. "I'll just go up there."

In his bedroom is exactly where I want him. Everywhere else in this fortress, there are people who can eavesdrop. Workers who care about his well-being. His parents, who love him. No, I don't want to be near any of them.

I want him alone.

Walking into his room, I find Monty lying in his bed, still sound asleep. He looks peaceful, really—until I grab the glass of ice water the maid must have put on his nightstand and dump the whole thing on him.

"What the fuck?" he bellows as he's jolted awake.

"Yeah, what the fuck is right," I sneer.

Monty squints, as if he's trying to figure out if he's seeing things. "Laiken?"

"Did you threaten Hayes into leaving me? And don't lie, because I swear to God, I'll kick your ass. I don't care *how* rich you are."

He sits up, using his comforter to wipe his face off and then sighs. "I was trying to help." I let out a dry laugh, and he continues before I can say anything. "I'm serious. I saw how much you hated needing to sneak around. I thought if I put some pressure on Hayes, he would tell Cam himself and the secret would be out."

"You don't fucking know him!" I roar. "You can't strong-arm Hayes into doing anything!" I huff, throwing my arms up in the air. "Anything except leave me, apparently."

Monty frowns, looking genuinely sad, but I have no sympathy for him.

"I'm sorry," he says. "I was just trying to help. The way that relationship was, with you being his dirty secret, it wasn't good for you."

I lace my fingers through my hair and pull in an attempt to relieve some anger before I kill the rich kid. "That wasn't for you to decide! God, I am so sick of people deciding what is good for me!"

First it was Cam with his constant overbearing attitude, telling every guy who looks at me the wrong way that they're not good enough. Then it was Hayes, saying that I deserve better than him. And now Monty, who I've known all of like five fucking minutes?

Yeah, no. Screw this.

He calls my name as I'm walking out the door, but that's another mistake, because I'm done.

"No! You've done enough," I sneer. "Leave me the fuck alone. I never want to see you again."

Laiken

CHAPTER THIRTY

I pace back and forth across Mali's room, my voice gradually getting louder until she shushes me, and the cycle starts all over again.

"I just can't fucking believe the nerve he has! What he said after the concert was one thing, but to actually go as far as to threaten Hayes? What the fuck is wrong with him?"

Mali sighs. "I totally get where you're coming from, and I'm on your side. He had no right to involve himself in... whatever it was you had with Hayes."

I narrow my eyes at her. "I'm sensing a *but* coming."

"But," she says slowly, "just to play devil's advocate here, do you think that maybe it really did come from a good place?"

Ha! "How could threatening someone to leave me come from a good place?"

She shrugs, looking like she's on the fence about it. "He might have actually thought it would be just the kick in the ass Hayes needed to tell Cam about you two."

Looking at her, I keep the straightest face I can manage. "Mali, an elephant could kick that guy in the ass and he still wouldn't tell my brother about us."

The mental image makes her giggle. "You know this, and I know this, but Monty doesn't. He doesn't really know Hayes, *or* how he is."

"Which is all the more reason he shouldn't have gotten involved."

I throw myself onto her bed, feeling exhausted from the lack of sleep and high range of emotions today. I didn't know someone could go from feeling sad, to happy, to upset, to absolutely enraged in all of an hour, but you learn something new every day, I guess.

"So what does this mean?" Mali asks, treading lightly. "Are you going to get back with Hayes?"

That question has been on my mind since the second Monty admitted to threatening him. Yeah, I knew Hayes wasn't lying when he told me about it. But I needed to hear it straight from the horse's mouth. And yet, the answer to the question still comes back the same.

"No," I tell her. "We want different things, and I can't continue to be his yo-yo."

"Oh my God!" she gasps. "I *love* yo-yos. I miss those things!"

I stare back at her, emotionless and blinking, and she smiles like a kid in trouble.

"Right. Not the time. Sorry."

Chuckling, I roll my eyes and turn over, getting some much-needed sleep in the only place I seem to be able to lately.

I NEVER THOUGHT THAT there would be a time

where I *don't* want to throw a bonfire...until now. It's not that I don't love them. They're so calming and peaceful, and it's always a good time. But I know Hayes isn't going to miss this one. Not after missing the last. And definitely not when he'll take any excuse he can get to see me.

He thinks I don't notice when he comes to the rink early enough to catch the end of my shift, but I do. I see him as he stands upstairs in the office, looking out the window. I just pretend that I don't. He hasn't tried to say anything to me, so I haven't had a reason to care.

Knowing that he's going to be here tonight is a strange feeling. Neither one of us have said a word to each other since I turned him down in the same place I gave him my virginity. But just because I didn't jump back into his arms doesn't mean that I don't still want to.

Sometimes it's all I can fucking think about.

But I meant it when I said I can't risk that kind of heartbreak again.

And I refuse to be with him while he hides us away like he's got something to be ashamed of.

For a moment, I consider staying in my room tonight. I'm not exactly in the mood to be around people, Hayes especially. But with that idea comes the possibility of him coming to find me—and that would be even worse. At least in a group of people, I'm not tempted to fall right back into him.

So, instead of tucking myself away in my room, I start getting ready for the bonfire, and mentally preparing myself to see him again.

Chapter 30

THEY SAY ONE OF the worst kinds of pain is wanting something you can't have. But what about the things you *can* have but know you shouldn't? When your head is battling against your heart, and the mere sight of them has you feeling like you're holding yourself together with tape?

Just because I let the ship sink doesn't mean I'm not drowning, too.

I curl into myself, watching the fire turn the wood into ash. Warmth surrounds me, but I still feel cold. Mali insists it's because I haven't been eating enough. She's probably right, but I still think a part of it has to do with Hayes. He had this way of warming me from the inside out, and now I'm colder than ever.

Every now and then, I can feel his gaze. Like he's watching me, trying to carve each one of my features into his memory. And I know the feeling, because I've done the same over the years.

After twenty minutes of resisting him like I never thought I could, I finally give in and let myself look over at him. But the sad smile we exchange makes me wish I hadn't. We're both dying inside—victims of our own crimes. When he doesn't look away, risking Cam seeing us in a way he never did before, I force myself to break the eye contact for him.

And that's when he cracks open the first beer.

Chapter 30

IT'S NOT LIKE HIM to drink excessively. Sure, we've had parties where he's gotten completely obliterated and spent the rest of the night expelling the alcohol from his stomach like a demon in an exorcism, but this isn't one of those. Bonfires are normally spent hanging out, joking around, and casually drinking.

Emphasis on casually.

But tonight, his emphasis is on drinking.

I know it's not my problem, and I shouldn't concern myself with it, but I can't help it. Hayes Wilder is my own personal bad habit, and it's going to take a lot more than a couple weeks to break it. Which is why I start keeping a tally of how many beers he's had in my phone.

Not being with him because I refuse to accept less than I deserve is not the same as not feeling something for him. I don't know that there will ever be a day that I don't. But even if there's a time when romantic feelings fade, I am *always* going to care.

And you won't hear me apologize for it.

"I have an idea," Owen says. "Let's play Truth or Dare."

Cam snorts. "Well, damn, I didn't know we were back in middle school."

"What's wrong? Afraid I'll finally get you to call chicken?" he taunts.

Chuckling, Cam shakes his head. "I've never done it before. I'm not going to do it now."

Owen shrugs. "Well, put up or shut up, Blanchard."

The game starts small, with petty shit like Owen daring Cam to shotgun a whole beer, or Aiden getting dared to prank call his own mother. Though, the way she screams into her phone that he woke her up for this bullshit makes me wonder what he'll be going home to later.

But the longer we play, the more dangerous it's becoming.

See, Hayes's drinking hasn't stopped. It hasn't even slowed down. Based on my tally, he's currently on beer number seven. And everyone knows that alcohol has a way of impairing your judgment.

Leaning over, I whisper into Mali's ear. "We have to figure out a way to get him to stop drinking so much. What he's had already is enough to make this game a bad idea."

She nods and winks at me before getting up. "Anyone need anything from inside?"

Everyone shakes their heads, and she starts to head toward the house, but as she walks by Hayes, she makes sure to kick over his beer—spilling the contents into the grass. And he's too drunk to notice.

"All right," Cam says. "Owen. It's payback time, fucker. Truth or dare?"

"Truth."

All the guys chuckle as Cam calls him a pussy. "Is it true that you're secretly dating your stepsister?"

My jaw drops as Owen throws his head back, laughing loudly.

"No, I'm not dating her," he answers. "I am fucking her, though."

"What the fuck!" Aiden yells, his arms flailing in the air.

But Owen has no shame. "What? It's not like we grew up together. We've never even lived in the same house."

Mali comes back out at the perfect time, squatting down next to Hayes's seat. "What'd I miss?"

Hayes must not have heard her coming because he jumps. "Jesus fucking Christ! Where the hell did you come from?"

"My mother?"

No one else is paying attention, but I watch as she switches out his spilled beer with what looks like another one. Judging by the fact that it's already open, however, I know she filled it with seltzer.

A trick she used on me when I got a little out of control one night.

"But seriously," she says as she stands up and comes to sit beside me again. "What did I miss? I heard yelling."

"Owen's got an incest kink," Aiden jokes.

Mali cringes as Owen defends himself. "Fuck off. We're barely even related. They've been married for all of like six months."

"Damn, O," Mali teases. "Didn't think you'd be the type."

"Screw all of you," he grumbles, and then he turns to Hayes in a way that has the hair on my arms standing up. "Speaking of people we're fucking… H, truth or dare?"

There's no easy answer to this. Either they're going to ask who it is, and I don't trust his ability to come up with a believable lie right now, or he'll figure out a way to get it out of him with a dare. Even Mali's breath hitches.

"Dare," he says confidently.

Owen leans back in his seat. "Call the girl you've been so hung up on lately."

Hayes manages to force out a snicker as he drops his head. "We, uh…We're not really talking anymore."

"Well, that explains why you've been such a dick this week," Cam jokes, but Owen isn't about to let it go.

"Not really what I asked, bro," he presses. "Unless you want to call chicken."

Hayes's eyes narrow at Owen before he pulls his phone out of his pocket. Thankfully, everyone is so focused on him that they don't notice the way I quickly slip my phone under my hoodie.

The second the ring starts to come through the speaker of his phone, I feel it vibrate against my stomach. And Mali, being the godsend she is, starts talking to cover the sound of it.

"Oh, I forgot to tell you," she says, as if she's talking only to me. "The other day at work, this guy came in with a woman who was *clearly* not his wife. His wife comes in all the time, so I obviously know who she is. Well, he had this bitch pick out some lingerie."

As Mali continues her story, I can't help but stare at Hayes. With each time my phone vibrates, the pain in my chest becomes stronger. And by the third ring, he looks up at me, making his actions clear.

I could answer the phone.

I could pick it up right now, and my voice would come through the speaker—revealing to everyone that it's me. That I'm the girl he's spent the last couple months all wrapped up in.

He's putting the power completely in my hands.

But what we had means more to me than what could very well become a drunken mistake in the morning.

The call goes to voicemail, and the little bit of sense that remains in him hangs up just as the first three numbers of my phone number are said. But the area code tells them nothing. It could be anyone.

I sigh, trying to ignore the way my heart feels like it's breaking all over again, and Mali leans against me to let her know she's there. Meanwhile, Aiden is looking at Mali in shock.

"Wait," he says. "You really sent the receipt to his wife's email?"

My eyes widen. Clearly, I wasn't paying enough attention to her story. But Mali smirks, shrugging carelessly.

"Yep," she tells him. "Well, technically the system did. I just rang it up under her account. It's not my fault he's a pig."

She has a point. I just hope her savage tendencies don't get her ass killed one day.

It's Hayes's turn next, and he looks anything but into it. But when he looks directly at me, there's something different in his eyes.

"Laiken," my name flows from his lips for the first time all night. "Truth or dare?"

There's no way I trust him enough right now to pick dare, so that only leaves me with one option. "Truth."

The corners of his lips raise. "What's been your favorite day of the summer so far?"

Aiden scoffs. "That's a shitty question. What a waste."

But he doesn't know that we've spent almost the entire summer together, and that most of my memories from the last couple months feature him. I know what he's doing. He's looking for something, anything, to hold onto. To tell him that I didn't wipe everything from my mind.

And I can't help but give it to him.

"I saw Thomas Rhett in concert. That was pretty epic." I pause and run my fingers through my hair. "But I think my *favorite* would have to be when I went out on Monty's boat. The sunset was perfect that day."

The way we don't look away from each other is intense, but the way he mouths *"mine, too"* hits me straight in the chest, forcing its way in and taking up residence right next to my heart.

And I feel it long after everyone moves on like nothing happened.

Chapter 30

THE GAME GOES ON for what feels like hours, but thankfully it's all mostly dumb shit you come up with when you're running out of ideas. But Owen is determined to finally defeat Cam.

See, the way we play is when you call chicken, you're out. And the game continues until you're the only one left—making you the winner of truth or dare. Usually, it ends with everyone calling chicken until there are two people left and Cam tells them to do something so outrageous that he wins by default.

This time, however, is different. We all start calling chicken over things we really don't care about, just for the sake of not wanting to play anymore. Mine is for not wanting to get Cam another beer. Mali calls it when she gets asked when the last time she had sex was, and then literally answers immediately after. And Hayes doesn't even pick truth or dare. He just says it as soon as his name is said.

Being as Aiden was already out from refusing to jump over the fire, that just leaves Owen and Cam. And it's Owen's turn.

Everyone knows this is his only shot. The look on Cam's face tells me he already has something insane that will get Owen to bow out, so if Owen can't get Cam to call chicken for the first time ever, Cam will remain undefeated.

Some may call it impressive, but I call it lacking shame.

"Hmm," Owen says, stroking his chin as he stares at

Cam. When he finally decides on something, he sits up and leans forward. His arms rest on his knees and he smirks. "I dare you to kiss Mali."

My brows furrow, wondering why the fuck he would waste the opportunity on something like that, but the confident look vanishes from Cam's face. He looks over at Mali and then down at his beer. The only thing you can hear is the sound of the fire crackling, until Cam exhales.

"Chicken."

His voice comes out so low I almost think I'm imagining it, but the way Owen celebrates tells me I didn't. I never thought I would see the day where Cam loses at truth or dare. I've literally seen him open the door of a restaurant bathroom with his pants at his ankles and yell for toilet paper while covering his dick with his hands. He just never gives a shit. Ever.

There are only three possibilities running through my mind. Either he just gave it to Owen for the fuck of it, he has a girlfriend I don't know about and doesn't want to cheat, or he has some kind of feelings for Mali.

But if it were the last one, wouldn't he jump at the opportunity to kiss her instead of throwing the game?

Aiden stands up. "Fuck it, I'll do it."

He goes to take a step toward Mali, but Cam acts fast and lifts his foot just in time, tripping him and sending him face first onto the ground.

"Leave the poor girl alone," Cam tells Aiden. "No one wants your herpes."

We all laugh, and Mali looks grateful for the save. But there's also something else about her I can't seem to put my finger on.

Chapter 30

THE FIRE BURNS OUT as everyone starts to leave, and once he sprays the pit with the hose, Cam heads inside. I run up to my room to grab some things while Mali waits for me outside. It's just safer if I sleep at her house instead of risking the chance of Hayes tapping on my skylight when he's stuck awake.

But as I walk out the door, I see him heading for his truck.

There's a level of panic that shoots through me, and I nearly drop my things as I run toward him. Just as he goes to get into the driver's seat, I push myself between him and the truck.

"What the fuck do you think you're doing?" I growl, ripping the keys out of his hand as he stays completely frozen. "Are you trying to kill yourself? Or someone else for that matter?"

He looks down, having at least a little sense to be ashamed of himself. "I was just trying to give you your space."

I sigh heavily. "I appreciate that, but I'm sleeping at Mali's so it's fine. Just go sleep in Cam's room."

But he doesn't move. "I can't do that."

What? "Hayes, I'm serious," I press. "You can't drive home. You're too drunk. So go inside and go to sleep."

"I. Can't." His voice comes out a little louder this time, and I am way too exhausted for this argument.

"Why not? You've done it a million times." I spin him

around and push him in the direction of the house. "You can drive home first thing in the morning. Just go get some sleep."

"I told you, I can't!" he shouts. "Don't you get it? Everything in that house reminds me of you! I can't torture myself like that!"

"Shh!" I say, throwing my hand over his mouth and looking around to see if anyone could have heard him. "Have you lost your mind? Cam is going to hear you."

His fingers wrap around my wrist as he pulls my hand away. "Let him! I don't give a shit anymore!"

With each word that leaves his mouth, he gets louder. And if I thought he knew what he was saying, I'd probably just stand back and watch the chaos unfold. But he doesn't. And I can't.

"None of it fucking matters when I—"

Bracing myself, I roll my eyes and grab the back of his neck, pulling him down and cutting off his rant by kissing him. As his lips move against mine, he sighs and immediately relaxes into it. Like an addict finally getting his fix.

When he kissed me the other day, I pushed him away, knowing it was going to be the last time I was ever going to feel his mouth on mine. And it hurt like a bitch, but I did it.

This time is worse, as I feel the pain of reopening a fresh wound.

"Get in the passenger seat," I tell him as I pull away. "I'll be right back."

He nods, but that must be a bad idea because his eyes widen, and he holds up one finger. I watch as he walks over to the bushes, getting there just in time to vomit all the beer and seltzer he drank all night onto the ground.

Can't say I didn't know that was coming.

After he's done, he comes back and mumbles an apology

before getting into his truck. I take a deep breath and go over to where Mali is waiting for me next to her car.

"So, are you sleeping at his house? What was that about?"

I glance back at Hayes and shake my head. "Just follow me, okay? I have to drive him home."

"You sure that's a good idea?" she asks, knowing I'm willingly putting myself alone with him.

"No," I answer honestly. "But I'm going to do it anyway."

"Okay. I'll be right behind you."

Mali unlocks her car and climbs in while I go back to Hayes truck. It takes a minute for me to adjust the seat, but I manage to make it work. The truck comes on as I turn the key, and I pull out of my driveway.

The drive to his house is quiet for the most part but I can feel him watching me the entire time. His eyes don't leave me once, even as I refuse to look at him. And it isn't until halfway to his house that he breaks the silence.

"I miss you," he tells me.

His voice is so raw. So broken. And I know he's telling the truth. This time there isn't a doubt in my mind that ripping my own heart out of my chest would be less painful.

"God," he breathes. "I miss you so damn much."

"Stop," I beg as my eyes start to water. "Please. I can't do this."

He goes completely still, and I glance over at him in time to see him sigh as he nods, finally taking his eyes off me as he turns toward the window instead. My heart sinks, and I feel bad, but *he* did this. If it were up to me, things would be so different.

We get to his house, and I park the truck before helping him out. Mali waits in her car while I bring him inside. He stumbles a couple times, having trouble getting up onto the porch, but we make it work.

I use his key to unlock the front door and hold onto him as I push it open. Devin is sitting on the couch. She looks back at us, and her brows furrow as she sees me.

"What's going on?" she asks as she stands up and walks over to us. "Are you two back together?"

But before I can respond, she stops, and her eyes widen as she backs away, clearly getting a whiff of Hayes.

"Jesus Christ. Did he bathe in a distillery?"

"He may as well have," I tell her.

Hayes lets me lead him to his room and then crashes onto his bed, drunkenly mumbling something about how it still smells like me. I slide his shoes off his feet and put them on the floor, covering him with the blanket that's scrunched up at the bottom of the bed. Giving myself another second to watch him, I hate the way I still have the urge to curl up next to him. To fall asleep wrapped in his arms, listening to the sound of his heartbeat.

But those days are gone.

As I turn to leave, I notice a sweatshirt hanging over the back of his chair. My first thought is that he had some other girl here, followed by *he might not be the only one to puke tonight*. But when I pick it up, I realize that it's mine.

"Can you leave it?" he murmurs.

My head whips over to him, and I'm surprised to see his eyes open, blinking back at me. I thought he was passed out already.

"I know you don't owe me anything," he continues. "But could you just..."

His voice fades out, but I know what he's asking. And while this hoodie may be one of my favorites, I fold it back in half and drape it over the chair before forcing myself to leave the room.

Devin is still waiting for me when I come out, and I hand her his keys.

"Hide these somewhere until the morning," I tell her.

She nods, but I can tell she's worried. "What the hell got into him tonight? He never gets this drunk."

I exhale heavily. "It's my fault. He tried to apologize and wanted to get back together, but I can't do it."

The look on her face is sympathetic, not at all judging, but her words hit home. "Can't, or won't?"

"Both," I answer honestly. "I'm crazy about him, Dev. You know that. But all I would ever be is a secret to him. And sneaking around may have been fun and exciting at first, but it became something darker.

"Every time he would look away too quickly so Cam wouldn't suspect anything or jump away from me because someone was coming into the surf shop, it was a painful reminder that none of it was ever real. Not for him anyway. Not in the way that it mattered."

She frowns. "But what if it wasn't a secret anymore? What if he told Cam about you two?"

I shake my head. "I'm not playing the *what if* game. It's too dangerous. He already made his choice there."

Devin nods in understanding, and I give her a quick hug before I leave. Putting one foot in front of the other, I focus on just getting myself to Mali's car so that I don't listen to the way my heart screams at me to turn around. Once I get in, she turns to look at me.

"Are you okay?" she asks carefully.

A stray tear slips out, and I wipe it away as I stare out the window. "Just drive."

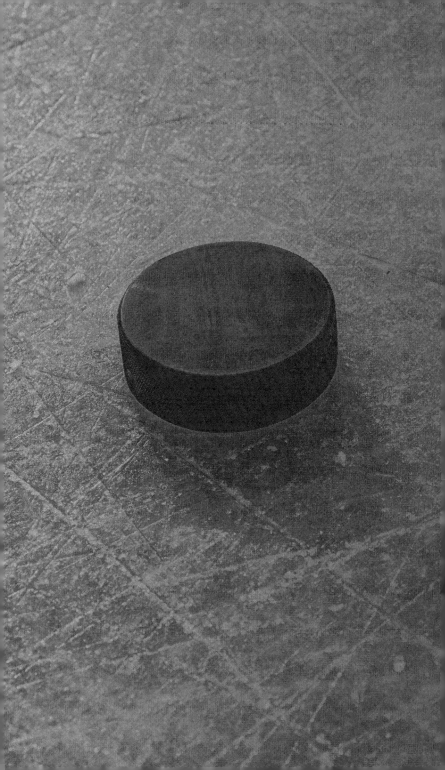

Hayes
CHAPTER THIRTY ONE

A stabbing pain shoots through my head, feeling like someone just put an icepick straight through my brain. My eyes are still closed as I wince and press the heel of my hand to my temple.

"Oh, fuck," I groan.

The sound of Devin chuckling comes from somewhere in the room. "Yeah, I figured you'd be miserable this morning."

I force my eyes open a crack to find her leaning against my doorway, but when I go to flip her off, I realize the mistake of letting go of my head.

"I feel like a garbage fire."

"I bet," she teases. "You smell like one, too."

My mom comes down the hallway and peeks head around to look in my room. "What's wrong with him?"

Devin smirks. "Oh, you know. Just drinking away his feelings."

"Hayes Beckett!" Mom yells, and I swear, a spiky ball ricochets around my brain.

"Don't yell," I whimper.

My sister laughs while my mom sighs and walks away. A couple minutes later, she comes back with two Advil and a bottle of water.

"Here, dipshit," she says, handing them to me. "Take them."

"There's no need for name calling," I whine as I take them from her.

She isn't amused. "Mm-hm."

I force myself to sit up and swallow the pills as she leaves. It takes me a minute to get over the nausea, but once I do, it sets in that I would normally be waking up at Cam's right now.

"How did I get home last night?"

"Laiken brought you," she says, shocking the shit out of me.

But as I sit there thinking about it, I slowly start to piece together the events of last night. And when I remember asking her to leave her sweatshirt, my gaze immediately goes to the chair.

It's still there.

I sigh in relief as Devin holds up my keys and tosses them to me. "I figure you're sober enough to have those now."

"Thanks."

She pushes off the doorway and walks away, and I groan as I crash back into my bed.

I don't think there's a single part of my body that doesn't hurt.

I SIT IN MY truck, waiting in the parking lot for Laiken's shift to end. I skipped hockey practice on the grounds of being too hungover to be trusted on skates. Taking a shower was difficult enough, let alone trying to focus on a small rubber puck.

Showing up here is a risk. If Coach sees me after I skipped practice, I'll be benched for sure. But I need to talk to Laiken. So, as I start to see kids coming out with their parents, I get out of my truck and head inside, hoping that Coach has already left for the day.

As I walk through the doors, I'm expecting to find Laiken on the ice. Since practice is before her shift on Saturdays, she usually stays a little past her shift. But instead, I find her standing by the stairs to the office, talking to the owner.

I'm surprised to see him here. Usually, he's only around for big events or when we make the championships. At first, I wonder if he's on her case again about how she's aging out of being able to go pro. But when she smiles and nods at something he says, I know that can't be it.

Her eyes meet mine, and she double-takes before putting her attention back on Mr. Zimmerman. They exchange a few more words, and she smiles again before he heads up the stairs—nodding when he sees me standing here.

"Next Sunday," he yells to her before he goes in his office. "Don't forget."

"I won't," she responds.

Laiken runs her fingers through her hair as she comes closer—no hostility anywhere to be found. I probably shouldn't, but I find comfort in that.

"Everything okay?" I ask.

She glances back at the stairs quickly and nods. "Yeah. We were just talking about me taking over the lessons department. Calvin is getting too old to keep track of a bunch of rambunctious kids, not that it hasn't been all me for the last year anyway."

"That's great!" I tell her, going in for a hug without thinking. But she allows it and wraps her arms around me. "I'm so proud of you."

"Thanks." We let go of each other a little soon for my

liking and she steps back. "We're meeting for dinner next week to discuss some of the ideas I have for revamping the program."

My grin only widens. "I'm sure they're all amazing."

"We'll see," she shrugs. "Was there something you needed?"

"Yeah," I tell her, rubbing the back of my neck. "I just wanted to thank you for bringing me home last night. I shouldn't have tried to drive. That was really stupid of me."

"It was," she says in that no-bullshit tone of hers.

I nod slowly, looking down. "I know. But you didn't let me. So, thank you."

Her chest rises and falls as she sighs, letting go of any leftover anger. "It's no big deal."

"Maybe not to you, but I really appreciate it."

She chuckles and shakes her head. "It's not like I hate you or anything."

It's so lighthearted, the way she says it, but it still manages to hit a soft spot. "I wouldn't blame you if you did."

Her shoulders sag as we stand there, looking at each other, and for the first time since everything was shot to hell, I feel like maybe I didn't completely screw everything up. We may not ever be more than friends again, and it might take some time, but as long as I eventually still have her in my life, I'll be okay.

"Mr. Wilder."

And just like that, the moment is ruined. I wince, hearing the way he says my name like I'm in trouble, and Laiken chuckles.

"Well." She claps her hands together. "I'm going to go, but you have fun with *that*."

I glare at her playfully. "You're pure evil. You know that?"

Raising her eyebrows, she looks at Coach. "Whatever excuse he tells you, don't believe him. He got blackout drunk last night and was too hungover for practice." My jaw drops as she smiles at me. "Now, *that* was evil."

As she turns around and walks out, giggling to herself, I can't help but watch her. Once she's gone, however, I'm forced to turn around and face the music.

"Step into my office," Coach tells me. "Let's discuss tonight's game and the importance of showing up for practice when you're one of my captains."

SOCIAL MEDIA IS THE best and worst thing to ever happen to the world. I tend to avoid it for the most part, but when I feel particularly self-destructive from missing Laiken, it helps. I scroll through her Instagram, looking at pictures and smiling at how gorgeous she looks. Devin catches me.

"Jesus," she says, appearing behind me. "When did you turn into a teenage girl?"

It manages to pull a laugh out of me. "I'm not sure, but if you find my man card, please give it back."

"Man?" she cringes. "Oof. Let's not get ahead of ourselves, big boy."

Narrowing my eyes to slits, I stare back at her. "Have I told you that I wanted a brother?"

"Yes, but I'm more fun." She comes around the couch and sits down. "I don't get it. If you're so hung up on this, why not fight for her?"

"I tried, remember?"

Her eyes roll. "No, you tried to get her back. I mean *fight* for her. Face your fears and tell Cam that you're banging his sister, and then claim your girl."

"Oh, so you want me to get myself killed is what you're saying," I say, only half joking.

She purses her lips. "Well, no. But that would be a great plot twist, wouldn't it?"

I grab the empty water bottle in my lap and throw it at her. She lets out a small laugh as she shields herself from it.

"All I'm saying is you're at a point where it's all or nothing with her. You either need to go all in and tell Cam or leave her alone and let her get over you. But you can't have it halfway anymore."

As her phone rings and she answers it, getting up and walking toward her room, I know she has a point. But the thing is, I don't even think that's an option. She had the ability to expose us when I called her that night, and she chose not to.

"Hey, Dev?" She stops just before the hallway and tells her friend to hold on as she looks at me. "What if that's not what she wants? What if she really *is* just done with me?"

I watch as my sister smiles sadly and shrugs. "That's life, brother. But that doesn't mean this is easy for her. It's going to take both of you time to heal."

As she goes back to her call, I'm left alone to think. I look down at my phone and admire the way she smiles. You can practically feel her happiness. It's contagious. Even now, missing her the way I do, I can't help but feel her warmth.

She deserves to be happy. She deserves to be this same girl, smiling brightly and laughing like the whole world is butterflies and rainbows. And as much as it may kill me, Devin is right.

I need to let her go.

Chapter 31

STAYING AWAY IS THE hardest part. I don't know if it was better when she was the one avoiding me, but when you lack self-control, it comes down to literally taking it one day at a time. That's all I *can* do.

And for an entire week, I manage to make it work. I go straight into the locker room when I get to the rink and hang out with Cam at places other than his house. I do my best to keep my distance, until I have no choice but to see her again.

Before last week's game, I was benched for skipping practice. Normally, that would mean having to watch the game but not getting to play. But I managed to convince Coach that I was better used in his office, coming up with new plays that use each players' strengths to our advantage.

It kept me tucked away in the locker room, where I didn't have to see anyone except the guys. And I waited until Laiken was gone to leave the locker room. I couldn't risk seeing her. It would only make me want to talk to her. And if she had come to talk to me, I would've been starting all over again.

But as I sit by my locker, lacing up my skates, I know that there's nothing I can do. Tonight, I have to play in the game —and playing in the game means I'll have to see her.

"You good, man?" Cam asks me.

I pull the laces toward me, making them tight. "Yeah. You?"

He nods. "Just ready to kick some ass."

"Fuck yeah!" Aiden agrees. "They're going to eat my snow."

Everyone goes quiet until Owen comes up and pats him on the shoulder. "That was only cool when we were like fifteen, dude."

"Mentally, he still *is* fifteen," Isaac adds.

Anytime that guy talks, I want to knock his teeth out. Owen may think he's cool, but I'm not about to sit here and listen as he talks shit about Aiden.

I finish lacing my skates and stand up, nodding toward Isaac. "And yet, his average is still better than yours."

The rest of the guys laugh while his face turns beet red, but I can't find it in me to care. He shouldn't be talking shit about his own teammate. Aiden may not be our best player, but I'd pick him to be on my team over Isaac any day of the week.

I head out of the locker room and walk over to the rink, stepping on the ice. All week, I've been putting in extra practice as a way to work off some energy. It's helped keep me distracted, and more importantly, it's made it so I'm able to sleep at night. Not well, exactly, but at least more than I was.

The only thing I have to do is get through this game without letting myself get wrapped up in all things Laiken. But as I skate around the goal and finally lift my head, I realize that's going to be a lot harder than I originally thought.

Because there she is, sitting in the stands with Mali by her side, and she's wearing my jersey.

Chapter 31

EYES ON THE PUCK. Stick on the ice. Nothing else matters except this. Right here. Right now. This game. The timer is winding down to the end of the third period, and by the grace of God, I've managed to keep my head in the game. But we're still tied 2-2.

If we don't score in the next two minutes, we're going into overtime.

I get in position and wait for the puck to drop. The guy across from me looks like he wants to taunt me, but I took a page out of Cam's book, and the earplugs do a great job at keeping me from getting distracted by shit talkers. You know the type. The ones who can't play as well, so they try to get under your skin instead. Those shitheads.

The moment the puck hits the ice, I don't miss a beat. I pass it over to Cam and get around my opponent. Between him, Owen, and me, we form a V and make our way down the ice, passing the puck between us.

Owen takes the first shot, but it hits the post. The clang you dread hearing in hockey is so loud that I can hear it through the earplugs. But Cam manages to recover it, and he passes it to me just in time for my stick to slap it straight into the goal.

We win.

The buzzer sounds and my teammates surround me, hitting my helmet. The energy in the room is amazing.

Everyone in the crowd is on their feet, screams echoing throughout the rink. And Mr. Zimmerman looks on from the big window in his office, smiling proudly.

As the game ends, we all pour into the locker room, high off our win. Every single one of us played our asses off out there and we deserve this. That team was not easy to defeat by any means. But we worked as a team and made it happen.

There isn't a guy in this room that I'm not proud of.

Well, except maybe Isaac.

Douchebag.

"So, where are we going to celebrate?" Cam asks as he opens his locker.

"My place is empty," Owen suggests.

Cam purses his lips and nods. "Can't turn down an empty house full of booze. H, you coming?"

I should. I should go celebrate the win with my team. But I can guarantee Laiken is going to be there, and nothing good can come of her and I being in a place with bedroom doors that lock. It would be too easy to fall back into old habits. And it's bad enough she kissed me just to shut me up the one night. I don't want to risk us getting drunk and doing something she ends up regretting.

"I would, but I've got work early tomorrow," I tell them.

It's not a lie. I do have work. And ten in the morning *is* early to me.

"Lame," Cam tells me.

But it's for the best. I know it is.

Chapter 31

I WALK DOWN MAIN Street, heading back to my truck after shopping for a birthday gift for Devin. I ended up buying her a gift card to the salon and a T-shirt that says *My Mom should have stopped at one.* It's meant for the oldest child, but that's what makes it great.

And it's typical of us to mess with each other, so I know she'll love it.

I'm only half a block away when I stop. The universe must really love seeing me suffer, because only twenty feet away, Laiken steps out of the restaurant. She looks good all dressed up, and if she were mine, I'd take her into my arms and tell her so.

There's no way I can avoid her, unless I turn around and head in the opposite direction, but that doesn't feel like an option either. If she saw me do it, it'll hurt her, and I've caused enough damage.

"Hey," I say softly.

She turns her head and smiles when she sees me. "Oh, hey. What are you doing here?"

I hold up the bag in my hand. "Birthday present for Dev."

"Shit," she winces. "Thanks for reminding me."

Nodding, I kick my feet against the ground. "How've you been?"

"I've been okay." Her voice is soft, like she's talking to

one of her favorite people. "What about you? I haven't really seen you around much."

"I'm all right. Just trying to keep busy. I think I practiced twice as much last week."

I consider telling her that I'm staying away for her. To make things easier and not risk putting her in more pain than I already have. But I don't think it would do any good.

"Well, it shows," she says. "You played really well."

"Thank you," I tell her honestly.

She looks down and away for a second. "I'm sorry if you didn't want me wearing your jersey. I'll give it back. I didn't even realize I still had it, but then I saw it hanging in my closet and I—"

"Laiken," I cut her off with a small laugh. "It's fine. You can keep it. It looks better on you anyway."

I watch as she blinks, her mouth falling open just slightly. At the risk of testing my luck, and really torturing the shit out of myself, I step closer and press a soft kiss to the top of her head. Her hand rests on my arm, leaving a burning feeling that lingers long after she removes it.

"I'll see you around," I tell her, and she stays silent as she nods.

But as I get a few steps away, curiosity gets the better of me, and I spin back around.

"Can I just ask you one thing?"

The corners of her lips raise. "Anything."

"Why didn't you answer the phone that night?" I blurt out the question that's been on my mind for the last week. "You could've answered the phone, and Cam would have known about us the second your voice came through the speaker. It would've been that simple. But you didn't, and I'm just wondering why?"

Her brows furrow, and it looks like she's about to answer, until an expensive car pulls up next to her. Mr. Zimmerman puts down the passenger side window and leans over the center console.

"Sorry it took me so long," he tells her. "I didn't realize I parked that far away." He turns his attention to me and nods. "Hey, Wilder. Great game last night, son."

"Thank you, sir," I reply. "Nice car."

He grins, knowing that half the money for the thing probably came from our hockey team. Laiken opens the passenger side door and slips into the car, her eyes never leaving mine. And as he drives away, the sad smile she gives me brings me back at least three steps.

MUSIC BLASTS THROUGH THE speakers as I drive toward my house. My fingers grip the steering wheel as my mind runs wild. She looked so pretty tonight, and while it may have been a work dinner tonight, I know it won't always be. One day, she's going to start dating again, and I'll be forced to watch her fall in love with someone else.

The only thing I wish is that Mr. Z pulled up a couple minutes later. That I could have heard her answer to my question. But if I'm not meant to know, then I guess that's just something I'll have to deal with, no matter how much it sucks.

As if she can tell I was thinking about it, my phone vibrates in my lap and Laiken's name appears on the screen.

The way my heart jumps at the sight of it still hasn't faded. Not even a little. I pick up my phone and read the words that have the power to change everything.

> Because you were drinking, and I might not know exactly how important I was to you, but you and what we had together mean more to me than a drunken mistake you'd regret in the morning.

My foot slams on the brake, my tires screeching as it comes to a halt. I read her words over for a second time. And then a third. Checking that I'm seeing this right, and it's not wishful thinking making me imagine things that aren't there.

It's the same reason I didn't go to the party last night at Owen's. She thinks I would have regretted it. Regretted her. But I could never, and it's time that she knows that.

Turning the wheel, I press the gas pedal to the floor, doing a burnout as I spin around. The car in the opposite lane lays on their horn as they're forced to stop short, but I simply don't care.

Some things are more important.

FLYING DOWN THE ROAD, I come to a stop in front of Cam and Laiken's house and jump out of my truck. It doesn't even occur to me that I left it running. There's nothing else I can think about except the determination running through my veins.

Laiken is in the driveway, standing outside of Mr. Zimmerman's car as they talk, but when she sees me, her eyes widen.

"What are you doing?"

But I don't answer. My gaze is laser focused on the light that shines from inside the detached garage. Cam must be in there working. My feet carry me toward it like I'm running on autopilot as Laiken rushes to follow me.

"Hayes," she shouts, swearing under her breath. "Hayes, stop! What are you doing?"

I ignore her, pulling the switchblade from my pocket as I walk through the door. Cam looks up at me as I spin the blade around, so the handle is toward him.

"You're going to need this," I tell him just as Laiken reaches the doorway.

His brows furrow as he takes it from me. "What? Why?"

"Because I'm falling in love with your sister."

To be continued…

A Drop of Pretty Poison
Available Now

A Drop of Pretty Poison

THEY SAY THAT WHEN A LOVE BURNS TOO BRIGHT, IT'S BOUND TO BURN OUT—ESPECIALLY THOSE WRAPPED IN SECRETS AND DOUSED IN LIES.

After a risk is taken and a confession is made, one relationship heats up while another hangs in the balance. When everything rests on shaky ground, we find the stability we need tangled up in each other. Guards are let down and trust is repaired, but all vulnerability comes with a side of weakness. And the betrayal that hits us is one we never saw coming.

Revenge is a dangerous game, especially when fueled by jealousy. We'll do whatever it takes to protect our own, even if it means seeking help from unlikely sources. While every favor comes at a price, choices made in distress have a tendency to backfire.

As our world comes crashing down around us, loyalties are put to the test. Nothing should be able to shatter the promises we made, but there's a fine line between tenacious and toxic.

Someone should've warned us that even a drop of pretty poison will spread until all that's left are shattered pieces and broken memories.

Continue with Hayes & Laiken
A Drop of Pretty Poison
Available Now

THANK YOU FOR READING!

I hope you enjoyed the beginning of Hayes and Laiken's story. If you did, I would greatly appreciate it if you could leave a review. :)

Who is she?

THAT GIRL, KELSEY CLAYTON

Kelsey Clayton is a USA Today bestselling author of Contemporary Romance novels. She lives in a small town in Delaware with her husband, two kids, and two dogs.

She is an avid reader of fall hard romance. She believes that books are the best escape you can find, and that if you feel a range of emotions while reading her stories - she succeeded. She loves writing and is only getting started on this life long journey.

Kelsey likes to keep things in her life simple. Her ideal night is one with sweatpants, a fluffy blanket, cheese fries, and wine. She holds her friends and family close to her heart and would do just about anything to make them happy.

For inquires: management@kelseyclayton.com

For social media links, scan below:

Books by KELSEY CLAYTON

The Pretty Poison Trilogy

A Dose of Pretty Poison

A Drop of Pretty Poison

A Shot of Pretty Poison

Malvagio Mafia Duet

Suffer in Silence

Screams in Symphony

Haven Grace Prep

The Sinner *(Savannah & Grayson)*

The Saint *(Delaney & Knox)*

The Rebel *(Tessa & Asher)*

The Enemy *(Lennon & Cade)*

North Haven University

Corrupt My Mind *(Zayn & Amelia)*

Change My Game *(Jace & Paige)*

Wreck My Plans *(Carter & Tye)*

Waste My Time *(Easton & Kennedy)*

The Sleepless November Saga

Sleepless November

Endless December

Seamless Forever

Awakened in September

Standalones

Returning to Rockport

Hendrix *(Colby & Saige)*

Influenced

SIGNED PAPERBACKS

Want a signed Kelsey Clayton book?

You can purchase them on her website.

Check it out.

Manufactured by Amazon.ca
Bolton, ON

41138803R00256